What We Deserve

A WISHBONE TATTOOS NOVEL

LIZZIE STANLEY

What We Deserve

To my mother, my hero and my touchstone, who did what needed to be done. She knows what I'm talking about. What an effing legend. Thank you for everything.

And

To M, the greatest of husbands, who is on every single page of this book in some form or another. Thanks for being mine, and for the endless love.

AUTHOR'S NOTE

On the advice of some fellow writers, and to bring a touch of realism to the pages, please kindly note that when Emily's the narrator, she will write in English English, with all the British spellings, ie colour, favourite. When Eli is narrating, he will write in American English, and will say color and favorite. Thanks!

Content warnings: this book deals with themes of relationship emotional abuse. There is also content regarding fertility and conception. Additionally, there is mention of a school shooting in America and post-traumatic stress disorder, but this is not a main plot point for this novel.

I'm used to being alone, until she changed everything…

When my ex-wife left, she said the cruelest words she could think of, and I took them to heart.

Now I work at my loveable bastard cousin's tattoo parlor and keep most people at arm's length. I have the occasional one night stand to take the edge off, but there can never be anything more than that for me.

I don't let myself think about how lonely I am. At least I'm not ruining anyone's life, right?

Then Emily walks into Wishbone Tattoos, asking about the receptionist job. And this shy, smiling, kind-hearted woman is everything I've ever wanted.

I can't help falling for her. But I don't want to be selfish, or torture myself with small tastes of a life that can never be mine.

But there's something about Emily I don't know. Something that will make her the exception to my rule…

She's battle scarred herself, and running from a dark past which snaps at her heels, but I'm not going to let anyone hurt her ever again, I swear to god.

And maybe, if we're lucky and we both want it hard enough, the two of us will finally get what we deserve

what we
DESERVE

A WISHBONE TATTOOS NOVEL

PROLOGUE

Eli

My cell phone rings while I'm setting up my tattoo machines for the afternoon, and I grin when I see the caller ID.

My Em. I smile because I can't help it. We hung up just five minutes ago, when she let me know she was just going to her place before heading back to the parlor, but my girl can call me as often as she wants. I'm curious, though. "Hey, *chere*," I answer, feeling that familiar warmth spread through my chest as I wait for her to talk. There's no response, just a few odd scuffling noises. "Hellooooooo, Em?" More sounds like an overfilled washer dryer.

I'm just about to hang up on the assumption that she's accidentally butt-dialled me with her cute-as-a-button ass when I hear shouting and a crash, like a slammed door and a dropped skillet, over the line.

And then my blood turns to solid ice and my stomach plunges through the floor as I hear my girlfriend yelling at the top of her lungs, her voice dripping with rage and fear, "Get—GET OUT! *GET OUT! GET OUT OF MY HOUSE RIGHT NOW!*"

"Fuck!" I bark. I'm running out of my studio and towards the shop's front exit before I even know what I'm doing, clutching my cell tightly. My heart feels like it's trying to force its way out through my throat with panic. Leo and Dean flinch when I burst into the reception area, but I don't have any time to explain. *She's in danger and she needs me NOW. I may already be too late.*

"What's—" Leo starts, but I'm already breaking into a run.

"CALL THE COPS TO EMILY'S!" I throw over my shoulder as I hit the street, hoping that he caught that. Thank fuck she only lives five minutes away. I'm going to be there in one, I swear to god.

I can hear someone running behind me, and in seconds Dean has caught up to me by running flat out. I'm grateful to have his unquestioning support, and backup in case shit goes bad. And to *maybe* keep me from killing the motherfucker and spending the rest of my life in jail.

I yell at other people on the streets to get out of my way, and they yelp behind me as I leave them in the dust. My adrenaline is pounding, and I'm going as fast as I can, faster than I've ever run in my life, not caring if I leave my cousin behind. I know exactly who's in Emily's apartment. She crawled out of the hell he dragged her into, and he's trying to force her back in.

Over my dead body. Over *his*, if he really pushes it.

My heart is racing in my chest, my temples are pounding with hot fury, and the streets are a blur. I put my cell to my ear to see if I can hear anything, as I never ended the call, but it's impossible. I'm breathing too hard and too loudly, and I can't hold the phone steady enough as I sprint. *SHIT.* Regardless, I don't want to pause for so much as a second, because I know. I'm certain.

Somehow, he's found her address.

But the moment I first held her in my arms, before I knew for certain that she was the one for me, before I told her I loved her for the first time, I swore to myself that this shitbag would never hurt or frighten her again, and I meant it.

This time, she's not alone.

chapter ONE

Emily

OK, *EMILY, DEEP BREATHS*, I TELL MYSELF FIRMLY. THE 'Receptionist Wanted' sign in the window of this tattoo parlour is heaven sent. I moved to Foxton-on-Sea two days ago, and I need employment. I have extensive experience of reception work from my years as a temp, so this is a no brainer, and it doesn't matter how scared of needles I am. When the most perfect and arse-saving opportunity presents itself to you during a grocery run, you put your big girl pants on, go for it, and hope for the best.

What would Janeway do, I think to ground myself as I tentatively push the door open. I've been watching my beloved Star Trek again now that I'm allowed to watch whatever I want, having it on in the background while I unpack and settle in, and it's been like having an old friend hanging out and keeping me company after years apart. Janeway is my favourite captain, and I recall with a small smile her saying that first contact must always be a positive thing. I'm by no means cool enough to be employed in a place like this, but I'm a hard worker, and that counts, I tell myself. *It DOES.*

I check out my surroundings while I tighten my ponytail.

The reception is stylish, with pale gold walls, healthy green plants, and an elegant black iron spiral staircase towards the back corner of the room. The words 'Wishbone Tattoos' are spread across the front window in artful black lettering, with 'Est 2009' underneath. There's a squashy, beaten-up leather sofa begging to be sat on, and an oak coffee table scattered with magazines and hardback tattoo art books. It needs a bit of a tidy, but it feels immediately welcoming and comfortable, more than I would have expected to find in a tattoo parlour.

There are a selection of framed photos on the walls, depicting what must be examples of tattoos they've done here in the past: a skull in a top hat with red and purple flowers bursting all over the brim on someone's calf, the surrounding skin pink and puffy; a woman's bare back tattooed with angel wings, the feathers so finely detailed and realistic that they look like a photo instead of a drawing; a replica of a still from Yellow Submarine on someone's arm, instantly recognizable and flawlessly rendered; passages from a Lord Byron poem in varying sizes, layered in perfect black and red antique handwriting script. I'm blown away by the talent involved in each of them. It's genuinely astonishing.

There's a low thrum of Disturbed on the sound system. It's *Deify*, one of my favourite tracks. I smile to myself; perhaps it's a sign that I could belong here, after all. Beneath David Draiman's toe curlingly sexy vocals, I can hear the faint buzz of a… I don't know what it's called; a tattoo gun, maybe? Like a piercing gun? It's coming from beyond the doorway to the right of the reception desk. My spine shivers involuntarily. I am a card carrying needlephobe, so as much as I would love to have a tattoo (and I know exactly what I'd get), I'm too much of a wimp to go through with it. Bottom line, though: this place is hiring, and I need a job like yesterday so I don't have to keep dipping into my secret savings to make rent. This job is perfect: walking distance from my new home, and I have the skills for it. I tamp down the anxiety as best I can, unwilling to let it persuade me to run back out the door. I can do this.

Just as long as I don't get squeamish about the needles. *No panicking, Em. For once in your life, do NOT make a fool of yourself.*

I'm not sure how long to wait. I straighten my clothing, painfully aware that my old holey jeans, Converse sneakers, and plaid shirt I threw on just to nip to the shops don't exactly scream 'hire this professional powerhouse', but then again, what *is* the best thing to wear for an interview at a tattoo parlour? A business suit? I wouldn't have thought so.

I notice a button marked 'Press For Attention ;-)' on the reception desk by the laptop, and nervously press it. A buzzing bell sounds through the doorway to my left as I face the desk. "Coming," a deep, masculine voice calls out. I take a steadying breath, telling myself not to be intimidated, and within seconds one of the best looking men I have ever seen in my life emerges from the back rooms.

Wow.

He's a great big bear of a man, or wait, no, he's actually more of a lion. Easily six foot three or four, broad shoulders, muscular arms covered in a multitude of tattoos and leather wrist cuffs and bracelets, and a golden brown mane of hair with blond-ish ends as though dyed by the sun, curling down to just past his shoulders. He has an easy, piratical smile framed by a very sexy beard, and a scar cuts through his left eyebrow. The imperfection only serves to emphasise how gorgeous this man is, and I blink in surprise.

He looks me up and down in friendly assessment. "Hi, can I help you?" he asks in a deep, Bagheera-like voice with a pleasant smile.

"U-um," I stammer, swallowing hard and clearing my throat.

Good start. "Hi, I'm here about the, uh, the receptionist job? I hope you don't mind, I...was just passing, and...I'm sure the position has already gone, don't worry if—"

Fortunately, he cuts in to stop me from rambling any more. "Fan fucking tastic," he crows, stepping forward and holding out a hand for me to shake. His grip is firm, warm, and dry, and very steadying. "Leo Mills. I'm the owner, and I'm really bloody glad you walked in." In spite of the 'bloody', there's the faintest American twang to his voice, like maybe he's lived in the States at some point.

Ha. Leo. Of *course* this gorgeous, leonine man is called Leo. "Emily." I hope my handshake conveyed more professionalism than my waffling did.

"Nice to meet you, Emily." He's so cheerful. To my great surprise, I find myself relaxing slightly. It feels so strange to not be intimidated by a man, especially one I've literally just met. "So, have you done any reception work before?"

"Yes," I reply, putting my game face on, "I was a temp for years, so I've had loads of receptionist positions. I just moved here a couple of days ago, but before I left, I was a PA at a legal firm, and I covered reception every lunchtime—"

"Good enough for me. You're hired."

I stop in surprise, and he chuckles, a rich, rumbling sound.

"Wow," I manage, and join him in laughter. "That was... quick? Are you sure?" Not that I want to discourage him, but how was it that simple?

He shrugs and leans against the doorframe, not breaking eye contact with me. "We need a receptionist like there's no freakin' tomorrow. You've got experience. I can't think of anything more straightforward than that."

He has a point there. There's bound to be a catch or two, but I'm just going to enjoy this time before I find out what they are. "Thank you," I say sincerely, trying not to sound like I'm pathetically grateful. This saves me having to sign up with employment agencies and pace in front of the phone every morning hoping for an assignment. I really didn't want to have to temp again. This job will hopefully get me settled into my new home town, at least.

"No problem," he says, "but before we go any further, I should give you a rundown of duties to make sure you're happy with it all?" He lifts his scarred eyebrow in enquiry, and I nod eagerly. I doubt he's going to suggest anything I wouldn't want to do, and fortunately reception work is much the same wherever you go. "Pay is twenty thousand a year. Working hours are 10am until 6pm Tuesday to Saturday, with the occasional Sunday paid at time and a half and with plenty of notice given. And yes, there *is* a staff discount for tattoos," he says with a wink.

I can feel myself starting to blush. "Oh, I, um…I don't have any," I admit apologetically. Maybe it's kind of a requirement. If customers come in and can see examples of their work on their staff, that's just good advertising. Maybe this is a bad idea… I start to slump inwardly.

He shrugs like it's no big deal. "We'll see how long that lasts," he says knowingly, "but there's absolutely no obligation." His eyes, which are a rather lovely golden hazel, turn kind, as if he knows how insecure I'm feeling and wants me to feel better. It sounds absurd, but it's as though he's known me all my life. I think he'd probably make anyone feel that way. It's that brotherly kind of energy, or maybe it's simply that he has bucketloads of natural charisma. But either way, I can't help warming to him.

"Anyway, day to day duties are…" he lists them on his fingers, "meeting and greeting the clients, making them feel comfortable, talking to them if they seem nervous—oh, are you first aid trained?" I nod, and he grins. "Even better—we get the occasional fainter. So yeah, meet and greet, book the appointments," he continues, resuming the counting, "Look after our social media—it's just Facebook and Instagram at the moment, but we get a lot of enquiries on them—keeping the place tidy, making sure the coffee machine is running constantly for Sadie, ordering supplies and taking deliveries, and just keeping us all running smoothly, really." One side of his mouth quirks up. "Sound good?"

"Sure, sounds *great*." Twenty thousand a year is almost as much as I was earning at the legal firm back home. As long as I'm careful, it will easily cover rent and living expenses. I'm never this lucky usually.

Well, maybe you were due some good luck after all that crap you went through, my often-smothered inner optimist murmurs to me, but I quickly squash the thought before it jinxes anything.

"Perfect," Leo says, pleased, "when can you start?" It's a huge relief to me that he seems to be such a nice person. It's a far cry from my last boss, a misogynistic dinosaur who never noticed any of my good work but pounced mercilessly on the smallest error. You know the type. The type whose coffee you spit in.

"How about tomorrow?" The sooner the better, as far as I'm concerned, and starting mid-week is my preference anyway: time to learn the ropes, rather than having to hit the ground running on a Monday.

"I was hoping you'd say that," he says with visible relief. "I'll get you set up on the laptop tonight. What's your last name?"

"Cole," I reply.

"Great. I'll sort it after work. Now, let me introduce you around," he says, beckoning back towards the back corridor

The walls in the long corridor are painted dark red, with beautiful sketches of dragons and statues and skulls—I'm assuming more tattoo designs—hung here and there. There are rooms off either side of it all the way to the end, and the buzzing noise of the tattoo needle intensifies, seemingly coming from slightly further down. Leo knocks on the first door on the left.

"This is the kit—chennnnn, whoah!" He quickly leans back mid-word to avoid getting smacked by the kitchen's swing door, which opens outwards as a woman around my age with long, curling ginger hair pokes her head around the door with a curious smile. She is possibly the most beautiful woman I have ever seen in real life.

"I thought I heard voices," she says, beaming at me. Her smile is knockout megawatt amazing, lighting up her whole face.

"Hi," I say shyly.

"Sadie, this is our new receptionist, Emily," Leo says with a smile bordering on smug.

Her bright, ocean blue eyes widen. "Seriously?" Leo nods happily. "Thank *fuck*! Hi, I'm Sadie, Leo's best tattoo artist. You have *no idea* how glad I am that you're here. When do you start?"

"Tomorrow," I reply, admiring her easy confidence. *Leo's best tattoo artist.* Love it.

"Yay!" She claps quietly. Like Leo, she also has a sleeve of tattoos on her right arm in soft greys, pinks, purples, and blues, like a watercolour, and I'm already dying to raid her wardrobe. Her black top is covered in a cool skull x-ray print, and just drapes so perfectly. I can never find anything like that. Maybe I'll ask her where she got it, now that I can wear whatever I want, and now that I'm finally allowed to spend my money on myself.

"I'm just showing her around. Dean back?"

"No, not yet."

Leo turns to me. "Dean's one of our tattoo artists. It's a family business. Dean and Eli are my cousins. Just to let you know now, Dean can't talk." His eyes turn serious. "Dean and Eli emigrated here from America a few years back, after…well, do you remember the Nolan High School shooting?" I nod. It was an awful tragedy in Louisiana about ten or fifteen years ago, when one of the school's teachers shot up a Senior Prom after getting sacked. "Dean was in it. Caught a bullet in the throat, can't make a sound. He was lucky to survive."

My heart sinks for him. "I'm so sorry." I can't think of anything helpful to say. How awful for him.

"Thank you." He clears his throat. "Anyway, you'll find Dean has his own ways of communicating, and he has a notepad and pen on him at all times, so there won't be a problem." The smile has returned to his eyes.

"And Eli knows American Sign Language, so he can translate when needed, or Leo or I can, though we're not as good, me especially," Sadie adds. "Dean's the best, and I'm sure you'll have no problem getting to know each other." She sounds genuinely fond of him.

"Sure." I wonder if I should maybe look into an online course in ASL to be able to help out. At least there are probably some YouTube videos that can get me started with the basics. I decide to look it up tonight.

"Come to think of it," Leo says, looking thoughtful, "one sec." He walks back through to reception and leaves me with Sadie, who gives me a bright smile.

"I'm really happy we have a receptionist again," she says, chatting easily with me with a total lack of awkwardness. I'm a little—OK, a *lot*—in awe of her. "We've been taking duty shifts at the front desk for the past couple of weeks—well, except for Dean, obviously. To be fair, the boys have been good about taking their turn, and haven't been relying on me to do it all just because I'm a woman. They're not into that sort of sexist bullshittery, or I'd have to break their kneecaps. But still, I could not be any gladder you're here!"

Her smile is impossible not to return. "I'm very happy to help. And it couldn't have come at a better time for me—I just moved here."

"Cool! Where from?"

Before I can reply, Leo's back. He's holding a black piece of paper covered in white writing, and hands it to me to read. "You'll need to hand these to all of Dean's new clients. He wrote it himself."

The arty white border around the page that frames the text is beautiful and intricate, swirling lines intersecting seemingly at random but so perfectly arranged that a lot of work clearly went into it. I imagine Dean designed that, too. I'm clearly going to be working with some exceptionally talented people.

I read the page.

Hi there –

My name is Dean, and I'll be your tattoo artist today.

A quick point before we start: I am completely 100% mute. This is due to an injury I sustained during a mass shooting in America, where I am originally from. Yes, it was one of the well-known mass shootings. No, I definitely do not want to talk about it (which is useful, given that I can't talk), so please do not ask me anything about it. Suffice it to say, I don't like guns at all, I emigrated to get away from them, and, having been a victim of gun violence, I hold the unshakeable opinion that gun control needs to be more of a thing in my country. End of discussion, and I will end your appointment early if this subject is raised again, even if your tattoo is incomplete. Boundaries are healthy, y'all, and that's one of mine. Please let me know any of yours so I can return the favor if needed.

Now, you may be thinking this will make your session rather quiet and stilted. Maybe even awkward. It ain't necessarily so, my friend. Think about it. You can talk to me about anything you want, and 1) I won't be able to tell you to pipe down if you go on and on, and 2) I am guaranteed to be able to keep it all 100% confidential. Tell me all about your secret affair with the mailman. Tell me why you hate your asshat boss, or your in-laws. Practice your TED Talk on me. I'll take it all to the grave.

If you need me to answer any questions that require more than a nod or a shake of my head, it's all good: I have an iPad I can type on, and if the battery dies on that, I have a pen and paper. Or I'll just tattoo the answer to your question on you. Kidding! Probably.

Nice to meet you, and let's get started.

Dean Gastright

PS: I'm sure this doesn't need saying, but you'd be surprised how often this happens: I'm mute, not deaf, nor cognitively impaired, so there is no need to shout at me or to speak slowly.

I chuckle. "I like him already," I say.

Leo grins. "Yeah, he's good fun. You'll need to make sure there are always plenty of those sheets available. He's popular with the customers. Anyway," he says, getting back on track, "That—" he knocks on the first door on the right, opposite the kitchen, "is Sadie's room, because it's closest to the coffee machine." He smirks at her, and she good naturedly gives him the finger as she heads back into the kitchen. I get the impression from the humour in their expressions as they look at each other that they have a very banter fuelled friendship, and they seem evenly matched.

"Mine is the one at the end. Dean's is the second door on the right, and Eli's second on the left. He's in, so we'll say hey." Sure enough, the buzzing is loudest outside Eli's door, and I take a deep breath to steel myself to watch someone getting tattooed. I'm going to have to get used to it, after all. *Just don't faint. Anything but that.* My knees shake a little, but I squeeze my hands into fists, clenching rhythmically, because I read online that it reduces the chance that you'll black out. "He probably won't look up, but don't take it personally. He's a good guy, he just really zones out when he's focusing on his work. But we might get a 'hello'. Maybe." He winks at me as he knocks twice on the door and opens up.

Eli is sitting with his back to the door, tattooing what looks like the bright stained glass window from the Disney cartoon of *Beauty and the Beast* onto his customer's thigh. The skin around it is glowing red and looks tender, but the girl doesn't react as he works. She has denim blue hair, and she's making it inescapably clear, with her burning hot looks and the way she's squeezing her ample cleavage together with her arms, that she's very, very interested in him. I'm surprised he's able to ignore the smoulder she's sending his way, but, as Leo said, he's so focused on what he's doing that he doesn't look up, even when we enter, or give any indication that he's at all aware we're there. The buzzing from the tattoo gun sounds like an angry hornet, and I try to hide a shudder, quietly taking a steadying breath so my throat doesn't close up at the thought of needles puncturing skin.

"Hey, Melissa," Leo greets the customer, and she smirks at him. "Eli, this is Emily. She's our new receptionist, starting tomorrow."

"Hmmm," Eli acknowledges vaguely, a deep rumble, concentration unbroken.

He's got his back to me, so all I can see is that, even sitting down, he's a giant of a guy, muscular as all get-out and maybe even taller than Leo. His hair is long, mostly straight, reaching halfway down his back. It's almost black, shiny, and luxurious in that way men's long hair often is. I couldn't get mine looking like that without industrial amounts of expensive conditioner. My own hair is dyed blonde and looking dull, with easily two inches of regrowth, and in sore need of a trip to a salon. I make a mental note to ask Sadie for a recommendation for a local hairdresser.

Leo sighs dramatically and shrugs. "I think that's the best we're gonna get from him," he says to me with a shrug, his eyes sparkling with mirth.

"He's too busy concentrating on my thighs," Melissa says

smugly. Snap decision: I don't like her. But I smile politely at her anyway. I'm well-versed in hiding my true thoughts and feelings.

"I hear you, Leo, I'm just in the middle of something right now," Eli mutters wryly, and oh my god. That voice…it's like honey and locusts, a stunning, deep Cajun drawl that makes me think of bayous and Mardi Gras and good jazz and jambalaya. He sounds like Gambit from the X-Men cartoons, but deeper. Gambit was always my favourite. It's toe curling, and completely out of place in a British seaside town, even one as cosmopolitan as Foxton-On-Sea. Leo raises an eyebrow comically. Melissa's jaw tenses very slightly and she scowls, as though he shouldn't be speaking to anyone else if he's not making conversation with her. "Nice to meet you, Emily, and I'm glad you're here," Eli says without turning his back. He's the third person to say that to me in quick succession. How hard have they been struggling without a receptionist?

"Y-you too," I say as we leave. After I speak, Eli starts to turn, but then Leo is showing me out, so I still don't get a look at his face. I realise as I leave that "you, too" could be taken to mean either it's nice to meet him, too—which was what I meant—or that I am glad he is there, which is weird. I eyeroll inwardly. *Typical doofy Emily.*

"So, apart from Dean, that's the team," Leo says as he shows me back through to the reception area. Having heard Eli talk, Leo sounds a lot more English by comparison. "Can you be here by 9:30 tomorrow? Be good to get an earlier start to show you a few things before the customers come." Right on cue, two girls who look to be in their early twenties walk in, giggling and taking furtive looks at him. "Hey, there, ladies. Here for your appointment with me?" he asks one of them with a wicked smirk playing around his lips. He clearly knows full well the effect he has on people. One of them nods, and the giggling continues.

Jeez Louise. Can't blame them, though. He's the sort of man you find on the cover of MC romance novels: built, with long hair, tattoos, and eyes that slay.

He raises that eyebrow at me. "9:30 ok?" Woops, I haven't responded!

"Sure," I say hurriedly, quickly getting my mind back on track. It'll be nice to have a boss who's bona fide eye candy, but it's not like I would do anything about it, and he certainly wouldn't. He's so far out of my league that it's not even funny. And in all honesty, even aside from that, I'm not truly interested in starting anything with anyone, not so soon after...

Nope, not going to think about it.

"Great. That'll let me make a start on showing you the ropes before we open. It's really not the most complicated job in the world. You just need to look after us and keep us all in line." He smiles at me. "See you tomorrow, Emily, and thanks for coming in."

"No problem, thank—thank *you,*" I manage. Even if he's just desperate for anyone to fill the role, he's been really nice and welcoming, and I resolve to do a really good job and not to let him down. "See you tomorrow." I walk through the door and damn near float back home. *I have a job. Problem solved.*

Eli

I wander out to the waiting room just as the door closes behind the new receptionist. I can't see her face through the glass door, just the back of her head as she walks quickly away. For some reason this irritates me. I just missed her when I turned my head in my studio.

I probably should have been more polite. Made with the pleasant conversation. We really need to keep this one sweet, so she stays longer than a month. I feel oddly guilty for not at least looking her in the eye when I welcomed her on board. Hmm. I'll make nice when she's next in.

Leo turns back and blinks when he sees me standing there. Normally, once I've started a piece, only an emergency can drag me away. My concentration on my work is absolute. I'm not really sure what made me wander out here. The girls in the waiting room were giggling like children as I walked in, but now they're just staring.

"That was a stroke of luck, eh," he comments.

I nod slowly. "Just do us all a favor and don't fuck this one," I say with a warning look. The waiting room goes silent. I will strangle him if he messes this up for us again. I'm not good on the front desk. I don't like answering the phone. I don't like greeting people. I don't like turning down appointments because I'm too busy playing receptionist to do my actual job.

He rolls his eyes. "*One time* I did that—"

"Please, *frère*. Not just one time. It's practically your MO. And look what it did to us," I point out, quite reasonably in my opinion. Leo shakes his head. He has no right to be so affronted. We've been struggling for the past two weeks because Leo screwed our last receptionist on a whim and then didn't declare his undying love to her afterwards. Same thing happened with the receptionist before her. *And* the one before *her*, come to think of it. "I don't want to have to do that job anymore, do you?" He huffs. "Exactly. Leave this one alone."

I wander back to Melissa, who, despite me pointedly ignoring her come-ons, still doesn't seem to understand that it doesn't matter how many times she asks me out for a drink, or how much she wheedles and cajoles and lowers her neckline, I'm still going to say 'no' because I'm just not interested in dating her.

Or anyone.

Regardless of how lonely I may ever get, that door needs to stay firmly closed and locked.

chapter
TWO

Emily

HE'S DOING IT AGAIN.

I roll my eyes in irritation as I scrub his plates and cutlery, but only because I'm sure he can't see my face. I make certain to leave the spoons bowl down on the draining board this time, like he told me to. He'll get angry again if I don't, and I don't want to be yelled at about spoons ever again in my life. Spoons, for god's sake.

I walk out of the kitchenette and sit next to him on the sofa, drying my hands on an old tea towel with a huge hole at one edge. He doesn't want me to waste money on a replacement. "Honestly," I grumble playfully, masking my disgust at what he's doing with my best approximation of a gently teasing smile.

He looks up at me, his eyes full of gleeful spite. He's colouring in the edges of an underwear model's torso from one of his magazines to give her a waistline more to his liking. He's been doing this more and more lately. He likes his women thin to the point of emaciation, hand span waists, but with large breasts. Very few women measure up to his exacting standards. I certainly don't. "What?" He grins with feigned innocence, but there's a sharp edge to his voice; I need to tread very carefully, or that sharp edge will cut me once again, and I'm tired of crying myself to sleep. "I'm improving her. If she went to the gym more, this is what she'd look like, the lazy bitch."

I look at the model. She's stunning, with a lovely figure that no-one in their right minds would consider overweight or un-toned. The electric blue lace underwear she models looks fabulous against her perfect golden tan. She's in much better shape than me, which, though unspoken, is as clear as day. He wasn't just calling the model a 'lazy bitch'. I'm a normal, healthy UK size 12, but that's practically obese in his eyes. He berates me every chance he gets for the food I eat and the fact that I don't live at the gym every evening, as he does. He loathes my cellulite, and my not completely flat belly has been blamed for him losing his hard-on more than once. I've looked at my body in the shower and cried so many times over the past few months. I'm getting more and more annoyed by his misogyny and nasty comments about people's weight, but I dread what would happen if I called him on it. Acid insults, or the silent treatment. I just can't face it, cowardly though it may be.

It might be easier for me to go to the gym if he was more encouraging and less scathing…and if he cut out the incredulous jeering. I can't believe you can't do this, *he'll taunt as he pushes me to perform like an experienced athlete rather than the beginner I am. It sets me up to fail every time, and I swear he delights in it.*

I will never be good enough.

"She can't be more than a size 10," I say, speaking up in defence of this model on principle, but smiling gently to show I don't mean any real harm. I don't want to be yelled at again, but, although my inner fire has become barely glowing embers, it's still there. Just.

What am I doing here, I think to myself. What's the point anymore?

"Too. Fucking. Fat," he declares in his I'm-not-to-be-argued-with voice. "She's an underwear model. That's her motherfucking profession. She should be half this size." He carries on shading with

his biro. "Her tits are pretty decent, but there's no excuse for her being this wide. It's just unprofessional, not to mention gross." *I look again at the photo, and he's colouring more and more.*

And then I see her face.

Oh my god.

It's no longer the underwear model.

It's me. It's a photo of me in that underwear.

And he's coloured nearly all of me in with deep, scratching strokes of his black biro that tear the page of the magazine.

I jolt awake.

My heart is pounding hard and my throat feels like it's closing up. I know it isn't, but I quickly sit up and have a drink anyway to ease the feeling, managing not to choke.

I can feel a panic attack hovering at the edges, and I whimper in desperation. The trembling, the nausea, the tingling chest, the tightness, the overwhelming need to cry...the feelings start to build. *Please, no. Not today.* I have to be at work in...I check my mobile for the time with sweaty hands...three hours. First day. I must be on time. I can't be dealing with this now.

He's not here. He doesn't know where you live. You don't ever have to see him again.

Do some square breathing, I tell myself, and take a few slow, deep breaths. *Quick, think of a colour...* I choose blue, and then I look around my room, counting how many blue things there are in here. My jeans. The antique velvet chair I dumped them on. The lid of my hand cream. Some of the stripes on my bed set.

I take a deep breath and do another grounding technique, noting everything I can hear. A couple of cars passing in the street below. The downstairs neighbour shutting a door. A seagull crying—I live among seagulls, this is so awesome—and, if I listen very hard, the distant sound of waves.

It's working. I'm no longer frantic.

Once my hands have almost stopped shaking, I reach for

my Kindle and pick up the cheap sci-fi romance I downloaded last night where I left off. I have a little while before I need to get up and start the day, and reading always calms me. Distraction is key.

Butterflies of nerves start fluttering in my gut when I contemplate my first day at Wishbone Tattoos, and I wonder if this was really such a good idea. What if I'm as hopeless as Gav always said I was, and I make a massive fool of myself? Cock up a stock order, forget to write down an appointment, faint at the sight of one of the artists working, that kind of thing?

What if they get angry with me, too? The thought fills me with terror. If they shout at me, I'll freeze, and I'll go to pieces, and then…

I get a tight grip on myself. They seemed like good people. Normal people, who don't shout and swear because someone messes up a little. I need to stop assuming that everyone is just going to act like Gav all the time. Because no matter what he told me, the way he behaved was not normal or understandable. *He* was the aberration, and what I went through was not acceptable. I left because I believe that now.

You need this job. You're not backing out. Just do it.

Eli

I have to admit, Sadie was right about this coffee maker.

When she told me how much Leo had let her take out of petty cash to buy it, I was shocked to my core. It's just a coffee machine, not a second hand car. But god damn, if this Americano doesn't hit the spot.

I'm alone right now. It's usually me that opens the parlor up because I'm up and at 'em before anyone else. I've never needed that much sleep, and I go to the gym or for a run early every morning before everywhere gets too crowded, so I might as well start work early. I'm usually the last to go home in the evenings as well, but I don't mind. My life is pretty quiet for a man of thirty-five. I work a lot; bragging aside, my appointments are always booked out months in advance and my waiting list is *long*. I'm as introverted as it gets, and permanently single, so I'm not exactly missing out on a pulsating social life. And at least I know for damn sure that the store's alarm is set properly. Leo never remembers the code, and I got sick of having to come back out to fix it.

I'm just re-tying my hair back into a knot for the day when I hear the gentlest of taps on the glass of the front door.

I sigh a little. It's amazing how many people can't, or won't, read signs on doors. "We're closed," I call firmly as I leave the kitchen and move towards the entrance, intending to bring their attention to our clearly stated opening hours, and then stop in my tracks.

She's maybe late twenties or early thirties, and looks as nervous as a turkey on Thanksgiving, but her tentatively smiling face is one of *the* very loveliest I've ever seen. She's in a green parka, and she's holding a grocery bag from the supermarket across the street.

"Hi, I-I'm Emily," she calls through the glass, and her breath mists it slightly. "Your new receptionist? I'm sorry I'm so early." She squirms a little, and something inside me that I didn't even know was frozen melts into liquid.

"Right," I say, shaking my head to clear it, realizing I've been standing here staring at her. "Sorry, I'll just..." I unlock the door and open it for her. It takes me a moment to realize that I'm standing in her way, because close up, damn, she's even more gorgeous. She's all big gray eyes, snub little nose, and soft, plump pink lips that need, *deserve*, a thorough kissing. Her hair is pale blonde, darker at the roots, and she's pulled it back into a neat ponytail. I gulp a little and stand aside so she can come in. I'm not saying I never appreciate a beautiful woman, but I don't normally react this strongly, this quickly. I'm not normally stunned like this. Any other time, I would smile and strike up a conversation, just for the pleasure of talking with someone this hot. But, even if my life was different and I could realistically allow myself to start sweet talking her and getting to know her better in the hope of dating her, after all the shit I gave Leo yesterday about sleeping with employees, she's the one woman in town I could never approach anyway without being a giant asshole.

Her smile is still nervous, and yet there's a happy warmth shining from it that makes me wish I had my sketch pad. Usually that's reserved for tattoo ideas, but doing a portrait could be fun. It'd certainly flex my creative muscles in a way I haven't in a while. "I think we met yesterday, maybe? Eli, isn't it?" She asks, and her voice makes me smile back before I know I'm gonna.

"Yeah," I say, with another shake of my head. She's going to think I have flies living in my ear if I don't quit it. "I'm sorry I didn't say a proper hey yesterday. I get kind of, uh…*fixated* when I'm working."

"No, no," she hurriedly assures me, "It's fine, you were busy." She seems to cast around for something to say. "It…it looked really pretty. I mean, the, uh, tattoo…that you were doing…it was nice."

I can't stop looking at her eyes, mentally mixing different blacks and blues and whites to get the irises just the right shade if I painted them. A brief image enters my head of her in the nude, curving over my couch, posing for me with that shy smile and a wicked look in those silvery eyes as I painted her, and it sends a flash of pure, uncomplicated arousal straight to my already twitching dick. I shift as subtly as I can, stunned to find I'm barreling towards full blown wood. *What's wrong with you?* I ask myself, and cough to clear the impossible daydream.

"Thanks," I respond. "Leo will be here soon, but I've just turned the coffee maker on, if you want to come through, get settled in?"

"Sure," she murmurs, and holds up her grocery bag. "I just picked up some biscuits as well, just...you know, as a first day gesture, or something." She's a little flushed, like she's second guessing the idea. Her eyes widen in sudden panic. "Oh, god—no-one's diabetic or lactose intolerant, or anything, are they?"

"No," I reassure her, and she looks relieved. I take the bag from her and take a look inside. They're chocolate ones, a sure-fire crowd pleaser in this establishment.

"Thanks, that's real nice of you," I say as I lead her to the kitchen. She smiles and takes off her coat, revealing the slope of her neck as it meets her shoulder. I think of scraping my teeth softly along the sensitive skin in that area, and soothing it with my tongue as she moans near my ear -

"Would you like some tea or coffee?" I ask quickly, to try and break the physical reactions this woman seems to have caused in me. I'm being ridiculous, and these thoughts are not helping my wood situation. I can't decide if I can't wait for Leo to arrive and take her away, or if I want to just stay in the kitchen with her all day.

Or, if she was willing, pin her to the wall and kiss her senseless.

"Erm...could I have a glass of water, please?" she asks, as if she's being impolite to me by wanting something other than what I offered. "I'm so sorry, I'm just not much of a hot drink person."

"Yeah, sure," I say, and fetch a glass from the cupboard. It's still a little warm after I unloaded it from the dishwasher this morning, so I run it under the cold tap for a few seconds before filling it up. "By the way," I say to make conversation as I hand it over, "when people say biscuits to me, that's not what I think of.

Those are definitely *cookies*," I say with a smile so I don't come across like a condescending ass. The contrast between our accents is stark: me, the boy from the Big Easy, and her, with her soft, bright British murmur. I'd be lying if I said I wasn't enjoying it, which is strange, because I've lived in the UK for years and I've long since gotten used to how British people talk. But this... hell, this is something extra.

She smiles as she accepts the glass from me. My finger brushes her for a split second, and the hair on my arms stands up. *This is ridiculous.* "I s'pose they would be. I'm not sure what biscuits are in America, if they even are anything?"

I whip out my cell and Google them quickly. She moves a little closer, and damn it, she smells like peaches, a perfume as petal soft as her mouth looks. She's maybe a foot away from me as she peers at the image on my screen, but my whole body lights up at her nearness. She's dressed professionally in black trousers and a loose cream blouse, nothing too fancy, but not as casual as we are in our jeans and band shirts. Still, I've had less potent feelings when previous lovers have dressed up in lingerie for me. Even my ex-wife never once got me to this eager, instantly hungry state, especially this early on in our acquaintance. She looks kind of fragile, though, as though she could use a cheeseburger, a stiff drink, and a long hug. I wish I could take her for one of each, but...

"Those look like scones to me," she says with a smile.

"Scones?" I ask.

"Well, *scons*, I suppose." She said it with a hard 'o' sound first of all, to rhyme with 'bones', and I frown a little in confusion. She chuckles at my expression, and the gentle sound makes something in the pit of my stomach glow like fireflies. It feels really nice.

Stop it.

"There's a bit of controversy about how the word is

pronounced," she says, "and I always used to pronounce it 'scones', but then someone I used to work with insisted it was 'scons', because you have one on a plate, and one minute it's there, next minute… *s'gone*."

I laugh.

And that's when Leo pokes his head around the door. For a second he looks nonplussed. "I'm gonna say that, since you made *Eli* laugh, you've passed your probation period, so congrats," he says, the ass. I love Leo, and not just cos he's my cousin, but the man is too observant for his own good. And it's true, I'm not known for being the smiley guy. It's deliberate on my part; I'm not as extroverted as Leo, and like to keep most people at a distance for a number of reasons. But Emily's had me smiling and laughing within five minutes. And now he's going to yank my chain about this every chance he gets.

"Hey, I laugh," I protest, wanting to make light of it.

He doesn't, Leo mouths silently at Emily with a brief shake of his head.

"I do when something's funny. Probably why you never hear me laughing around you, *frère*." I sip my coffee.

Leo grins but he still looks curiously at me. Reassured that we're just messing and aren't truly giving each other shit, Emily smiles at us both, which makes my gut tingle in the best way. In a way I haven't felt in a long time.

My other cousin, Dean, wanders in and makes straight for the coffee machine. His jeans are rumpled and dirty, and his leather jacket isn't straight, the collar hanging awkwardly over the scar on his throat. He doesn't look like he's washed or combed his hair in a couple of days. He's looking dog tired again, his pallor almost gray. I make a mental note to check in with him later. He's probably having another spate of bad nights.

"Dean," Leo says, "I'd like you to meet Emily, our new receptionist." Dean looks up, and his tired and drawn face instantly warms into a friendly smile, like the genial guy he is. He nods at her, and I'm genuinely stunned when she silently signs back, in *American* Sign Language, *Nice to meet you.*

Dean blinks, and basically melts, as does Leo. As do I.

Emily's gone bright red, hunching her shoulders and placing her hands in her back pockets, suddenly bashful about this really considerate thing she's done. She's won us all over now, not that she even needed to, but all the same...

You know ASL? Dean signs to her.

Her eyes widen. "Um... I'm sorry, I-I'm still only learning. I looked up some key phrases last night," she explains sheepishly. She signs again to demonstrate the extent of her knowledge. "Please, thank you, good morning, tea or coffee..." She puts her hands down. "But I'll learn some more, I promise."

Dean chuckles soundlessly. *Thank you, I appreciate it.*

"He says he appreciates it," I translate, trying hard not to grin like an idiot, pleased that she went to this effort for my cousin. She's never even met him before this moment, and she still took the time to start learning how to communicate with him in anticipation, even though that meant a pretty heavy investment of her time and effort. That, to me, is a great human.

Dean quirks an eyebrow at me. *Also, I've never seen that look on my cousin's face before now. I'm pretty sure he'll say yes if you want to ask him out?*

Emily looks at me to translate, and I'm going to kick Dean's ass later. His eyes, always expressive, are alive with mischief, and I know from his amused cough that Leo got the gist, even though he's not as fluent as me. Dean and I learned basic ASL in high school, and then became fluent as a project to focus on after he was shot, so he could talk to us all again. The rest of the family did the same, and Leo and Sadie took courses, too.

"He says he hopes you have a good first day," I say firmly. Dean snorts quietly as he turns back to the coffee maker.

"Thank you," Emily responds, beaming at Dean, who returns the favor. I can think of about twenty reasons off the top of my head why this sudden crush of mine is entirely futile, and for the first time, it bothers me.

"Hadn't you better start training Emily *now*, Leo?" I grate out, and turn back to wash my mug up. Gotta put some distance between me and her, right this second.

Leo opens the door, entertained at my expense. "Right this way, milady," he says, grinning warmly at her and oozing easygoing charm that I simply don't have. I've seen Leo turn it on for people almost every day for years, and this is the very first time it's made me grit my teeth in annoyance.

What. The. Fuck.

When they've gone, I turn and glare at Dean for a long moment. He shrugs and gives me a wide eyed, exaggeratedly innocent look in return, as if he can't begin to guess why I'm pissed at him. "Asshole," I mutter, and retreat away from his silent laughter to the safety of my studio.

chapter
THREE

Eli

SHE'S ON THE PHONE, SMILING AS SHE BOOKS A NEW appointment for Dean in four weeks' time, as I see my last client of the day out the door. I never used to bother doing that—it's not like they don't know the way to the exit—but since Emily started working here last week, I've found myself doing it every time. Leo and Dean have both noticed, and I've seen them nudge each other and grin, but they haven't said anything yet. It's probably only a matter of time, but I need to head that off at the pass. It's not like I'm mooning over her, or hanging around her like a moth around a bonfire, or doing anything more than treating our new employee with polite respect, right?

But it's not just showing them to the door, either. I've been emerging from my studio a little more often generally, making my own beverages instead of people bringing them to me because I've hyperfocused on my work and lost track of time. Sometimes I pass her in the corridor, and she does this cute thing where she hunches her shoulders, trying to make herself smaller so she can get by. And sometimes she says 'oop' as she scoots past, and I secretly melt every time.

It is oddly fascinating to watch her work, too. She fidgets

a lot when she's on the phone taking messages and booking appointments, twirling her pen around her fingers, and sometimes doodling random shapes or flowers, unable to stay still. And I know the callers can hear her smile as she talks. I just know it. She's great with clients face to face, too, chatting and enthusing with them sincerely over their requested designs and assuring them that we'll take the best care of them. I've seen a couple of the regulars get a little *too* friendly with her, and it never fails to set my teeth on edge, but she's managed to keep them at arm's length while still being nice to them. More than those pussy hounds deserve; if I had my way, I'd throw them physically through the door.

Another thing: she always makes sure we have everything we need, from the essentials, like sufficient stock of inks and numbing cream and antiseptic wipes, to little things that she's gone out of her way to find out about. Sadie's favorite brand of coffee, for example, and Leo's favorite potato chips. And I haven't skipped lunch once since she got here, because she always brings me back a Subway or a pasta salad when she goes out, just to make sure I have to take a break to eat it. She places it next to me so gingerly, and then hurries away before I can say thank you. I found out this morning that she does the same thing for Dean, too, and my heart clenched in my chest with how sweet that is.

Plus, she's getting better at ASL every day; she must be cramming every night.

I was hoping my crush would die off as quickly as it came, but I'm shit out of luck there. She's gorgeous, my exact type, *and* she's a really nice person.

Stick a fork in me, I'm done.

How many times do I have to tell myself to just forget it before I'll listen…

She looks up when my client leaves. He's pleased with the Dali-esque melting clock I inked onto his arm. Her eyes brighten a little. "Hi!"

Although I know better and have given myself a pep talk every morning since last week about keeping my distance, I can't help smiling back. "Hey. Had a good day?"

She nods, finishing an Outlook calendar entry. "Lovely and peaceful for a Friday." I really, really like her voice. *If whipped cream could talk…*

I don't know where these silly thoughts have come from; they're out of character for me.

"Good," I respond a beat too late, casting around for something else to say to prolong the moment, but knowing I should probably just go back to my studio and clean up for the day.

Fortunately, she comes to my rescue. "How about you?"

"Not bad at all," I reply, smiling again. I haven't stopped fucking smiling since she got here. "I've got an interesting one tomorrow. He sent me the design. Wanna see?"

She nods happily, and I whip out my cell and search through my emails until I find the right one, handing it to her. "He wants this done on his back." It's a war horse, its face protected by metal armor. It's hyper-realistic, looking more like a photo than a drawing. Fortunately, that's my specialty, and I'm really looking forward to this one.

"Oh, wow," she breathes, genuinely impressed as she studies it, "that looks incredible."

As she leans over, her hair—loose and straight today—brushes ever so slightly against my arm, and I can smell her coconut shampoo. I manage to restrain a sigh.

Forget it. She's not one of your one-night-onlys. One night with her and you'd be a goner, and you know it, and you know why you can't. Don't waste her time.

"I wish I was brave enough," she says, so quietly that I almost miss it.

I look at her in surprise. "Are you thinking of getting some ink done?" I ask, trying hard to force my mind away from the mental image of her naked back spread out in front of me on my wine-red leather chair in my studio, her gorgeous ink-virgin skin under my hands and needle, my very own canvas. Like placing fresh footprints in new snow. *God. Yes. Please. I'll do anything.*

She looks up at me with those big, pretty eyes and chuckles grimly as she shakes her head. "I'd love to, but I'm terrified of needles, and much too much of a sniveling little coward to feel the fear and do it anyway."

There she goes again. I frown. I've noticed she never misses a chance to insult herself. The slightest mistake has her calling herself a dumbass under her breath. It's hard to listen to without wanting to throw all the compliments I can think of her way. "Is it the pain you're worried about?" I ask gently and with genuine interest.

She looks up at me again, seeming surprised I asked, and shrugs uncomfortably. "Not so much the pain. I can take pain. It's…I don't know, it's the idea of the needle piercing my skin over and over. Makes me feel…" She shivers a little.

Our eyes meet, and lock. Neither of us looks away.

God damn, those eyes of hers…I never knew slate gray could be such a warm color.

It's a beat too long for it to be purely innocent now.

And still it continues.

Her eyes darken, and the expression in them is kindling into…something. Probably the exact same one I find myself wearing. She bites her lip, and I groan inwardly, trying not to imagine leaning forward and running my tongue over the indentations of the bite mark she's creating before slipping it inside her mouth for a taste of her. Goosebumps break out along my arms, tingling down my spine, and my heart beats a little faster as my breath catches. I can smell her perfume. I want to pull her to me and breathe her in…

I have to look away. I *have to*. But my fingertips tingle with the urge to touch her, and a soft breath escapes her lips, like a tiny gasp, and *she's* still not breaking eye contact, either...

"Guys, have you seen my phone charger?" Sadie chooses that moment to wander in, searching all the power outlets, and the moment is broken. I'm torn between relieved gratitude and wanting to growl at her like an irritable mutt.

But ultimately it's a good thing. Emily is now distracted, helping Sadie look around, so I slip away, back to my studio.

I need to do much, much better than this. There's a reason I've got to be single forever, or at best until I'm too old for it to matter, and I cannot allow myself to get sucked down this path. It leads only to hurt. It doesn't matter how much my belly dips when she smiles; nothing can start, and even if it did, there's no point in torturing myself with a small taste of a heaven that I can't ever really have.

Usually I can face down being romantically alone with a fatalistic shrug, but not this time. This time, the prospect seems disappointing, and depressingly bleak. A waste. Long, lonely, empty years stretch out in front of me, and, instead of my usual calm acceptance, I resent each and every one of them. It's as though I've poked an old sore injury and woken up the raw nerve endings.

Resolutely distracting my mind from Emily Cole for what feels like the hundredth time, I start wiping down my leather chair, ready for my next client tomorrow.

There's a tap at my door, and Leo's head appears around the frame.

I nod. "Where y'at," I murmur, a traditional New Orleans greeting, because after all, half of Leo is a NoLa boy.

He grins. "Awrite. Pub? To celebrate Em's first complete week?"

I'd love to. "Thanks, but I'll pass," I say, not stopping what I'm doing, hoping that he won't try to persuade me.

Once again, I'm shit out of luck, but I suspected this would be the case. "You'll pass?" he says, sounding surprised, walking in and putting on his leather jacket. "How come?"

I look at him sharply, and, although he's acting all puzzled, we know each other too well. I can see in his face that he knows exactly what the problem is, and bullshitting him will be a waste of his time and mine. "Because it's not a good idea, and you know why," I reply, quietly but firmly.

For a split second there is a hint—just the barest trace—of pity in his expression, but my cuz knows better than to do anything other than smother it immediately, which he does. "Mate, you don't know if that's something she even wants," he says gently, the British half of his accent sounding stronger.

"Everyone deserves to still have choices open to them," I mutter darkly.

"She likes you." My heart gives an extra beat at his blunt words, and I clear my throat wishing he'd leave the subject alone. I can't afford to even think about it... "She does," he insists kindly, "and you like her. And that's OK, Eli. Seriously—"

"She's our receptionist," I retort, "and after giving you shit for chasing the last two or three away, I'm not going to be a fucking hypocrite." I smirk, hoping he'll let it go now.

"Ah, but," he says with a bigger smirk than mine, "you wouldn't do what I did with them. Or what you do with the women you've been with since your divorce. You wouldn't punk out after one night." He gives me one of his Serious Leo looks. He sees himself as very much the Older Brother Figure out of the three of us, even though I'm older than him by nearly three months and Dean's only a year younger. "Not with her."

I shake my head. I'm not budging on this. "I'm not gonna go there, and you shouldn't be encouraging me," I snap to put him off continuing this nonsense. I'm not sure why he's pushing this. It could only lead to heartache and loss, and I thought he was smart enough, and sensitive enough, to get that. He's an intuitive guy, with all the insight into my situation he could possibly need, and normally he's kind enough to let it be and to respect my decision, even if he disagrees with it. I don't know why he's doing this now.

He shrugs. "Alright," he says, shaking his head. "Shame. I was hoping we could all get to know her better, as a team. Find out more about her." He wanders over to the door, very obviously knowing how tempting the idea is to me, to be able to get to know her better while everyone else does as well. The perfect cover. My jaw tightens. "Like what she likes to do in her spare time. What music she likes. What tattoo she'd most like, and where she'd have it... *So* many questions." He says, and gives me a final knowing look. I smile slightly as I jerk my head in the direction of the exit. He's bugging the living shit out of me, but I know he means well.

He has, however, deliberately left me with a massive pile of temptation to wrestle with.

"Em," I hear him call further down the corridor, "we're taking you to the pub. Drinks are on Uncle Leo." He knocks on a door. "Sadie, let's go." There is a pause. "Dean, pub?" His voice becomes muffled as the door to reception closes, but the tone of Emily's voice as she responds sounds happy, so I guess she's accepted his offer. Well, his order, really.

I lean on the head of my chair and take a beat to think. I picture clearing up in here double quick and going with them. I picture maybe sitting next to her in a beer garden for the entire evening as we all drink and relax after a hard day's work. I picture making her laugh, and that smile I spend way too much time thinking about...

I shouldn't go.

I really, really shouldn't.

Emily

"Definitely your round next, Sadie. You're prettier than me, so you'll get served quicker," Leo comments as he sets another tray of drinks down on the table in front of us all and passes them around as he sits opposite me. We're in a beautiful and relatively busy beer garden, with clematis draped over a trellis and a brand new barbecue grill standing inactive in the corner.

Sadie raises an eyebrow, and he winks. He hands me my second diet coke of the night. It means so much to me that they didn't put any pressure on me to have a 'proper' drink. I don't drink a lot of alcohol generally—usually just at Christmas—and that usually invites unwanted comments and peer pressure. Not a bit of it this time.

They're a great crowd, and I am very aware how lucky I am. It's been a long, long time since I sat in a pub with friends. *My* friends, that is. I'd forgotten how good it feels. I smile at the thought.

"What's that big ol' smile for?" Leo asks me with an answering grin. That accent of his is intriguing, a perfect mix of English and American; since I started working at Wishbone, I've heard him say ass and arse in a near equal ratio. And I've learned over the past week and a half that nothing, and I mean absolutely nothing, gets past Leo's eagle eyes. He knew without asking that Sadie had a headache on Tuesday and simply dropped some Nurofen on the table next to her with a glass of water without a word. And he already seems to sense stuff about me, like when my thoughts wander to a darker place. A more perceptive, empathetic human I don't think I've ever met.

"Oh," I mumble, casting around for a reason to be smiling like a dingus at a half pint of coke, "it's...just been a really good week." I don't want to tell them the truth: that a simple trip to the pub has me feeling on top of the world; that I've laughed more in the past week and a half working at the parlour than I have in the past four years of my life; that I'd forgotten what it was like to have friends of my own, that the four of them were worth the move, and that I'm touched beyond words that they've adopted me as one of them, with no questions asked.

Because they truly have.

"I've gotta say, I am *so glad* you answered the ad," Sadie says, sipping her Doom Bar next to me. "It's great to have some professionalism from reception for once."

"Ouch," Leo chuckles.

She gives him a sardonic look. "Morning, Leo, can I get you anything at all, Leo, *ooooohhhhhhh, Leo,* you're *sooooooooo* talented," she mimics with an eye roll. "Meanwhile, we had no black ink for a *week* because they were too busy dribbling over you to order sufficient stock."

"Can you blame 'em?" Leo says with an innocent shrug, and Dean chuckles silently. He's looking a bit brighter and less worn out than he has for most of the week.

"I can when I don't have my inks," Sadie quips back. "Put your ovaries away, darling, and do your frickin' job. Emily can manage to get shit done, so there's no excuse. And you know why you hired them all, especially that last one. What was her name? 'Becky', or something?" She says sarcastically.

"Hey, sweetheart, you had all the eye candy you could want in the three of us. We all deserved some."

"Nice to know I didn't count," she laughs good-naturedly. I love their banter. It's great fun, and makes me laugh whenever I catch it during the day.

"You have Peter," he reminds her with a quirk of his scarred eyebrow, "or believe me, we'd all 'dribble' over you, Red."

She rolls her eyes again and shakes her head, giving him an amused exasperated look. I haven't yet met Sadie's partner, but he really must be something if all three of these men are like water off a duck's back to her. She and I have lunch together every day, and she talks about Peter a lot. He's an up and coming Economics lecturer at the University of Foxton, and she's fiercely proud of him. They've been together around four and a half years, and I've only seen one photo of him on her Instagram. He's in the shadows at a distance, so I haven't had a good look at him. She says he doesn't like being in photos much.

Leo, on the other hand, is whipping out his mobile. "Selfie time!" he declares, waving his hand to get us all to bunch up.

Sadie nods, and waves me closer to her. "Go on, then," she says to him, and slings her arm around me. I'm still so in awe of her confidence and her wardrobe; today she's rocking the Thelma and Louise look in an old band t-shirt and ripped jeans, but what would look slovenly on me looks chic as all hell on her, and I don't know how she does it. Though I imagine the raging, unstoppable natural beauty must help.

Dean leans next to me, his head resting lightly on my shoulder. His mop of bronze hair tickles my jaw a little. He's got what you might call a 'nice' face; not as obviously, jaw droppingly handsome as Leo and Eli, but he's appealingly expressive, and when his blue eyes light up with a smile, he's sex on legs. We're getting on really well. I'm trying to learn a little more ASL every night, and the gaps in my knowledge are easily accommodated with his iPad's notepad app. He's very patient with me as I learn, and we haven't found the communication barrier to be a big problem so far.

And then there's Leo, always with a ready smile. He's leaning back at a bizarre angle against Sadie's stomach, holding his phone up until he finds an angle where we all fit, snapping a shot once we're all smiling. "Beautiful," he says, sitting up again and fiddling with his phone. "Straight onto Instagram." Leo has been the soul of patience as he trained me up, and not a day goes by without at least five hugs, or an arm slung around my shoulder as he tells me something to make me laugh, always cheerful, never moody. At least, not that I've seen.

While Sadie asks Dean about his client this morning, I covertly whip out my phone and Google until I find Leo's post.

Congratz to our Emily for a great first week with us at @wishbonetattoos! You'll speak to her lovely self if you call up to book an appointment with us. Best hurry, the month is filling up fast! ***#NewReceptionist #OneOfUs #WeLoveYouEm***

I swallow hard over the lump in my throat at his kind words. Everyone in the photo looks happy and relaxed. Even me. I take a screenshot, even though it'll always be there on Instagram, and email it to myself. I don't ever want to lose this pic. I might even make it my phone's background.

I put my phone down and look up. Leo is watching me, and winks. I flush and smile.

"So, yeah, isn't it a shame Eli couldn't join us," Sadie observes as she takes another drink. Leo and Dean both give her a funny look, which I can't decipher, but I don't try.

"Well, we've shown him what he's missing," Leo replies, shaking his smart phone which is still open on Instagram and winking at her. I look down at my fingers, willing myself with all my might not to blush or do anything else to give myself away.

I have *such* a crush on Eli Gastright.

There, I admitted it.

It's completely ridiculous and laughable. He's so far out of my league it's not even funny. As if a man as ludicrously hot as that would ever look at a plain Jane like me.

But there's no harm in looking at him and wishing, I tell myself every morning, and, after the past few years I've had, it's nice—and a real surprise—to have a quiet, harmless crush on someone, safe in the knowledge that it can never go anywhere. Kind of like having a book boyfriend, but he's a walking, talking feature of your daily life that you can sigh over as you watch him in action.

"He should have come," Sadie says, with a definite tone, into her beer. Maybe he doesn't often join them?

"Mmmm," Leo agrees. "I did try, but you know our Eli. Wanted to get some stuff finished up." He gives a wry smile and stretches his jaw slightly as if to say, "meh, what are you gonna do".

Dean shakes his head and signs. I know enough to know he's said "works a lot" or "works too much", and, I think, "idiot".

I thought Leo was ridiculously handsome when I met him, and he is, but Eli seems to have been created to my own exact specifications of Dream Guy. That, long, almost black hair paired with those amazing, Mediterranean blue eyes and perfect olive skin. That wide, beautiful mouth, and that deep Cajun rumble that comes from it, never failing to send shivers of lust down my spine. I swear, I nearly lost myself entirely and collapsed in a swoon when I actually heard him say New Orleans' motto, "laissez les bon temps rouler", this morning to Leo. Especially when it was paired with the rare grin that splits his face in two and crinkles his eyes with laughter lines. And I never realised how much I like tattoos on a man until I saw Eli's arms, which are muscular and covered with intricate repetitive geometric designs, chevrons and zig zags and cross hatches and infinite detail. Even better, I saw the most amazing skull design on his rock hard abs when his t-shirt lifted a little as he reached to the top of the cupboards for the new coffee drum for me in the kitchen earlier this week. Managed to be cool, but did have to surreptitiously run my fingers along the corners of my mouth in case I was drooling.

He's a quiet one, that's for sure. Leo and Dean are both gregarious people in their different ways, and there's often a lot of laughter between them and their clients in their studios. Eli, on the other hand, gets the job done, no small talk, very little chit chat, just him and his laser focus. But it doesn't affect his popularity; I have to tell people who call asking for an appointment with him that there's a ten week waiting list.

Thanks to that tall, broad shouldered, mostly silent, inked up American, my battery operated boyfriend has been doing some serious overtime, and I need to remember to pick up some more batteries the next time I go grocery shopping or I'm screwed. Or, you know, *not*, as the case may be.

I shiver a little, even though there's not much of a breeze, as I imagine Eli running his tongue down my stomach on his way further down, to give me what is of course going to be the best head of my life…

"Anyway," Leo says, and I jump slightly, racing my mind back to the here and now and hoping no-one picked up on where my dirty mind was headed, "what made you move to Foxton?" They all look at me.

My throat goes dry. "Ah…well, it was just time for a change," I say, trying to sound breezy, as though I'm the sort of cool person who will completely uproot her life and relocate on a whim; however, I also don't want to sound unreliable to my employer, so I hastily add, "and I visited here a few months ago, just for a long weekend because it was off season and I could afford those sorts of prices, and I fell in love with the place. There's such a…I don't know, a vibe here. Like everyone's so inclusive, and life is about fun. I wanted that."

Dean signs something, and I catch the word 'family'.

"Your family must miss you," Leo translates.

I take a steadying sip of my drink. "Nope. My parents died when I was six, and my grandmother…she died about seven years ago." It's true. I'm alone in the world. The thought eats me up at night when I'm trying to get to sleep: there's no-one who loves me, no-one to care if I'm ill or hurt, no-one to mind if I'm in trouble. I sometimes wonder if that's part of the reason I stayed with Gav for so long: to have *someone*…

"I'm so sorry," Sadie says softly, giving my hand a gentle squeeze. Leo and Dean's eyes look sympathetic, too.

I shrug. "It's OK," I say with a smile, but I have to grit my teeth against the threat of some surprise tears. It's been so long since anyone sympathised with me that I don't really know what to do with myself.

Dean signs again, and I catch "who" and "all of us".

"Who's your favourite out of all of us," Sadie asks with a grin, letting go of my hand.

"Sadie," I say without skipping a beat, and Dean laughs, not making a sound. His head goes back, and his scar—a knotted, torn looking mass at his throat—is more visible. I try not to think about it, and I never ask him or anyone about that night, but the idea of someone shooting such a great person makes me want to break something.

"Hey," Leo says in mock affront, "what about all the times I showed you how to order stock and make appointments? Did they mean nothing to you?"

I shrug. "I'd just rather raid Sadie's wardrobe than yours," I say flippantly, and she fist bumps me.

Leo looks down at his t-shirt, a plain olive green that, while simple, really works with his golden skin tone. "I think you'd look cute in this," he asserts. Then, to my amused shock, he whips it off, leaving him bare chested in the middle of the beer garden, and throws it to me. "Here, try it on."

"Oh my god," Sadie drawls with an eye roll, "any excuse." Leo chuckles, and I gape at him a little. Dude is ripped, and covered in amazing ink, two full sleeves that must have taken hours, flashes of script here and there, and even a few mandalas I immediately recognise as Sadie's work. The women in the rest of the beer garden are staring in ill concealed lust, and I can't blame them. But hey, if you've got it, flaunt it, I guess, and Leo is many things, but he's definitely not a shy guy. "She doesn't want to wear your sweaty, smelly boy shirt," Sadie laughs.

I look down at it, and then sling it on over my loose fitting blouse. I want to join in with the spirit of things. I want them to like me. I want to be one of them. "Ta-dahhhh," I sing, holding my arms out, and get treated to laughter, a little applause, and a whistle from Leo.

"Save my seat," Sadie says suddenly, standing.

"I will personally rugby tackle anyone who tries to snag it," Leo assures her as he finishes his pint.

"Now, *that*, I'd pay to see," she replies without looking as she walks through the door to the bar. Leo turns his head and watches her go before turning back to me.

"That's a nice colour on you," he says.

I chuckle a little. "Thanks."

"So, are you happy with how everything's going? The job, I mean?" he asks me seriously, and Dean looks up, too.

And this is why I love working with them. They all treat me so well, and care that I'm OK.

"Absolutely," I say sincerely.

"Is there anything we can do to make life easier for you, or anything you think we can do better?" he asks.

I think hard. "Not really. Everything's been remarkably straightforward. Your systems were all there, you just needed someone to run them."

He nods. "Well, yeah. Someone consistent and reliable, who wouldn't dribble on us or throw tantrums..."

Dean snorts silently, eloquently for someone with no voice. Leo smirks at him, and I giggle.

"I keep hearing about these receptionists, and it sounds like there's a great story—"

"Look who I found!" Sadie exclaims brightly as she wanders back to the table, eyes sparkling a little.

And behind her, holding a dark looking pint, is Eli. My stomach plummets. He blinks as he looks at Leo, half naked, and me wearing Leo's shirt. I hastily take it off and hand it back.

Shit. *Shit.* Why did I have to be sat here looking like a wally when he walked in? Why??

"Buddy," Leo says brightly as he puts his t-shirt back on, and there's a gleam in his eye that I don't understand. "You made it!" He seems to be highly amused about something.

Sadie quickly sits at the end of the table. This leaves her old seat next to me as Eli's only option.

"Yeah, thought I'd drop by. There's nothin' that couldn't wait," Eli murmurs as he sits down, and my heart rate picks up. I'm frozen in my seat. God damn, he smells so good, like wood and rosemary. Whatever his aftershave is, I want to soak my pillow in it and let it send my dreams to a sexy place where clothes are optional.

"We were just talking about which of us is Em's favourite," Leo says, looking mischievous. Eli puts his pint glass down slightly hard on the table.

"And I won," Sadie crows, sticking her tongue out sweetly.

Eli smiles slightly. "Good choice," he says quietly without looking at me, taking a large swallow of his pint. I chuckle nervously, casting around for something to say.

"Was it the photo that got you down here? Caught the FOMO?" Leo asks, and really, I don't know why his expression is so entertained and challenging, but it makes me squirm a little.

Eli gives him a long, even look. "Sure, Leo," he drawls, "if you like."

"I saw him come in," Sadie explains, grinning, "so I thought I'd let him know where we were."

"You got a good table," Eli observes. He raises an eyebrow to Leo. "Though I wouldn't have said it was so much in the sun that you needed to strip, Cuz."

Leo stretches comfortably. "What do you mean? The weather's pretty god damn fine."

"For British people, perhaps," Eli drawls, pulling on the long sleeve of his black Henley. "In NoLa, this would count as chilly."

Leo makes a scoffing noise. "You delicate little flower. It's sixteen degrees and downright balmy."

I grin. I can't help myself.

"Oh, Em, you have *got* to let me in on why you're smiling like that," Leo says, leaning forward and resting his chin on his fists.

Crap. God, he doesn't miss a thing.

I shift uncomfortably in my seat. "Um…it's just…I love how you're blood relatives, but your accents are so different…" I trail off.

Leo grins, and when I risk a look at him, Eli's starting to do the same, though he looks away again. He has the most incredible smile, white and even. It completely changes his face, making him look…warmer. Less formidable and intimidating. And it makes my stomach squirm even more. *Damnit, does he have to be quite so pulsatingly gorgeous?* At this rate, my vibrator is going to break through overuse, never mind needing new batteries.

"Leo's ma used to be a Gastright. My dad's and Dean's dad's sister," Eli explains. "She married a Brit, and they settled here. But one of Leo's sisters lives in Louisiana, so there's a Mills-Gastright trade-off," he jokes.

"And then these *aaaaaaaahss-hawls* immigrated, what was it, eight years ago?" Leo muses.

"Almost ten, *arrrrsehole*," Eli quips back.

So, that would have been, what, four or five years after Dean was…

My eyes flick over to him, and he smiles gently at me. His fingers on his right hand move slowly, spelling something out, and I focus hard so I can keep up.

B-E-S-T-D-E-C-I-S-I-O-N-I-E-V-E-R-M-A-D-E

I smile, and slowly spell back, *S-A-M-E-H-E-R-E*. I think for a moment, and then add, concentrating, *N-O-R-E-G-R-E-T-S*. I don't think I made any mistakes. He smiles, showing teeth, and lifts his glass in our own private toast.

I notice Eli shift, and glance his way. For a brief second our eyes meet, and I can't quite read the look on his face. There's a gleam in his eyes that seems to have just slipped out in spite of himself. Then he looks away and clears his throat, and takes a drink. His pint is nearly finished already. I inwardly moan as he licks his lips to clear them of the traces of foam. It sends a flicker of heat straight to my clit with near pinpoint accuracy.

He won't look at me anymore.

I look away. *Don't get too lost in the fantasy,* I tell myself sternly. *He'll never be interested in you. Just enjoy the crush and take it out on your vibrator later.*

Leo

With the possible exception of Sadie's arse in her low rise Wranglers, this is the cutest thing I have ever seen.

They're into each other. They are *so into each other* that it's tangible, an extra guest at the table.

And this is so unlike Eli. I've never seen my cousin this mesmerised by a woman in my life. He's trying to act normal, and that in itself is telling: he's *having to try*. Almost finished his pint already because he keeps sipping it for something to do. He keeps looking around the beer garden, the plants, the fairy lights, the doorway to the bar, pretending he's thinking about anything except the fact that Emily's sitting next to him (nice work, Sadie!). But someone who knows him as well as I do, and pays attention as much as me, will notice that his jaw is pitched ever so slightly to the right, in her direction, and that he keeps sneaking furtive looks at her when he's fairly sure her attention is elsewhere, as though he can't stop himself. In spite of his actively affected Eli-style nonchalance, which is normally as natural as breathing to him, she has his undivided attention, even when he's not directly looking at her, and he's hanging on her every word.

You know what, this is *great*. I know he gave me shit when I hired her, and warned me not to pursue *this* receptionist, so in fairness I could give him shit right back for being hot for her himself, but I'm not gonna do that. I'm not gonna piss all over something this awesome. Eli's ex-wife really screwed him over, leaving him with the cruellest, nastiest fucking words she could muster to justify her actions in her own mind, and it was completely unnecessary. Plus, the damage she did is ongoing. She left scars rawer than if she'd physically cut his heart out.

Now, he just won't entertain the idea of anything approaching a meaningful romantic life. I know he has the odd extremely casual one night only fling here and there, because he's still a red-blooded bloke with needs, but he makes damn sure it goes nowhere. No sleepovers, no breakfasts together, no calls back, no exceptions. He's ethical about it, at least, and establishes his ground rules upfront—I've seen him refuse to kiss a woman until he'd made this clear and got her consent to his terms—but it's still sad that he doesn't allow for anything else to develop.

This is different, though. I've seen the way he looks at Emily in passing during the day. It's hungry. You have to know him well to catch it, but, in his own way, he lights up. A lingering glance, a quickly smothered smile at something cute she says. I can tell he likes her much more than he's comfortable with. She could never be one of his one-and-dones, and that must scare the shit out of him.

I study Emily as casually as I can. Sure, she hasn't been with us that long, so I can't claim to understand the inner workings of her mind, but I'm actually pretty good at reading people. And that's why I liked her so much straight away. She's one of life's genuinely lovely people, always so considerate and eager to go above and beyond. She's pretty jumpy, though. I definitely get the impression that there's a lot more to her relocating to Foxton than just fancying a change of scenery. Sometimes she gets this look, like a veil coming down over her face, and she seems to go elsewhere in her mind, and to a rather unpleasant place at that. She's haunted by something, or someone. I wish I knew the score. I don't like the idea of her being afraid or upset.

I just know, with bone deep certainty, that if Emily and Eli ever got it together, I'd end up going to their wedding one day. No doubt in my mind. They'd look after each other in their own ways; she'd soften his rough edges, and he'd protect her from life's knocks, and have someone to coddle and love, which I know he secretly longs for. They're *exactly* what each other needs, a perfect dovetailing fit.

Because she definitely likes him, too. She went a little pink when he sat next to her, and it suited her. If you ask me, and lord knows not enough people do, a pretty woman going pink in the face because of a crush is one of the most gorgeous sights life has to offer. And right now, there's a suggestion of a smile playing about the turned up corners of her lips. She seems to be trying to repress it, but she can't quite manage it. She won't look at him, and her shoulders are a little hunched, but...yup, she's just turned ever so slightly towards him, too. Boom, there it is.

Ah, *shit.*

I know exactly what's going to happen here. They're both going to stand well back from each other and let happiness slip through their fingers, Eli because he still believes his ex-wife's bullshit, and Em because she's too shy, or something. Neither of them will make a move, and all that well-deserved happiness for them both is gonna go to waste because they'll pretend it's not there for nonsense reasons that mean fuck all in the long run.

Well, not on my watch, son.

I look up at Sadie, and she's grinning into her beer. Yeah, she knows what's up. Sensing my gaze, she looks up to meet it, and her eyes sparkle. I look at the star crossed lovers, and then back at her. She winks. I wink back. We understand each other.

I glance to my right at Dean. He and I can communicate very effectively with only facial expressions, so I know he'll know exactly what I'm saying when I look at them, look back at him, and raise an eyebrow. He and Eli are like brothers, so he'll have noticed what's going on with him. *Yeah?*

One corner of his mouth quirks up in amusement. He nods, nearly imperceptibly, and masks it with a sip of his pint. *Yeah.*

I smile. They're both on board.

Excellent. This is going to be fun…

chapter FOUR

Eli

IT WAS SO WORTH JOINING THEM ALL.

Tonight I learned that Emily's favorite color is yellow, because it reminds her of the rapeseed fields she grew up next to in Suffolk. I learned that she's going to be thirty this year, and that the best birthday she's had so far was her twenty second because she had a nice meal with friends and ended up getting a free slice of cheesecake, which is her favourite dessert. I learned that she cracks up adorably at puns and Dad jokes, her nose wrinkling as she giggles in a way that makes my stomach dip, and I owe Leo around ten beers for keeping them coming in rapid succession so I could quietly enjoy her laughter for a while.

But there's a lot I didn't learn. She's happy enough to talk about these pretty basic details, but doesn't volunteer anything deeper than that. We're still no clearer as to why she left her hometown because she deflects those questions. She doesn't strike me as the sort who's in trouble and on the run, so maybe it's some personal stuff. Or maybe she really did just want to try a new town, and I'm reading too much into everything.

I did find out that she's not much of a drinker, but I didn't learn any reason why. Some people just don't like it, I guess, but...I don't know, I'm getting the impression that there's more to it.

I don't want this evening to end. I want to sit next to her all night and not sleep so I can try and learn more. I want the secrets she's hiding in her large gray eyes. I want her to lean closer until our heads almost touch so she can quietly tell me—and only me—everything.

But we've all got work in the morning, and she's been starting to stifle yawns behind her fingers.

"Keeping you up?" Leo chuckles.

"Sorry," she says with a rueful smile.

"Nah, you're right. We should make tracks," Leo observes, standing and stretching.

"Cab?" Sadie says, waving her phone.

"Oh, no, it's OK, I can walk," Emily replies.

"No, you should share a cab with us," I say. "We'll see you home safely."

She blinks, and smiles. *At me.* And the hard-on that's been plaguing me ever since I sat down next to her slams to attention.

Fuuuuuuuuuck, I'm so screwed.

"Only if you're sure. Thank you so much, that's really kind." She seems rather grateful for something pretty standard. We always make sure we see Sadie to her door after a night out, and I for one am definitely always going to extend the same basic courtesy to her.

"Cab for four, please, Jackie," Sadie says into her phone. She gets to know literally everyone on a first name basis. It's just her way. "From the pub. No, The Red Lion. Ah, awesome. Perfect, thanks, doll." She hangs up. "Apparently there's one that's two minutes away."

Dean gives her the thumbs up. He's looking a bit more rested, but still not back to his usual self. My guess is that the nightmares are back.

And then I remember.

I check my watch for the date just to be sure, and…yeah.

Shit.

It's almost Callie's birthday.

Her birthday doesn't trigger him every year—in fact, for the last couple of years or so it's come and gone without incident—but sometimes he suffers in the run-up. Even after nearly fifteen years.

Making a mental note to talk to him as soon as I can, I stand and wait for Emily to do the same. We say goodbye to Leo, who needs to go back to the studio to finish up some bookkeeping for the brand new tax year, and the black cab pulls up just as we step outside.

Dean and Sadie jump in first and sit next to each other with their backs to the driver. It buys me a few more minutes sitting next to Emily, and it's as though they know…but when I study their faces, they look genuinely innocent, like their minds are on other things. We always taxi home together; Dean lives in the flat upstairs from mine, and Sadie lives around the corner.

"Ooh, Em," Sadie says, playing affectionately with Dean's hand, "wait until you see my ten thirty appointment tomorrow." She fans herself. "I can never remember which one is Chris Hemsworth and which one is Liam, but he looks like one of them."

"Chris Hemsworth was Thor," Emily offers.

"Yes, that one," Sadie decides. "Girrrrrrrl, if I keep from biting his butt during the appointment, it's going to be a miracle." The women laugh and chatter about the hotness of a few of the actors from those Avengers films while Dean and I roll our eyes and shake our heads.

I find myself wondering if she likes pretty boys. I sigh a little. If the answer is yes, then I am definitely not her type; nobody would ever call me 'pretty'. I'm probably not even the kind of guy she'd be into, and not just in terms of looks. She's sweet and sociable under the layer of shyness. I'm quiet and distant. She needs a Leo type to bring out her brightness and encourage that spark.

I tell myself to consider myself out of the running. A blessing for her. A damn shame for me.

I ignore the cold, hollow feeling that settles in my gut at the idea of her dating somebody else, which, let's face it, is inevitable because she's so fucking awesome. Whoever he is, he'll be the luckiest man on the planet.

But he's not me.

"Just here," she says to the driver after what seems like the blink of an eye. I didn't even get the chance to start a conversation with her, to my regret. I peer out the window at her neighborhood, which is all brightly painted maisonettes. Huh. She really is a stone's throw away from Wishbone. Probably not even five minutes of walking. I'm glad. It'll be safer for her in a few months when the nights draw in sooner. Maybe I can walk her home...

Just as friends. For safety reasons.

The driver pulls over and she smiles at us both. She takes out her wallet. "Here's my share of cab fare—"

"Don't worry about it," I tell her firmly.

She looks at me, eyes softening, her teeth worrying her lip. "Are you sure?"

"Positive." I try not to let her smile distract me.

"Thank you," she says sincerely. It's just the price of a short taxi ride, and once again she's behaving as though I've given her a gift. The thought that just this small kindness has been absent from her life before now bothers the shit outta me.

She opens the door with a final smile and brief wave to us all. "See you tomorrow."

"Bye, hon," Sadie sings, Dean holds his hand up, and I nod and grunt.

The door closes, and the driver starts to change gear to move on. "Wait until she's inside," I tell him sharply, pissed that he'd drive off before she's safely in her home, and I watch as she unlocks her door and goes inside. Once the door closes behind her, I nod at him, and we drive off.

Sadie and Dean both give me a look. A look that speaks of amusement at my expense.

I try to ignore it, but then they both shake their heads and chuckle. "What?" I ask, shrugging.

"Didn't say anything," Sadie says nonchalantly.

"Just being a decent person," I mutter, and look out the window, at the driver's ID, at the No Smoking sign…anywhere except at my friend, who can suddenly read me like a book, and my cousin, who is sucking in his cheeks in an effort to keep his face straight.

I've got to let this almighty attraction to Emily go, fast. It's already gone too far if their expressions are any indication. If I ignore it long enough, it will go away. It *will*, I insist to myself, but there's an uneasy sense in my chest that it's not going to be that simple this time. Not with her.

We make sure Sadie gets dropped off next. She gives me a kiss on the forehead, which she doesn't do normally, and a final smirk. I make a bit of a show about making sure we wait until she's closed her door—and the cab driver doesn't need to be told this time—but this only makes Dean give me a knowing, *you're fooling no-one* look as I tell the driver where to drop us off in the next street. I know exactly what's going through his mind right now, because he and I can have whole conversations without words, but there is one talk I do need to be having with him.

"Where y'at?" I ask him seriously.

Awrite, he signs automatically, smiling slightly. You can take the boys out of the Big Easy… *How about you, loverboy?*

"You know what I mean," I say quietly, ignoring his comment. "You've been looking pretty tired lately, and then I checked the date." His smile fades, and I feel bad, but I know from experience that he does better when things are stated plainly and dealt with, rather than pretending he's fine. "I'm sorry I forgot," I tell him quietly.

It's OK, he says immediately, and rubs a hand over his face and stretches his shoulders. He sighs. *Sneaks up on me sometimes. Probably always will.*

"I know, man," I say as the driver pulls up. I pay him, and we head inside.

"Dean," I say before he trudges further up the stairs to his apartment. I'm on the second floor, he's on the third. I made damn sure we were neighbors when we moved here just under ten years ago, in case he needed me. I was there through every step of his rehabilitation process, and I'm here for him twenty four seven no matter what; it's just the way it is. "Do you need to call Gabriel?" Gabriel is his therapist. He used to talk to him regularly, but now he only reaches out when the flare-ups happen, and only with a lot of convincing.

He shakes his head in certainty. *Nah, I'm good. They're just nightmares. Same old, same old.*

I sigh. If Mr Whitmire hadn't blown his own brains out at the end of the shooting, I'd have choked him till his neck snapped for what he's done, what he's *still* doing, to my cousin. And I'd have done it with a smile on my face. Although I've been told I look intimidating, I'm not a violent man by nature, but I'd make an exception for that sick bastard. I don't take at all kindly to people hurting my loved ones. Dean went through hell that night at his prom, and saw terrible, horrifying things that most people can't even begin to imagine. I've seen him in the throes of countless nightmares and post-traumatic stress disorder episodes, and it's gut wrenching. He's doing much better now than he used to. His meltdowns used to happen a lot more often, with many more triggers than he has now, so just once in a while is serious progress. Still, I keep a watchful eye on him. "OK, but you know where I am."

He gives me a nod, then starts up the stairs. He pauses, and climbs back down them again, looking me squarely in the eye.

You didn't even look at Charmaine the way you look at Emily, he says. I blink. He never, ever mentions my ex-wife.

I wish he wouldn't mention Emily, either. He knows the score as well as Leo; I confessed everything to them in a state of numb, drunken despair the night Charmaine left, needing to offload in spite of the humiliation I felt. They know to leave the subject well alone, and I don't know why they can't do the same this time.

"Stop reading shit into things," I grumble. "OK, fine, she's hot, but I'm not int..." I sigh. Jeez, I can't even say that I'm not interested out loud. I shake my head, like this is all just tiresome.

Dean shrugs and holds his hands up in an 'alright, if you say so' gesture. *Whatever, man, I know what I saw.* He gives me a long look, and whatever he sees there puts him off continuing the conversation. *Night,* he says, and heads up to his place.

I probably shouldn't have gone tonight, as it's only made me like Emily more, which I can't afford, but I can't bring myself to regret it. Watching her talk with Dean—even in the most rudimentary ASL—made my heart ache in the best possible way. Family is the most important thing in the world to me, always has been, always will be. I'm protective of Dean in a way I never have been with anyone else, and seeing her make the effort to talk to him without leaning on anyone else to help...it did something to me. It took everything I had not to take her free hand and kiss each individual knuckle in gratitude.

My apartment seems quiet, dull, and empty after this evening. I sigh and throw my keys on the coffee table, briefly considering turning on the TV before giving in to the idea of just going to bed. I grab my iPad and turn it on, waiting for it to load while I brush my teeth.

Once in bed, though, I can no longer ignore the insistent and relentless throb of my boner. I turn my iPad off, all thoughts of catching up with my emails now forgotten, and sigh hard. My dick is demanding a greater and greater share of my attention as the seconds tick by, a heavy fullness and admittedly pleasurable sensitivity swelling through me and making me glad I took my jeans off because *shit* this would be uncomfortable otherwise. When it comes to self-gratification, I'm normally an every-morning-in-the-shower kinda guy, but I'm pretty sure I won't get a moment's sleep until I take care of this. It won't wait.

Fine.

I snake my hand down, into my boxers, and grasp my cock. I blink. I'm rock hard, even more so than I'd anticipated. Close proximity to Emily had a stronger impact on me than I realized. Giving it a quick experimental pull sends a tingle down my spine. For me, this is usually a brisk and efficient race to the necessary release, which is kind of depressing, now I think about it. I'm not even allowing myself this much of an indulgence, and why? The gun is still loaded, even if it only fires blanks.

Indulge. The word flickers through my mind, where a crystal clear picture of what I want waits patiently for me to give in.

Give in to *her*.

In my thoughts, my wildest dreams, I brush my lips over her naked, soft-as-silk skin, slowly kissing down her collarbone, across her breast, and finally to the tip of her nipple. I circle it with my tongue before gently biting, and I can almost feel her fingertips digging into my shoulders.

Reflexively, my hand tightens. My imaginings are more vivid than they have ever been, and it's making everything feel stronger, sharper, more piercing. My pulse is pounding hard with anticipation. I rub myself the way I know I like, a few slow, thorough strokes to wake my entire shaft up, before gradually speeding up. Only this time, my grip is harder than normal, and I'm starting to ache. It feels…god, better than I can say.

I think of her, of the noises I could coax from her if I ran my tongue down her belly, over her mound, to her clit, and my helmet feels like it lights up. I always find that V of flesh on a woman so tantalizing… My balls tighten as I imagine being able to taste her, her flavor on my tongue, licking her over and over, *mine,* and I feel the brush of electric shocks just under the head, where I am most sensitive. I'm closer than I thought. A few hard pulls would push me over the edge, *already,* but I want to push it back, I want to enjoy this, I want more…

But then my mind flits unbidden to thoughts of her returning the favor. I picture her looking up at me with sharp, lust filled eyes as she engulfs my dick in her warm, wet mouth, her lips dragging over me, teasing me…

"*Chere,*" I gasp, desperately trying to hang on, but it's no use. I'm past the point of no return. I'm acting on pure instinct now, stroking myself hard and fast until I come in hot, throbbing waves, grunting and cursing through the heart pounding ecstasy.

Jesus, that was intense.

As my breathing and my pulse return to normal and I clean myself up, I start to feel like an idiot. Moping like a lovesick ass, and then frantically pleasuring myself like a horny teenager the moment I'm at home alone after seeing her, unable to withstand more than a few seconds of imagining her blowing me before I shoot my load. Ironically, considering what I just did, I need to get ahold of myself.

I can't wait to see her tomorrow.

I can't help that feeling. I wish I could. I wish I could turn it off and go back to normal. It would save me a lot of sadness.

It's the absence of possibilities that's really starting to hurt. I wish I was a normal guy, one able to offer her everything she could want. I swear, I'd treat her so right. Take her to nice places, stay up all night talking to her just to find out more about how she sees the world, and make sure she knew every day just how important she was to me.

Maybe she won't care that you're broken?

I can hardly believe I even thought that. It kinda gives me hope…

…but then, I wouldn't be that lucky.

I just want a normal life, Eli. I can't believe you'd be so selfish as to want me to give that up, just for the sake of being your wife. You're defective. Being with you would leave me as empty as your ballsack, and that's not a fair thing to ask. Any woman would feel the same, it's not just me, so don't make out like it's my fault here. YOU'RE the one with unreasonable expectations. It's asking too much of me, of any woman. You selfish piece of shit… You can't expect me to still love you after this…

Grimacing, I turn my mind away from Charmaine's ugly words, pushing them back to the past where they belong, and try to settle down to sleep.

chapter FIVE

Dean

I LOVE WALK-IN DAYS.

Once a month we run a promotion where the clients can call in without an appointment and select from a pre-drawn chart of small tattoos, each no more than a couple of inches long, for thirty pounds a pop. Letters, skulls, all seeing eyes, stars, flowers, representing a selection drawn by each of us. We set up stations in the front of the store, and it's first come, first served, depending on whose design you selected. Easy money, and good for tattoo virgins wanting to try it out. It often leads to repeat business.

Right now, Eli and I are occupied with clients, and Leo and Sadie are relaxing behind the reception counter with Emily. I'm inking runes that say 'Old love does not corrode' onto my client Rob's shoulder for his twentieth wedding anniversary, but I have half an ear on their conversation.

Leo seems to be going for the needling Eli approach, much to mine and Sadie's amusement. He's not exactly flirting with Emily, as I know he'll be careful not to overstep boundaries with her, but he is showering her with affectionate attention. I get the idea behind drawing her out for Eli's benefit. I know him well enough to know that, no matter how much he stares at his work, his focus is devoted to her, same as in the pub a few nights ago. So Leo's definitely giving him an easy route to finding out more about her.

Slinging his arm around her shoulders and kissing her cheek? Calling her 'babe' and 'sweetheart'? That's just baiting him, and it could be a stroke of genius.

Or Eli's going to grind his teeth into dust.

I smile to myself. It's about fucking time he found someone to be happy with. And seeing him trying to pretend he's not all bent out of shape about it is brilliant, after all these years.

Just gotta convince him to admit it, shed the past that's been holding him back, and go for it.

Piece of cake.

Eli

I'm finding myself grateful that my latest client has gone for my most complicated and intricate miniature, a realistic rose bud with fine shadowing and dewdrops on the petals. Gives me something else to concentrate on other than Leo's shenanigans.

I don't think he's really making a play for her. I may not be able to pursue anything with her myself, but I'll be damned if I watch my cousin live out my fantasy in front of me. *Surely the universe wouldn't be* that *cruel…?*

I look up for the millionth time. Normally I don't even register the outside world when I'm working, even during walk-in days where I'm forced to leave my studio and work out front. Usually I can tune out the background noise.

But today, it's my cousin teasing and laughing with the woman who features strongly in my dreams.

Nah, I reassure myself. He's doing this because he

figured out I like her, which makes me want to kick myself. He wouldn't do that to me for real in a million years.

But it doesn't make this any more pleasant to watch.

"Hey," Leo says to her, "while it's quiet, I want you to update our Spotify with your favourite songs." The music in our parlor is basically a team Spotify account. It's eclectic, to say the least. My ears prick up. I wonder what she'll add? Any new information about her likes and dislikes is like a drug to me. All I ever want is my next hit.

"Oh," she fidgets, "that's OK, you've got a lot of my favorites anyway." I frown. Something is definitely going on with her if she thinks expressing her preferences even to this small degree is too much.

"I insist," he says smoothly. "I'm sure we don't have every single one. Indulge me, I'm curious." I look up just as he lowers his head to meet her gaze. "Pleeeeeease?" he cajoles comically, but I see the concern hidden in his eyes. I've gotta hand it to him, he's good. She seems to both melt and squirm as she nods.

Dean signs to her, and in my peripheral vision I catch the words *Eli* and *his Britney collection*, some words spelled out to allow for her being an ASL beginner. I shake my head on a small smile, and she grins when she gets the gist of what he's said.

My turn to squirm.

Enough. Back to my tattoo.

"There are a couple of songs that we don't allow on the playlist," Leo murmurs to her quietly, "but I'll let you know if I see you add any of them."

I glance across at Dean. By the twist in his mouth, he heard, but it hasn't upset him. I'm relieved. And it's important for Emily to know not to add them.

A Metallica track I added to the Spotify ends, and then she plays something vaguely familiar to me. It's loud metal, which surprises me. She looks like she's more of an indie pop girl, but I'm liking her choice a lot. Leo whoops.

"Ratfinks!" he exclaims. "Jesus, I haven't listened to any White Zombie in *years*. Good shout!" He high fives her.

She flushes, pleased. "You don't mind it?"

"Absolutely not," he assures her, and then gives her a third kiss on the cheek, and can feel that muscle in my jaw tightening again.

Back to the god damn tattoo, for the final time. Seriously.

"Play all the White Zombie you want, we all dig it." He leans towards the screen. "Let's see what else you're adding…" He whistles. "Damn, girl, you got taste."

"What's next?" Sadie asks, looking up from her phone.

"Let's see, we got some Motorhead, Rammstein, Divyded…" He punches the air. "No way, Madness! Em, you *have* to marry me."

I'm gonna spit in the next coffee I make him.

Wait a second…

"Did you say Rammstein?" I ask, almost hoarsely. *Oh, come on, universe, that's not fair, stop making her so perfect…* Rammstein are one of my all time favorite bands, and I count their gigs among the best I've ever been to.

"Mmhmm," she replies with a shy smile. "I've added *Ich Will*. Are you a fan, too?"

I nod, wondering what else she can throw at me to prove how much she fits the bill of My Ideal Woman. It's almost funny at this point.

But I'm not laughing. Not when it's starting to chafe like this.

"I'm liking this one," Sadie comments. "White Zombie, was it?"

"Yeah," Em replies. "I'm not sure why, but I always find Ratfinks incredibly relaxing. It's a song I used to listen to when

I was having a bubble bath at the end of a long, hard day. That, and Africa by Toto." She laughs.

I turn my needle off and manage to quietly disguise a growl as throat clearing. Emily. Naked. In bubbles. I picture her in *my* tub at my home, waiting for me there to surprise me after work…the heat of the bath water flushing her pale skin, the suds and droplets of water running down her body as she stands…

My dick hardens to the point of chafing along my fly. The zipper's going to leave a bite mark at this rate. *Quit it,* I snap at myself mentally. I groan inwardly. That image of her is not going to let up once I'm home. I've been jerking myself raw like I'm in high school all over again since I met her, and after this, tonight will be no different.

"Sounds like we need to add the Emily Cole Having a Bath playlist to our Spotify," Leo drawls, "don't you think, Eli?"

Sadie's attempt to hide a bark of laughter as a cough is not convincing. I hold my jaw steady as I take a couple of slow, even breaths through my nose. I can't shake off the mental images of Em in the bath, and that bastard cousin of mine is deliberately making it worse.

"Fuck yeah," my client pipes up, sitting up slightly. "What else do you play in the bath, sweetheart?" He waggles his eyebrows at her suggestively.

I press harder with the needle, making him hiss through his teeth. "Shit, watch it," he complains.

I give him an even look. "My apologies," I mutter, wishing I could just pull him up and sling him out for making that double entendre.

The others seem to have moved on when I next look up. Leo's marching like Ric Flair to a Madness song, I think it's called *Our House*, to make both women laugh.

I will never understand British people.

"So, you gonna have a little tattoo, sweetie? While we're

doing them?" Leo asks Emily, giving her shoulders a little squeeze. I look up once again, waiting for her response with bated breath. I can't decide whether I want to choke Leo for the idea, or hug him in gratitude. I'd *love* for Em to be sitting in my chair, trusting me as I ink something beautiful onto her skin, leaving my mark on her forever... *Fuck, don't pick someone else to do it, pick me...*

She flinches, and the hope dies. "Um..." She winces. "I mean, I'd love one, but...I'm so sorry, I just... I can't." The more she goes on, the more I want to stop what I'm doing, stride around the counter, and hug her and say it's OK.

"No worries, petal," Leo says easily. She clearly thinks she's letting the team down by declining, and I want to rip into him for putting her on the spot. "It's not a prerequisite of working here. But if you ever change your mind," he says, nodding towards us all, "any one of us will be more than happy to pop that tattoo cherry. Isn't that right, guys?" he says, but looks directly at me.

Oh, fuck you, I tell him with my eyes as mental images of being the first to ink her virgin skin fly through my mind. Followed swiftly by the idea of having been the lucky guy to have taken part in Emily Cole's sexual debut. I shake my head, not daring to pursue that line of thinking. I scowl at his smug, shit-eating grin. *Thanks so fucking much, asshat.* He lifts his eyebrow at me, not bothered, and amused at my expense.

"Sure," I bite out, and then I make the mistake of looking at her.

Her eyes are smiling gently into mine in the way that's starting to make me ache when it happens. Once again, our soft gaze is a beat too long to brush off as meaningless, pinching my gut with both joy and despair. Her hair is tied back today, and some of the strands at the front are escaping down her cheek. My fingers tingle with the desire to tuck them behind her ear...to cup her face, and just spend a few short, stolen moments looking at her, taking in her beauty, the sweetness in her face that can never really be mine.

Shit.

I'm going to fall in love with this woman, I realize numbly. *If I'm honest, I'm already halfway there. And there's not a damn thing I can do to stop it.*

I sigh, making myself look away from her and back to my work, bracing myself for what this is inevitably going to mean.

Later that night, on the EmEli WhatsApp channel (members: Sadie Stewart, Leo Mills, Dean Gastright)

Sadie Stewart: Leo, you prick, what if she'd said yes and chosen one of your doodles? Or Dean's, or mine? Risky game!!

Leo Mills: Then I'd have needed either of you elsewhere for now, and/or mysteriously developed hand cramp and Eli would have taken over. He can mimic anyone's design. I'm not just a pretty face, Sades.

Sadie Stewart: …OK, fair enough. But you're still a prick ;)

Leo Mills: Love you, too, princess [kiss emoji]

Dean Gastright: His face when you asked tho [laughing emoji]

Leo Mills: IKR.

Leo Mills: I just had a genius idea

Leo Mills: Night out on the town. Those two. Some alcohol. Dancing. Bam chaka wow wow. Guaranteed ;)

Leo Mills: God damn I'm a smart man

Leo Mills: I surprise myself

Sadie Stewart: That's actually not the worst idea I've ever heard

Leo Mills: *takes a bow*

Sadie Stewart: I'll come, and I'll bring Peter

Leo Mills: Sure

Sadie Stewart: A few Jaegerbombs, get your DJ mate to play some Rihanna, and…

Sadie Stewart: [GIF of Edward and Bella's first kiss from the Twilight movie]

Leo Mills: LOL ;)

Sadie Stewart: Deano, any further inside track for us?

Dean Gastright: Nothing beyond what I already told y'all. He definitely likes her, but he's still got Asshole Charmaine's shit in his head

Sadie Stewart: :(glad I never met her, and that I don't know the full story. NEVER tell me what she said cos I'll lose my shit

Dean Gastright: BTW something is def going on with her

Dean Gastright: Emily, I mean

Leo Mills: Yeah, totes. Wish I knew what.

Dean Gastright: Her face when you asked her if she wanted a tattoo…

Leo Mills: Her face when I invited her to add her music, too

Sadie Stewart: Does anyone else get the battered woman vibe from her

Leo Mills: Oh shit

Leo Mills: Now you mention it

Dean Gastright: I fuckin hope not, but it would make sense

Sadie Stewart: If that's the deal, I am definitely hunting down the shithead in question >:(

Leo Mills: Me too

Dean Gastright: Me three

Sadie Stewart: Honestly, no shit, I want her and Eli to live happily ever after more than I want Christmas

Sadie Stewart: And you know how much I love Christmas

Leo Mills: Can't wait to see those spiral pointed bell shoes again, my little Christmas elf ;)

Sadie Stewart: ;) sometimes I wear them just to do the housework

Leo Mills: Just them, or...?

Sadie Stewart: Perv

Leo Mills: [GIF of Leonardo DiCaprio rolling his eyes and biting his knuckles in Wolf of Wall Street]

Dean Gastright: [Eyeroll emoji] And on that note, I'm off to bed

chapter SIX

Emily

"I WANT TO GET MY PIERCING CHANGED."

I look up from my computer, where I've just entered a new appointment onto Eli's calendar. The man in front of the counter is very handsome in a probably-plays-in-a-hard-rock-band kind of way, all spiky hair and pierced eyebrows and 10mm ear gauges, but his eyes are wild. He looks like he's not slept in weeks and is manically awake, and he's clenching and unclenching his jaw at an alarming speed. He points at his nose ring, and that nostril does look a little pink and inflamed. "While we're still young," he adds.

Great. A customer with an attitude an hour before closing time. The perfect end to an otherwise great day.

"Oh, I'm...not sure that's a service we offer," I say, smiling apologetically. I mean, they've never mentioned doing any kinds of piercings, and I haven't booked anyone in for one before. Surely they'd have told me about it during training. "I'm not sure where to recomm—"

"I had this done here, so I think you do," he says rudely, glaring at me.

"Oh...I'm...sorry," I stammer, "I'm new, I'll..." He rolls his eyes. "I'll check," I say quietly, picking up the phone and dialling Sadie's extension with fingers that are starting to shake. Sadie's perfectly capable, but I get the definite impression he'd respond better to someone with a penis; unfortunately, Leo's out, and Eli and Dean are occupied. *He's not Gav…he's just a little moody because his piercing hurts…you're fine…you can handle this…*

"Yeah, you do that," he snaps, placing both hands on the counter in front of me, closer than I'd like, and huffing impatiently. "And I'm not too happy that it's become infected already. Wouldn't be surprised if you used a dirty needle. Fucking disgusting." I flinch at the accusation more than the swearing. That's something I know we'd never, ever do, under any circumstances, and we can't have him badmouthing us around town.

The phone rings, and I seriously hope that I'm wrong and that we can sort this out for him. I really don't fancy telling him 'no' again.

"S'up, babygirl?" Sadie says on the end of the line.

"Hi, we, ah, have a gentleman here who wants his nose piercing changed," I say quickly, feeling my pulse starting to race and my head start to feel a little lighter with panic, "and he says we did the original piercing, so—"

"No, we don't do that," Sadie says, confirming my worst suspicions, "we've never done that, so he must be mistaken."

"We don't," I repeat, my guts sinking, "OK, thanks, Sadie."

"No worries," she says, and ends the call. I want to call her back and plead with her to come through, and not to leave me alone with this man. The thought makes me feel low and pathetic. *This is my job. I need to handle this. I need to be a grown-up, not a feeble little child.*

I turn to him and quietly take a steadying breath. It doesn't work. "I'm-I'm sorry, sir," I say quietly, trying not to let my voice tremble, "we don't offer any services connected with piercings—"

"You bloody do," he barks at me, "because I had this done

right here two months ago, so try again. Stop trying to weasel out of it and sort your fuck-up."

Fuck-up.

My stomach clenches as the memories assault me. *God, you really can't do anything without fucking it right up, can you, like, not a single thing,* a familiar masculine voice sneers nastily in my head, and my throat clenches in remembrance. I'm hot. I'm too hot. It's stifling in here out of nowhere. My skin is too hot. Need air. Open a window. AIR.

No. Focus.

"I'm…I'm sorry, sir, but we've been open for almost ten years now, a-and I've just been told we don't do—"

"Are you fucking calling me a liar?" He nearly roars the words, and I cringe, pushing away from the counter. The door opens, and another guy, a friendly looking Jim Halpert of a man with vaguely familiar eyes, walks in. "I don't fucking believe this," he continues, clearly stewing up and whirling on the new customer, "I'm being called a liar."

"N-no, no, please," I beg him, because I really don't want him levelling that accusation at me, even though I am basically telling him he's wrong. His eyes are dark and livid, and his anger is escalating. I know the signs too well. *De-escalate NOW, calm him down, quick…* "I just…I…" Oh god, my mind is going blank. I can't handle this. I'm out of practice. I never thought I'd have to do it again. Icy cold fear spreads through my gut, and my eyes aren't working properly. I'm dizzy. I'm blurry. I can't inflate my lungs all the way. My throat is too tight for me to be able to swallow anymore.

"I just, uhhhhh, *uhhhhhhhhhhhhh,*" he mocks me viciously, slacking his jaw, and a little of his spit flicks onto my face. I freeze. "Get me your manager, now. NOW." He yells the last word, and I flinch and cringe again.

I knew this would happen. I knew something would happen

and I would show myself up for the useless waste of life I am and crumble under any sort of pressure. I want to go home. I want to be in my bedroom, alone, under the covers, where nothing can hurt me.

"Hang on a minute, mate," the other customer starts to say in a calm tone, his hands up in a placatory gesture, and then I hear Sadie's voice as if from a long way away, but she's just by the door to the studios, which *is* a long way if you have jelly legs, I guess. All I can do is gulp and clear my leaping throat and whimper.

"What's going on?" she says sternly, and I can see that she's frowning a little, and I try so hard to breathe and to find words to tell her what's going on, but I....

"Finally! Are you the manager?" Angry Man demands.

I can't do this.

"Can I help you?" Sadie says frostily, lifting her chin and narrowing her eyes, steady as a rock, clearly unimpressed by Angry Man's tone. I wish more than anything I could be her, and be unafraid, and stand up to him like a pro. Instead, I'm stuck being me. Jellyfish, lily livered, stupid, useless me.

"Yes," he snarls, and points at me. "This stupid bitch called me a liar, and I want to know what you're going to do about it! AND the piercing you gave me is *fucking infected...*"

Like the coward I am, I cut and run, ditching Sadie to deal with this client on her own. A horrible thing to do.

Yeah, go on, Em, Gav's voice drawls through my brain, *run off and leave someone else to clear up your mess, that's what you do best, isn't it,* isn't it, *you useless, selfish...*

My legs are numb and shaking and then I'm in the kitchen and I can't breathe through my throat because it's closing up and I'm burning hot and everything is too close to me and too loud and I can hear him still yelling at Sadie and I want to go home and I want my mother but she's dead and I can't breathe I CAN'T BREATHE

Eli

BAM BAM BAM

I stop drawing small designs for next week's walk-in tattoo promotional offer and rush to my door to see what the problem is.

Dean was about to slap my door again when I opened it. "What's up, what—"

His face is hard, eyes looking angry and worried, and he points at the kitchen next door. I walk over, and I hear her before I reach the doorway. "*Hgggggggghhhh…*"

Emily is holding onto the counter, her knuckles white, and she's knocked a glass of water over the work surface. It's dripping onto the floor. She's leaning forward and seems to be struggling to breathe, frantically dragging air through her lungs in desperate, shallow huffs. Her eyes are wild, and tears are streaming down her face. I can see her legs shaking; they don't look like they'll hold her up much longer.

I rush over to her and take her hands, which are clammy and cold, and place them on my shoulders. "Emily?" She struggles for control, but she's too far gone. I know what's up. I've dealt with this with Dean more times than I can count. The urge to hold her and protect her floods through me even harder than normal. "Panic attack?" I ask. I've found it's better to keep questions as brief as possible when Dean is struggling. She manages to nod, just barely, and I go into calming mode. I know the drill. I just want to destroy whatever has frightened her, wipe it from this earth, but first things first.

Her hands are clutching at my sleeves, biting a little into my skin with a death grip like I'm all that's keeping her alive right now. I ignore the pinching pain and speak in a low, clear, calm voice, holding her wrists gently but firmly. "Emily, look at me.

Look at my face." She's staring unseeing at my chest. "Tilt your chin up just a little bit and look at my face." After a couple of squeaky pants, she lifts her gaze up to my chin. "Good," I say quietly, "now look at my eyes." She swallows tightly, as though it hurts, and lifts her eyes to mine, and I see a world of pain and terror that shocks me to my core. "That's real good," I murmur calmly, "now, keep looking into my eyes—no, keep looking," I gently encourage as her eyes dart about all over the kitchen in a panic, "and breathe with me." Out of the corner of my eye I see Dean set the tipped drinking glass upright and then leave the room. He doesn't like an audience when he's having a meltdown, and I guess he's satisfied that I've got this. And I do.

"Breathe with me," I say again slowly, and take a deep, slow inhale through my nose.

She clutches tighter onto my sleeves, not breathing in or out. "I can't," she croaks, sounding strangled, trembling as more tears spill over her face.

"Yes you can," I assure her, and pull her a little closer. "Hold on to me all you want, and just follow my lead. Breathe in and out for the count of four. OK? We can do this." Again, I take a slow, deep breath in through my nose. *One, two, three, four...* I hold it and look at her. She gives me a look filled with desperation, and finally breathes in, a little harder and faster than me. "Good," I praise her, watching her try to hold it. She manages, and then breathes out for maybe two, two and a half. We try again, with me setting the example and her following, doing a little better each time.

I hear some yelling, and then a loud crash and a slam. It makes her jump and she cringes in my arms, clutching on to me tighter, but I murmur soothingly and get her to refocus on our breathing. *She's safe with me. Nothing, and I mean* nothing, *is going to hurt her while I'm around.* I say this aloud to her in as comforting a voice as I am able.

When her breathing settles back down, she dissolves into tears in my arms. "I'm sorry, I'm so sorry," she cries, and I let her cry it out on my shirt.

"It's OK," I whisper, slowly rubbing the middle of her back in a circle to try and ground her. I can't help but enjoy holding her, though obviously I wish it was for a more pleasant reason.

Sadie pokes her head around the door, frowning, and then looking with sympathy and concern when she sees the state Em is in. "Oh, honey," she says gently, "don't cry." She walks forward and squeezes her arm. "He scared you, eh? He's a nothing. Just a stupid little coked out dipshit. And he's gone, I promise."

"I'm so sorry, Sadie" Em sobs, and she clings to me tighter. "I shouldn't have ditched you with him—"

"You have nothing to be sorry about," Sadie says firmly and kindly. "That guy was a dickless wonder. I sorted him. He won't be coming back, *ever*. Lifetime ban on this shithead," she says, showing me a photo she took on her phone. White male, tattoos definitely not done by us, wild and angry eyes, didn't like his photo being taken. Looks like the asshole he clearly is. I'm glad Sadie was able to handle him without needing to call the police. She can be scary when she needs to be.

"You got it," I say. After seeing what he did to Emily, if I ever see this guy around, I will grab his hand and break every single finger one by one, leaving plenty of time in between each snap.

"He knocked a plant pot over as he flounced off," Sadie quips with an eyeroll, "So I'll go clean that up. Tim's out there, too, and he said he'd give me a hand." Tim's her brother. Nice guy.

"N-no, I should," Emily mumbles.

Sadie shakes her head and gives Em a kiss on the temple. "Stay with Eli," she advises her, "And don't worry how long you need to take time out. Even if you need to go home, we can cope for the rest of the day. There's, what, an hour left? And I'd rather you had the time you needed to feel better than anything else, and I know everyone would say the same." She looks up at me. *You got this?* She mouths.

I nod briefly.

I'll cover Reception, she continues, and leaves us alone together in the kitchen.

Emily's breathing more normally, and her color is looking a bit better, but she's still very upset. Almost broken.

Dean's meltdowns are different. Silent, obviously, and with more obvious triggers, like a slammed door (hence why we have slow close doors here, and why I was a little surprised that he banged on my door so hard). He sweats, hyperventilates, shudders, and kind of bunches in on himself and goes someplace else in his mind. Comforting him is more about bringing him back to the here and now and out of the flashback.

Emily's pain is palpable, and she's still muttering "I'm sorry" over and over.

"Nothin' to be sorry for," I assure her. I gently, very gently, guide her chin up. "What happened?"

She takes a deep breath. "That man," she chokes out in a hoarse voice. "He wouldn't stop shouting." She bites her lip and looks like she's holding her breath again. Just as I'm about to start a new external focus exercise with her again, she lets out the breath she was holding in a mirthless huff of laughter. "I'm sorry, I know this is immature, but I just can't stand being shouted at. I can't stand shouting at all anymore, even when it's not...aimed at me."

I find myself listening intently. Dean doesn't really say much when he's coming down from an episode because his hands shake too much for ages afterwards. So it's really hard to hear Emily so upset, but I'm glad she's confiding in me.

"It's stupid," she mutters.

"It's not stupid," I say gently but firmly. "He frightened you, and that's not OK." Once again, I'd *love* to get my hands on this fucker.

"Yeah, but this is a pretty extreme reaction from me. Overreaction, really," she says, and her face crumples again. "Shit. Do you have any tissues?"

There's kitchen roll behind me, and I give her a handful. Way too much, really, but at least that makes her smile a little. She blows her nose delicately and wipes under her eyes, smearing a little of her make-up. "I'm so sorry about this," she mumbles, not looking at me. "You must think I'm really weak."

I lean down to catch her eye. "Not at all," I tell her firmly. "I definitely *don't* think that." She needs to hear this, and I'm happy to tell her the truth.

Pressing her lips together, she looks like she's deciding if she wants to tell me something.

I wait, not wanting to influence her one way or the other. Maybe she's like Dean, and needs to get everything out in the open before she can properly deal with it. Or maybe it's none of my business.

I wish it was.

She looks me in the eye, and seems to see something there.

"It's because of my ex," she says in a rush, holding her forehead in her left hand. "He…shouted at me a lot. And he also… *didn't* shout at me, but was still mad at me all the time regardless. *All the time.*" Her shoulders hunch, and she holds herself by the elbows, staring at the floor again as she starts to tell me more. I can feel in my bones that this is gonna be bad.

"It started out with just little things," she continues. "Snapping at me for very little. Taking it out on me when he had a bad day at work, which was *always,* because he hated his job. Then he started disagreeing with everything I said. I couldn't say or do *anything* right. And then I became the butt of all his jokes." Her hands are trembling. "I became a nervous wreck because he was such a seething cauldron of rage, and it always seemed to be my fault. Like, if I'd tried harder, or worked harder, or not done whatever it was I had done to annoy him, it wouldn't have happened. But the truth was…I wasn't doing anything wrong. It took me a long time to realize that. Too long." She picks at her thumbnail like a nervous habit. "To begin with, he was always sorry later. I forgave him every time, of course, because I was so relieved that the latest mood was over and done with, that I just didn't fuss. And besides, he had depression, and what kind of awful girlfriend would blame their partner for depressive outbursts? They can't help it, right?" She sighs sadly. "So, yeah, I forgave him, and forgave him, and on and on, and then the apologies stopped. And the insults started. He'd tell me I was lazy, or fat, or boring, or a drag…and I believed him. He'd do it a lot when he was drinking. He was a mean drunk, and he'd get through a bottle of vodka every weekend. It's why I don't like drinking myself, even though he jeered at me for it. Too many bad memories."

I'm so angry right now that I can't speak. How the *fuck* dare he?! I steel my jaw, determined to let her finish. She needs to let this out.

"It got to the stage where I used to wish he'd hit me, so I could have some physical evidence that nobody could deny, just…I don't know, proof that he wasn't the nice guy he pretended to be for everyone else except me. We'd have his friends over, and he'd be the life and soul, and then as soon as they left, he'd be back to normal, moody, and saying as many mean things to me as he could think of. It's so easy for people to judge me and say I should have been feistier and not taken any shit, but if he'd hit me, they'd have been sympathetic. So I wished for that black eye, just so people would support me instead of thinking I was weak for taking it. Isn't that sick?"

"No, it makes sense," I reassure her softly. Too softly. This is the voice that happens when I am burning with acid fury. I can't stand the thought of anyone demoralizing Emily, breaking her spirit that way. She's one of the best people I've ever met, no harm in her at all, and I cannot understand why anyone would want to hurt someone so sweet. It's as senseless and brutal as crushing a butterfly in your fist.

Her eyes soften in the desperate relief of being understood. Suddenly, so much makes sense. The layers of shyness hiding the sunshine of her personality. How agreeable she makes herself, even happy to keep our Spotify account as it is rather than assert her preferences. Her panic attack now after being yelled at by some asshole. I'm so sad for her right now, but I refuse to pity her. Anyone who went through such shitty treatment from someone who was supposed to love them and *still* smiles for people…that's a strong woman right there.

And I make myself a promise, here and now, that I will never allow her bastard ex anywhere near her ever again. If he shows up, *I'll* be there, and he won't get the first word out before I throw his ass out and teach him some god damn manners. I swear to god, he doesn't even get to lay eyes on her if I can help it.

"Is that why you moved to Foxton?" I find myself asking.

She nods. "I wanted to get away. In a four and a half year relationship, I stayed three and a half years too long. Three and a half *years*," she says tiredly, frustratedly, like she blames herself. "And I only left when I found out he—" She halts and flicks her eyes to me. "Sorry, I'm waffling."

"Sounds like you need to talk more than you need waffles."

She laughs, and I feel all crawly and happy in my gut because I made her smile. "He cheated on me," she admits, "shockingly enough." She shakes her head. "Found out on my birthday. Apparently it wasn't 'actual cheating', though, because he was just having cybersex with them, and never actually physically touched any of them." She giggles again at what I imagine is a starkly incredulous, disgusted look on my face. *Someone cheated on her? Why the fuck...* "Oh, and get this: they were his 'emotional support system' because I was such an awful girlfriend who couldn't give him ki-" Her eyes widen. "Kids," she falters, as though she's just realized she revealed too much.

My heart stops at her words, certain I heard her incorrectly, not daring to hope that I didn't.

There's silence for a beat, and then she shrugs in defeat. "Well, I certainly blurted that little bit of TMI out, didn't I," she says, clearly embarrassed. "I'm so sorry, I shouldn't have—"

"Did you just say you...that you..." I shake my head, impatient with myself. "You can't have kids, either?"

Her eyes widen. "Um... When you say 'either'...?" She asks. I don't even blink, don't even move. I can't. Because if what she said is true, then all bets are off and everything has changed.

Slowly, she nods.

"I can't have them, and moreover, I don't want them," she says, quietly but clearly.

Something inside my chest explodes into fireworks.

"Hard same," I say slowly, and I'm trying not to smile because that's kind of poor taste, but I can't believe my luck.

Holy. Fuck.

We're in the exact same boat.

I lean back against the counter, in shock. I never thought this could happen. I never thought I would find a woman who didn't want children. I've spent so long believing the terrible things Charmaine said when she left that I resigned myself to being alone forever. I've heard friends talk about wanting children in the not too distant future, like it's a certainty. I've had a couple of women I've slept with give me looks of total pity and regret when they mentioned what would happen if the condom broke, and I told them why they didn't have to worry about taking the morning after pill and that the condom was for common sense reasons rather than birth control. After finding out that I was unable to father a child, they were never bothered that we'd have a one night only thing, because they immediately disqualified me as any kind of prospect, and I could see it, I could tell. It all led me to believe one thing: I was a reject, I was *defective*, and any woman I had anything more than a meaningless fuck with would be making an enormous sacrifice and it was too much to ask. Just like Charmaine said.

And now the woman who has more of an effect on me than any other woman I have met before, the one I've been eating my heart out for, has just told me the one thing that frees me from my self-imposed isolation. The one thing that means I take nothing from her by liking her, ruin nothing for her by pursuing her.

Maybe…just maybe…if she likes you back…

We look and look at each other, and something that feels like hope settles into my chest.

chapter SEVEN

Emily

I FIND MYSELF TELLING HIM EVERYTHING.

All the anger, all the pain I've been carrying around inside since I left Gav…no, since things started to go wrong with him, actually…it all comes pouring out all at once like a busted dam. I must have really, really needed to offload, more than I knew, because I hadn't had the opportunity, or anyone to talk to, before now. But I suppose panic can do that to a person. I tell him about the ridicule, the constant angry nitpicking until I was a nervous wreck scared to speak or act, the way he made me spend some of my inheritance from my grandmother on stuff for him and to bail him out of credit card debt. I think, after holding this as a boulder of a secret inside myself, I just needed to talk to someone about it all.

And Eli listens patiently, without judging me.

He judges Gav plenty, though—especially when I find myself confessing to him that I had to have sex with Gav whenever he wanted or he'd throw a fit. Eli's nostrils flared and his face went pale and his jaw tightened, and I really thought that he'd lose his shit, but he didn't because he's not an animal. So all he does is tell me, in a voice that's not to be argued with, that I did nothing wrong. His judgement and anger with my ex is soothingly validating. Eli's a good guy, and he's on my side.

And he doesn't want children, either.

I haven't pushed him for more information about that, even though I'm gagging to know the deal. But I know from my own experience that that's intensely personal.

Parenthood is something that has simply never been on my radar. There's just never been any interest. When I found out that I had almost no chance of conceiving ever in my life without a lot of expensive procedures and a few miracles, the doctor held my hand and broke it to me gently, and she seemed almost offended when I shrugged and blithely accepted it. But where is it written that every woman has to be a mother?

Gav took it as more evidence that I wasn't woman enough for him, and right now I'm glad. I'm glad if I'm 'broken' in his eyes, because it's part of the reason why I'm safe from him now.

That knowledge settles warmly over my shoulders, bringing me a wondrous peace.

I'm safe now. I'm not going to be hated anymore.

I smile a little in relief. It's still not going to be easy to deal with the internal scars and wounds caused by years of Gav's rage and abuse, but that realisation does help a lot.

Eventually, I feel all talked out. I feel more tired than anything else. Tired and a little embarrassed at my panic attack, tears, and subsequent offloading, but not embarrassed enough to regret it. Not yet, anyway. That will come later, I'm sure, when I'm in bed cringing as I think back over the day. But not yet.

Especially since his hand has been rubbing my shoulder in gentle circles with his thumb for a little while as we stand barely a foot apart....

"I'm really sorry," I say, binning my tissue and rubbing my sore, puffy eyes, "I've been banging on..."

He smiles and shakes his head. "Forget it. Sounds like you needed it."

Oh, that voice. It's so deep and rumbly and...gentle. I barely hide a sigh.

Then I see the clock.

"Oh!" It's almost twenty minutes past closing time. "Bollocks. I, er..."

He follows my gaze to the clock face. "Don't worry about it," he assures me. "The others will have straightened it all out in there. If you give me a second to sort out my room, I'll walk you home."

"Oh, y-you don't have to," I mumble, but he gives me a steady look.

"I'm walking you home," he says, quietly but firmly, and truth be told, I'd be grateful tonight. If that awful man from earlier is hanging around, I don't want to be alone, and it would be even better to have someone as tall, built, and intimidating as Eli next to me. I have to admit, although I always get butterflies around him, I feel absolute calm whenever he's near. Like nothing bad can happen to me on his watch. It's the strangest feeling, but I'm not complaining. At all.

Having settled that, he nods and wanders out of the kitchen, where he's spent almost an hour and a half patiently listening to me pour my heart out, without so much as a whisper of complaint.

As if my crush on him needed to be intensified further.

Stop it, I scold myself. *He's not for you. He's* never *going to be interested. Particularly after your dramatic outburst.*

I hunch in a little on myself. This afternoon has brought up a lot of Gav stuff for me, and I can't help but think about how angry he was with me whenever I was upset. How he'd shout, and jeer, and slam doors, leaving me with my face damp from both my own tears and his spittle from his yelling.

But not Eli.

He listened. He let me waste the rest of his work day...and not once did he snap at me to get to the point, or to get over it.

I almost don't know what to do with myself.

He comes back pretty quickly, shrugging on his old, beaten up leather jacket, and I don't think he could look hotter if he was actively trying.

"It's OK, you really don't have to," I assure him, "It's in the opposite direction from where you live."

"I like walking," he says with a grin, and he shakes his head. "You won't persuade me not to," he warns with a sexy one sided smile.

"OK," I cave in happily, and wander through to reception to grab my things and pick up my coat.

A plant pot is missing, and I remember Sadie telling me that the arsehole broke it; bless her, she swept it up for me. The whole place is pristine, and I feel such gratitude for their understanding—something that nobody else has ever shown me—that if I wasn't almost dehydrated from crying so much, I'd well up again.

Eli unlocks the door and opens it for me, waving his hand to indicate that I should go first. The cool early evening breeze is refreshing, but also highlights how drained and tired I am. I think about the night ahead, and the bath I'm going to run for myself, and the slab of Oreo Dairy Milk chocolate in my fridge, maybe the potential to have takeaway delivered if I'm still hungry. Screw the calories. I don't have to suffer the withering disapproval of my ex for occasionally eating unhealthily anymore, and every now and again I am going to enjoy the shit out of it.

"So," Eli begins, "what are your plans for the rest of the night?" His natural stride is bigger than mine, but he matches my pace.

Briefly I consider telling him I'm doing something cool, like club hopping or a hot yoga class, but I don't want to pretend I'm someone I'm not. Not with Eli. Not after this afternoon. "Honestly? I'm going to have a bath, put on some Princess Leia pyjamas, have a takeout, and watch some Deep Space Nine." I risk a look at him, looking for the jeering expression I'm used to getting from people when I reveal my Trekkie tendencies. "I'm a terminal nerd, I'm afraid."

He quirks an eyebrow. "Terminal, huh?"

"Mmhmm. I'm a die hard Trekkie. And not just that. I'm into all of the sci-fi shows. Battlestar Galactica. Babylon 5. Stargate. And the movies, too. I like Marvel movies, but I think DC has the edge with TV shows. I watch the Arrowverse series in chronological order, episode by episode. *And,*" I say, going in for the knockout punch for any chance that he'll ever find me sexually attractive, "I used to play Dungeons and Dragons, before Gav put a stop to it. And I miss it. And I'd love to do it again."

"D&D?" he asks, perking up. "I used to play that when I was a teenager. I was always the Ranger. Human or Dwarf, usually."

I stop walking.

"You're kidding me," I breathe.

"I am not," he says, a chuckle lurking in his voice. "Played a Cleric once. Hated it. Went straight back to Ranger." He looks at me, and one side of his mouth curls up in the most attractive smirk I have ever seen. "Don't tell me, let me guess... You tend to play a Bard."

I nod, slightly stunned that a man like him even knows what D&D is. He doesn't strike me as a fellow geek. "Always. Their skills are the best. I mean, I sometimes play a Sorcerer, but only to ring the changes. I mean...I *used* to." I cannot seem to stop grinning. Devastatingly handsome, incredibly kind, *and* into my guilty pleasure? I may dissolve into lust filled girly mush right here in the twilight street.

He grins back at me. "We should get a Wishbone-only game going. I haven't played in years, but it was always fun. Dean was pretty into it, too. And I'm sure Leo and Sadie'd be down. I don't think they've played before, though."

I nod, my mind racing with possibilities. If he's serious…I could run a game of The Curse of Strahd, the fifth edition, which is a campaign I've been *dying* to play, and looks new-player-friendly from what I've seen. I squash it, taking care not to get carried away, but even the thought makes me so happy.

"We should," I agree, trying not to sound too enthusiastic or to get my hopes up.

All too soon, we're back at my flat. I wish I lived another five minutes away. And another five minutes away from that. Basically I would happily walk the streets with him all night, tired as I am, just because being around him makes me feel… good. *So* good, about everything.

"This is me," I say, nodding at my front door, and he mutters something that sounds like, "Already", but I can't be sure. "Um…thanks for walking me back. I really appreciate it." And I do.

"No worries," he says in that Louisiana drawl, like it's no big deal. There's silence for a few beats as we look at each other, and, curses, I can feel myself going red as I smile like a total wally. We say "see you tomorrow" simultaneously, and then both give a nervous laugh. He walks backwards for a few steps, watching for me to get up the front steps, unlock my door and get in safely, and he doesn't start turning around until I'm in and closing the door.

Like a dreamy idiot, I sigh as I lean against my front door, warmth radiating through my body and sparking at my fingertips. I have butterflies. Again. It's been so long since a man gave me butterflies, and no man has ever made them flap harder.

I don't want to push the feeling away right now.

I don't want to tell myself to shut up and stop hoping.

I don't want to smother it.

So I don't. Just this once, I let it be.

Eli

I don't remember much of the journey back to my apartment.

All I can think of is her. All of her, from the way she smiles to her taste in TV shows, everything about her.

She's captivating to me.

The things she told me about her past was jarring, but all I can feel for her is admiration. If I'd been emotionally and psychologically abused that insistently and that cruelly for that long, you'd best believe I wouldn't be able to work up a smile for *anyone*, let alone everyone I meet. God, she's strong.

Dean is waiting in the lobby when I get back, and the knowing smile in his eyes doesn't reach his mouth.

Is she OK?

"Yeah," I assure him, "Just…that asshole scared her."

Badly, he agrees. *I texted Leo. He's pissed. He's talking about getting a panic button installed for her, so this doesn't happen again.*

He looks like he wants to say something else, and it's not like him to hesitate.

"What?" I ask.

He sighs awkwardly. *I heard some of what you two were saying. Didn't set out to eavesdrop, I swear, but I was checking on you guys periodically, to see if Sadie and I would need to close up, and…*

Oh.

I sigh. "How much?"

He grins awkwardly. *I know you both have something in common.*

I take out my front door key. "Ah."

Aren't you psyched? He asks incredulously, his face animated with happiness for me.

Dean hated Charmaine. *Hated* her. He never said so while she and I were married, but I knew. He can be inscrutable when he wants, but when he thought I wasn't looking, he let the facial expressions fly behind her back. And when I told him why she'd left me after our bad news from the fertility clinic, and what she'd said the night she left, when I was drunk off my ass and humiliated, it's one of only two times I've ever seen him truly mad. The other time was when he was told that Mr Whitmire had escaped justice by blowing his own head off after the shooting.

"Man, there ain't no guarantee she even thinks of me in that way," I mumble, but I can't seem to help the grin that spreads across my face.

She might like me.

We've had a few eye meets that got so intense my dick jumped, and I can't help but hope.

It's a little wrong, though. She's our receptionist. I have no desire to be the new Leo and chase away the office savior by blurring the lines.

But what if it worked out?

I can't remember ever liking someone so much. She's my idea of heaven, and she has been since I met her. Every time I see her, I just...I don't know how to describe it. But I feel like my entire body would glow bright as Mardi Gras lights if it could. Her warmth, her kindness, the strength of character that I now know is behind it... And she says the most interesting things. I would never have imagined she'd have been into D&D, and the passion with which she spoke was inspiring, and made me want to rediscover something I haven't had in years.

And the way her lips look so soft and like they're begging for a kiss...

Dude, I'd say snap out of it, but it's too fucking good to see you so happy, Dean says, and he's god damn beaming at me.

I sigh. "I just don't want to…I dunno, count my chickens."

And I get that, but also, you like her and she likes you. He gives me his best one-plus-one, are-you-a-moron look, and I can't help but grin.

"Baby steps," I say, unlocking my door. I pause, and then, like a hopeful teenage boy, I glance at him and ask, "You really think she likes me?"

He gives me a look of amused exasperation. *Yes, dude, I do. This is by no means a one sided deal. You look at each other, and everyone's hair gets static from the electricity in the air. I keep expecting Teddy Pendergrass songs to start spontaneously playing and, I don't know, fucking doves to swoop in and start lighting candles and whatever.*

I shake with laughter. "Poetic, man, that is…some poetic shit you got there."

Poetic, but I'm not wrong. He gives me a pointed look, and starts towards the stairs. *Don't waste this. It doesn't come around every day.* He leaves me with that little nugget to think on, heading up the stairs as I unlock my front door.

chapter EIGHT

Emily

I GIVE UP.

I huff to myself as I throw yet another top to the floor in frustration, growling for good measure as I flop my butt to my bed. This is hopeless.

Curse Leo for coaxing us all into a night out clubbing.

I know this is a cliche, but I genuinely have nothing to wear. All my club appropriate clothes are things that Gav bought me, or made me buy, and I hate every last one. They are all considerably more revealing than anything I would choose for myself, and he always used to take great pleasure in sneering at me and pointing out how much hotter other women at the club were while I cringed and tried to keep my jacket on for cover. I'm going to donate the lot to charity. Which, you know, feels great and empowering and all, but doesn't help me right now.

My only other option is a dress I wore to a wedding once, and it's way too special occasions-y for a night out with friends.

I'm seriously considering begging off with a headache when I have a lightbulb moment.

Sadie. My new friend and style crush.

I do want to go tonight. I don't want to punk out. If anyone can find something wearable in the outlandish mish mash that is my wardrobe, it's Sadie Stewart.

I reach for my phone and fire off a quick text, hoping I don't sound like a hopeless case.

What are you wearing tonight? I can't decide & my wardrobe is a disaster area. X

Within a minute, she fires one back.

Meet me at my place in half an hour and bring some possibilities. I'll sort ya. Xx

Thank god.

I scoop up the clothes I spent the most time umming and ahhing over, grab my handbag, and head out the door.

"Yeah, I can definitely see what you mean," Sadie says, pursing her lips to one side as she holds up an old black lace top and gives it a doubtful look.

Her place is so cool. Aubergine purple walls and skull art and quirky lamps all over the place so the dark decor looks cool rather than oppressive. I wish, I wish, I wish I had her sense of style.

But I don't, and that's why I'm here; so I don't end up going clubbing in work clothes.

"I mean, this is a nice top," she says thoughtfully, "But if I may..." She looks at me appraisingly. "It's not really *you*. This isn't what I'd pick out for you. You're more rock chick, and this is a bit...*fussy*."

She's bang on the money.

And I very much like that she sees me as a rock chick. I haven't been able to indulge that much over the past few years, but the fact that she can see it in me still... I want to punch the air in happiness at the prospect of being the real me again.

"Yeah, that's exactly what I think. I definitely need to go clothes shopping with my first month's pay packet," I add, hoping she will offer to come with me to show me where the hell she buys her stuff.

She picks up another top. It's the wrong shade of red for my skin tone and makes me look drained of all colour in my face, and the neckline is achingly low. "Yikes," she smarts. "So I'm thinking Gav inflicted this monstrosity on you?"

"Christmas gift," I mumble. They all know about Gav now. I felt I owed them all an explanation for the scene I caused. I was expecting awkwardness, and was sure I'd make them uncomfortable. Not for a second. Sadie roared about misogyny and emotional abuse and wrapped me in a fierce bear hug, promising to loan me her Jessica Valenti books. Leo looked incredibly sad and quietly held my hand for a little while, and had a panic button installed under the reception desk. Dean checks in on me regularly throughout the day. I think he likes the idea of watching over me, being the caretaker for once.

I love them all so much.

"Let's approach this from a radical new angle, chickie pie," Sadie says, patting the space on her bed next to her. "What do *you* like?"

I sit next to her. "In terms of…?"

"What do *you* like to wear, and how do *you* like to look?"

I look down at my fingers. "I don't really know," I admit, "except to say…none of *this*." I take a slightly shaky breath. "It's all just coming home to me how…I don't know, how pathetic this all makes me feel. Like, I didn't even have the lady balls to dress the way I wanted when I was with him. I wore clothes *he* approved of, even if I hated them. He preferred blondes and wanted me to have hair like Daenerys, so I did that, and I still wasn't—*it* still wasn't good enough. *He hated me anyway*." I flinch a little at having said the words.

She takes both my hands and squeezes them, giving me full eye contact. "And well done you, because you got out, and now you can have all the fun in the world just pleasing yourself." She and I both burst out laughing at the same time; one of the things we have learned about each other during our many lunch breaks together that we both have dirty laughs and a filthy sense of humour. God, it's good to let loose with a girlfriend again. "Well," she smirks, "I didn't actually mean that this time, but sure, that, too, I guess! Tracy's Dog, baby. Battery operated boyfriends for the win. Much less trouble." We high five, and everything seems lighter.

"OK," she continues, "let's start with your hair. I mean, sure, the kind-of Targaryen look is cool, and you've almost got an ombre thing going on because of the regrowth, but I get the impression you'd prefer something different?"

"Shorter," I say instantly, indicating just below my chin, "and probably brunette." I look at her hair, gloriously thick, gently curling, and red, and feel pure and unadulterated envy. The Demelza Poldark look would never suit me as much as it does Sadie. It's like her trademark.

She nods in agreement. "Brown would definitely suit you," she says. "Your eyes would just," she makes a popping sound, "pop. And I think a little curl would look cute, too."

"You read my mind." That's exactly what I've been envisioning. I hate my long, dull, pale blond hair. I hate the roots. I hate how washed out it makes me feel.

"So book an appointment," she suggests. "I use Chaos Hairdressers, which is on the street just behind Wishbone's. They take online bookings, so let's book you in for next week. Let's just do it." She grabs her iPad from her bedside table and fires it up. "I'll try to get you in with Lindsey. She's your girl if you need a makeover."

I nod, excited at the prospect of looking completely

different. We agree on next Monday, as that's one of our days off, and in a few quick taps, I am booked in with Lindsey for a total restyle.

I look at the intricate mandala tattoo which I happen to know she inked on her own left forearm. I've gotten to know each of the artists' styles now, and can pick them out on tattoos I see on strangers in the street. Sadie is amazing with delicate designs. Dean's speciality is script, and I know I'm biased but I think his calligraphy work is second to none. Leo loves to use as much colour as possible, and can copy pretty much any design you give him. And Eli…his work looks like photographs, it's so realistic. I wish I could just get past the fear enough to have something as beautiful as Sadie's ink on my own skin. I'd feel truly transformed then.

"Right," she says decisively, "clothes. Let's see what we can find in my wardrobe. We're the same size, as far as I can tell. And can I pleeeeeeeease do your make-up?" She laughs as I punch the air. "Come on, you. I'm going to make you look like a wet dream."

Eli

It's been fucking forever since Leo dragged me on one of his nights out. Months and months.

My idea of a good time is not really watching my cousin throw shapes and dry hump random women on the dance floor. Leo dances with everything he has, every time, cos to him that's fun and he never does a damn thing by halves. Go big or go home, that's just the way he's always been. And the women flock to him, because he has the charm and they know by reputation that he's a good lay. And he just lets it happen because he needs the distraction from being hopelessly in love with someone else, a state that I have recently come to sympathize with.

I go now and again, because sometimes the loneliness gets to be too much, and I do the exact same thing as he does, but for different reasons.

Looking at it through new eyes, it all seems so cheap and half-assed now.

I don't think I've hurt anyone's feelings, which is good. And there's nothing wrong with casual sex, as long as everyone gets treated respectfully and nobody gets hurt.

But now I've met someone who makes me want more. And for the first time in a very long while, there's an actual possibility for this to become a reality, and with a woman I really, really like. It's exciting, and it's making my blood pump wildly out of control. And it's nerve wracking as all hell.

I knock on Dean's door. He answers in pajama trousers and an old Bray Wyatt t-shirt.

"I guess that's a no to coming out tonight?"

He nods. He doesn't tend to join in very often. Parties make him uncomfortable, for obvious reasons, and he usually ends up drinking beer in the corner and pretending he's somewhere else before taking the first excuse to leave. If the wrong song plays, it can even trigger a PTSD meltdown. But for all that, and as much as I'd never want him to be uncomfortable, I don't ever want him to feel excluded, either, so I always ask, and sometimes he tries.

I've got Minecraft to keep me company, he smiles. His eyes spark up with mischief. *Will I need my headphones tonight, or will you be going back to Em's?*

"Come on, man," I say sternly.

He holds his hands up. *I was kidding. Kind of.* His eyes narrow. *Tell me you'll make a move tonight. For fuck's sake, how you've managed not to all week is beyond me.*

I narrow my eyes right back. I may be wearing a brand new black shirt, and I may have spent a little more time than normal grooming my beard, but I'm not allowing myself to anticipate anything happening between me and Emily *tonight*. And I'm actually fairly glad, much as I'd love to have her in my arms as quickly as possible. I don't want to rush things. I don't want just a quick fuck with her, the kind I've picked up at the club with various other women before now. I want...all of it. The first kiss. The second kiss. Dates in restaurants and movie theaters and anything she wants to do. Staying up all night talking. Holding her hand at every possible opportunity. Buying her roses on our one month anniversary.

I've become a sap. But I'm feeling more optimistic about life than I have in a long time, and it's all thanks to her.

"We'll see," I reply shortly.

What's stopping you? Literally, what's stopping you? Dean's seeming both curious and argumentative. It's done with love, though.

"Several things. You know she's been through a lot. Like, a *lot*, a lot. And she might not be interested in me in that way."

You must be blind, he says in obvious exasperation, shaking his head.

"I just don't want to crowd her, or make her uncomfortable. And she *is* an employee."

You are literally the only one of us that cares about that. Leo might give you a little shit, but he'll just be happy for you. And why would you care about a little teasing? She'd be worth it.

Sometimes I forget that Dean is a year younger than me.

"I know," I say quietly, "and you're right, I wouldn't give a shit about any teasing. I just feel kind of bad about giving him a hard time and then turning around and doing the same thing. I'm not a hypocrite."

Nobody thinks you are.

I shrug. "I'll have the chance to get to know her better tonight, maybe. But as she's literally just gotten out of a bad relationship not even three months ago, she might not be ready, and that's OK."

Dean sighs with a smile. *You're a good man, bro.*

I shrug again, and smile. "Thanks, man. Wish me luck."

I'm not quite running to the club, but I'm not just walking, either.

chapter NINE

Emily

I CAN HEAR THE THROBBING BEAT OF *BONKERS* BY DIZZEE Rascal pouring from The Lair nightclub along the seafront as I jump out of the taxi and pay the driver. Sadie got a text from Peter asking for her to meet him at his office, so she's joining us later, but she hooked me up with a taxi from her mate's all-women-drivers company. In this day and age that's a genius idea, and I make sure I keep their card.

I smooth down the dress she loaned me as I walk towards Eli and Leo, who are both chatting as they wait outside. I love this dress I'm borrowing. It's a dark forest green, knee length, and tight but still with plenty of freedom of movement. The top is shaped, and there's underwire under each of my breasts; I'm only one cup size larger than Sadie, and let's just say it works. It's been a while since I willingly rocked any cleavage, and I'm secretly loving it. She did my hair in messy waves, and my make-up is a little darker than I normally wear—my lips are wine red—but, again, it *works*. I feel like someone else, someone confident and more interesting, and I wonder if this will help me cut loose tonight.

Eli turns, as though he can feel me staring at him like a

touch. He looks awesome in a black shirt and dark grey jeans, and his hair is in its usual knot. I swear his blue eyes flash and set alight for a split second when he recognises me, and it sends a tingle down my spine that makes my breath catch, but his expression settles quickly and I tell myself it was wishful thinking on my part. I'm not sure if I'm relieved or disappointed.

I think I'm leaning more towards the latter.

Leo follows Eli's glance and he gives me a bright smile. "Hey Pumpkin," he says as I approach, giving me a friendly kiss on the cheek and a cheeky whistle. "Nice dress, you look *great*," he says, looking at Eli briefly and then behind me. "No Sadie?"

"Thanks—um, no, Peter texted. He wanted her to call by first." Leo's jaw clenches slightly, but his smile remains in place. "She says she'll meet us inside later."

"Hmm, I'll believe that when I see it," Leo drawls derisively. It's a little out of character. "Peter doesn't like coming out, so we probably won't see them tonight." He stretches his neck from side to side like a warm-up. "Still," he says, flipping back to his jovial self, "The three of us are going to have an epic night, regardless, right? Shall we?" he nods at the door. "The first round's on me, so get your sweet butt inside." He grins, already a little hyperactive, and raises an eyebrow, the one with the scar.

We start to make our way inside, up some steps through two large oak doors manned by bouncers, one of whom Leo low-fives. The entrance is a little crowded with other people, but nothing too uncomfortable.

"You *do* look great," Eli says quietly next to me in his deep rumble. I know I'm starting to go pink, and my goofy smile is unstoppable.

"Thank you," I murmur back, glancing at him from the corner of my eye as we walk in—*damn*, he looks good—and making a mental note to buy Sadie a good bottle of wine for the sterling job she did on my appearance tonight.

Once we pay the entry fee, Leo leads us through a mirrored corridor opening on to a thriving dance floor with a bar to the right hand side. The energy in here is good; people seem happy and in the party spirit, lots of dancing and laughter and a few hollering cheers as shots are downed by a group next to the bar. Dizzee Rascal is just finishing up and segueing into *All the Single Ladies*, and the lights that dance across the room are a stunning aquamarine and mauve. Around the edge of the room on a raised platform, protected by railings lined with fairy lights, are a mishmash of unmatching seats with small tables, just large enough for trays of drinks.

"You guys grab a seat, I'll get the drinks in. Diet Coke?" Leo asks me, and I nod, oddly touched that he's memorised my regular order. He turns to Eli. "How about you?"

"Any cider will do," Eli replies over the noise. Leo nods and walks to the bar, and Eli gently taps my elbow, which feels nice. *Very* nice. It's a *gentle elbow tap*, and yet it goes straight to my clit. I need to pull myself together. "Up here?" he says, indicating with his thumb towards a group of four chairs facing the dance floor.

"Sure," I say, and we nip over quickly before the seats are claimed.

The people in this place are amazing looking, and I am reminded again how fashionable an area Foxton-on-Sea is. The men look like they're all in bands, with obscure fandom t-shirts and curly hair and perfect stubble; the women wear rockabilly dresses from Lindy Bop, maybe, and have neon hair, shaved undercuts, and tattoos of Betty Page on their arms, probably done by Sadie or Leo. I love this town so much. I completely see why it's known as 'Camden by the sea'.

Eli picks the chair directly opposite mine. I smooth the dress over my legs nervously, casting around for something, anything, to say.

"I haven't been clubbing in years," I call over Beyonce.

"I don't think you'll find it's changed much," he calls back with a delicious wry grin, leaning forward to make conversation easier. His shirt sleeves are rolled up over his forearms, and my eyes slip to his ink. The urge to trace my fingers over the black patterns covering his skin is strong. "Though this club is actually pretty cool. Leo knows the DJ, so..." He shrugs. "I've been to worse clubs, I know that."

"Do you come here very often?" I ask, and then gape at the corny question. His eyes sparkle and we both laugh.

"Now and again. Not for a while." He gives me a direct look, and I think he's trying to communicate something, but I'm too mesmerised by how unutterably handsome he is to be able to clear my mind enough to understand precisely what.

The moment is broken when Leo arrives, deftly holding our drinks. "Right," he says decisively, "lubricate, and then it's dance-floor time. You all down?"

Eli looks at me.

My face heats up as cold panic runs down my body, an interesting and entirely unpleasant combination.

"I...um..." I take a deep swallow of ice cold Diet Coke as I try frantically to come up with an excuse. "I...can't dance," I finish lamely, looking at the floor.

Unpleasant memories intrude, uninvited guests at what is supposed to be a fun night.

I remember loving to dance on nights out with friends, never caring whether or not I was good at it, until I met Gav.

I remember him hanging around on the sidelines when I took him out with my friends, never joining in, telling me to go and have fun but standing alone and obviously bored if I did so. I remember the increasing moodiness, how quickly he became openly rude, and eventually stopping saying 'yes' to any invitations for nights out with my friends so they wouldn't see it and I wouldn't have to pretend I didn't see their speaking looks to each other. I remember dancing at one wedding once a few years later, out of practice, feeling a little stiff and unsure of myself…and Gav grabbing my wrist, pulling me to one side, and hissing in my ear that I was embarrassing him with my crap dancing and ordering me to stop.

I shiver involuntarily. He's not here, but his presence in my mind still stifles me.

It was a mistake to come tonight, I think sadly. *Why come to a nightclub if not to dance? What's the point? They were all expecting a fun evening with somebody who'd join in, and here I am ruining it with my chicken shittery…*

"I'm…sorry," I say quietly.

"Hey, no harm, no foul," Leo says sincerely, reaching across for a gentle hand squeeze, "you don't have to dance if you don't wanna." He nods towards his cousin. "Eli will keep you company, won't you?" He grins.

"Sure," Eli responds easily, seeming untroubled.

"Oh, but I wouldn't want to hold you back, or—"

"Nah," he assures me, "Leo's the one with the rhythm. I'm good sitting here with you. We can point at him and laugh." His eyes warm up with a hint of mischief. He's the most relaxed I've ever seen him.

"Laugh it up, I don't give a shit," Leo says quite happily, downing some more of his drink before stretching his arms and sides like he's about to start a marathon. He looks good tonight himself, in jeans with a sleeveless shirt with loose threads on the shoulders. His tattooed arms are as muscular as Eli's, and his hair is loose and curling haphazardly down his smiling pirate face. "Feast your eyes, babygirl, and enjoy watching me bringing sexy back." He winks at me before leaping deftly over the railings with one arm and ploughing straight into the busy dance floor as Eli rolls his eyes good naturedly.

Ho. Lee. Shit.

Leo can *dance.*

I've never seen anything like it. It's as though he is the music and the music is him. He's fearless, snake hipped, throwing shapes and pulling off complex moves without seeming at all wanky about it; just a hot guy having a good time. The women on the dance floor watch him like hawks, and I can't blame them; the guy is sexy as balls. They almost start sniffing around him, moving closer, like wild animals in heat. I half expect David Attenborough to start narrating the scene, going into detail about the mating rituals of the adult male Leo.

"Leo Mills!" The DJ crows into a microphone. "Ladies, your evening has begun."

Leo throws his head back and laughs, and the DJ switches to *I'm Sexy and I Know It* by LMFAO. As Leo gives it everything he's got, spinning and thrusting his pelvis and making the song all about him, I can't help but laugh, too. When I look up, Eli is grinning at me. He points to the seat next to me. "May I?" he says.

My eyes widen slightly as I nod. *Don't get too excited. He's stuck talking with you, and moving closer will make it easier to hear.*

He sits next to me and takes a long drink of his cider. I get a brief whiff of his cologne, all woody and masculine. My legs cross and I squeeze them together involuntarily for a little relief from the heat blooming there. That causes the most delicious tingle, so I stop quickly.

"I didn't know Leo was such a dancer," I comment.

One corner of his mouth tips upwards. "Yeah. Total show-off. And Steve—the DJ—he's an enabler. Plays whatever he feels like, and Leo will dance to a fire alarm given half a chance."

I laugh at the thought.

"I've been meaning to ask him where he got that awesome scar," I mention, running my finger along my own eyebrow.

Eli's lips tightens very briefly, and he looks a little sad. "Um...probably best you don't ask him if Dean's around," he says.

"Oh...OK," I reply, sorry for bringing it up. "I just thought, Leo being Leo, there'd be some cool story about wrestling lions, or something."

"Nah, he saved a mermaid from sharks," he deadpans. "You should see the shark, though. He'll never play the piano again."

I laugh; Leo sure is built like Aquaman. "Well, maybe he can still be a piano *tuna*," I joke, hoping Eli's not a pun hater, and I'm more than a little gratified when he laughs back. *Land sakes, that's a sexy laugh*. Deep, rich, and lighting up his face like Christmas.

He looks towards the dance floor and rolls his eyes with a smirk, pointing. "Here we go," he says, shaking his head knowingly.

I follow his gaze. There's a gorgeous woman wearing her chocolate brown hair in a retro cool Rosie the Riveter updo having serious eye contact with Leo. He's still doing his thing, strutting his apparently funky stuff, but there's a spark in his eyes as he looks at her, and she's moving closer to him, as though he's magnetic. Which, in many ways, the charismatic bastard is. I may be hung up on Eli, but I'm not blind and can absolutely see Leo's appeal. Especially when he can dance like he's in a damn music video.

"Next up, he'll take her hand and give her a twirl," Eli murmurs in my right ear as we watch in amusement, and oh boy... My ears are one of my most intense erogenous zones, always have been, so his breath tickling over it is... Unnnnnnnnffffff. I squirm slightly and watch as Eli's prediction comes true, and Leo takes the woman's hand and twirls her until her red skirt swirls, pulling her back to him and giving her an intense look and a smile that promises the hottest sex of her life if she carries on down this path. From the way she looks at him, she's gonna.

"Nice," I say approvingly, and turn my head, nearly bumping noses with him. I catch my breath a little at the proximity, but then he moves slightly back as he holds up his hand for a high five. "Called it," he crows.

I return the high five, but my angle is off, and our ring and pinkie fingers are the only ones really involved. I wince and laugh. "Sorry, that was really bad—"

"Mmm, ya gotta align the elbows," he tells me, holding his hand up again. "Redo." I hold my own hand up, and he pulls my arm closer to his until our elbows touch. I look, and then my eyes travel up to his face, mesmerised. Leo is by no means the only magnetic man here. "See?" He gently taps my hand with his own once or twice to demonstrate how much better our hands line up.

His hand stays put for a few brief seconds.

Our eyes meet, and I could swear…

I could swear there's at the very least awareness of me as a woman in his warm gaze. And I'm pretty sure he looked at my mouth for a split second. I bit my lower lip self consciously and—yeah, he looked again, and this time, I think his eyes darkened a little. My insides warm with this new information, even as my stomach plummets with nerves. *Careful now.*

Our hands are still touching. It's been around five seconds, which is actually a pretty long time to touch hands with someone, especially when you're into them the way I'm into Eli.

My nipples tighten, and I hope like hell this dress is thick enough to hide them. Because of the underwire, this dress did not require nor allow for any bra.

"So," he clears his throat, "again." Looking each other in the eye, we high five, and this time it's perfect.

"Nice," he grins. "Good job."

I grin back, thankful that I'm too scared to dance so that I can have this one on one time with him. He's a really nice man, and great company. He comes off as a little forbidding at first glance, but that's just because he's six foot five and built like a brick shithouse, and doesn't smile at the clients as much as Leo and Dean both do. But when you get to know him, he's such a warm and gentle soul. He's rapidly becoming my favourite person to be around.

I remember something I found boxed up at the back of the store room earlier, and I feel myself smiling cheekily.

"What?" he asks.

"So I found something interesting today when the delivery showed up, and I was putting the new inks away," I say, trailing off mysteriously. He raises an eyebrow, and the familial similarity between him, Dean, and Leo is never more pronounced than when they do that. "There were these boxes tucked right at the back…" Understanding dawns, and he closes his eyes, chuckling in embarrassment.

"I swear, they were Sadie's idea," he groans, shaking his head slowly. "I was against it from the start."

"What? They're good t-shirts," I tease, "100% cotton, good quality, good cut…and the printing is high standard. No cracking or—"

"I still want to burn every single one of mine," he admits. His eyes light up. "Any chance I could persuade you to 'accidentally' drop a match in the—"

"None whatsoever," I say with a laugh. "They're too awesome. I think I might take one of each. Team Leo. Team Dean. Team Eli."

His eyes flick to me as I say the last one. The Team Eli shirts are black with writing a similar shade of blue to his eyes. The Team Leo ones are a gingery red with black writing, and the Team Dean ones are purple with a darker purple writing. All of them have doodles in the style of each artist covering the front underneath the script.

"So, want to tell me what happened?" I ask, holding back a giggle at the cringe on Eli's face.

He sighs. "One hundred percent Sadie's idea," he sighs, "and y'know Leo would do anythi—well, he, er, gives Sadie free reign for a lot of things," he says quickly, "and apparently she thought a lot of the women who come to the parlour would go for it, because, well..." It's his turn to squirm uncomfortably.

"Because the three of you are obviously as hot as hell and it made sense to cash in on your fan following?" I finish saucily.

He gives me a look that makes my clit jump to attention. I swear the wretched thing salutes him. "Hot as hell, huh?" His wide mouth spreads in a slow grin, and I feel myself going pink.

"In other news, grass is green," I crack back at him trying to cover my tracks, and he laughs, never breaking eye contact with me. I'm the one to break it, in the end, taking a sip of my drink to have a quick breather from how much I want to launch myself at him and bite his bottom lip. "And you're forgetting, I monitor the social media accounts. I see how many phone numbers and tit shots are sent for the attention of one or other of you." Every. Single. Day.

He rolls his eyes good naturedly. "Yeah, that can be, ah...a lot." His eyes twinkle. Yeah, he definitely knows how many lewd offers are addressed to *him* in the inboxes. "So, yeah, Sadie ordered the shirts, and it's fair to say they sold well. But it just got embarrassing. Some of the women who bought them got a little...*forward*. very reluctant to take 'no' for an answer, y'know? And then Leo got wind that Dean's were selling quicker than his, and he wanted to start a sweepstakes on who would sell the most each month, and..." He grins. "I don't know if you've known Leo long enough to see his competitive streak, but I could see him coming up with ideas on how to charm people into buying more of his, and then he started talking about a spreadsheet, and I just threw them all into the back of the store room and told him if he did anything except sell them casually on our website, I'd quit and take Dean with me. Every now and again Sadie wears one of them while she's working, and to be honest they still sell well online, but there's no way I'd let that spreadsheet shit happen. Over my dead body."

"Well, maybe I should start wearing them, too." He gives me a *Really?* look. "Hey, it's good advertising," I protest, laughing.

"Which one would you wear?" He asks, looking me straight in the eye with a challenging smirk.

It makes my pulse race a little, and I bite my lip. To buy myself some time—and, if I'm honest, to keep from blurting, "yours, and only yours" like a total wingnut—I glance back over to Leo, who is now bumping and grinding with Rosie the Riveter. I incline my head towards them. "Probably on a rotation so they'd all get a good airing," I reply, squirming slightly. I look towards the dance floor to deflect, and joke, "Well, we all know which one *she'd* be wearing."

When I look back, he looks slightly disappointed for a brief flash, and then grins. "Probably."

I try to think of something to say to change the subject, so I don't end up fangirling all over him. "So, no Dean tonight?"

He shakes his head. "No. Not his scene. And because of what happened, sometimes this sort of environment, or the wrong song playing, can trigger off his PTSD, and that's not good."

I frown. "God, I'm so stupid, I didn't think..."

"Hey," he says firmly, reaching out and gently tilting my chin towards his, making sure I'm looking at him, "don't say that. You are *not* stupid. At all." His face is deadly serious, determined, even a little pissed off. But not with me, *for* me, and not in a way that I find intimidating. In a way that makes me feel...valued.

He lets my chin go, and I probably imagined the short, light stroke of his thumb.

"You've learned a lot of ASL in a short time," he remarks.

I give a tentative smile. "Thanks. I found a decent course online that you can complete at your own pace. I do a little every night. I still flub it a bit sometimes, but I'm getting there."

His smile is soft. "So if I signed this..." He signs, *Same again?*

I grin. *Yes please,* I sign back. *No I-C-E.* I have to spell sign 'ice', as I don't know the sign for that word yet, but Eli's smiling face tells me it's not a problem.

He wanders away, and I take the opportunity to check my reflection in the compact Sadie loaned me. I touch my lipstick up lightly, to make sure the darker colour stays even, and lift my hair a little with my fingers. *Good enough.* Thanks to Sadie's mad skills and good quality make-up, I'm actually not looking half bad.

My mobile buzzes on the table in front of me. Crap, I forgot to let Sadie know I arrived OK. I fire her off a quick text, and then check my messages.

Huh. That's a surprise. It's a text from Kayleigh, an old mate from back in Suffolk. Well, she's Gav's mate, really, but she and I always got on well.

Kayleigh: Hey, lovey. How are you? Thought I'd check in and see how things are now—where have you moved to? Xx

Hmm. I have nothing against Kayleigh—she was always sympathetic to me—but Gav is one of her oldest friends. Her loyalties will always lie with him by default. I don't want to tell her where I've moved to just in case she lets slip, accidentally or on purpose.

I tap out a quick response.

Emily: Hi! Lovely to hear from you :) I'm fine thanks, moved to the coast. Settling in really well. How are you? Xx

The response comes very quickly.

Kayleigh: I'm fine thank you xx how are you after everything?

I purse my lips.

Emily: You mean after the split?

Kayleigh: Yeah

I'm a little surprised she's asking. I mean, don't get me wrong, she was a really nice person—raucous and good humoured—and we were friendly enough when we saw each other, but we were never particularly close. She might just be curious.

I decide to tell her the truth. I'm not going to stress about that whole situation anymore. I'm out of it. She's asked. I'm telling her. And if she feeds it back to Gav… I realise I don't care one way or the other. His grip on me has significantly loosened.

Emily: Honestly? I'm 100% happier. Life is good :) x

Her reply to this takes a bit longer to come through.

Kayleigh: Good good. Pleased for you. x

I put my phone away and look up to see where Eli is at the bar, but he's actually already on his way back with the drinks.

He sets mine down in front of me, and I have to hide a happy smile when he sits back down, still next to me.

He smiles back at me, and he looks a little nervous. I'm intrigued, and more than a little charmed by this unexpected version of Eli. "So I was wondering—"

"Hey, handsome."

We both look up to see a woman with blue hair, fishnet tights, and possibly the very coolest LBD I have ever seen smirking down at him. It takes a couple of seconds, but then I recognise her.

She's the person Eli was tattooing when he and I were first introduced. I can see the brightly coloured Disney tattoo on her thigh through the fishnet. Eli's work. The place he spent hours touching her.

My heart starts to sink as I picture him ditching me for her, because she's probably way more fun than me, and will almost definitely at least be willing to dance with him.

"Hi, Melissa," he says.

chapter TEN

Eli

SHIT.

"Hi, Melissa," I say, hoping she doesn't see the eye roll I'm repressing. We're in a nice secluded part of the club here. Why did she have to see us? Why did she feel the overwhelming need to barge in and interrupt? Just as I was working up the courage to ask Em if she wanted to go out to dinner with me sometime, just the two of us. I'd spent the entire time at the bar psyching myself up to do it, to say the words, and now I've got to deal with this pushy pain in the ass instead.

"Didn't expect to see you here tonight," she drawls, bending forward and placing her palms on the table in front of us. Her arms squeeze together just enough to make a Grand Canyon of cleavage as stark and noticeable as she can get it without literally rubbing it in my face. I deliberately keep my eyes trained on hers, ignoring her display completely. I can see this throws her off her game, and pisses her off a little.

An idea occurs to me. *No. I shouldn't. Or…maybe I could? Fuck it.*

I sling my arm around Em's shoulders and squeeze slightly. And then, because I can't resist, I gently run my fingers along her shoulder. I can feel her holding back a tremble, and it's all I can do not to howl like an alpha wolf over the song playing from the DJ decks about being in love back in 2002.

"Do you mind? I'm kind of on a date here," I say clearly.

Her eyes widen, and then narrow. "A date?"

I squeeze Em's shoulder again. She has gone still, but I'm hoping she'll just go along with this and won't rat me out. Melissa has been the very definition of persistent, and it's been getting more and more irritating. The answer is no, and it would be even if my ideal woman wasn't sitting right next to me. "Yeah. So, if you don't mind..."

Melissa straightens slightly. "I was gonna ask you to dance with *me*," she says, trying to sound inviting, or like a better offer, but she just comes off as desperate and bratty.

"No thanks," I say coolly, "I'm happy with my girl." She looks pissed, but doesn't make a move; she just stands there, looking annoyed.

Time to go for broke.

I turn to Emily and lean to whisper sensually in her ear. "Help me out here, and I'll tell Leo to give you a pay rise and an extra day of paid vacation. I'm frickin' begging you."

She gives a sexy chuckle that goes straight to my groin and runs her hand up my thigh. It's my turn to smother a shiver. I wish to holy hell this was for real.

"Wow, Eli. Not normally on the first date," she says flirtatiously, clear enough that Melissa will be able to hear, "but if you play your cards as well as that for the rest of the night...I may have to break my rule."

I'm torn between admiring applause for her easy deception and begging her to tell me more about exactly *which* rule I allegedly suggested she break.

Especially when she rests her forehead on mine and runs the tip of her nose along the side of my face.

If I was standing up right now, my knees would be weak.

And then she grazes my neck softly with her teeth.

I'm lucky that the music is pretty loud right now because a growl of pure want escapes my lips. I swear I feel her tongue on my skin. Sure enough about it that my hand tightens its grip on her...

Just as quickly, she pulls back, right back so the only physical contact we have now is my hand on her shoulder, and I want to curse enough to make my momma mad and pull her back to me. I *want* her. I want her so badly I can't even think straight anymore.

"Ooh—all clear," she says brightly, "she's gone."

Who's gone?

OH.

I look up, and sure enough there's empty air where Melissa stood before.

I take a deep, steadying breath, and notice my hands are shaking slightly. I remove my hand from Em's shoulder with regret and crack my knuckles, hoping it will somehow help them to still.

"Thank you," I say sincerely.

She smiles, and I am gratified to see she's flushing all over. This is a god damn excellent dress on her. I pull my eyes away, not wanting to be a creeper, but the image lingers in my head.

"No worries," she says, taking a sip of her drink. Even watching her swallow is turning me on. Are her hands shaking slightly, too?

Pull it together, man.

She looks towards the dance floor, which is packed, and squints. "Can't see Leo," she remarks. She stands and leans on the railings, looking down and scouring the crowd, colors from the fairy lights on the railings dancing along her dress. That. That is how I'd paint her if I could.

She doesn't realize how hungrily I'm looking at her figure from behind, and I mentally slap myself before walking over and standing next to her. I don't want to push my luck.

I'm fairly sure she feels *something*, though. I'm hook, line, and sinker for her, but that doesn't mean she feels the same for me yet.

I can wait, though. I'm a patient man. If there's even the chance that she could be interested now, and that it could grow into the same way I feel, I can have infinite patience.

"There he is," I say, pointing to Leo doing a sexy and fun fake tango with his Sadie substitute of the night. I can't believe I nearly let that little fact slip earlier. Emily is so easy to be with that I forget to keep my mouth shut.

She giggles at my cousin's antics. God, I hope she doesn't have the hots for him. She doesn't look envious or disappointed, so I don't *think* she does. Their scene is more like best friends, or big brother/kid sister. They laugh together a lot, wisecracking at work with the ease of old friends, but the air doesn't crackle between them. It's not like ours. I swear I'm not imagining the chemistry between us.

And then I notice it.

She's tapping her toes. Ke$ha is singing *Blow,* and Em is tapping her toes to the beat. Her fingers move along the railings, and her hips are gently swaying. For someone who said earlier she can't dance, she's sure halfway there right now. Her actions are subconscious, involuntary, and I wonder why she didn't want to dance when it's so clear she likes it... Until it hits me.

I'd bet my last dollar Gav has a hand in this reluctance, and for the billionth time since I became aware of his existence, I want to punch his head clean off his body for mentally abusing her until she can't enjoy anything without fear and anxiety spoiling it.

I'd love to dance with her. Feel her body sway rhythmically

next to mine, and how perfectly I know we'd fit together. Jesus. I can picture it so clearly that it taunts me.

And I decide to take the risk.

Taking a page out of Leo's book, I reach next to me and take her hand, giving her a twirl that catches her slightly off guard. Her eyes are huge and a little terrified when the spin finishes, but I spot a hint of exhilaration in her silver depths, so I keep going, dancing to the music to try to encourage her to join in. I'm no Leo, but I can dance pretty well. I don't touch her; I just do my thing and smile at her like it's no big deal. She doesn't want to dance in front of other people? No problem. We'll dance here, in our own little corner of the club, where no-one will notice or care.

Her hunched shoulders drop as she starts to slowly relax towards me, and by the time the second chorus belts out, I can see she's made a conscious decision to join in. Maybe it's simple pity, to keep me from being embarrassed by dancing by myself. I don't care. I feel like a million dollars when she starts shaking her moneymaker and getting really into it. I feel like the king of everything because she's no longer too afraid to dance with *me*.

She's good, too. Particularly when she completely lets go and leaves the self-consciousness behind. As the song becomes bouncier and more upbeat, she jumps around energetically, and I cannot help grinning because I've never seen such a cheerful dancer in all my born days. How very Emily. And as the beat settles again, her body undulates mere inches from me until, in spite of my mental determination not to get a boner, my cock is so hard and heavy I could chip concrete. I can feel a drop of sweat inching down my spine, and my heart is racing, both from dancing and straight up happiness.

This is the best night I've had in many a long year.

At one point in the song, she spins so energetically and fearlessly that she crashes into me, and then my hands are at the base of her back to catch her before she falls, my pinkie fingers mere centimeters from the curve of her ass, and she's giggling softly, pleasantly giddy from the twirling, and I'm a little dizzy, too, because she's so close, and we're looking at each other and smiling, and her lips suddenly look so temptingly, tantalizingly close to mine.

I catch her hand and place it on the back of my neck, wanting to groan at her soft touch. Our mouths are mere inches apart. All I need to do is just lean forward and touch her mouth with mine, and maybe I could, maybe it's what *should* happen. Maybe everything has been leading to this all along. Her eyes are huge, and they're in control of me right now, pulling me into their depths…

She does a double take over my shoulder, and her eyes light up. "Sadie!" she exclaims.

I look over, and, yep, sure enough, with perfect timing, I see Sadie and Peter loitering five feet away. To her credit, it looked like Sadie was trying to make a hasty exit, and her eyes are full of apology when they meet mine.

"Heyyyyy, girlie," she says to Em with an awkward beam, and they hug. She mouths, *I am SO SORRY* over Em's shoulder, and I smile and shake my head, making a 'forget about it' gesture with my hand. It's not her fault she accidentally interrupted. And to be honest, I'm just glad she made it tonight. I don't think much of her boyfriend, Peter, and not just because he comes off like a self-important ass. He never seems to take much interest in things that matter to Sadie, or be willing to put himself out to do something *she'll* enjoy. He ducks out on as many of these nights as he can, and if he can convince her not to go, he does. So I was in full agreement with Leo's assessment earlier, and I'm genuinely surprised to see them here. Of course, I am biased in favor of my cousin, but even without knowing that Leo's always been desperately in love with her, I still think Sadie could do a lot better than this dullard standing next to her.

Take now, for example. He gives me the barest polite nod, and doesn't say much or even smile as he shakes Emily's hand, even though she gives him the most gorgeous, friendly beam, and tells him it's great to meet him after hearing so much about him.

Jackoff. If he's not charmed into politeness by *Emily,* the sweetest person in the world with her adorable manners, he's clearly beyond hope.

"Drinks?" Sadie asks, seemingly oblivious to the awkward silence that was starting up. For all Peter's expensive education and personal wealth, his manners suck.

"Sure," Emily replies.

"We'll stay for one," Peter decides in his cut glass British accent, running a hand through his hundred dollar haircut. Sadie doesn't say anything, but I roll my eyes inwardly. Yeah, he definitely didn't want to come tonight. What a dick. This is literally a duty visit, and Sadie got all dolled up for all of probably an hour of club time. What a waste, and what a god damn shame for her.

Anyway, we all make our way to the bar. The seats will probably be gone by the time we get back, but we can stand.

I see Leo look up from bumping and grinding with the same brunette he's been macking on all night, and notice us. Or rather, notice *Sadie*. The split second of raw pain, mixed with a more lingering look of surprised happiness that she made it after all, makes my chest ache for him. I honestly don't know how he deals, sometimes. He's confided in both me and Dean, and I know how much the situation hurts him behind the grinning and the Leo charm. He loves Sadie, body and soul, always has. I can see in his face his evening has spun from pretty freakin' sweet to a punch in the gut. He quickly turns back to the woman he's with, who fortunately didn't notice him looking at another woman while she was twerking against his crotch. He collects himself enough to give us all a convincing carefree wave, like it's no biggie, and then forcibly turns his attention back to her.

Emily looks at me, and then back to Leo. Shit. I think she just saw everything. My suspicions are confirmed when she darts her eyes towards Sadie, who is laughing happily at whatever Peter just said and playing with his hair.

"Did I just see..." She glances over her shoulder at Leo, who is now back to normal and grinning at tonight's woman. Em's eyes are huge and soft with sympathy as she looks up at me. "Leo's into Sadie," she mouths. It's a statement, not a question. She's nobody's fool.

"Yep," I say quietly. She's figured it out. No sense in hiding it.

"Awwww," she says sadly, patting her chest where her heart sits. "And she doesn't know?"

I shake my head. "Not as far as I can tell. She's all in with..." I nod towards her and Peter.

Em sighs. "Poor Leo," she says very quietly.

"Yeah, it's rough on him," I agree. "He does this every so often as a distraction, but...there's no-one else for him. No-one else measures up." I shrug sadly. I do feel bad for him. And for Sadie, who'd be much better off with my cousin, but she can't seem to see past Asshole Peter. But Leo never lets his mask slip to her for a second. Just keeps on keeping on, not wanting to spoil their admittedly cast iron friendship. I admire the shit out of him for it.

"Guys!" Sadie calls, eyes bright with laughter at something apparently funny that Peter said (though I doubt it, she was probably just being nice). "What're you having?"

After a couple of drinks, Emily surprises me further by pulling my wrist gently to the dance floor of her own accord without any prompting.

Helping her feel confident enough to do that is the high point of my month—of my *year*—so far.

Now that she's warmed up to it, her dancing has become completely uninhibited, and she's gorgeous to look at while she's lost in the music. Leo catches my eye as I dance a respectful yet still intimate distance from her. I'm not letting another man near, and I glare at a few that are eyeing her up, making a few subtle fists at my side which flexes my biceps, until they back off; I'm a big guy, and there are few who would size me up and be willing to take me on. It makes Leo laugh as he bumps and grinds with his band aid lady of tonight, and mouths, *Fucking go for it.*

I raise an eyebrow and look back at Em. I'm never normally this shy in a club, but, though I would love to pull her hips towards me and dirty dance with her the way Leo is with his date, I do believe in waiting for very clear signals before I make a move. The only reason Charmaine and I got together was because she made the first move, and to be honest I think her go-get-it attitude was one of the parts of her personality that drew me to her. But I don't want to crowd Emily, or misunderstand anything. She's been through so much. I don't want to get this wrong and misread any signals and make her uncomfortable. That's the last thing she deserves, and besides, I wouldn't want to ruin our friendship in any way. Being her friend is too important to me, above and beyond my feelings for her.

But then she looks at me.

There's a pulse between us, and we both move imperceptibly closer together, not breaking eye contact for a second. The air between us is charged like static electricity, and in spite of the muggy heat inside the club, I feel my arms prickle with goosebumps. Haim sings breathlessly about the heat of the moment, and if the heat they were singing about is anything like this moment right now, I'm amazed the mics didn't burst into flames as they sang. I realize my hand was starting to inch towards her waist, that mouthwatering hourglass figure of hers, and I pull it back, digging my fingers into my palms. Her cleavage jumps a little as she dances, and I'm only a man, and my cock once again starts to harden towards her. I pray my jeans and boxers are tight enough to keep the fucker under control and discreet. The last thing I need right now is a tented crotch region giving the game away and making shit awkward.

Em has started mouthing along to the lyrics, and she's still not breaking that supercharged eye contact with me. Her gray eyes look like silver in the flashing blue and purple lights of the club, and I wish she was saying these words to me for real, and not just singing along to a Calvin Harris song.

I can't look away.

"Guys, we're off," Sadie declares to us, effectively severing the moment for the second time tonight. "Peter's got a cab waiting." Peter stands back, nodding a brief goodbye to us both. He barely said anything all night, and was very obviously bored out of his haughty skull the entire time. I glance back at Sadie. I know from previous nights out just like this one that my friend loves to get down on the dancefloor. Tonight she hasn't been near it, stuck babysitting her man on the sidelines. Peter is a selfish *ass.*

She and Emily hug, and she also gives me a quick squeeze. "Leo's right, fucking go for it," she murmurs in my ear, and I blink. She pulls back and winks at me, and then she walks with her asshole boyfriend to the exit.

Leo notices, and the longing in his face seems worse than usual as he watches her leave, his eyes following her though the crowd until she's gone. Like a snap decision, he spins the woman he's with around, and in a split second he's cupping her face and kissing her, hard and deep, like she's the love of his life and he hasn't seen her in a year. Or, more accurately, like she's the woman who just walked out the door with Peter. He's lost, desperately chasing comfort in the last place he should be looking, and the woman responds with alacrity, hooking her arms around his neck and giving as good as she gets.

I shake my head. He is officially out for the evening. He'll take her home, fuck her to deaden his own pain for a few hours, and never call her again. And next week he'll do it all again with a different woman.

"I guess that's Leo occupied for the rest of the night," Emily jokes wryly, echoing my thoughts.

"Guess so," I agree. I look back at her, trying not to think about what would happen if I pulled her close and did the same thing, trying to ignore the thud in my chest urging me to do it. Her face is flushed and her eyes are sparkling. She's so stunning it's like a jab to my ribs.

"I'm kind of done, too," she admits.

"Sure," I say, wishing the night could last forever. "Let me walk you home." She lives closer to the club than Sadie does, so there's no real need for a taxi. Plus, I want to prolong the amount of time I have with her.

She looks up at me, and I half expect her to politely say that she doesn't want to put me out, like she usually does. But instead, she smiles a little, and says, "OK."

chapter ELEVEN

Meanwhile, on the EmEli WhatsApp group (members: Sadie Stewart, Leo Mills, Dean Gastright)

Sadie Stewart: DEAN

Sadie Stewart: Deeeeeeaaaaaaaannnnnnn

Sadie Stewart: It's definitely working

Dean Gastright: Yeah? :)

Sadie Stewart: I swear they were about to kiss when I rocked up with Peter. I tried to vacate, but she saw me. I was like shiiiiiiiiiiiiit I'm such a cockblocker

Dean Gastright: Aw man

Dean Gastright: But the fact that they got to that point…lookin good :)

Sadie Stewart: I left them dancing together

Sadie Stewart: They weren't quite bumping and grinding, but I don't think it'll be too long, and when I said goodbye I told him he should go for it

Sadie Stewart: Shit a BRICK I hope he does

Sadie Stewart: Their eye meets were EVEN MORE INTENSE THAN NORMAL and COMPLETELY ADORBS

Dean Gastright: LOL

Dean Gastright: I'll get my earplugs ready then ;)

Sadie Stewart: LOL

Sadie Stewart: I swear if nothing happens between them tonight I will CRY

Sadie Stewart: Or bash their heads together

Leo Mills: They just left

Sadie Stewart: Yeah??

Leo Mills: Yep. And his hand was on the small of her back as he led her out ;)

Sadie Stewart: Goooooooooood sign

Sadie Stewart: Ugh I have zero chill about this

Sadie Stewart: Surprised you noticed them go, Patrick Swayze ;)

Leo Mills: They came and said goodbye. Also, Patrick Swayze??

Sadie Stewart: You and Miss Thing were dirty dancing ;)

Leo Mills: Not Channing Tatum? I think I could rock a Magic Mike movie ;)

Sadie Stewart: Swayze is the OG. Original and best. There would be no Channing Tatum without Patrick and his moves.

Leo Mills: I've never actually seen Dirty Dancing

Sadie Stewart: . . .

Sadie Stewart: [GIF of Kevin Hall staring in offended shock]

Sadie Stewart: WTF LEO

Leo Mills: Just never got round to it

Sadie Stewart: We can't be friends anymore. We just can't.

Dean Gastright: Lol

Dean Gastright: Even I've seen it

Dean Gastright: How you've managed not to is beyond me

Leo Mills: Jeez, OK, is it on Netflix?

Dean Gastright: Amazon Prime.

Sadie Stewart: Do NOT tell Miss Thing you haven't seen it or you're going home alone tonight

Leo Mills: Her name is Sheryl, and I'm sure she wouldn't care

Leo Mills: Not after the moves I just pulled ;)

Sadie Stewart: OK, 1. Eww and 2. You sure you want to take that chance?

Leo Mills: ...maybe you're right. I really do want to get laid tonight.

Sadie Stewart: Ugh

Sadie Stewart: You are so gross

Leo Mills: [GIF of John Goodman laughing raucously in Roseanne]

Sadie Stewart: BYE

Leo Mills: LOL

Dean Gastright: [Eyeroll emoji] Have fun, everyone

Eli

I can almost hear my heart pounding as I walk her home.

These are the streets I use for my morning run. They're perfect for training; up and down hill, and with the roar of the ocean to keep me company. We can hear the waves crash now as we stroll next to each other, though, as we climb the hill towards the studio, it's becoming muffled. It's like an AMDR track, the ones Dean uses sometimes for relaxation. I pound these pavements every day in the early morning; sometimes with my iPod, sometimes without, but either way I'm always tuned out.

Walking with Em now, with the roads lit by a bright half moon and dim street lamps, these old roads that I've taken for granted all these years somehow look so much better. I have no regrets about emigrating with Dean to the UK; much as I love and miss New Orleans, I felt the same as he did about being unable to stay in a country without gun control after everything that happened to him, and it allowed us to spend more time with Leo and get in on doing something we both love. But Foxton itself used to be simply where the parlor was. Now, I can appreciate what a great place to live it is. Great architecture surrounding us. A clean, broad seafront with a clear blue ocean. Nice places to take her on a date, maybe, if she's up for that.

God, I hope she is. Just the idea of taking her out to dinner, sitting across from her all evening in a first class restaurant, maybe reaching across the table to take her hand, makes me smile to myself.

I'm glad the streets are deserted as we talk about random stuff. It makes this all feel more intimate, like the town is just ours for the night. I'm also pleased by the increasing ease between us. Yes, Leo does indeed have the moves. No, you wouldn't automatically put Sadie and Peter together based on appearances. Emily's careful and tactful and sweet, but I can tell she's not impressed by the guy, either. Em, I've learned, sees the good in everybody she possibly can; if *she* thinks you're an ass, you're definitely an ass.

I jump slightly as her fingers accidentally brush mine when she checks her handbag. She's panting a little after the climb up this street, and it's making me think about making her pant on purpose for less wholesome reasons than a brisk walk. My entire right hand is tingling after the brief touch, which she doesn't seem to have even noticed beyond a quick, "Oops, sorry".

I stretch my fingers to try to clear the feeling so I can pretend it didn't happen.

Until I start to wonder.

What if I did it again?

Silently, I take a deep breath and hold my right hand in just the right place to brush her fingers once more. It takes a few seconds, and I try hard to focus on what she's saying about how Steve the DJ played some of her favorite songs at the club. But then it happens. Her knuckles skim accidentally across mine. Somehow it's fucking electric.

And I take a chance.

Suddenly deciding to go for it, my fingers catch and hook on hers, gradually, gently taking her hand until our fingers are laced together.

A second passes…

Two…

I hold my breath as I look at her from the corner of my eyes, wondering if I've misinterpreted, blown it, and made her uncomfortable…

…until I feel her gently squeeze my hand.

Holy shit.

This is the exact opposite of what I feared.

I feel all tension leave my body, melting through the pavement along with my spine at the gentle pressure of her hand. I'm beaming at everything in the surrounding area. This is not an expression that often crosses my face, but I couldn't stop it if I tried.

I sneak a direct look at her, and her shy smile is excruciatingly beautiful as she looks towards the ground.

We walk the remaining blocks to her home hand in hand, all conversation at an end, just enjoying the feeling. Something in my chest, cold and empty for so long, starts to spark and glow like a lit firework.

I don't want this walk to end. I want to walk these streets all night, just holding your hand.

To go from assuming I'd die single to walking hand in hand with a woman who was tailor fucking made for me is jarring. But in a good way. In the best possible way. I've secretly longed for this connection. I've been lonely. But maybe, just maybe, those days might be over.

Shit, already? I think as we reach her home. We stop in front of the doorstep.

"Thanks for walking me home," she says to my feet, and there's a light wobble to her voice, like she's nervous. I wish she'd look directly at me so I could figure out what would be an appropriate goodbye.

"My pleasure, *chere*," I murmur back. *Huh*. It's the first time I've called her that to her face, and I did it without thinking.

Her gorgeous smile deepens. Her eyes slowly flick up to mine, and for a brief second they seem like quicksilver in the light of the street lamps. And then she takes half a step forward, leans up, and kisses me on the cheek, soft and sweet.

My knees tremble ever so slightly at the scent of her. Peaches. Coconut shampoo. *Em*.

"I appreciate it," she adds. Pause. "I'll…see you tomorrow?" she asks.

Tomorrow is Sunday, and I don't have any appointments this time. Leo or Dean must have one, or she wouldn't have been asked to go in, either.

"Sure," I say. I mean, I'm sure I can think of a reason to go into the shop. No way am I missing out on some extra Emily time. And the smile she gives me in return sends a wave of happiness straight through me.

We do this awkward shuffle, and then we smile as she begins to walk up her steps and I start to take a couple of steps backwards. "Bye," we say in almost perfect unison. More laughing. She opens her door and walks inside, waves, and closes it.

Damn it, I think to myself as I trudge back to my own apartment a few streets away. *I should have…*

I really *should have…*

Fuck.

I stop in my tracks and rub my chin, weighing the pros and cons of what I'm pretty sure I'm about to do.

I take a deep breath.

She squeezed my hand back. I can still feel the lingering feeling of her touch if I close my eyes and concentrate.

I look back at her front door.

Her light is still on.

I look at the streets ahead.

My walk home suddenly seems much too long, even though it's all of ten minutes if I stroll.

My feet are moving before I realize I've made a decision.

Fuck it.

I take her steps two, three at a time, and then I knock before I can change my mind. One-two-three-four, not too loud, not too soft.

I wait.

My heart may burst out of my chest, and I wonder if this was actually such a good idea.

I can see her walk towards the door through its frosted glass. Too late.

Take the chance, asshole. She's amazing. Don't punk out.

The door opens. Hey eyes look surprised, but…she's smiling. Genuinely. I'm not unwelcome.

Thank god.

"Hello," she says brightly, "did you forget something?"

You could say that.

"Um…" I start, leaning on the doorframe, and the moments tick by as I realize I haven't prepared a cool line for this. *Say something, say anything, god damn it.* "I..." I chuckle nervously. "I forgot to come up with an excuse to come back," I manage honestly. I straighten up. *It's now or never. You've come this far.* "The only *reason* I have," I say, swallowing my nerves, "is you."

Her eyes widen, like she's stunned.

"Can I come in?" I ask quietly.

Her surprised face starts to smile, and she pulls the door wider, wordlessly nodding.

Answer enough.

I don't have a plan. I have no idea what I'm going to do next. I just wanted to be in the same room as her again, just for a little while longer.

I walk through the door and turn to her as she closes it behind us.

Her hall is cream and light blue. There are small blue and white flowers in a purple pot on a small table behind me, and several unopened letters just next to it. She's clearly not a fan of receiving mail.

I look at her face. The flush in her cheeks. Her front teeth softly scrape her lower lip, front to back. *Fuck me.* My cock, which was almost at half mast, jumps at the sight. My jeans are now almost painfully tight.

"I want to kiss you," I say in a low voice.

Her eyes go wide.

"Only if you want me to," I continue quickly to reassure her, unable to look away from her astonished gaze. *Why astonished? Has she not looked in a mirror lately?* "But if you do—"

She takes a step closer to me, smiling nervously as she returns my look, not blinking as an inviting warmth ignites in her beautiful eyes. "OK," she whispers, biting that gorgeous lip again.

"What?" I say blankly.

She giggles a little. "I said, *OK*," she replies in a very sexy murmur.

Do it.

I step forward and place my hands on her hips, gently pulling her towards me. Her eyes are huge, and she's holding her breath.

I lean forward until our noses touch, my mouth so close to hers, and then…

Then…

Her lips are so soft against mine as they touch gently, one small kiss to dip our toes into the waters before I slant my mouth against hers.

Holy fucking god.

She makes a faint noise that sets my blood on fire as my mouth moves again of its own volition, coaxing her lips open so I can gently slip my tongue into her mouth. She tastes so sweet, fresh as berries, and her mouth is so invitingly warm. I briefly think of how her silky lips would feel in other places…and then her tongue slides smoothly, delicately against mine and I lose my head entirely. I pull her close, closer, still not close enough, until she is engulfed and wrapped in my arms. This is where she belongs. The kiss deepens, becomes almost frenzied, and the rumbly groan I hear, when she begins clutching at my shoulders, is my own. My hands tangle in her hair as her fingertips trail slowly down my back, sending a tingle along my spine and a live wire straight to my aching cock. I slide my hands to the top of her ass and pull her closer, grinding gently against her so she can feel it, feeling a primal need for her to know precisely what she's doing to me.

This is the best first kiss of my life. No question.

I become dimly aware of her fingers starting to fumble against my belt as she fights to undo it. *Damn, baby, you read my mind,* I think in a fog of lust, until it hits me that she really is about to -

She's going to -

I gently take her fingers, holding them still.

Not yet?!

"Hey, whoah," I murmur against her lips, "what are you…"

She grins at me as we catch our breath, but this is not the same Emily smile that has made every day since she arrived a lot brighter. I search her eyes, confused and a little concerned. *This is not the Emily I know, full stop.* The look in those eyes of hers has become calculated, artificial…fake. It's a front. There's heat there, but no warmth. There's a wall up between us that wasn't there before. She's not with me in this anymore. What happened?

No. No, honey, come back to me.

"It's OK," she says in an exaggeratedly sultry voice, "just relax and enjoy it." She reaches for my belt again, but once again I hold her fingers still. She looks up at me, confused.

Maybe I should just go with it, even encourage her. Maybe many men in my position would. But I don't like that she seems to be trying to impress me by acting a certain way. She doesn't have to do this. She just has to be…*her*. Just her genuine self. *That's* what's sexy to me, not this sudden artifice she's brought to the table.

"I didn't come here for that," I say to her with a laugh, and I really didn't. I came here for a few extra minutes of her company. I hoped to kiss her. But I don't want to rush everything. I want to savor every moment. I don't want to push for a home run.

She flinches like I struck her. My mind races to find the words to put this right, to turn this from unintended rejection into what I actually mean. I shouldn't have laughed.

"I mean, you don't have to—I just meant—"

"It's fine," she says numbly, her voice dull, and she backs off. Fuck. "I'm…sorry…" She hugs herself and starts to turn away, embarrassed. Withdrawing from me. Shutting down.

FUCK.

"Em, no—" I hurry to assure her, reaching for her, but she

takes a step back to avoid my touch. Her lips are still pink and swollen with my kisses, and now I've made her feel like…

Shit, shit, shit.

"It's…late. I'm gonna go and get some sleep," she says in a small voice. "I'll see you later, OK?"

"But you don't under—"

"Please leave," she pleads.

My heart sinks.

"OK," I say quietly. I'm going to put this right later. I don't think she's in the right frame of mind to listen to my explanation right now. But still… I can't bear to leave it like this. "I just didn't want you to think I was just fixin' to get lai—"

"It's fine," she cuts me off.

I sigh, defeated, but only for now.

I walk towards her door, mad as holy hell with myself for going from kissing my ideal woman as though our lives depended on it—easily the most passionate, toe curling kiss of my life—to offending her and having to show myself out.

Unfortunately, the door does not hit me in the ass on my way out.

Her hall light snaps off straight away once the door closes behind me.

FUCK. I blew it.

chapter TWELVE

Emily

IT'S INCREDIBLY TEMPTING TO CALL IN SICK THE NEXT DAY, go back to bed, and just die of embarrassment, but I don't. That's something Old Emily would have done.

Instead, I put on my favourite ripped skinny jeans and a Patti Smith t-shirt, and spend ages perfecting a cool eyeliner flick, or near enough. War paint. I feel more like the real me like this, anyway. I can dress how *I* want, and starting today that's exactly what I'm going to do.

My hair is still slightly curly from the night before, and I take the time to refresh it a little with my curling iron. Tomorrow's hair appointment can't come soon enough for my liking. But in the meantime, if roots laden blonde curls can work for Miley Cyrus, they can damn well work for me.

He laughed.

I'm feeling the urge to text Sadie and just vent it all out, but that's a little awkward since we all work together, and I'm not sure she's clocked my crush on Eli, and I don't much fancy starting from the beginning. Plus, she's probably still with her surprisingly boring and nothing-to-write-home-about boyfriend. With his thick brown hair and even features, he's not at all bad looking, but his snootiness ruins it. I cannot for the life of me understand what she sees in him. She's far too vibrant for such a disdainful git as that.

I check my reflection, ignoring how badly my stomach is churning, before I go. I don't look half bad, actually, especially considering I barely slept. Huh. I add my leather bomber jacket to complete the look, because that's what badasses wear, right? Leather jackets?

I stomp a little bit on my walk in, to build up my confidence, and to mask the sound of my heart thudding in rising panic. Bollocks to whoever booked an appointment on a Sunday for making me come in to help out. This is going to be super uncomfortable. Although it would be a little offensive if he really did so, I kind of hope Eli just ignores me, and then I can ignore him, and then we can only interact when he needs me to book an appointment or take a payment, and in time everything will settle down and be fine again.

Why did he stop me?

I sigh sadly to myself. It serves me right for being conceited enough to believe he and I could actually have anything, that a man like that would truly be interested in me. 'Agonisingly humiliated' is an understatement. The first time I decided to try going for it with someone new since my break-up, and he rejected me when I offered it to him on a plate. I...don't get it. Sex was the one thing, the only thing, Gav ever said I was good at. I have good techniques. I was willing. I'm always undemanding in bed. I never expected Gav to go out of his way for me or my pleasure; I was happy as long as he was happy, as long as *he* got off. It was all that used to make him pleasantly inclined towards me at times. So if I was good enough to stave off Gav's bad moods...why doesn't a nice guy like Eli want me?

And why did he take my hand while we were walking home? Why grind his cock (which *was* hard, I don't care what anyone says) against me as he kissed me, if he wasn't that bothered?

And what was all that with pretending to Melissa that I was his date? I mean, admittedly it was all for show, but all he had to do was just tell her, 'Hey, Melissa, I'm on a date right now'. He didn't have to run his fingertips around my shoulder, or whisper in my ear, or turn me into jelly.

Is it me? Maybe it was a pity kiss. Or maybe one kiss with me made his skin crawl and put him off for life. Oh, god. Did I have bad breath? I mean, he was gentle enough in his rejection, but...

Oh. Maybe he thought I was a slut? Well, if that's the case, Eli Gastright can DO ONE. He doesn't strike me as a slut shamer, but any man who can't accept that women like to have sex, too, and might even be upfront about it, is definitely not the man for me.

So there.

I've been through enough for one year; I was stupid to consider getting into something new so soon after ending a shitty and abusive long term relationship, anyway.

I didn't get a brilliant night's sleep last night, due to that exquisite cocktail of indignant outrage and cringe-inducing mortification, as well as having these same thoughts about the whys and wherefores of him turning me down running through my brain in a relentless, insistent loop. I've got to dig up some moxie from somewhere, so I resolve to add *Rebel Girl* by Bikini Kill to the parlour's spotify and play it a few times really, really loudly.

All too soon for my liking I approach the shop door, and Oh. My. Crap.

He's waiting on reception.

He's leaning both hands on the counter behind my desk. I guess my vain hopes of being able to largely avoid him, at least for today, were exactly that: vain. He's clearly determined to have this out.

Urgh, no...

He looks up and his face relaxes slightly when he sees me through the glass of the door, and then becomes serious once again.

Probably better to just get this over with, I try to convince myself, but I also briefly consider just turning around and running back to my place. But no. That's what Cowardly Emily would do. New Emily is fierce and stompy and is wearing her clumpiest Doc Martens and will not be cowed, damnit.

I just wish my legs weren't shaking as I open the door.

I shrug my jacket off and hang it up, managing not to look at him. I'm just starting to wonder if I should just say 'good morning' and then leave it at that when he speaks.

"Can we talk?" God, I wish, I wish, I WISH his voice was just a fraction less sexy. I might stand a chance then.

"I don't think there's any need," I mutter with a throwaway smile to try to get him to drop it. "It's fine. We don't need to—"

"Please," he says quietly, and I finally look up at him. He looks…sad. His eyes are filled with regret and concern, and he's leaning over the counter and pressing his lips together. The lips that kissed me and then told me 'no.'

Oh, buggeration and all things bollocks, I *cannot* take a gentle 'it's not you, it's me' talk. I don't want to hear it. Not now, not ever. But he looks like it's eating him up, so I guess I'll have to just stand here and let it happen and take it on the chin. And then lick my wounds later when I'm alone. I'm used to that, aren't I? Once more won't hurt.

Who am I kidding? One more will hurt like holy hell.

"OK," I mumble reluctantly, and take a deep breath to brace myself for the fresh humiliation to come.

There's silence for what feels like a bloody hour.

"I wasn't saying no because I didn't want you," he finally says, firmly and with plenty of squirm inducing eye contact.

I blink. "Well, that's certainly what it—"

"I promise," he cuts in seriously. "On my mother's grave, it was not that, at all. What it *was,* was..." He pauses, apparently struggling for the right words. He gives a wry laugh. "I've had all fucking night to think how to say this," he mutters. He looks back at me at last. "You weren't yourself, and you didn't...seem into it," he finally says.

I gape. "I'm sorry?" I splutter. "I seem to recall basically th... throwing myself at you," I trail off in a humiliated mumble.

"But it wasn't real," he blurts out, seeming frustrated. "It was like some...performance, or something, that you were turning on for my benefit, and you really, honestly didn't have to d-"

"Alright, morning, guys," Leo says tiredly, but with a big grin. He's wearing the same clothes as last night. Walk of shame alert. At least *someone* had a good time. "All recovered from last night?"

There is a pointed silence as Eli keeps looking at me and I keep fidgeting uncomfortably, and Leo's smile starts to drop.

"Yes," I reply quickly, plastering a smile onto my face. "All good. Cup of tea?" Without waiting for a response, I dart towards the kitchen, not looking at either of them.

Childish though it is, I can't resist lightly slamming the kitchen cupboard doors. I can hear the quiet thrum of their conversation, which I can't make out and don't want to. I'm glad that the noise of the kettle boiling blocks it out some more.

How in the hell can he say I didn't seem into it with a straight face?!

He kissed *me* first, and I *kissed him back.* With considerable enthusiasm. I made it clear I was up for it. Jesus H Christ, I was the one who tried to kick things up a notch by undoing his belt. I thought he'd be pleased. I still don't fully understand why he wasn't.

I close my eyes. Once again, my best performance isn't good enough. This is the one thing, the *one thing,* that I bring to the table, the *one thing* I'm good at in relationships. Without that... what can I really offer him that he'd want?

Nothing, I realise numbly. Absolutely nothing.

Dean

She hasn't seen me watching her, and it should stay that way.

I stop peering around the kitchen door and head back to my studio.

Slamming cupboard doors is not like Em, and while it's not triggering one of my episodes, it's making me uncomfortable. And Eli hasn't been himself all morning. You have to really know him to see it, but because he and I are close, I've been alarmed since he arrived and I saw how downcast he was.

I'm puzzled. Leo and Sadie both fired a text to me last night, on our dedicated EmEli WhatsApp group, saying that they seemed to be getting on really well. Like, *really* well. Apparently there was dancing and lots of cute eye meets, and it was, according to Sadie, 'adorbs'.

What the hell happened?

Well, whatever it is, it needs fixing, and it needs fixing now.

Eli would probably murder me if he knew what I was thinking of doing, and it's not something I would normally even consider, but I want him to be happy. He's seriously good to me, better than worthless shit like me deserves, and I owe him more than I can ever repay, even in two lifetimes. He deserves to be happy with someone who gets him, and damn it, I'm going to see it happen, even if it means sticking my nose in where it isn't wanted.

Even if it means breaking a confidence.

Screw it.

Emily

He's retreated to his studio, and he doesn't seek me out for the rest of the morning, which is a relief, but also makes my mood slither downwards. As uncomfortable and infuriating as the discussion was, we do need to sort this out. We passed each other in the back corridor mid-morning, and it was precisely as awkward as you'd imagine. I just kept my eyes trained on the floor as we passed each other. I heard him sigh, but he said nothing, apparently as much at a loss for words as me.

Leo, observant as ever, has noticed, and he's plainly concerned. He keeps glancing at me out of the corner of his eye and trying to jolly me along with wisecracks and funny comments about last night. I try to join in, and I appreciate his efforts, but I wish he'd stop. I wish he could just send me home early so I could escape this atmosphere I've caused. Part of me wants to just tell Eli to forget everything I've said and apologise, just to put an end to it. But that's an old, bad habit of mine, and I'm pretty sure it's too late to backtrack now.

Dean is watching me, too, when he comes through to collect his client, but his expression is more thoughtful, his gaze narrower. I wish I knew what he was thinking. Probably sees his cousin is down in the dumps and thinks I'm a shit human being for causing it. Well, fine; I'm upset, too, and that's allowed.

I'm just completing a new booking in his calendar when my phone pings with an instant message from him via Google Hangouts.

Dean: Did Eli ever tell you he was married before?

I blink. No, I didn't know that.

I pause for long moments, wanting to ask a million questions but wondering if I should instead say a more polite version of, 'so what?' for the sake of saving face. But no. I keep it simple, but he has my undivided attention.

Me: No

My heart starts thudding. Eli had a wife? Who was she? Where is she now? Did he love her? Stupid question, of COURSE he did. Eli wouldn't marry anyone he didn't love; he's too honest for that. I bet she was everything I'm not. I bet she was beautiful, and sweet, and sexy, and smart as a whip, and utterly sure of herself. I'm picturing Scarlett Johansson as Black Widow levels of stunning. She must have been something truly special to have gotten to marry *him*. Dimly, I wonder why it didn't work out, why anyone lucky enough to marry such a great guy would let him slip through her fingers. Because he *is* a great guy. My heart sinks slowly to the soles of my feet, even more dejection setting in as I watch the three dots indicating Dean is typing flicker across the screen. The impatience builds until I'm clutching my mobile so hard I'm surprised I haven't cracked the screen.

Dean: Yeah. They were married for about two years, maybe? Divorced for the last three.

Me: That's sad

I worry my lower lip with my fingers. I'm sorry Eli had to go through a divorce. He doesn't deserve that.

The three dots dance along the bottom of the screen again.

Dean: Nah. She was a heartless bitch who destroyed his self-esteem and nearly ruined his entire life. The divorce was the second best thing that ever happened to him.

I flinch, and my stomach clenches. Even the notion of anyone hurting Eli fills me with outrage. Underneath the somewhat introverted and gruff exterior is the kindest man I know; I only need to recall how gentle and sweet he was during my panic meltdown to know that. I've never fully understood why he seems to keep some people at a distance. I thought maybe it was because he's always thrown in direct contrast with Leo, the living embodiment of extroverted charisma, but perhaps there is something to it.

Perhaps it's a defence mechanism.

Many wayward strands start to fall into place and add up. Like how he studiously ignores the way some of his clients—even the most gorgeous, sexy, confident women—come on to him.

My phone pings again.

Dean: I'd say the first best thing that's ever happened to him was meeting you, but y'all seem upset this morning.

I wince.

Dean: It's none of my business, and I don't want to pry. But I DO want to see him happy, because he's a good guy and deserves it. And you're a great person, too. You suit each other.

I bite my lip. This is obviously awkward bordering on inappropriate to discuss him behind his back with a member of his family, but I have to admit I'm desperate. Particularly now I know he's got this history which might explain how things went last night.

I go for it before I can change my mind.

Me: That's sweet, but…I'm not sure he's that into me

Me: He made a move last night but then he backed right off when I responded and tried to turn it up a notch. I don't know if I pushed him too hard or what. I'm so confused. And kind of hurt. And very, very embarrassed.

My gut fills with butterflies. I really shouldn't be doing this. But Dean brought it up. And I might actually learn something.

Three dots dance on the screen once more.

Dean: That he backed off doesn't altogether surprise me.

I blink, waiting for more dots to turn into sentences. I'm hanging on Dean's every word. *Please,* I think, *just tell me what I'm missing.*

Dean: So, the thing you gotta bear in mind is, Charmaine (aka Evil Ex Wife) said some terrible things to him when she left. The kind of things that make a man feel worthless. And he fully expected to never be in a relationship again because he took her words to heart and believed they were all true. So he shut down. I'll be honest, though: even before he closed himself off, I've never seen him like this about a woman the way he is about you, not even Charmaine, and I know it's really not my place to do this but I'm full on pleading with you not to give up on him because you are not a regular occurrence for him.

My heart aches.

Dean: I know you've got scars from your past. Please consider that he has his own, too. The fact that he tried last night is HUGE. Never thought he'd put himself out there ever again. This means you are special, honey. Very special to him indeed, more than you know. I don't know what he said or did last night, but I'm really hoping y'all can get past it. I know I shouldn't be getting involved, but... please talk to him? Betcha anything it can be straightened out ;)

I rest my forehead on my hands.

I've been so short sighted. He always seems so solid and together. I never even considered he had his own dark past, his own burdens. I feel sick at the idea that I've apparently only been considering myself this entire time.

I think back over last night, how maybe he really did just want to slow things down, pace himself as much as me, before going further. Maybe it wasn't truly a rejection after all. I still think he could have handled it better, because the laughing wasn't great, but that may have just been nerves, and I'm suddenly determined to hear him out.

Maybe there's hope. If I can just find it in me to have one moment of outstanding bravery and take that leap of faith and *talk it out honestly*... I might get the answers I need.

chapter THIRTEEN

Emily

Both Dean and Leo's clients are done by 2pm. I realise suddenly that Eli didn't have any appointments today. It's beginning to look a lot like he came in just to see me and try to sort this out, and has stayed the entire time even though I gave him short shrift first thing. How adorable.

As they leave, Leo gives me an encouraging look and a wink, which I return with a wan smile. Those penetrating eyes of his see all, and I'm certain he knows more than I think he does. Dean gives my hand a little squeeze with a sheepish look. I smile at him gratefully. I'm sure many people would think that the exchange we had this afternoon was wrong, but I cannot help being thankful that he gave me the inside track. *Be gentle with him,* he says to me. I nod. "I will," I whisper. He nods, and knocks on the counter as he leaves, like he's knocking on wood.

I lock up, and then take a deep breath as I approach Eli's studio door, steeling myself for the conversation ahead. It's probably going to be uncomfortable, maybe even mortifying, but I know deep down that he's worth it.

I knock lightly.

"Yo," he calls back, and I gingerly enter.

He's sat at a table in the corner, surrounded by balls of screwed up paper from his sketch pad, in which he seems to be idly doodling now. He looks up, and his eyes sharpen when he sees it's me. He stands, and the sketch pad gets knocked to the floor, forgotten.

It occurs to me too late that, much like when he knocked on my door last night, I haven't prepared anything to say.

But then words come out of my mouth anyway.

"Screw it," I say decisively, "I trust you."

His eyes widen.

"I'm so sorry I was so…I should have listened better this morning—"

I don't manage another word before he strides over to me and engulfs me in a warm hug, stroking his thumb over my shoulder and resting his face on the top of my head. He takes a deep breath, as though steadying himself. All at once, I feel safe. I feel like this has all been a stupid misunderstanding, and that everything's going to work out. I don't feel afraid. Not of him. And I wasn't afraid to disagree with him this morning, either, which is *astonishing* and completely out of character for me. I want to tell him exactly that, because it's maybe the biggest compliment I can give him.

"I'm so fuckin' sorry, Em," he mumbles into my hair. "I really didn't mean to make you feel bad, or to give you mixed signals—"

"It's OK," I assure him in a whisper.

"It's not OK," he insists. "I should never have made you feel that way. I just…*fuck,* I *do not* want to ruin this…"

"You haven't." I take a shaky breath and pull back. "I'm… sorry I tried to force things." I'm excruciatingly embarrassed, but I need to apologise and make this right. It wasn't cool. "I didn't mean to be so…pushy, or to force the issue. I just thought you'd like it if I…" I trail off, my face on fire.

"Hey," he says, his voice full of feeling as he tucks my hair behind my ear, "you have *nothing* to apologise for." He says it so sincerely that I instantly feel better. One thing about Eli is that he doesn't say anything he doesn't mean. "And I'm being one hundred *thousand* percent honest when I say that it really and seriously wasn't that I didn't want you. As I hope my body made clear," he says with a half smile. It's enchanting to see this big guy blushing, and I feel my own face warming some more as well at the reminder of his erection pressed up against me as we kissed. "That kiss was…fuckin' amazing…" He trails off, looking a little uncomfortable.

"Until it wasn't?" I ask softly. He gives me a guarded look. "Go on," I encourage gently. "I won't get angry. I need to hear this stuff. I have to admit, though, I don't fully understand what you said this morning, about…"

He sighs. "When you reached for my belt," he manages, looking like he's trying to be careful with his words, "it felt like…I don't know how to describe it. Like I wasn't kissing *you* anymore. It felt like you wanted to impress me, and do just what you thought *I* wanted to do, or what you thought I expected of you, y'know? And like the real you had vanished…when the real you was all I wanted." He leans down and rests his forehead gently on mine. "You don't have to pretend, or put on a show. Not for me. I don't want fake. I want *real*."

I think about what he's said.

He's…not wrong. Which is kind of a shock.

I hesitate at first, but then I just go for broke. "But sex is what I bring to the table," I tell him in a choked voice. "It's… always been the one thing I can contribute. The one thing I'm good at in relationships…the one thing I'm good *for*."

"Em," he says sadly, "that's just not true."

I feel tears well up in my eyes. I'm touched by his words, but also painfully confused by them. "I don't know what you want," I burst out, a catch in my voice as I hang onto his ever-so-sexy muscular arms. He's an absolute dream, and I'm almost certain I'm going to ruin this, which makes me more desolate than I thought. *Shit.* Turns out, though I'm afraid of something serious developing between us, I'm finding myself more afraid of nothing developing at all. "I don't know what you need from me, but I don't want to lose…whatever is happening. I really don't. I'm… completely lost here. Please, just tell me what to—"

"It's OK," he soothes me gently. There's a tear spilling down my cheek. He leans back and carefully wipes it away with his thumb. "I want *you,*" he whispers. "The *real* you. Good mood, bad mood, happy, sad, angry, whatever…just as you are in the moment, with no hiding and no fronting. *That's* what I need from you."

I press my lips together to try to keep from bawling in his arms at the bewildering and wonderful thing he just said. "Eli… I'm a mess," I say falteringly. "I'm battle scarred and scared shitless. You cannot *possibly* want to have to deal with that, especially not without…I dunno, like, me making it worth your while…"

He looks at me thoughtfully. "We've all got shit to deal with," he says finally. "But maybe, we've both earned a reward, and it doesn't need to be any more complicated than that. And that's what we could be for each other. Maybe we fuckin' well deserve it." He runs a hand gently up my neck to tangle in my hair. "You don't just bring sex to the table, Em. I mean, not to be an arrogant jackass or nothin', but if that's all I wanted, I could do what Leo does, go out to a club and get laid for the night pretty easily. And I've done that a few times. But with you…I want more than that, because I don't just *want* you…I *like* you. I like who you are. I want more with you. And I'm not going anywhere. I'm here, and I'll deal, and I volunteer for this, OK? I am officially signing up for all of you. *All* of you, for good or bad," he says, very sincerely, and oh my holy wow, I actually believe him.

I slide my arms around his waist and cuddle into him.

Without hesitating, he wraps his arms around me, smelling my hair as he sighs.

One moment of outstanding bravery, I remind myself. I have no clue where I get the courage from, but I find myself opening my mouth and asking, in a quiet voice, "What if…what if I asked you to be mine?"

"Then I'd be yours," he whispers back immediately, with zero hesitation. He pulls back and cups my face with his left hand, making my legs weak. I've always found that to be one hell of a sexy move when I've seen it in films, and I am no proof against it in real life. "I want us to try this, Em. For real. I want you to…be my girl." He looks me in the eye, searching for my reaction, and I'm touched by the nervousness I see there.

I take a deep breath, and, though I cannot deny my anxieties and my scars left over from Gav, I also cannot deny that every cell in my body breathes a sigh of relief whenever Eli walks into the room, as though everything is going to be OK because *he's* there. And that's not the kind of feeling I can walk away from, no matter what's happened to me in the past. No…*because* of what's happened to me in the past. "OK," I reply, very, very softly.

His eyes light up with relief, and I close my eyes and relish every second as he kisses my forehead. We stay in each other's arms for long seconds, and then another impulsive idea comes to me. I smile. It's perfect. It's the best way I can think of to show him I do actually trust him. So I take a deep breath and look him in the eye. "I want you to give me a tattoo," I say, decision made.

"Yeah?" He blinks in surprise. I nod. He gives me a searching look. "Are you sure? I know you said you're nervous of getting some ink done. You have nothing to prove, you know that, right?"

I run a finger over his chest thoughtfully, enjoying the way his flesh quivers slightly under my touch. *Well, that's…gratifying.*

"I know. But I want one, and I want to feel the fear and do it anyway. It seems appropriate to do it right now." I lean forward and hide my face on his scrumptiously well-defined pecs. "And... obviously my first tattoo should be done by my, uh...my super talented...*boyfriend*." I stay still, trying out the word and waiting with baited breath for his response.

He rubs my back. "Fuckin' A," he says, and I can hear he's smiling before I lean back and see him grinning down at me. *Jesus, that mouth of his is gorgeous.* "I've been hoping you'd let me do this someday. And, I mean, yeah, no way would I want anyone else tattooing my girl." He kisses the top of my head, and I squirm happily. I'm someone's girlfriend again. Scary? Yes. But also pretty exhilarating. I feel a lot more comfortable with my decision to give this, us, *him* a chance. "What would you like?"

Ah. I hadn't actually gotten that far yet. "I...don't know. I mean, I know what I've always planned to get, but I want to start off with something small, just to test the waters. Cos everything else on my tattoo wish list is a bit too large for my first time."

He nods thoughtfully. "Yeah, I mean, you're doing the right thing. Start small, and then maybe build up if you're alright with it." He lifts one corner of his mouth. "But you best believe I wanna be the one doing it. Every time."

I grin. "Promise. No-one but you." He smiles one of his rare face splitting smiles, and I love that I put it there.

"Come take a look at my sketches," he says. "See if there's anything you like. I mean, my specialty is for larger work, but I can do smaller. 'Specially for you." He winks, and it's hot as hell, and I can't help but think how much being cheerful and laid back suits him. And how lucky I am to be the one to see it.

He picks up the sketch book that had dropped on the floor and flicks through it until I see a couple of pages of tiny designs. I smile as he hands it to me. They all have a high level of detail, a spin that's pure Eli. A small set of Valkyrie wings, the feathers so fine and tangible I expect them to have a soft, fluffy texture when I run my fingers over the page. A black wasp casting a shadow mid-flight. A tiny daisy that looks more like a photograph on the page than a sketch. I take a steadying breath. I've wanted tattoos for a while, and I know he'll do a great job, and be as gentle as it's possible to be while jabbing someone with needles. Plus, the designs are so small, they shouldn't take more than a few minutes, probably. Maybe? Either way, I'm doing this.

And then I see it, and it's perfect.

A red and black ladybird holding on to a seed from a dandelion clock, riding the air currents. I don't know precisely why, but I relate to the image. I point to it. "That's the one. Definitely."

I feel his chin on my shoulder. While I've been perusing, he's moved behind me, and I find myself leaning my temple against his like it's the most natural thing in the world. He smells *so good*. Clean and fresh and warm. Although my heart rate has picked up, I relax to the soles of my feet. "The ladybug?" he asks, that baritone Cajun voice turning my stomach to jelly, particularly as it's being murmured directly into my ear. My spine tingles, and I shiver. "Sure thing. I doodled it a few weeks ago. Bit cuter than my usual work. It'll suit you." He picks up my hand in one of his and runs his thumb slowly along the delicate skin of my wrist, making my toes curl. At this rate, he won't be able to tattoo anything on me at all because I'll have turned into a puddle of swoon at his feet. "Where do you want it? Your wrist?" He turns my hand over and runs a finger over the back of my hand, over a freckle between my second and third knuckle that I've had since birth. "Back of your hand?"

Taking a deep inhale, torn between just relishing the pure sensuality of the moment and putting a stop to it before I lose the power of coherent speech, I raise my arm and indicate somewhere between the crook of my elbow and my wrist. "I thought maybe here-ish?" My own voice is a little huskier than normal.

His energy is clearly contagious. I haven't the first clue how to play this, since he doesn't want to rush any sexy times, but I have to admit…this feels good. *Really* good. And actually pretty comfortable, like it's right, though the air around us seems to hum with possibilities.

"OK," he says, giving my shoulders a quick squeeze, "take a seat."

Eli

My girlfriend is sitting in my red leather chair, waiting for me to mark her, and Jesus take the wheel, or pinch me, or something, because having the woman of my dreams sat here waiting for me to ink her makes this one of the hottest moments of my life.

Quickly but carefully, because although I'm eager to do this I don't want to screw it up by hurrying, I prepare the needles and inks and put on my rubber gloves, and then I'm sat on my stool in front of her, marveling at how the day has done a complete one eighty. Thank god I haven't ruined this with clumsy words, and that she's opened up to the idea of us.

"Ready?" I ask her. Her eyes are wide and unblinking, and she's been fidgeting while I prepped everything; I felt her tremble when I did the alcohol swab, and her pulse was throbbing fast. But my brave girl nods, placing her trust in me to do the thing that scares her and to do it right.

It's very humbling.

"Tell me if you want me to stop," I say gently, and then begin freehanding the small doodle halfway up her arm.

She jumps slightly at the first touch of the tattoo needle, and gives a soft little grunt of surprise at how it feels. I'm burning with curiosity about her thoughts as I work, and keep looking up so I can enjoy the changes on her face, from the initial wince to the realization that it's been built up in her head as worse than it is. "How does it feel?" I ask.

"Um..." She smiles briefly, watching the drawing take shape. "I mean, it's not the best feeling in the world, but, ah, it's...not as bad as I thought it would be." She winces. "Ow." Her face clears quickly, and, while she is still watchful, she's less tense. She even laughs.

I grin. I'm relieved. "I'm glad you're alright with it," I murmur, carrying on, "I mean, you wouldn't get people like me covered all over in the damn things if it was as bad as I'm sure you've imagined." I smile at her. "Maybe this will be the first of many, after all...?"

"Probably," she agrees softly, watching what I'm doing.

I cannot stop thinking about the conversation we had just before this. The fact that she thinks her sexuality is all she brings to the table, as she puts it, explains a lot about last night, but it is so incredibly sad that she's based her worth on that. This is going to take some careful handling. She's not only gunshy—to the extent that I'm amazed she's agreed to give us a try—but she's also got a *lot* of toxic bullshit to unlearn. And that's not going to be easy. But I'm good. I don't care how long it takes: I'm going to make her understand how awesome she is, both in the bedroom and, more importantly now I know what she believes about herself, out of it.

At the thought of her in my bedroom, I sneak a look up at her face, my eyes drawn to her mouth. She has beautiful lips, plump and soft and delicious. I can't wait to taste them again. And, for all I told her I didn't want to rush straight through to the bedroom, the anticipation of those lips running down my neck, across my chest, and brushing down my abs—shit, I'm getting hard, back up, back up—but god, those thoughts are tempting, and set my blood racing. I manage to disguise a slight groan as I clear my throat.

All too soon—because damn do I love inking *her*—the tattoo is finished, and I'm taking her through the aftercare. She listens carefully, but a bright, ecstatic smile spreads across her gorgeous face. "I did it!" she crows, throwing her arms around my neck exuberantly. I laugh, cheering with her. "Thank you so much! It looks amazing!"

"My absolute pleasure, *chere*. Knew you could do it," I say sincerely. I love the feel of her face nestling into my neck, and my stomach fizzes happily with the realization that such pleasures are going to become a regular feature of my life, all being well.

She sits back, staring at the little ladybug with gleeful triumph. It's a great feeling to overcome a fear, and I'm genuinely pleased for her.

Her eyes meet mine. "How much do I owe you?" she asks.

"Pfft," I say, waving my hand, "on the house. I'm not gonna charge ya."

"No, really, I should pay you for this," she insists.

"Oh, you should?" I ask playfully. "In spite of being a staff member, *and the artist's girlfriend*,"—god damn, I will never get tired of that word if the buzzing joy running through me is anything to go by—"*and* it being something I really enjoyed doing for you?"

She smothers a smile and nods decisively. "Yes."

"Hmm," I pretend to think. I grin. "Give me a kiss and we're square."

My heart thuds happily with anticipation as her eyes widen. "You're…um, you're sure?" she asks.

I nod wordlessly, giving her a meaningful look. God, yes.

She scoots forward, tentatively resting her hands on my knees as her lips slowly come closer. "Just, um," she mumbles uncertainly, "just tell me if I…go too far, or…"

I lift a hand to her face, and god, her skin is soft as thistledown. "Let me be completely clear," I say slowly. "As long as I'm kissing *you*, and you're *one hundred percent* with me in it, you're making me the happiest I've ever been." It occurs to me that reassurance is the best thing I can give her, and that this is likely to be the case for a while, at least until she gets used to being able to rely on me. She says she trusts me, and I believe her and recognize that for the honor it is, but I can't take that for granted, and it's going to need reinforcing. I'm not fantastic with words, but I give it my best shot. "I just want to know for damn sure that every step we take is a conscious decision you've made because *you* truly *want* it to happen. If we kiss, if I'm going down on you, if you judo flip me onto your bed and ride me into next month, I want to know it's your choice, that hasn't been influenced by anything but your own wants, and you're not just doing things for my benefit. Like right now, for example. I've asked for a kiss, but if you don't want to, or don't feel like it right now, it's all good."

Her eyes soften, and her mouth comes closer still. She hesitates a hair's breadth from my own lips, but I wait, though my blood is roaring for me to close the distance and take her mouth in a hard, desperate kiss that shows her better than my words can how I feel about her. This has to come from her. She has to know it's OK to kiss me all she wants, as long as it's from the heart.

The brush of her lips is like a little electric shock, and I sigh as she fits her mouth against mine. She gains confidence pretty quickly, seeing how receptive I am and hearing the groans of pleasure I allow to slip out as her tongue licks into my mouth. Her hands run up my arms, down my chest, and I bite at her lower lip as I deepen the kiss. My stomach is liquid. My cock is hard as granite, *again*, but I ignore it. No matter how badly I want her, no matter how tempting the thought of pushing her back on the chair, pulling down her jeans and panties, freeing my dick and sliding into her in one smooth thrust, I'm not a damn hypocrite. Nor do I give mixed messages. We literally just got to the point where I'm her boyfriend; the rest will come in its own time.

Probably counting that in days rather than months, though, because *Jesus*…

It seems an age goes by before we stop kissing, and her face is flushed, her lips puffy and swollen. Her eyes glitter with lust into mine. I imagine my own face looks much the same as pure happiness settles into my chest.

"Y'all busy tomorrow?" I ask, nipping her softly just under her ear.

She bites her lip. "Unfortunately, yes. I have plans with Sadie. Hair appointment and shopping."

"That's OK," I assure her, slightly disappointed but already looking forward to seeing her Tuesday. I get an idea, and grin inwardly. *Oh yeah, that's happening.* "I'd best get tomorrow's kisses in now, then," I tease, relishing her smile and capturing it with my mouth as I kiss her again, addicted already, and refusing to think about the fucking bedroom upstairs in the parlor.

chapter FOURTEEN

Emily

WE SPENT THE REST OF YESTERDAY JUST HANGING OUT together at Wishbone. I suppose we could have gone out for dinner, or gone back to his place or mine, but we were happy where we were. We kissed. We talked. We kissed some more. Kisses for their own sake, not leading anywhere except for increased intimacy. At one point I was straddling him, and his fingers ran gently up and down my spine as I leaned forward to catch his lips with mine as we chatted and got to know each other even better. It felt delicious, and I bathed luxuriantly in every one of his smiles, all of which I earned. And not just by using my body, because it's *me* he likes. Not just what I'm willing to do.

I learned more about him, and not just that I could make him shudder and growl low in his throat by gently biting his bottom lip, or groan softly by running the tip of my tongue along the seam of his mouth. I also learned that he went to California Institute, where he was aiming to complete a BFA focusing on painting, but dropped out when Dean got shot so he could be there for him. I learned that his mother passed away not long before he moved to England, and his dad has since married a woman Eli describes as 'a real nice lady', and they're spending their retirement travelling around the world. I learned that the thing he misses most about New Orleans—pronounced 'Nawlins'—is the food. He taught me some Nawlins slang, as well; like when he says 'Where y'at' to Dean and Leo, he's asking them *how* they are rather than *where,* like 'where are you at in life', and that the correct response if he asks me (and if I'm fine) is to say, "Awrite". When he started fiddling with the music coming through on the sound system, I learned to my delight that the majority of the Disturbed and Rammstein on the Wishbone Spotify was his. And when we ordered a pizza, I was even more delighted to find out that he agrees with me about pineapple on pizza, ie. it's sick and wrong and a total abomination and perversion of something good and pure and delicious.

It wasn't easy, having a cloud of doubt and fear lingering over me while we enjoyed each other's company, but I have to believe that this will pass over time. My gut told me to take the chance, and that he is worth the effort. He's never given me any *reason* to doubt him, and I'm not counting last night's misunderstanding. Because it was exactly that: a *misunderstanding. Each day as it comes,* I soothe myself. Besides, given my thumping great crush on Eli, I'd have to be the biggest dumbarse in town to turn him down.

It was dark out by the time we agreed to call it a night, and of course he walked me home after locking up, my hand in his as though we've never done anything else. He spends ages kissing me goodbye on my doorstep, but, though it's tempting, I don't invite him in, and he doesn't seem to expect it. After last night, it would just have felt wrong. But I find his determination not to rush things...well, intriguing. It's so foreign from any experience I've had with anyone else since I started having proper boyfriends, all of whom just wanted to get laid as fast as possible with the minimum effort from them to get there, and I find myself feeling more excited anticipation for each step of what is to come with Eli. When he talked about wanting me on board if he was going down on me or if we were having sex, the thrill at the ideas, the prospect of savouring each of them in turn for my own enjoyment…I wanted it. All of it. And I wanted it on those terms: a slow burning build up that we can both revel in, not just a one woman mission to get him off with nothing given back in return. This time, *I* get to enjoy it, too.

"Oh, holy sh—" I exclaim, clapping both hands over my mouth and gasping with delight, "I *love* it! It's exactly how I picture it in my head! Thank you *so much!*"

I've just spent around three hours in the hairdresser's chair, and Lindsey, the woman Sadie recommended, has completely transformed me. I can hardly believe my eyes when I look in the mirror; my hair looks exactly how I wanted it. She grins at me, and says, "Bugger, we should have taken a before and after shot for the salon's website!"

Gone is the regrowth and the pale blonde ends. My hair is now a glossy, rich milk chocolate brown that suits my skin tone so much better and makes it glow rather than draining me. When I walked in this morning, my hair was mostly straight and a couple of inches past my shoulders; now it's wavy and cut just past chin level. I have in the past felt a strong urge to do something drastic to my hair when big life changes have occurred, but this one has been the most meaningful of all to me. My hair looks the way *I* want it to look. I haven't based the colour, cut, or style on anyone else's preferences but my own. I feel free. I feel like *me*, more than I have in years. And I'm hard pushed to hold back the tears welling up in my eyes, but I manage it.

Sadie walks in just as I'm paying. She agreed to come

shopping with me for clothes and makeup once my hair was done, because I'm going all out with this makeover and don't want to half-arse it. No more same old, same old for this girl. Her eyes light up, and her mouth drops open as she beams with glee. "Oh, wow, Em, that looks *fantastic*!" She hugs me and takes a step back, holding both my hands. "You were so right about the colour."

"You like it?" I ask, feeling like a million quid.

"God, *yes*, but more importantly, are *you* happy with it?"

"Couldn't possibly be happier," I confess on a joyous giggle. I'm so happy I could burst. I turn back to Lindsey as she hands my card back to me. "Genuinely cannot thank you enough."

Lindsey waves a hand at me. "My pleasure. I love a good transformation." We say goodbye, with me assuring her I'll be back very soon for a trim.

I cannot stop touching my new bob as we leave. The ends feel soft and delicious and healthy. Sadie chuckles at me.

"So, ready to complete the look?" she asks. "Clothes or makeup?"

"Whichever we get to first," I reply. I'm looking forward to the rest of the day, and can't wait to get back and enjoy my haul. So many possibilities are in front of me, and I feel like a kid at Christmas.

My phone pings. It's a text from Eli. *My boyfriend*. My stomach dips happily.

Eli: Hey, beautiful. How's your day so far? X

I melt a little, and I quickly tap out a response while Sadie chats to me about a cool vintage store she likes.

Me: It's going great, thanks. Hair all finished, and just met up with Sadie. How's your day? X

His answer pings back within thirty seconds.

Eli: Sounds good :-) I'm just about to go for a run. It's nice out, so I'll probably get a little sweaty. When I get back, I might have a good long hard think in the shower about my girlfriend and the cute noises she makes when I kiss that soft patch of skin just under her ear ;) X

My jaw drops. Oh. My. *God*, that's hot. Eli, sweaty. And naked. In the shower. Masturbating. While thinking about *me*. I can feel how wet the idea has made me as I walk, saying a distracted "hmm," to whatever Sadie is saying. I am absolutely loving this new, flirty, sexy side of him. It's *awesome*.

I send him a :-O and a little fire emoji.

Me: Jesus, are you trying to set me on fire or something?? X

Eli: Baby, I might be ;) X

"Oh my god, *please* tell me that's Eli you're texting and grinning about," Sadie's eyes are alive with amusement.

I tuck my phone away in my jacket pocket. "Sorry," I say with a sheepish smile.

"Babe, you only need to apologise if you're not going to give me all the deets," she says, linking her arm through mine. "Seriously, tell me he made a move on Saturday night. *Please*."

I grin, and can feel myself going pink. "Well, erm..."

Her eyes widen and she stops us in our tracks. "Oh my god, he did!"

I smile at her. "So, uh, I have news...Eli's...kind of my boyfriend now."

Without another word, she takes me by the hand and drags me towards the nearest pub as I laugh. "Drinks, and you're telling me *everything*."

I decide to join Sadie in ordering a Rekorderlig as I lay it all out for her. My schoolgirl crush on Eli. The way he gently encouraged me to dance at the club until I was letting my freak flag fly when I'd had no intention of doing any such thing. The kiss. The misinterpretation. The way we fixed it by honestly talking it out in a way I never have before with anyone else. And, of course, the hours spent liplocked in his studio after everyone else went home yesterday. Shivers of remembered pleasure echo through me as I remember the taste of him, the gentleness of his lips, the hot, tender slide of his tongue against mine. She listens intently, eyes sparkling as she rakes in every last detail. It's as though she's been anticipating this for a while, maybe even hoping for it.

"So, do you think what he said was fair?" she asks I've finished.

"You mean about the way I acted when he first kissed me?" She nods. I sigh. I've thought about this a lot. "He's not wrong," I admit. "I don't want everything to always come back to Gav, but I did kind of go onto autopilot. I was definitely on board, but I was very much acting the way I thought he wanted me to, rather than just letting it be what it was."

She squeezes my wrist, eyes softening with sympathy. "Conditioned behaviours are hard to unlearn. It's totally understandable. But, I mean, Eli's a great guy. You know he'd never treat you the way your dickbag ex did, right?"

"Oh, for sure. I'd never have been able to get this far if I even thought it was a possibility." I run a finger around the rim of my glass of cider as I consider the whole business. "I'm still pretty blown away that he even picked up on it, when I didn't realise that's what I was doing. I thought Leo was the perceptive one in that family, but…" I shrug.

"Oh yeah, I mean, *Leo*," she says with a fond eyeroll, "he knows everything about everyone. That man knows what you want before you even think of it. But Eli's just as shrewd. Sometimes I think when introversion was doled out in that gene pool, Eli got Leo's helping, too. But he's still got the gift."

I smile at her description, but find myself fidgeting with my sleeve. "I'm still scared," I say quietly. "If I'm honest, I really wanted to be single for a while. Relax, just be by myself for a bit so that I could take stock and rebuild to suit myself, without having to take anyone else into consideration. But...he's so lovely, I just couldn't resist." She beams at me. "Honestly, he's just...I couldn't gush about him enough. He's the sweetest, kindest, smartest, *hottest...*" Sadie giggles, and I join in a little. "But what if..."

She waits patiently after I trail off.

I make a grumbly noise, irritated by myself. "What if it's just too soon? What if the scars are too raw, still, and I ruin it?"

She thinks for a moment, eyes wandering around the room as she contemplates her response. I've seen her do that sometimes when she's deep in thought. "I'm not going to tell you not to worry about it," she says, "because I would have the same thoughts if I was in your shoes. Which, by the way, are some *lovely* Doc Martens." She leans down to have another look at them, and I waggle my toes. "Cherry red. Classic." She sits up straight again. "But honestly, I think you'll be OK. It's Eli, right? He's good with people who need a little extra TLC. He's amazing with Dean when he has a breakdown. I'm sure he can cope with whatever you throw at him."

She's right, of course, but... "I wish he didn't have to."

"I know. But you have to play the hand you're dealt, and Eli is an ace. A tall, muscular, sexy ace with a massive crush on you." She chuckles as I grin and go a little pink.

"I still can't believe he likes me back," I admit. "I mean, look at him. He's ridiculously hot. I swear to god my knickers burst into flames when he looks at me with those *eyes...*"

She laughs, loudly and unselfconsciously, drawing the bartender's gaze. He smiles slightly, and doesn't look away from her right away. Sadie draws a lot of looks from men, I've noticed. Passers by while we were shopping, people in any pub we've ever visited, moony-eyed clients. And I personally don't think it's *just* because she's a stunning redhead. Sure, that's a factor, but she's simply got this way about her. It's a friendliness, a spark, an easy-going confidence enhanced by fire that makes you want to be around her.

Wasted on Peter.

"Well, I think his pants do much the same thing whenever you give him *that* look. You know the one. You look up at him, and you're all shy but smiley, and your eyelashes do this thing..." She flutters her eyelashes a few times in different ways, but then shrugs. "Meh. I can't do it." I blink. "Oh, you thought we hadn't noticed?" She laughs at my expression. "Babygirl, we all saw the looks, we all knew, and I guarantee you that everyone is going to be just as thrilled for you both as I am."

"You all knew?" Oh, man...

"Yep. And we all totally shipped you both." She finishes her cider and hands it to the bartender with a smile. He's randomly decided to do a sweep of glass collecting, even though there's hardly anyone in here. He glances my way briefly, and I take the hint and quickly finish the rest of mine while he returns his eyes to Sadie. She skilfully ignores him, and carries on talking to me as I hand him my glass, and he has no choice but to go away. "Just, I dunno, don't lose sight of how he makes you feel, so that when you do have a wobble—and heaven knows you have a right to them after everything Gav put you through—you'll have that to cling to and see you through to the other side of it."

I consider her words. "That's...actually pretty wise. Thanks."

She winks as she gathers up her things so we can leave. "In spite of what some may tell you, I do have my moments." A cloud passed across her eyes, but it clears as quickly as it came. "Right, you," she continues before I have a chance to ask her what she means, "Boots or Superdrug? It's makeup time."

The next hour is a flurry of makeup counters, where I find myself focusing on lip colours more than anything. Having stuck rigidly to unremarkable nude pinks all my life, I want to expand my horizons. Being an artist with a good eye for colour, Sadie is the perfect person to give me advice, and she persuades me to pick up some more adventurous shades: berries, plums, and even a dark claret similar to the one she loaned me the other night.

She keeps up her usual steady stream of cheerful chatter as we follow this up with clothes shopping. She gives me armfuls of clothes to try on in the sorts of shops that she frequents, all of which have the Camden rocker chick vibe I love and want for myself so much. Some of the things she insists that I try are items I would never have bought before ordinarily, not because I don't like them but because I would have thought they wouldn't suit me. Turns out I was wrong, and they do, which fills me with delight and excitement for my new look.

When I get home, I'm in seventh heaven as I pore over my purchases and put them away, making plans on what to wear and when.

And then it hits me.

I met her boyfriend for the first time a couple of nights ago, and neither Sadie nor I mentioned him once.

That's odd.

Eli

So, are you gonna tell me why you've been grinning like Jason Momoa this entire time? Dean asks, catching his breath as we take a break mid-run. I pull the lightweight rucksack off my back and pull out two bottles of water, handing him one. I also take out my towel and run it over my face.

I grin wider and take a swallow, glad I remembered to put

the bottles in the refrigerator first thing this morning. "Jason Momoa?" I ask in amusement.

Have you seen his Instagram? Non-stop smiling. But with Lisa Bonet for a wife, can't really blame the guy, he smirks.

"Hey," I shrug, "it's a beautiful day. Look around you. What's not to smile about?" It is, actually. The sun is shining, and there's just enough of a breeze to be refreshing while we have a break. The oceanfront is busy but not packed. Foxton is known nationwide for its award-winning pebble and sand beaches, and the air smells salty and fresh. I stretch, utterly contented.

Dean gives me a shrewd gimme-a-break look. *Come on, man. There's more to it than that.* He squirts a little water over his face and wipes it with his hand. *I'm hoping it's that you and Em sorted out whatever was going on between you yesterday.*

I grunt. "You noticed that, huh?" I take another drink, running the bottle across my forehead when I'm done. "Yeah, we straightened it out." Yet another grin spreads across my face. "In fact, I went one better..." Dean raises his eyebrows, his eyes clearly saying, *keep going?* "I asked her to be my girlfriend. And she said yes."

A huge smile breaks across my cousin's face, and he punches the air before holding his hand out for me to slap. *Congrats, man. Pleased for you.*

"Yeah, me too," I say, thinking back to my little texting session with Em earlier. Now that I'm allowed to flirt with her, my floodgates have opened and all bets are off, as far as I'm concerned. I am going to drive my woman wild in the best possible ways, and I can't wait. I grin as I swallow some more water.

Dean looks thoughtful. *So she's taking a chance on you.*

I screw the lid back on my bottle. "Guess so."

He smiles briefly. *Well, if anyone is the right guy for the job, it's you.*

"How do you mean?"

He thinks. *She's been through a lot. Got to be honest, I thought it would take more time for her to agree to this. No offence to you, just…* He waves his hand in the so-so gesture. *She's going to need a lot of reassurance. Lots of patience. And you are without a doubt the most patient guy I know.*

I consider his words. He's not wrong; she will need me to be understanding. While she comes to know first hand that I'm a completely different person from Gav the Fuckwad. "Prepared for that. She's one hundred percent worth it."

I think so, too. Really. I like her. I think she's wonderful, and I think you suit each other perfectly. Just…know what you're looking at. You can do it. You're good with me, so I don't doubt you're capable. Just, I dunno, make sure you get support, too. I'll be there if you want to talk about it.

Touched by his words, I hold my fist out, and we bump knuckles. People often remark on how much I gave up for my cousin—dropping out of college, emigrating—but he gives back a great deal. He's always got my back, and I've never regretted stepping up for him for a second.

So I gotta ask, he says as we finish off our drinks, *why are you on a run with me when you could be with her?*

I lift one side of my mouth. "Honestly? I asked her if she was busy, and she said she was. Can't say I wasn't a little disappointed, but I also respect the fact that she had other stuff to do, and I don't want her to feel suffocated, or like I'm some demanding-ass Gav type who'll insist she cancels her plans to suit me. She needs to feel free to be herself and to do her own thing, y'know?"

He purses his mouth and nods as he stretches his hamstring, understanding completely. *Sure, that makes sense,* he says.

"But what I *am* gonna do," I continue, "is swing by her place tomorrow morning so I can walk her to work." I smile a little in anticipation. "I mean, maybe I should ask her first? I dunno, just thought it would be nice to surprise her."

He nods. *Do it. The surprise thing is romantic. I think she'll like it.* He gives me an uneasy look, and stops stretching. *Hey man, I...* He sighs. *I have a confession.*

I frown. "OK?" I ask. This is unusual.

He looks me in the eye. *I told her about Charmaine.*

I blink. OK, that was unexpected.

I could see how miserable you both were yesterday, and I wanted to help. I realize it wasn't my place, but... He stretches his neck, looking sheepish. *I thought she needed to know that she wasn't the only one who'd had it rough. I didn't go into chapter and verse or nothing, but she knows the score. And...well, she took it on board, and now you guys have sorted shit out, so although I feel bad for spilling my guts, I'm also...not really sorry.*

Hmm. "I respect that," I tell him quietly. "I'm...well, I'm not crazy about you telling her, but I guess I can't be that mad if it helped." I take a deep breath. Dean's normally a fortress of discretion, but I understand he had the best of intentions. "It came from a good place," I say at last, "and I get it. Just...please don't do it again."

He grins. *Man, if I'm right, there'll be no reason for me to ever mention it to anyone again. Because you know and I know...she's your girl. I think she's, you know, it. For you.*

"She's my lobster," I joke. We watched a lot of Friends reruns while Dean was in recovery, so I know he'll get the reference right away.

I really do think Emily's The One. I've never been so crazy or so sure about a woman before. Ever. And the thought doesn't scare me at all. It's more exhilarating than any runner's high I've ever experienced. I want this. I want her, and I don't envision that ever changing.

We finish the run in companionable silence, while I'm mentally composing my next text to her.

chapter FIFTEEN

Emily

I'M SURPRISED BY A KNOCK ON MY DOOR THE NEXT morning, just as I'm gathering my things to head off to work. I frown, until I remember I *am* expecting a couple of Amazon packages. The postman must be early.

But when I open my front door, it's not the postman. It's Eli. My boyfriend. And he looks *gorgeous*. I swear leather jackets were made with him in mind, and his butt looks totally edible in dark grey, slightly ripped jeans. "Hi," I breathe, devouring him with my eyes. His hair is in its usual knot, but the sea breeze has fluffed it up a little, and a couple of dark strands have escaped. I know he'll redo it when we get to Wishbone, but right now my fingers itch to play with it, to tuck them behind his ear, twirl them around my fingers. It occurs to me that I'm allowed to do that, being his girlfriend and all, and I can't help smiling. Nobody pinch me; I've decided I don't want to wake up if this is a dream.

His eyes widen and his grin is gratifyingly quick as he looks me up and down, taking in the new hair and the different clothes. It's truly amazing just how invigorating it is to wear clothes that *you* chose. I feel like a new woman in my black leather pencil skirt, and a scoop necked maroon bodysuit with a black skull pattern down the spine. The cleavage it gives me is awesome. And I'm loving my fishnet tights and DMs. They make me feel like *me*.

"Wow," he rumbles low in his throat, and it goes straight to my clit, "you look amazing..."

"Thank—" I am interrupted by his lips covering mine, and I giggle as he smiles against my mouth, pulling me a little closer with his hands on my hips. "Thank you," I finish softly.

He lifts a hand and runs it gently through my hair, tugging it in a way that is so sexy and so achingly hot, and I shiver a tiny bit. He notices, of course he does, and his lips gently brush mine, soft as thistledown, electric as a live wire, and I'm hard pushed not to swoon.

Confession time: I was actually having serious doubts about us this morning, and second guessing my decision to give us a try. I nearly convinced myself that seeing him was going to be super awkward and uncomfortable, and that he needs more than I am able to give. But right now, in his arms, being kissed in a way that makes my knees tremble, all my fears go away. That sense of bone deep relief at being with him is back in full force, and it feels like heaven.

"It's like I'm meeting you for the first time," he murmurs, and I blink, surprised again by how perceptive he is.

"You kind of are," I reply, getting lost in his eyes. God, they really are stunning.

He smiles, running his thumb along my jaw. "Don't get me wrong, since the moment we met you have always been the most gorgeous woman in the world to me, but...damn, baby," he chuckles, "you look *even more* fantastic."

I melt at his words. "Really?" I ask shyly.

"*Really*," he says firmly, and starts to run gentle kisses

along my jawline, to that patch of skin under my ear that he mentioned in that super hot text he sent me.

That reminds me...

"So, did you have a nice shower yesterday?" I ask mischievously. He chuckles against my neck, his breath tickling my skin in the most delicious way.

"I sure did," he whispers into my ear, and I giggle again, blushing at the very thought of what he did to himself and biting my lip in a state of pure want. *God, I wish I'd been there.*

When he laughs, I realise I spoke that last part aloud, and I feel myself going pink. But screw it: like the hair touching, I have his approval to do this. "Me too, *chere*," he replies, dropping a kiss on my forehead, "me too."

I smile up at him. "So, to what do I owe this pleasure?"

He smiles back, tucking my hair behind my ear. "Thought I'd surprise you. I'd like to walk you to and from work from now on, if that's cool?"

My stomach flutters. He is *so cute*. "Yeah, sure," I assure him. "That sounds...well, absolutely great."

"Oh, that reminds me," he says, holding up a white plastic bag that he'd left at his feet. "I'm not sure if you've had breakfast, but I picked up some bacon, ah, *sarnies*, apparently, on the way." His face when he says 'sarnies' in that New Orleans twang makes me laugh. "British words are so weird."

We head down my steps. "Hey, sweetie, you have po'boys, we have sarnies."

He grins at my use of 'sweetie' and slings an arm around my shoulders. "Baby, a po'boy will kick a sarnie's ass any day of the week, and I'm gonna make you one someday. You ain't *never* gonna wanna go back. It's all in the way you fry the shrimp..." I reach up to my shoulder and take his hand, and we wander along chatting easily in a way I haven't experienced in a very long time. Perhaps never.

Eli

I love having my arm around her as we're walking down the street to work. I love that it's allowed. I love that she likes it.

This is already the best morning I can remember for a long while, and we haven't even gotten to work yet.

I dig out my keys as we approach Wishbone. "So, uh," I mumble as I open up, "I told Dean. I hope that's OK?"

She gives me a reassuring smile. "Totally. And I told Sadie." She shrugs. "Well, I mentioned in passing that you're my boyfriend now, and she frog marched me to the nearest pub and pulled out every last detail…" She giggles, and I grin in return, kissing the top of her head because I'm having the worst trouble keeping my lips off her.

"So, nobody's told Leo…" We exchange a highly amused look.

"Gird your loins?" she suggests, and I chuckle, running my hand through her new, shorter hair again. I love her new look. It's sexy; plus, she looks happier in her own skin, and that to me is a huge deal.

She pulls back, lifts on tiptoe, and kisses me full on the mouth. "Now, about these bacon sandwiches that are definitely the way to my heart…" She grins as she wanders over to the reception desk and begins to set up for the day.

"Sure," I reply, unwrapping them. "I wasn't sure if you'd already had breakfast, but, you know. Wanted to give you something." I nod my head towards the kitchen. "If you want any sauce, there's some in the kitchen."

She shrugs. "As it comes," she says, taking a healthy bite and giving soft moans of enjoyment. I never thought I'd ever get an erection from watching a woman eat a bacon sandwich, but here we are.

Once we're done, I move so I'm standing behind her with my arms around her waist, because a) I can't stop touching her, and b) I think it's probably a good idea to provide constant reassurance of my affection for her. Woe is me, right?

I'm just putting her off her stride as she chats to me about how busy our afternoon is, by gently kissing the back of her neck, running my tongue up the delicate skin there, when Leo walks in. He takes one look at the compromising position we are in, which I am smug to note leaves no room for any doubt, and dramatically collapses on the sofa with an elaborate sigh. Like a jackass.

"Thank fuuuuuuuuuuuuck," he hoots, "you two finally got it together." He lifts his head. "You did, right?"

"Ah…yes," Emily giggles, turning and burrowing into my arms as she goes a very cute shade of pink.

"Christ on a bike, at *last*," he sighs. "You guys had me worried." He wanders over to us, wrapping us both in a growling bear hug that makes my girl giggle. He kisses the top of her head, and then the side of mine, loudly and exuberantly. This is the moment Dean walks in. He shakes his head in amusement at Leo's antics. "Deano, it finally happened," Leo announces, "EmEli is officially a thing!"

"EmEli?" Emily and I both look a little confused.

"It's our Brangelina name for the pair of you. I think it's a pretty awesome one, though I do say so myself."

I like it, Dean adds, and then he smiles at Em and crooks his finger to her, pulling her into a hug. She responds with surprise and laughs. *Welcome to the family*, he says to her, and I beam at him.

"Aww, thank you," she replies, signing as she talks, and she looks so happy that I can't resist giving her a little squeeze.

Nice hair, by the way, Dean adds.

"Yeah, was gonna say, your hair looks hot as fuck," Leo

pipes up, giving her a twirl and a wolf whistle. "Suits you, Pumpkin."

The door goes again, and Sadie wanders in, scowling and preoccupied. Definitely not her usual self.

"Yo, Sades," Leo says, clapping his hands once and raising them in triumph, "EmEli is a go!"

"Yeah, I heard," she says, clapping her hands together quietly and smiling. "Congrats, guys, I'm really pleased for you."

"Are you OK?" Leo asks, zoning in on her expression.

"Yeah," she says, distracted, "Just…bit of a shit night last night."

"What's up?" Emily asks.

Sadie sighs. "It's nothing, just…Peter stuff." She looks at Em. "Think some girl chat later would be good." And then she points to the third finger of her left hand. It's currently bare, but then she adds, "I think he's thinking of proposing," she says quietly, "but, like, there's some other stuff going on, and I'm pretty frickin' confused, so…" She trails off.

Emily's eyes widen. "Whoah," she says, and I catch her glancing briefly at Leo, who has gone very still. "Let's…let's have a quick chat now, while you set up for the day."

Sadie looks at me and winks, more like her old self. "Glad you finally did it." They both move through the door leading to our studios.

"Shit, man, I'm sorry," I mutter, and Dean squeezes Leo's elbow in sympathy. That seems to bring him back to the here and now.

"I've been wondering when this would happen," he says, very quietly. He sighs and squeezes the bridge of his nose briefly before rubbing his hand over his face. "I kidded myself that he was taking too long, but…here we are at last, I guess." I've never seen that look on his face before. Total desolation. "I'm not ready. I tried to prepare myself for it, but…" he shakes his head, taking one deep breath.

"You gotta tell her," I begin, but the look on his face stops me in my tracks.

"There's no point," he says firmly. "She doesn't feel the same way. She will *never* feel the same way. She just doesn't see me like that, and she loves the prick." He huffs mirthlessly. "I hate him," he mutters darkly. "I *fucking bloody hate him.* If he loved her properly and appreciated her, it wouldn't be half so bad and I could cope because I'd know at least she was loved, but he *doesn't*." Leo slams his fist on the counter on the last word, and then he turns and walks to his studio, leaving me and Dean looking at each other uneasily.

chapter SIXTEEN

Emily

"So, what's up?" I ask as soon as I've closed her studio door behind me. Sadie's room is beautiful. She's done a graffiti style mural on the walls, with the words, 'Nevertheless, She Persisted' stylised in beautiful shades of blue, orange, and purple. She often burns cinnamon scented candles in here, as well, so there's a lingering smell of Christmas.

She flops onto her stool and sighs. "So, he told me last night that he's going to have the tattoo I did for him removed," she says, and for the first time since I've known her, she looks forlorn. "I know it sounds stupid, but I'm really upset by that. I did that for him. That's my artwork *on* him. It's something special, and was *ours*, and it really meant something to me." She smiles ruefully. "I shouldn't be so attached to it, but he got that done when we were first together, and showed me how much he was willing to loosen up, and that he liked my art so much he wanted to wear it permanently. Now, it's as if he's embarrassed by it, even though no-one else other than me can see it…and I can't help but feel really, really hurt."

I sit next to her and squeeze her hand. "I imagine I'd feel the same way if it was me," I tell her honestly. "What was the tattoo of?"

"A bird of prey. It's cheesy as fuck, but when we first went to bed together, he told me that loving me felt like he was soaring like a hawk. It was cringey, but also...kinda nice. And then he pulled off his shirt and told me to mark him permanently. Gave me carte blanche, told me to give him any tattoo I wanted, so that he could remember that night forever. It was..." She shakes her head and giggles softly. "It was so corny, and romantic, and the one impetuous thing I think he's ever done. Other than me, of course," she grins, winking at me.

I smile, but I can't quite summon up a laugh. The idea that he would want to get rid of something with such an intimate story behind it sounds genuinely sad.

She makes a 'tsk' noise. "So, on the one hand he's planning to destroy something I consider quite meaningful. On the other hand..." She beams gorgeously. "On the other hand, I walked into his study over the weekend and found him Googling engagement rings."

"Wow, that's—wow," I say lamely. I have to admit, I found the sum total of things to like about Peter was the fact that, in looks, he reminded me of Lee Adama from the more modern Battlestar Galactica series. That was it. Otherwise, I thought he was an ill-mannered bore, and nothing like I imagined any boyfriend of Sadie's to be. She's such a live wire, so talented and charismatic, and gorgeous to boot. I thought Peter would be much the same.

Come to think of it, I thought he'd be more like Leo. The cheeky-chappy life of the party, the soul of charm and gregariousness. That'd suit her personality more.

She's giving me a searching look, probably wondering why I'm not full of squee for her news. I bite my lip, and decide to ask the hard question. I think our friendship is certainly strong enough to withstand some very tactful honesty.

"Look, I...wish there had been someone to ask me when I

was with Gav, but..." Sadie's eyes become curious and guarded. I squeeze her hand again. "By all means tell me it's none of my business, but I...just don't *get* you and Peter. I'm sorry, I really don't mean to be rude or anything, but you just seem so different. He's...not what I was expecting. And I just want to know that it's simply that I haven't spent enough time around him to get to know him yet, and that you're really, genuinely happy, and I need to just butt out." Besides which, my heart is breaking for Leo, who must be in pieces right now. Part of me is astonished that she hasn't picked up on how he feels about her, because it seems obvious now that I know, but, to be fair, he's very good at hiding it. I only picked up on it at the nightclub when his mask slipped for a brief moment when he didn't know I was watching, or I'd still be clueless as well.

She closes her eyes and smiles tolerantly. This is definitely not the first time she's been asked this question.

"So Tim, my twin brother, became a father when he was fifteen," she says, looking to one side thoughtfully. "He and I are the youngest of four, and for years he was the sweet, well behaved twin, along with Jacob, our practically perfect older brother, and I was the opinionated black sheep bundle of mischief in the family. And then suddenly, this pregnancy bombshell was dropped on my parents out of nowhere." She grimaces. "Thing is, they're seriously good people, but they have high standards, and were always a little on the strict side. After Tim got Nat pregnant, it stepped up even more. They really just wanted us to either be at school, or studying at home. I get it, you know. Eleanor's arrival really shook up their world, and their preconceptions about Tim, and about our safety. But it was stifling. Tim took it on the chin as the consequences of his actions, because he was always very well-behaved generally. Well," she smirks, "apart from the underage sex and getting his girlfriend pregnant. That was the one and only exception. But I found their old ideas a bit much, so their new rules were definitely met with rebelliousness from me. Not being allowed out without all sorts of restrictions and conditions...well, it got to me."

"That sounds rough," I comment.

She shrugs. "Don't get me wrong, everything worked out OK, and they love and adore Tim's daughter. We all do, and he's a fantastic dad. But I was the kid who used to roar with rage at a kiddie harness when they took us shopping as toddlers, so being tied down and having even bigger expectations for achievement and success placed on me, and feeling like I almost had to make up for what Tim did...well, I've always valued my freedom and being able to run my own life my way on my terms."

"I can imagine."

She sighs. "But then I saw my mum crying in the kitchen once, not long after Nat's parents came over with the news that she was pregnant. And it was the first time I realised that my parents were only human, not just strict authority figures, you know? And they were scared, and they were trying their best. And I didn't want my mother to cry anymore. So while I snarled and slammed doors, I didn't sneak out, or do anything to worry them."

I nod. "Makes sense to me." I'm not too sure what this has to do with Peter, but she'll be getting to that.

She gives me a small smile. "So, I went to university to do my arts course. Cut loose, just a little. Had a great time. But after I graduated, I was pretty directionless. I didn't want to be an artist in the traditional sense. And then I found my niche being a tattooist, but I had to pay my dues. Had to go through a few shitty little restaurant jobs on the side while I trained and found a job in a parlour, living hand to mouth. My parents were *not* impressed. They were already frustrated by my insistence on doing my arts degree, and not something more vocational, like Tim and Jacob, who both did IT and had stable, steady jobs with prospects. I think they maybe hoped I'd be a secretary who ended up marrying my boss, or something. And, well, look at me. Do I look like that kind of woman?" I giggle and shake my head. Definitely not. That would have been like putting a lioness in a tutu.

She grins, and it lights up her face until her blue eyes almost sparkle. "And then one day this handsome guy in a suit sits at one of my tables where I was waitressing at the time. And he acted like I was the most gorgeous woman he'd ever seen. He'd stumble over his words and took three different trips to my cafe to ask me out. I liked him right away." Her forehead hits my shoulder and she stays there for a few seconds. "I know he comes across a bit stiff-arsed, but I promise you he's really awesome underneath it all. He's just a bit socially awkward. Comes with being a professor, I guess. But anyway, he was absolutely fascinated by me. It was…kind of weird, but also exhilarating, and very, very flattering. He's a Professor of Economics, and all buttoned up and maths-y. Maths-y?" She wrinkles her nose and shrugs. "New word. Anyway, it was a great laugh, expanding his mind and seeing him get all excited about the art I liked, and the clubs I went to, and the clothes I wore.

"But he was also the perfect man to bring home to my parents. He's well dressed, smart as hell, successful, and from what they consider to be a good family. They're so happy that I've found someone so…upwardly mobile, and presentable. And because *I* won the love of someone like that, even though I'm a scruffy, stubborn tattooist, they aren't so worried or disapproving anymore." She grins. "And his *arse…*"

We both laugh, and I know she's trying to diffuse the tension.

"And besides, I'd already coloured a little outside the lines where they're concerned. Can you imagine if I'd made that even worse by bringing back someone like, I dunno, Leo?" I start slightly at the mention of his name. "Precisely," she says, reading my response wrongly as alarm. It was actually sadness. Sadness that she feels so much pressure to appease her parents' well-meaning vision for her that she's maybe convinced herself she loves this guy, and that it's worth her precious time putting up with his nonsense. Sadness that she's either knowingly or unknowingly putting her blinkers on when she looks at Leo, who is, the more I consider it, utterly perfect for her.

And I find it interesting that Leo's name was the first one she thought of when giving an example.

Still, much as I dislike it, I can see where she's coming from, but I still don't get why she accepts the disdainful way Peter treats her friends. But I suppose I have to respect her choices, even if every single part of me wants to grab her by the shoulders and shake her and scream in her face that she's making a mistake. The most important thing is what *she* thinks of her boyfriend. If she's happy, or has convinced herself that she is, then what can I do? Nothing that isn't going to alienate her or make me lose her friendship.

I can't help but feel really uneasy about Peter having that tattoo removed, though. It seems like a really shitty, rude thing to do.

I run my fingers over my new ladybird tattoo absently. Even if Eli had completely bodged it and the drawing had been ugly as all hell, there is nothing that would ever persuade me to remove it, because he put it there.

I remember another time, when Sadie was showing us one of her new designs—a mandala style fleur de lys—Leo instantly invited her to tattoo it on his neck, right then and there. And I know he would never, ever burn it off, no matter what.

Leo is the diamond to Peter's rhinestone, and I wish more than anything she would magically see the light and choose him. He's devoted to her, and I know in my bones they would be so happy. They suit each other so well, and it sucks that she's otherwise engaged, pun intended.

I suddenly feel incredibly lucky to have Eli. Sure, we've only been together all of five minutes, but it's been remarkably straightforward so far. Once we were both sure of each other, that was that. No bullshit. No nonsense. Well, except for my colossal misunderstanding, but that was sorted out within twenty four hours.

And I realise something.

This happiness is mine to lose.

If he and I don't work out, it won't be because of him. It won't be because he yelled at me, or bullied me, or made me feel worthless.

It will be because I walked away from the best thing that ever happened to me.

Eli

"Eli," Emily says softly at my door, and I pause tattooing my current client straight away and look up.

She's blushing as she smiles, and Leo is cracking up laughing behind her.

"What's so funny?" I ask, grinning at my girlfriend.

Leo leans on her shoulder and smirks. "I've been calling your name at this door several times, so I went to get Emily. One word from her and you look up." He kisses the top of Em's head. "I'll add 'get Eli's attention' to your contract and give you a small pay rise accordingly," he tells her, and she giggles.

I frown, and look at my client, a man in his early twenties with a fauxhawk. "He was," he confirms, "he must have tried three or four times."

I grin and shrug. "She's prettier than you, Leo," I remark.

But I rather like that she's the only one who can call my attention when I'm in the zone.

Leo gasps in fake indignation before laughing. "True," he says, and wanders off again, leaving me smiling into Em's eyes.

"Your next appointment is here," she tells me.

I glance at the clock on my wall. "OK, I'll be another two, three minutes here," I say, "and then I'll come get 'em." I crook a finger at her and grin, not caring if I'm being rude to my client by doing this.

She gives me a curious look and steps towards me. I lean up and kiss her lips, thrilled that I can do this whenever I want now. She giggles against my mouth, and I swear there is no better feeling in the world.

Well, not yet, anyway.

There's still lots of firsts for us to look forward to, and I have no doubt each one will be better than the last. I shift slightly as my cock twitches at the thought. Can't sit here sporting wood, which is why I deliberately don't look at her ass as she walks away.

I look back at the tattoo, a black widow spider I was asked to make as realistic as possible, and finish off the shadowing under the legs.

"Your girlfriend's cute," my client tells me. I look up. His eyes are friendly. I've been talking to him a little more than I do my other clients—in fact, I've been making more of an effort with *all* my clients since Em showed up—and he seems OK. It's not like he's leering at her or trying to be all bro-ski with me.

So I smile. "She sure is."

Leo drags us all out for drinks after work. I was going to take Em to a nice bar this evening anyway, but I think he needs the company, and I want to take her out on a proper date as well, so I don't really mind postponing a little. I want to do something special for her, though. Something she will really enjoy. Something a bit more personalized than dinner and a movie. I mean, I'm looking forward to nights like that, too, but I want to wow her a little for our *first* date.

I'm racking my brains, but nothing has jumped out at me as a stellar idea so far.

I'll think of something.

In the meantime, it feels incredible to be sat in the Red Lion once more, this time with my arm around Emily. She snuggles up a little shyly, and it's so cute. Her head fits perfectly under my chin, and her hair smells so good. Happy peace settles over me when she stays put. It gives me hope that I can be a real part of her healing. And maybe my own, too.

Leo is usually the life and soul, but he's Leo on speed tonight. Dean and I share a look. He's talking a mile a minute, getting fresh rounds in almost quicker than we can drink them, and spitting out jokes like teeth after a fight he's lost. He's not OK. Not by a long shot.

"Jeez Louise," Sadie remarks, her eyebrows raising at Leo, "what's got you in such a hyper mood?"

He gestures to me and Em. "EmEli is a thing now," he exclaims. "Isn't that reason enough? In fact, a toast." He grabs his glass and raises it exuberantly, spilling a little of his Magners on the table. "To the happy couple! May they always be this happy and this *hot*."

There's a slightly awkward silence as everyone clinks their glasses against his.

"Oh, *shoot*," Em mutters, staring at her phone.

"What's up?" I ask her.

She looks up at me. "I got sniped on eBay," she says.

"Urgh, I hate it when that happens," Sadie sympathizes.

What were you bidding on? Dean queries.

"Oh, it—" she starts, shaking her head slightly and waving her hand, but then she stops. She takes a breath, and then, much to my delight, she actually tells us. "There's a card game I like, and I, ah, well, Gav got rid of my copy of it, and I've been trying to replace it since I started earning again. I had the winning bid right up until the last second."

My jaw tightens. *That asshole threw her stuff away. What the ever loving fuck.*

"Gav is a douche," Sadie comments mildly.

"Yep," Emily agrees.

What's the game? Dean asks, and it's great to see him and Emily interacting so easily. Charmaine never really bothered herself with Dean after the first year or so of marriage, and bitched and moaned if he ever needed my help with anything, or if he had an episode, and if I had to get up in the night to sit with him. If that wasn't a red flag, I think grimly, I don't know what was. Looking back, now I've met Em, I can't imagine what I was thinking with my ex-wife. But hindsight is always twenty-twenty, especially when you have such a gorgeous point of comparison.

"It's called Sentinels of the Multiverse," Emily replies. "It's a cooperative game, bit of nerdy fun, but I used to lose whole evenings to it."

"Hey, nerdy fun is still fun," Leo protests, "it's right there in the name. Nerdy *fun*. And I say we trash Gav's house for *daring* to spoil it for you. C'mon. What's the motherfucker's address? Road trip. I call shotgun."

I shoot him a warning look, but Em chuckles softly. "Nah, he doesn't get any more of my time or energy." I'm thrilled to hear her say that, and I kiss the top of her head to make my feelings on that subject clear. She squeezes my hand, and I don't care how much of a sap I look as I smile down at her, because happiness like this is worth anything you could name.

"Well, I also say we trash the dickhead that sniped you," Leo rambles on. He's halfway to being hammered by the looks of things.

"Or she could just check out other sellers," Sadie says, frowning slightly at how over the top Leo is tonight. If even Sadie has noticed...

"Oh, I'm sure I'll find a good deal at some point," Em replies. "It's just that this was the lowest price I'd found for it, and unfortunately being a literal card carrying nerd is pricey."

"So, how does the game work?" Leo asks, and while she explains, I have a lightbulb moment. There's a shop in town that sells board games, comic books and action figurines, that kind of thing. I even saw a replica of a Cylon from the original Battlestar Galactica in there when I walked past once, and she mentioned liking the modern series, so I bet she'd really enjoy a look around. Maybe that could be our first date? Only trouble is, it closes at five thirty...

"Hey, Leo," I say suddenly. "Can I ask a favor?"

"Sure," Leo replies, "what do you need?" He seems to be calming down a little, but I can see in his eyes the storm is still quietly raging.

"Can Emily and I finish work a little early tomorrow? My last appointment will end around three. Can I steal her away after that?" Her eyes fly to my face, and I grin.

"That could be arranged," Leo says with a knowing grin.

"Thanks, boss."

"Hey, far be it from me to get in the way of a good time," he winks. He seems to be calming down slightly, eyes down at the table and tracing the grain of the wood with his thumbnail. His glances at Sadie now and again, and there's something about him that's just...slumping.

I feel really sorry for him, and genuinely wish I could help.

"What are we...?" Em trails off.

I kiss her briefly. "It's a surprise." I'm pretty sure I've got this right, but I can't wait to find out.

chapter SEVENTEEN

From the EmEli WhatsApp group (members: Sadie Stewart, Leo Mills, Dean Gastright)

Sadie Stewart: THEY'RE SO CUUUUUUUUUUUUUUUTE!!!!!!!!!!!

Sadie Stewart: The way they look at each other… I can't EVEN

Dean Gastright: Yeah, it's awesome :)

Dean Gastright: Really pleased for them

Sadie Stewart: [GIF of Buddy the Elf jumping up and down in excitement]

Sadie Stewart: Hey Leo

Sadie Stewart: Leo

Sadie Stewart: ….?

Sadie Stewart: LEO

Leo Mills: yeah

Sadie Stewart: Were you OK tonight?

Leo Mills: Sure, why

Sadie Stewart: I dunno, you seemed pretty hyper

Sadie Stewart: Just wanted to check

Leo Mills: I'm fine

Sadie Stewart: OK

Sadie Stewart: As long as you are

Leo Mills: [Thumbs up emoji]

Text message from Dean to Sadie: *I really think he's fine, don't worry x*

Sadie to Dean: *Hope so. He seemed a bit OTT tonight. Or was it just me?xoxo*

Dean: *It wasn't just you. I think maybe he was just tired and over-compensating. I think he's had a few late nights.x*

Sadie: *Ah, OK. As long as that's all that is. I don't like the idea of him NOT being ok xoxo*

Dean: *Don't worry, he's fine.x*

Sadie: *Cool. While I think about it, Tim said one of his colleagues at the university wants a first tattoo, and it's writing based, so I passed your details on.xoxo*

Dean: *Cool, thanks x*

Sadie: *No probs. She's not going to be available for a few weeks or months, so it's not a straight away dealie. Apparently she's a little quirky, so be prepared lol xoxo*

Dean: *OK :) I consider myself forewarned lol x*

Text message from Eli to Emily: *So I just checked Netflix and the entirety of Star Trek is on there. I've caught the odd episode here and there before now, but never a complete series. Where do I need to begin? The original, or…? Xx*

Emily to Eli: *[Heart eyes emoji]*

Emily: *You're gonna watch Star Trek for me? Xx*

Eli: *Of course. I need to catch up so I know who to cosplay as when I take you to a Star Trek convention someday xx*

Emily: *That's so sweet!!!!!! Um…start with TNG. This is a big old commitment, are you sure you want to? Xx*

Eli: *Sure. I mean, it'll take me a while, so gimme a chance to plow through it, but yeah, absolutely. It's important to you. Xx*

Emily: *They really have the whole thing on Netflix? Xx*

Eli: *Yeah, the Original Series, The Next Generation, Deep Space Nine, Voyager, Enterprise, and Discovery xx*

Emily: *THEY HAVE DISCOVERY [Open mouthed emoji]*

Eli: *Yep xx*

Emily: *Yay, I haven't seen that yet! Xx*

Eli: *OK, I take it you don't have Netflix xx*

Emily: *No, sadly xx*

Eli: *You can have my login if you want, but better yet, we can watch it together at my place :) xx*

Emily: *I am so in xx*

Eli: *[Big grin emoji] xx*

Emily: *Thank you xxxxxxxxxx*

Eli: *No problem, especially if I can pick those kisses up in person sometime [wink emoji] xxxxxxxxxxxx*

Emily: *You betcha [wink emoji] xx*

Eli: Good. Now, *what are you wearing?xx*

Emily: *LOL really xx*

Eli: *Yep, I'm going there lol xx*

Emily: *Well, honestly, I'm tucked up in bed right now, and I only ever wear knickers to bed, so… [wink emoji] xx*

Eli: Chere *[fire emoji x 10] what are you doing to me xxxxx*

Emily: *Hehe I love when you call me chere xx*

Eli: *You are my chere, toujou xx*

Emily: *Toujou?xx*

Eli: *Means always xx*

Emily: *[Heart eyes emoji] xx*

Eli: *So these panties… I'm thinking a barely there wisp of lace, yeah? Xxx*

Emily: *Mmhmm. They may even be a trick of the light lol [wink emoji] xxx*

Eli: *unnnnnnnnnnffffffff*

Emily: *LOL*

Emily: *How about you? Xx*

Eli: *Yeah, same, flimsy lace lol [wink emoji] xx*

Emily: *LOL xxx*

Eli: *Nah, I'm just getting into bed. Standard issue black boxers xx*

Emily: *Boxers or briefs? Xx*

Eli: *Now you mention it, briefs xx*

Emily: *unnnnnnnnnnnnnffffffffffffff*

Eli: *Lol my girl likes briefs, then? *mental note* xx*

Emily: *Hell yeah. Especially on you. Xx*

Eli: *Shucks, ma'am xx*

Eli: *What are you doing xx*

Emily: *Texting my boyfriend [wink emoji] xx*

Eli: *I love when you call me that [heart eyes emoji] but what else xx*

Emily: *Thinking about how nice it would be if he was here with me xx*

Eli: *Baby me too xx*

Eli: *Wanna have a little fun? [wink emoji] xx*

Emily: *YES xx*

Eli: *Lol OK then. I've never sexted before. Be gentle as you pop my cherry [wink emoji] xx*

Emily: *Ugh you are TOO HOT FOR WORDS xx*

Eli: *LOL well thank you xx*

Emily: *Seriously, I'm probably going to burst into flames [fire emoji] xx*

Eli: *Well, you ARE crazy hot xx*

Emily: *[blushing emoji]*

Eli: *And if I was there I would definitely be running kisses down your neck round about now xx*

Emily: *That's pretty much going to have me in a pile of horniness at your feet—my neck is one of my zones [wink emoji] xx*

Eli: *Noted xx*

Emily: *Hehe xx*

Eli: *So what else is a zone for you? Might as well ask in advance [wink emoji] xx*

Emily: *Lots of things where you're concerned. It's not a zone as such, but I love your voice, for example. Xx*

Eli: *My voice? Really? Xx*

Emily: *Absolutely. That accent of yours drives me wild. Xx*

Emily

My phone rings within seconds.

I giggle as I answer. "Yes?"

"That being the case, I thought maybe we could move from sexting to phone sex," he rumbles in my ear, definitely exaggerating the Cajun drawl somewhat. It sends a pulse of warmth straight to my pussy.

Oh boy. Things are definitely hotting up.

"Sounds good to me," I purr. In spite of everything, sex is an area in which I've always enjoyed a certain level of confidence. I love sex. I always have, and I'm good at it. Lying here right now, almost naked, talking to the sexiest man I have ever known, is making me feel seriously good. Powerful. Turned on. This is me in my element. I stretch, luxuriating in how good it feels, and let out a sigh of contentment.

"Hmmmm," he growls, "what are you doing to make that sort of sound?"

I grin. "Just a stretch," I sigh again to tease him a little. "Felt really good."

He makes another feral noise, and I giggle. "Man, just thinking of that gorgeous body of yours stretched out in front of me...god, baby, that'd be fan fuckin' tastic right now."

"You think my body is gorgeous?" I hate self-doubt, but it is so unbelievably good to be with a man who apparently likes my body after years of Gav's derision that I can't get enough of Eli's admiration.

"*Fuck* yeah. I can't look at you for too long while we're at work or I get hard."

"Holy shit," I breathe, imagining his cock lengthening and hardening for me. I've felt the indisputable evidence of his arousal pressed up and ground against me when we've kissed previously, and it feels amazing even through his clothes. Just tonight, for example, he had me pressed so tightly up against him when he kissed me goodnight that I swear I felt him throb against my mound through his jeans. I can't wait to feel him bare, to run my hands, my lips, my tongue over his cock, to drive him as wild as he's making me. I want to make him crazy. Throbbing, restless, eyes-rolling-backwards crazy. Each careful step we're taking is making us hotter and hotter for each other, and I spent most of today weak kneed and needful.

His breath comes a little faster. "Are you touching yourself?" I ask him.

"Mmhmm," he sighs, and my clit jumps at the thought.

"Jesus," I mutter, running my hand over my breast so I can tweak my nipple. It sends a spark through me, and my pussy throbs. I wish so badly that I was there to see it. Watching my men masturbate has always gotten me hot in the past. Watching Eli do it will incinerate me. "How does it feel?"

"Fucking aches," he grunts, sounding like he's speaking through gritted teeth, and I bite my lip in sympathy and yearning. Eli is painfully hard for me, and I want to be lying next to him so I can both ease his pleasurable suffering and torture him further. "Tell me you're touching yourself, too."

I place the phone to my other ear so my right hand can snake down into my lace briefs and feel myself. *Oh wow.* I tease him with a soft grunt. "I am *so wet,*" I murmur to him, my breath catching as I start to rub my clit in firm circles with my middle finger the way I like. It normally takes a little longer for me to become this slick and sensitive, but right now my whole body feels alive with tingles like static electricity. Guess this is what happens when Eli Gastright is your boyfriend.

He groans, and I feel like an absolute queen for making this man, this particular man, weak for me. "Someday soon, sweetheart, I am going to lick up every last drop of that honey of yours, and I'm gonna spend hours doin' it. I'm gonna make you dizzy." He exhales, and it sounds like he's shuddering. "I bet you taste *so good...*"

Oh my god.

Even the thought of his tongue on my pussy, smoothing and flicking and devouring me until I explode for him, is making me crazy. Receiving head is my kryptonite, and I can picture it so clearly that I can almost feel the wet sweep of his tongue in the exact right place.

This is the hottest thing I've ever done, and he's not even in the same room as me. He's mere streets away.

Why don't I call a cab?

Why don't I just open my front door and run to his flat?

But oh, blast it, I *am* enjoying this as it is. The tease of the so-close-and-yet-so-far quality to the phone sex. So I decide to be more Eli and just let it be, and not try to force things.

After all, it feels really, really *good...*

For long moments we carry on pleasuring ourselves, punctuating with quiet, feral grunts and shaky sighs and throaty words that spur us both on. He tells me I'm beautiful, and the almost primitively sensual sounds he is making are pushing me closer to the edge. I love it. I'm so glad he gives voice to how turned on he is. It's made me sad in the past when previous lovers have been silent. I do so love to hear my partner's enjoyment and appreciation, almost to fetishistic levels, and Eli's deep, soft, tameless sounds are beautiful to me.

The noises I make become earthier, more honest, less delicate as the feeling builds and spreads mercilessly through me. I groan because I simply cannot help it. As I rub harder and faster, my flesh makes wet, dewy noises. "I wish I was there," I confess to him, hungry and needy, because *shit* that would be stupendous right about now. "I just want to jump on you and…and…I want to be filled by you…" I gasp. My orgasm is within fingertip reach, and I strain towards it.

He growls. "That's it, *chere*. I want your legs wrapped around my hips. I want your pussy clamped around me." His voice is sounding breathless, like he's struggling to talk through the erotic haze we are both in. "I want those tits of yours in my mouth… while you grind into me…" His scorching words sound like they're being torn from him. He sighs, and I am done for.

"I'm coming," I manage to bite out, before my whole body tenses as tight as a harp string and my core just bursts with the fizziest, most electric pleasure I have ever known, throbbing and pulsing for longer than ever before. I gasp and cry out and make the dirtiest moans, surprising myself with their guttural filthiness. I am dimly aware of his gasping and groaning as his own climax breaks. It's the hottest thing I have ever heard in my life, and sharpens the last beats of my own release. I love the sound of a man coming.

Especially *this* man.

"Fucking hell, Em," he sighs in my ear, coming down from the high. "That was…wow."

"It sure was." I have to admit, I was a little concerned that he wanted to take things slow because he wasn't completely sure he was sexually into me or something. I grin to myself. Tonight has dispelled that notion entirely.

He lets out a long sigh. "I wish you were here so I could hold you," he admits, and it makes my heart clench.

"Soon, yeah?" I murmur hopefully.

"Abso-fucking-lutely," he agrees firmly. "Now that you're mine, it's a done deal as far as I'm concerned. Your nights of sleeping alone are numbered, so make the most of them."

I hum happily. "I won't miss it," I assure him. "So...how are you feeling about the pace? I mean, is this OK?"

"This is fine, baby." God, that Louisiana drawl just tickles me right in the clit every time, even now in the afterglow. "I may want to pace us, but that definitely does *not* mean I wanna dawdle. But if you're OK with it, I'd like to reach a point real soon where I sleep with you in my arms every night, whether at your place or mine. It feels... I don't know, inevitable. And I don't want to put it off much longer. I want to wake up with you next to me every day. I want that to be my life."

I shiver with pleasure at the idea. "Deal."

chapter EIGHTEEN

Eli

As soon as she opens her door to me when I pick her up the next morning, I am on her, pinning her to the wall and kissing her until her chuckles of amusement become moans vibrating against my lips, and I'm struggling not to back her into her apartment and do a live action replay. Last night was unbelievably hot, and if it wasn't for the fact that I have clients booked until mid-afternoon, I would do it.

We look at each other with intensified hunger whenever our paths cross throughout the day, turning our heads as we pass each other for killer eye meets that make my heart pound with longing. I want her. I've heard her come, and I want that again and again, this time in person. I want to feel that, feel *her*, in my arms and tight around me as she comes apart.

But, although we can't indulge the way every part of my body wants to right now, the tension is delicious. I'm enjoying every second, even the frustration. And it's the most ordinary and casual things that turn me on with her. She kissed my neck as we sat on the grass in a nearby park over lunch, and it did more for me than I thought such a simple gesture could possibly do. When she takes my hand and we lace our fingers together, I feel complete. Every time.

I have never felt like this before, and I'm glad.

She's the one.

I have a few nerves squirming in my belly as I see my last client of the day out the door at three o'clock. I hope I've guessed right and that she likes my idea. Her eyes are bright and curious when she looks up at me. "Ready, baby?" I ask.

"Ready," she agrees, just as Leo wanders in. He looks tired, with shadows under his eyes, but his smile is easy and natural.

"Alright, lovebirds, off you go. Have fun." He ties his hair back as he sits at Em's seat, ready to cover reception for her.

"Thanks for this, *frère,*" I tell him sincerely. He just winks at us.

She and I head off hand in hand to enjoy the afternoon.

"He's suffering hard," she says quietly.

I sigh. "Yep." I squeeze her hand. "I feel bad for him, but he won't tell her, for obvious reasons."

"It just sucks. They'd be so good together, and Peter is such an obtuse piece of *flotsam.*"

"A what?" I grin.

She smiles sheepishly. "That's my Trekkie side making itself known again. That's an insult from Q. He's, ah, one of the more interesting antagonists. And I'm a giant dork for remembering it."

That's good. I'm feeling increasingly confident that I made the right call with this date location. My adorable little geek will like it.

"So, moving swiftly on…where are you taking me?" She dimples up at me, and my heart flip flops. I know the first days of any new relationship are special, but this is just magic.

"You'll see soon enough," I tease, laughing as she joke pouts and leaning forward to kiss her full lips.

"I'm intrigued," she says as I sling an arm around her shoulders, holding her hand on the other side. She puts her arm around my waist, and I guide her through the streets as we chat a little more about the Leo and Sadie situation. "I hope she doesn't actually marry Peter."

"Same. He's an ass. I don't want to have to put up with him for the rest of our lives," I agree. "It's like socializing with a paperweight."

She laughs. "Pretty much."

Oh. Damn.

As we walk down the street to the game shop, I remember, just a few paces away, that there's a sex toy shop right next door. I've never been inside, but it's very obvious from the name *Climax* and the artfully displayed chains and leather harnesses in the window what you can expect from the place. I don't want her thinking I'm marching her straight to a purveyor of every vibrator known to man, so I stop a few feet away. Fortunately she is looking at the shops on the other side of the cobbled street: a French cuisine cafe, a silver jewelry store.

"OK, so I'm going to place my hands over your eyes, if that's alright?" I ask.

Her eyes light up. "Sure!" I cannot resist kissing her shoulder, and I guide her gently past Climax and to the entrance of Fonteyns, the gaming store. It's not a huge place, but there's a nice display of cards for a game called Magic: The Gathering in the window, as well as Funko Pop figurines for Marvel and Star Wars movies. I've never been inside myself, but I can see that there are shelves filled with board games floor to ceiling, with tables in the center of the store covered in the same. I think I read on their website that they sell books, too, but I can't see them right now.

"OK?" I ask her, and take my hands away. "Boom."

I watch her face from the side, and she gasps in delight, her face lighting up. I smile in relief. This was definitely a good place to take her. "Oh my gosh!" she squeals, and I laugh as she charges for the door. She stops and turns back to grab my hand and pull me inside, as excited as a hungry kid in a candy store.

Her mouth drops open as she takes everything in. "This is…just…YES!" She turns and beams at me, throwing her arms around my neck and kissing me soundly on the lips. "I had no idea there was a place like this in town. Thank you for bringing me here," she murmurs.

"No problem, *chere*," I tell her, returning her smile. "Worth it to see you so happy."

Her attention wanders to the shelves of cellophane wrapped games. "Oh, wow," she breathes, reading the titles. I don't know enough about them, but seeing her so excited has me interested. My knowledge of board games is limited to Monopoly and Sorry. A lot of these have beautiful artwork, and some of it is so stunning that I make a mental note of some of the titles so I can look up the artists. They're getting my own creative juices flowing. Some of these would make great tattoos.

She lets out a delighted cry and grabs one of the boxes. "They have Lords of Waterdeep!" She carefully turns the box over and winces slightly at the price. "I used to love this game. Must be…" she purses her lips as she thinks, "easily six or seven years since I've played." She puts it back and carries on looking. "I could bankrupt myself in here, I really could."

As she moves on, I check the price on the box. Forty pounds. Oh, man. She must really have to watch what she spends if forty is too big a splurge to consider.

I am going to spoil her.

"Ooh!" She peers to a galley in the back. "They have books, too!" She disappears into a cubby, and I take the opportunity to grab Lords of Waterdeep and take it to the counter, where a man with a sandy colored hipster beard and a Borderlands 3 hoodie is playing with his phone.

"Dude," I say quietly as he looks up, "keep this behind the counter. I'll be back later to pay for it, but it's got to be a surprise for her, so be cool, OK?" He looks towards where she's peering at their book collection and winks at me, unsmiling. He gets it. "By the way, do you have any Sentinels of the Multiverse?" I'm glad I remembered what it was called.

He points to a shelf behind me. "Yep. Full collection of everything that's out and available right there."

"OK, I'll take one of everything," I say, peering around the corner in case she's getting suspicious, but fortunately she must be engrossed in whatever they have back there. "I'll pay now, actually," I tell him. He rings everything up very quickly, nodding conspiratorially at me. I pay as fast as I can, not giving a shit that it comes to over two hundred pounds. I can afford it. "Can you hide it while we're still here, and I'll come and pick it up as soon as I can?"

"Sure, what's the name, so I can label it?" The bag is *huge*.

"Eli Gastright. G-A-S..." I spell it for him.

"Cool, man, I got ya." He places the bag under the counter.

"Thanks." I wander through, hoping she hasn't noticed I've been absent for a while, and find her poring happily over a large hardback book. It has her undivided attention. I breathe a sigh of relief; I've lucked out.

She looks up, smiling brightly. "They have it!" she enthuses, showing me the cover. It's a Dungeons and Dragons manual for a game called *The Curse of Strahd*. A vampiric looking man sits on a throne on the cover. "It's the fifth edition version. I've wanted this for *ages*." She bites her lip adorably as she smiles. "I'm going to get it. I shouldn't after the amount I blew on new clothes, but screw it, I'm gonna."

I smile at the happy look on her face. "Awesome. We'll have to organize a game."

She bites her lip, making me want to press her against these shelves and kiss her til she's dizzy. "Do you really think people will want to play?"

"I'm sure something can be arranged." Honestly, I do think the team will be up for it if they know it will make her this happy. She's loved at Wishbone more than she realizes.

When we get to the counter, the guy doesn't betray my other purchases at all. He's good. But he does wink at me again when I tap my card on the reader to pay for Em's book while she rummages in her purse for her wallet. She looks so touched that it makes me feel fantastic. I could definitely get used to this, and my determination to spoil her kicks up a notch.

"You didn't have to do that," she says softly, her eyes looking almost glassy.

I pull her towards me by her waist, kissing her cheek. "It's my pleasure."

She snuggles in, squeezing my back. "Thank you so much, that's so kind." She kisses me, and I smile against her lips. "I really appreciate it."

"Honestly, you're welcome." I can't wait to see her face when I give her the other games I secretly bought.

We leave the store, and I'm pleased to see the French cafe is still open. I've been in there before, and the food is always good, so I take her inside for a snack.

We talk for hours. We have to keep ordering drinks so they don't get pissed off with us for taking up a table, but it's worth it. We talk about D&D, and our favourite character archetypes; it's so good to reminisce over something I used to enjoy a lot as a teenager, and I'm looking forward to playing it with her. We also talk about New Orleans, and I promise her, and myself, that I'm taking her with me the next time I go home for a visit. She'll love the French market, and the Mardi Gras museum.

I can't resist pulling her knuckles to my lips for a kiss every so often. The memory of everything we said and did last night heats my blood as I watch her smile. There are times when we just silently look at each other with raw need.

I don't want to push her, though, so when I walk her home when dusk sweeps over the horizon, although I spend ages kissing her at her door, I don't try to come inside.

I don't think I can resist much longer, though.

Dean is arriving just as I get back. He smirks at my face, which, if it reflects how I'm feeling at all, must look like I'm on cloud nine.

How did it go? He asks, giving me a knowing look.

"Mmhmm," I say with an absent grin.

He laughs silently. *You look like a lovestruck teenager.*

I sigh. "Well, except for the teenager part…yeah."

He raises his eyebrows. *Oh yeah?*

I lean against my front door and smile at him, happily resigned to my fate. "Dude, I am so in love."

He claps, grinning at me with glee. *Knew it. At least you picked the right woman this time.*

I grin back. "I sure did," I say as I let myself in, digging my cell out of my pocket so I can text the woman I'm already impatient to see again. "'Night."

Goodnight, he responds, chuckling as he walks up the stairs to his apartment.

Emily

He's too freaking adorable for words.

For a second I honestly wondered if he was going to take me to the sex shop I noticed as we approached, but he seemed very keen to avoid me noticing that, so I pretended I didn't see. As much fun as it would have been to visit with him, I think I'd rather wait until we've at least slept together before we go inside. It's definitely on my to-do list, though. As is he, I joke to myself.

I can't believe he bought me the Dungeons and Dragons book. I hug it as I fall backwards on my bed, enjoying how puffy my lips feel after his kisses at my doorstep.

Right now, I wish I'd invited him in.

But I also think things are progressing as they should.

It's really nice not to feel any pressure to perform for him, and to get to know him properly first rather than race to get his rocks off to keep him liking me. I smile, daydreaming about our conversations in the cafe. I've never been to America, and it'd be so wonderful to go with him. He spoke with such affection about his hometown, and I want to visit the place that had such a huge role in shaping him.

My email alert tone goes off on my phone, and I pick it up idly, hoping it's him.

But it isn't.

Frowning, I sit up and read it, going cold as my stomach starts to churn.

It's Gav.

Hi Emmy, I read, and *ugh,* I hated that nickname, and I hate that I can practically hear his voice as I read on.

You've deleted your social media. I can't reach you by phone. You've vanished without a trace. It's just sheer chance that I remembered I can still contact you by email. Do you have any idea how that feels? To be just…cut loose? Like I'm nothing?

I can't believe that after all those years, this is what you think I deserve.

I fucked up, OK? I get it. I wish I could say this to your face so you could see that I mean it, and so you could see what you've done to me by running off.

But I don't believe in my heart that I fucked up badly enough for this. To be ruthlessly deleted from your life. I know we said we'd leave it for you to make contact when you were ready—that was ***when****, Emmy, not if—but there's some stuff I really want to say to you.*

And I'm hurting too, sweetheart. I admit there's a lot I could have done differently, but you can't say you were perfect, either. You pushed me to give more than I was ready for. I tried my best to give you what you wanted, but you put me through a lot of strain. So you can't lay all of the blame and shit on me.

But look, I really hope that you're OK, and that wherever you are you're safe and well.

Just tell me where you are, and I'll come see you so we can talk. Whenever I call your number, I get put straight through to voice-mail, and that eats me up inside. You blocked me? Really? It's not like I was violent and knocked you about, for fuck's sake. Even when I was provoked, I never laid a hand on you.

Throwing away four years is just unnecessary drama. You remember us, right, babe? The sex was good, wasn't it? I could get you off so fast, and I can still hear you screaming my name.

So I'd say we've got plenty to talk about, and we've both got stuff we should work on, but don't you think it's going to be worth it? Or are you really going to just chuck it all out without even having the decency to hear me out? Surely that's the least you owe me?

I love you, Emmy. Always have, always will.

Your Gav xx

My heart is racing and I can't stop shaking, but this time, it isn't in fear—at least, not entirely.

This time, it's in piping hot rage.

Piece of shit.

I sneer at my phone and delete the email. He's getting nothing from me. 'Your Gav' indeed. What a manipulative arsehole. I shake my head, knowing exactly what's happening here. He's missing his emotional punching bag. Can't help but notice he didn't say the word 'sorry' once. Just more of the same.

Everything's my fault, and he's taking none of the blame on himself.

After experiencing just a few days with Eli, where I've been respected, listened to, and just basically *liked*, there's no way I'd ever go back to that stifling misery.

And even if I'd never met Eli, if Gav thinks even for a second that I would so much as entertain the idea of him again, he has another think coming. He doesn't have to worry about me 'provoking' him anymore.

I add his email address to my blocked sender list, surprised that I forgot to do that when I left—but then, he was never a big one for sending emails, to me or anyone else, so it didn't occur to me.

My phone chimes, and this time it's from the right person.

Eli: *How do you feel about a home cooked meal tomorrow? I have a family recipe for authentic jambalaya that I'd love to make for you. Best you'll ever have, I guarantee it xx*

I bounce slightly on the bed, gradually calming, all thoughts of my ex discarded like yesterday's trash.

That sounds wonderful, I text back. *Count me in. xx*

chapter NINETEEN

From a new WhatsApp group (Members: Eli Gastright, Dean Gastright, Sadie Stewart, Leo Mills)

Eli Gastright: Hi, I didn't want to use the Wishbone group because Em will see

Eli Gastright: I wanted to ask y'all for a favor

Dean Gastright: Sure, anything

Sadie Stewart: Absolutely, if I can

Eli Gastright: Thanks

Leo Mills: I'm in, what do you need

Eli Gastright: So I bought Em that card game she mentioned, and some other board game that she likes

Eli Gastright: She doesn't know, I haven't given them to her yet

Eli Gastright: I'm picking them up between appointments this afternoon

Sadie Stewart: AWWWWWWWWWWW <3

Leo Mills: [GIF of Idris Elba giving an approving wink and thumbs up]

Eli Gastright: And she hasn't been able to play these games in a while, and I know if would mean a lot to her if we could set an evening aside, all of us, sometime soon so she can do that

Sadie Stewart: You are so effing bloody adorable

Dean Gastright: For sure, count me in

Dean Gastright: Not sure how to play, but I'm sure we'll all pick it up

Sadie Stewart: YES

Leo Mills: I'm down :) that's really nice, man

Eli Gastright: I've looked up the rules of the games and they're reasonably straightforward

Eli Gastright: And I know she'll love it, even if we're not experts. She'll be able to explain everything for us, and we can all look some stuff up in advance

Leo Mills: :) so when's good

Sadie Stewart: I'll check my diary tonight

Dean Gastright: I can be free whenever :)

Eli Gastright: I'll sort something out with her tonight. Can't wait to give them to her :)

Leo Mills: She's gonna love it

Sadie Stewart: And I imagine you'll get a great big thank you [wink emoji]

Leo Mills: Hey hey [wink emoji] Have fun

Emily

I wonder if I'll ever become accustomed to the way it feels to walk down the street hand in hand with Eli Gastright.

He reaches for my hand automatically now that we're a couple, straight away without hesitation. I love it. It makes me feel so liked, so wanted, so utterly secure. Even when I see the way women who pass us gaze at him with ill-concealed admiration. I can't even blame them, even if it does give me an unpleasant inner pang to see it. He's so gorgeous, and he comes across more warmly, and seems less serious and distant than when I first met him. He's started smiling more, showing the sweet soul hidden within, and even when he's not actively smiling, his expression is somehow lighter.

And I thought he couldn't get any hotter.

He chats with me easily as we stop off at the supermarket to pick up some andouille sausage for the jambalaya he wants to make me for dinner tonight. Wandering around the aisles with him feels deliciously domestic, a taste of what I could have on a regular basis if this works out. It's enticing.

It's also a little chilling.

Tamping down the unease of enjoying something too much, I follow him around quite happily as he grumbles about how tiny British prawns are in comparison to the shrimp he used to get in Louisiana, and I snuggle in a little as he hugs me from behind while we queue for the checkout.

I could definitely get used to this.

The thought makes me freeze. Since Gav selfishly reminded me of his existence on this planet last night, I've been getting these moments where I feel intensely anxious when I start to think about this new life with Eli. It's daft, and counterintuitive, and frustrating beyond all measure, but I don't feel completely comfortable with romantic happiness right now. I just feel like it's something I could lose, and that I need to safeguard myself from the emotional consequences of such a loss. The urge to run can be quite strong, and I've been fidgeting and fretting all day. After all, I was happy with Gav to begin with. I would never have dreamed he'd have had me crying myself to sleep, ever. Nobody would volunteer for that. In my soul, I don't believe Eli is cut from the same cloth, or we'd never have gotten this far...but I got it badly wrong once before. There are no guarantees I won't ever get it wrong again. And that thought chills me to my bones like a bucket of ice water dumped on me.

"Are you OK?" he asks me.

Shit. He noticed.

I turn and beam at him. "Yeah, just...someone walked over my grave, I guess." I shrug, making light of it. It's not his fault, after all, and I'm not willing to let him get punished for things someone else did to me. I need to stop dwelling on it.

He's still giving me a searching look, so I tiptoe up—jeez, he's so much taller than me, and I'm not a short person—and kiss him to distract him.

Thankfully, it seems to work. His lips are so gentle on mine that I wonder how I could ever think this man could have it in him to hurt me.

In case I needed proof, his phone rings when we're leaving the supermarket.

"Sorry, I need to take this," he says to me just before he answers it. "Hey, Aunt Wendy."

I melt inside. Family really does mean the world to him. I can't hear what Aunt Wendy is saying, but I can hear that she's got that gorgeous Cajun drawl.

"Awrite. How's ya mama an' them?" He grins at me when he sees me gape and sigh appreciatively. Since our phone sex incident, he knows what it does to me when he uses New Orleans slang, and he's definitely got a broader accent while talking to family back home. "Yeah, fixin' to make my girl some o'dat Gastright family jambalaya like y'own tonight." He winces and holds the phone away from his ear, and I giggle as I hear happy squawking from the other end of the line. "Yeah, I got me a girlfriend now. Few days. Emily. At the parlour." He grins at me and raises his eyes to the sky as I giggle. We're walking much slower as he continues his conversation. "Yup. Andouille sausage. Well, naw, not so fine as back home, but it's the best I c'n do. Yeah, I'm sure. Gon' do y'all proud." He laughs. "Ain't no jambalaya like Aunt Wendy's, but I'll do." He crooks his arm at me, nodding towards it insistently, and I take it, loving his determination to have some sort of contact with me as we walk. "Yeah, Dean's all good. Look like he sleepin' better this week. Only had to sit up with him one night. Uh-huh. Yeah, his colour's better. Not as grey. Yeah, I think he's eating more'n he was." His face has gone a little serious. "OK. Yeah, you know it. OK. Yeah. Love to the family. Bye." He rings off. "Dean's mama," he explains to me. He chuckles at my expression. "What?"

"You go super Nawlins when you speak to family," I tease.

He grins. "Don't be acting like you don't love it," he teases right back, putting his arm around me and squeezing my shoulders. He leans down to kiss my temple and whispers in my ear in his soft growl, "*Laissez les bon temps rouler, chere.*" He laughs, a deep, gorgeous, throaty rumble as I comically shiver with a lust I genuinely feel.

Eli's flat is nice. It's in what I've come to know is a desirable neighbourhood, and it's clean and well-kept. It's minimalist, and all the furniture is black, but he clearly looks after it all. It fills me with more confidence. Gav lived in a pigsty and expected me to be his maid. Eli clearly doesn't need me to fulfil that role, to my tremendous relief.

He puts the groceries on the kitchen counter and then turns to me, smiling a little bashfully. "I, uh, have somethin' for you," he says with a smile that's slowly starting to glow, like it's being turned up by a dimmer switch.

"Oh?" I ask softly. Is this his way of propositioning me? Because I've got to say, I'm a little surprised that this is the route he chose.

He nods, and gestures behind me. "On the sofa."

I turn, and there's a very large carrier bag that seems to be filled with boxes.

I stop in my tracks.

The logo on the side is for Fonteyns, the gaming shop he took me to.

I gape at him. "What's this?" My voice has gone all high.

He smiles shyly. "Take a look."

Tentatively, I peer in the top, and let out a squeaky yelp of surprise, covering my mouth with both hands.

Sentinels of the Multiverse. My favourite game. I had almost all of the boxes, and Gav made me throw them out because he was sick of them taking up space when I never played with them...

I gently take the top one out, and am even more astonished when I peer into the rest of the bag.

Eli has not only replaced all the box sets of cards that I lost, but has bought me the ones I didn't have yet. Villains. Vengeance. OblivAeon.

And there, at the bottom, is the Lords of Waterdeep board game I showed him.

He's spent easily two hundred pounds in one fell swoop, maybe more. This must be the errand he dashed off to do in the middle of the afternoon. I have no idea what to say.

"Oh my god," I splutter, trembling a little. "You..." I take a shaky breath, tears pricking at my eyes. "You didn't have to...I mean...this must have—"

"Did I get the right ones?" he asks me gently, cutting over my squawks.

"Yes..."

"Thank fuck," he says, visibly relieved. He folds his arms and nudges the floor with his beaten up biker boots. "You like 'em?"

At a loss for words, I nod helplessly and throw my arms around his neck. He immediately holds me back. "Thank you so much," I breathe, shaking a little, trying hard not to lose it.

"You're so welcome." He pulls back and leans his forehead against mine. "You're gonna have to teach us all how to play. I sounded out the others, and they're all down for a game night soon, whenever you want."

"Thank you," I say again, the words insufficient. Trying to get across how grateful I am for this amazing and extravagant gift, I press my lips to his. "I don't know how I'll ever be able to repay you," I breathe.

"Nah, *chere*, they're a gift." He leads me towards the kitchen. "Thank me by enjoying them."

I stare at him in bewilderment as he unpacks the ingredients for the dinner he's making me. This is by far and away the kindest gift I've ever received, and he's shrugged it off like it's no big deal and told me to just enjoy them. My mind is so completely blown that he has to say my name twice to get my attention.

"You up for cooking with me? Need to chop some stuff," he says.

It takes me a couple of beats to answer him. "Um, sure."

He hands me a couple of peppers, one red, one yellow, and a knife, pointing me towards a chopping board. "Thanks. Can you dice these, please, and I'll get started on the chicken."

Not once does he criticise how I chop the peppers. He simply gets on with cubing the raw chicken, rather expertly, and begins chatting to me as we work side by side.

This is so great, I think to myself. I never realised the simple pleasure of cooking with someone, splitting the duties companionably, could be so...peaceful. And so much fun. I find myself smiling at him, laughing at a comment he makes about trusting me with his top secret family recipe, trusting me with something so intimate as this, and he's so together and responsible and takes care of his possessions and I'm one of his possessions now and my heart starts to race in my chest and oh god oh god please not now...

My throat starts to close up. I cough once, trying to clear it, but it doesn't do anything.

Icy cold fear creeps up my spine, and my hands start to shake until I can't chop anymore.

I can't feel my legs.

Shit. Run.

"Are you OK?" he asks, taking in my frozen expression.

I gape at him for a second before dropping the knife on the chopping board and rushing to pick up my bag.

"I have to go," I mumble, my knees shaking, my heart rate picking up further.

"What?"

"I'm sorry, I...I can't...I have to leave. I need to leave right now."

"Hey, whoah," he says, putting his own knife down and rushing towards me as I make for the door, "what's wrong?"

I stop, rooted to the spot between the kitchen and the front door. I don't want to leave at all. I want to stay, and let myself be comforted and soothed by him. I want to be persuaded that it's all right. I'm also desperate to run out the front door and just forget I ever knew him because the loveliness of it all is too much and it's overwhelming and terrifying me. My mind is racing, and my throat still feels tight.

"Baby, talk to me," he says in a calm voice with the tiniest hint of pleading, which breaks my heart. *I'm hurting him. How can I hurt him? How can I bring myself to do that?* He takes both of my elbows very gently and turns me around to face him, but I stare at the ground. I can't look at him. This poor man... Why am I such a basket case? Why am I so petrified of just making dinner with him? It doesn't make any sense. "Talk me through it. Did I do something to freak you out?" he asks.

I manage to shake my head jerkily.

"OK, that's good. Keep talking to me. Help me understand so I can help." His hands are cold and gentle.

"I don't know," I mutter very quietly.

"That's OK. Is it OK if I ask you about it?"

God, what's the matter with me? He's so sweet. "Mm-hmm." I still can't look at him, and he gently tips my chin up with one finger. His eyes are so kind, and very concerned, and they both steady me and make me feel like such a shit for freaking out.

"I'm so sorry," I whisper.

"It's OK." He sounds like he really means it. "Take a couple of deep breaths."

It takes me a few seconds, but once I do, the next one is easier. My shoulders, which were hunched, start to relax by degrees.

"Come and sit down with me," he says gently.

If I do that, I'm not leaving. I look at the door, both hating it for tempting me and yearning for the freedom on the other side.

I look back at him.

All of a sudden, the panic ebbs. His dear face…he's staying calm and solid for me, and I can't believe I ever thought running away from him was a good idea.

"What happened?" he asks, and one of his hands is still on my arm, gentle but firm. I know he'd let go if I pulled, and that's the difference, I realise.

Eli will never deliberately hurt me, no matter what. No matter how much I irritate him, or freak out, or however many bad days I have, he will never yell at me, frighten me, exert force, or harm me in any way. He will never consider himself 'provoked'.

What have I been so afraid of?

"This is gonna sound really stupid," I say as we sit, forcing the words out of my throat with difficulty. I can feel them like a blockage choking me. I find this so hard.

"It's OK. I won't laugh. I won't be mad." He means it, too.

I take a deep, steadying breath. "We were happy," I say.

"Mm-hmm," he says, waiting for more.

I look at him helplessly, tears threatening, but I won't give in to them. "That's it. We were happy. *I* was happy. Just in that moment, and…" I take another shaky breath. "It felt like too much. Like I have so much to lose now, and I never meant to put myself in that position again, but…it's you, so of course I have, and of course I want to. I do. Your lovely gifts, and just…just chatting normally while we cooked, like a *healthy* couple would, and the laughing, and… I got scared. Scared of being *happy*. It's so… It's messed up."

He lets out a soft sigh and gently rests his head on mine. "It's OK to be happy," he says quietly, as though not to spook me. Poor man, I think. Having to tread this carefully with a girlfriend who's scared of feeling good. "It's what you deserve. And…I'm afraid you're going to have to get used to it, *chere*." He kisses my forehead and strokes my hair. *He still wants me. The man I tried to run from still wants me, even with all my nonsense.*

"I'm sorry," I say again, but he catches my lips gently with his.

"Don't be. We'll get there. Just…don't run, OK? Promise you'll always talk to me first." He looks me straight in the eye, and I'll promise this warm and patient man anything if he won't give up on me. If he'll always help fight my demons next to me. "If you really want to go, I won't make you stay, but…please don't just run." He gives me an assessing look, seeing how much of a flight risk I still am. "OK?"

I nod. "OK," I say calmly.

He smiles, and I feel a whole lot better. Embarrassed, but like it's all going to be fine. "OK, so, I have chicken-y hands and I put those hands on you, so why don't you, ah, hop into the shower, and I'll get the rest of dinner done," he says, smiling gently.

"But don't you need a hand?"

"Nah," he says with a cheeky grin, "been making jambalaya since before I could spell it. I'm good."

chapter TWENTY

Eli

THE REST OF THE EVENING SEEMS TO HAVE GONE OK. SHE took a shower while I was finishing off dinner, and I nearly sliced my fingers off twice thinking about that. About the droplets of water running down her body, following trails my fingertips ache to trace. I nearly let the jambalaya catch by thinking about how joining her in the shower and catching each drop with my tongue would be a fantastic way to spend the evening…

Christ, I'm on fire for her pretty much all day every day now. It's a taste that won't leave my mouth, a favorite song stuck in my head. I've never known this with any other woman before.

Anyway, she loved the jambalaya, and had an extra helping when she was done. That was flattering, I have to admit. There was a primal kind of pride in feeding my woman so well. Chest beating caveman bullshit, but fun. I'm over the top for Emily, that's for damn sure.

And I am so scared.

I didn't say so when I was talking her round from her panic attack, but my own heart was racing the entire time. I know we can count the days we've been a couple on the fingers of one hand, but she's got me. I am wrapped around Em's little finger, and I want to stay there. I don't want her to leave me. Not now, not ever.

I've been comforting myself with the knowledge that she really has calmed down, and that our dinner conversation flowed really well. No awkward silences, and most importantly, no more signs of nervousness or panic from her. It was just a momentary blip. And she did promise to talk to me if it happened again, and that she wouldn't just leave. I believe her.

I think back to what Dean said, about how she's going to need a lot of reassurance and patience going forward. Something settles in my chest. If that's what she needs, I'll be more than happy to give that to her. And I'll just keep hoping that, eventually, these moments will become fewer and further between, until they're a distant memory because she feels so safe and happy and secure that there's no room in her poor torn heart for anything else.

I can't imagine what it must be like to be afraid of relaxing and being happy. Fearing that it's all going to come crashing down and turn into more hatred, more abuse. She fights battles I will never truly know. But I'll hold her hand while she does, always.

We're both lying stretched out on the sofa—well, actually, she's stretched out on top of me, all of her body touching all of mine, which feels awesome—and we're watching a couple of episodes of *Star Trek: Discovery*, literal Netflix and chill time with my lady. She's never seen it, and it's been as much fun watching her enjoy it as it has been watching the actual show (which, I gotta say, I'm enjoying, too). She's got all the excitement of a long time fan given brand new material, and it's delightful. She's peppered me with little explanations about context, and why a certain aspect of the show has made her Trekkie heart happy. There are few things I'm as enthused about, and I love that about her, that a sci-fi TV show can get her so fired up.

Her head rests just above my heart as she faces the TV. The rest of her body is tucked so neatly against mine it's as though it's always belonged there, in this exact position. I can smell her hair, sweet, like flowers and sweet fruit. I find myself running my fingertips through it, spreading my fingers outwards, and back, outwards, and back to the center, enjoying the silky feel of it.

My fingers move down her neck, and she makes a little purring rumble in her throat. My already hard cock jumps in my jeans. Against her. *Shit*. There's no way she didn't feel that.

I don't want to stop.

I will if she's not ready, but if she is…

If she is, I'll make damn sure she doesn't regret it.

I carry on the trail down her spine, slow and gentle. She makes a soft noise and squirms, moving her body against mine in very interesting ways. I sigh quietly. This is the life I want. It's what I've always wanted: a quiet evening at home with the right woman, feeding her good food, telling her I love her with my touch…

…and feeling her affectionate embrace in return.

Jesus. She's started to trace patterns on my chest with a single fingertip. If I concentrate, I think she's spelling something… *E—N…no, M… E, M, I…* Her name.

And then a heart.

And then my name.

That does it. I gently lift her head and capture her lips with my own, cupping her jaw with my hands. I move back to look at her, check that she's alright with this, but she pulls on the collar of my shirt and brings my mouth insistently back to hers. I grin, my heart roaring with joy, and don't keep my woman waiting. I kiss her again, harder, deeper than last time, feeling the first shocks of the pleasure still to come as her tongue peeps out to meet mine.

Very well, *chere*. It's on.

She lets out a little squeak of surprise, her lips still pressed to mine, as I gently roll her under me. Our arms are around each other, and it's like a cocoon of us. There's a sense of coming home at last. This is where we belong. I've never been more grateful for anything in my life.

Our kiss snowballs, picking up speed, becoming more and more passionate. There's a rush of hands, moans, sighs, dizziness as it becomes something we can't fully control anymore. My hands slide over her body of their own volition, sliding under her shirt. Warm skin, soft as silk. A denim waistband. It's in the way.

I could make her come.

The idea flits across my feverish mind, and I latch onto it, the weight of weeks of wanting this woman barreling down on me. I want to focus on her, show her what I can do, what I've craved since she walked into the parlor with a bag of cookies and a shy smile on her first day. And I won't ask for anything in return, I insist to myself, tamping down the raging need to fuck and claim and come that's coursing through my body and making me grit my teeth. She needs to know…she needs to be given something without any expectations…

I tug on the button of her jeans in question. "OK?" I ask, my voice husky and deep and breathless from so much kissing.

Her eyes are fever bright. "Yes." She does not hesitate.

I undo them and she shifts, holding her hips up so I can pull them and her panties both down in one fell swoop. I hear her gasp, and her thighs widen a little, showing me the prettiest pussy I've ever seen. I know I'm biased, but it just *is*, pink and soft and apparently freshly shaved. My lips twitch. She prepared? It's glistening for me, a clear sign like nothing else that I'm not alone in my arousal. *Thank god.*

"Please," she whispers.

I groan. Hearing her plead flips the sparkwheel on my inner

lighter, unlit for so long, and I don't keep her waiting. The need is too great for that.

I part her inner lips with my thumb, and she's like hot liquid silk. Collecting some of her honey on my thumb, I press it against her clit, gently but firmly massaging it in a circle, figuring out how she likes it.

"Uhhhhh..." It's the softest little grunt, and I want to hear it again. And again. Her breath comes faster as my thumb quickens. With my other hand, I dampen my forefinger in my mouth and slowly, slowly insert it into her, meeting no resistance because she's so wet, *Jesus* she's so wet. She groans, and her thighs tremble. One fraction at a time. Just like if I was using my cock...

I grit my teeth even harder as my cock throbs in my pants at the thought. *Shut the fuck up*, I tell it. *This is for her.*

I gently feel inside her for her g-spot, grinning to myself when I find it, that small, cushiony, slightly rough place that can really kick things up a gear if touched just right. I keep stroking her clit with my thumb as I crook my finger inside her, firm but not hard, until I find a rhythm she likes. I know because her hips jump, and she lets out the most gorgeous moan that boils my blood and makes me want to stay here forever, doing exactly this for the rest of my life.

It's amazing, and telling, how often my thoughts run along the lines of forever when it comes to Em.

My fingers get wetter and wetter, and her breath comes faster, and eventually I can't resist the temptation any longer. Parting her legs just a little more to make room for me, I dip my head closer, and run my tongue from her entrance to her clit, one long taste, and my god, she tastes good. Sweet and light and smooth. Addictive. I let out a feral groan because I just can't help it. This is as arousing as fuck, and I want more. I lick her again, and again, replacing my finger so I don't neglect her g-spot; at this rate I will never be able to hold out before I shoot my load.

I've hardly even begun to stroke that sensitive place again when her cries take on a desperate quality, and she starts shaking in earnest. Her pussy squeezes my finger rhythmically, and her cries sound so pretty, worthy of a sex scene in any movie you'd care to name.

She's good, I'll give her that. I could almost have believed it.

I have two choices here.

I can play along, spare her the embarrassment, let her think she's fooled me...

...or I can trust what we're building here, and let her know she never has to do that again. Not with me.

So I lean back up to her and give her a light brush of a kiss on her lips. She smiles up at me, still feigning satisfaction, but I can see in her eyes the walls are up again.

Gotta get 'em down. Especially after earlier.

"*Chere*," I say gently, "you know I can tell the difference between a real orgasm and kegel exercises, right?"

Emily

Oh.

Oh, god.

Oh, crapping, bloody HELL.

How did he know? How the hell did he pick up on it? I've NEVER been caught out before. This can't be happening. I'd perfected the act.

At least, I thought I had.

I feel myself gaping at him for a second before giving in and covering my face with my hands. Can you actually die of this cringe-y awful feeling? Because if so, I'm definitely going to. I groan even more when I feel his hand stroking one of mine, soothing me.

"I'm sorry," I say, muffled by my hands. No point in trying to deny it; he caught me bang to rights.

He takes both of my wrists and tugs gently, but I look away from him, too guilty and embarrassed to meet his eyes.

"It's OK," he murmurs gently, over and over. A single tear spills down my face, and he wipes it away with careful fingers. "It's OK, *chere*, I promise."

I nod, but I still want to implode with embarrassment. That's twice this evening I've made a total and utter fool of myself.

He gently turns my head so I face him, and waits long moments for me to look him in the eye. There's no hint of judgement or annoyance in his gaze. He leans down and kisses me as though nothing is wrong, as though I didn't just...

"Were you enjoying yourself?" he asks softly.

I nod miserably. Because I was. I really, really was.

"So was I," he says, taking my hand and pressing it against his crotch, grunting just a little at the contact before looking me in the eye once more, unashamed.

Holy shit. He is iron hard, the sort of hard that speaks of super-human restraint in not simply opening his fly and ramming into me just for the sheer physical relief it would bring. I flex my hand, and his cock throbs wildly. "Careful," he murmurs with a low chuckle, "I'm just barely hanging on as it is."

"Wow," I say weakly.

"That's pretty much how I feel," he replies, letting go of my hand. I don't move it, and his eyes light up with heated warning as he grins at me. "I was enjoying doing those things to you," he says to me in a firm voice, and indeed, with this sort of proof under my hand, I can do nothing but believe him. "This is not a chore to me. I'm not sitting through this until it's my turn. I'm doing this because I genuinely..." he sighs, "*seriously* want to. I love the way you feel on my fingers. I love the way you taste. I *like* doing those things, and I want to carry on. And I don't want to stop until you've genuinely come, and maybe not even then. I have all the time in the world, and I'm in no rush. There's nothing else I'd rather be doing." He runs a thumb over my lips. "If you don't think you want to come this time, that's OK. And if what I'm doing isn't working for you, tell me and I can try something else. Or stop. Whatever you want." He shifts back down and kisses my belly, just above my mound. "Just don't pretend. I don't want anything fake between us. And don't stop me because you think I'm finding this boring, because believe me, it's the exact fuckin' opposite."

How does he understand me so well already? Because that's exactly why I did it. Why I've always done it, with every other lover. He was better than any of them ever were, though. I was marvelling at how much I enjoyed his touch, how likely bordering on inevitable an orgasm seemed with him...and then I panicked. The old impulse to hurry things along so he didn't get bored and irritated...so I could proceed with delivering *his* pleasure like a service I was providing... I sigh. "I'm sorry. It's just... Old habits die hard..."

Both his thumbs run over my hips, and the feeling is compellingly delicious. "Old habits can be overcome," he murmurs confidently. He lowers his head until I can feel his breath on my pussy. "May I carry on?"

This guy. Seriously.

"OK," I say in a tremulous voice, resting my head back on the sofa and promising myself that this time I won't pretend, that I'll just enjoy what he does, and if an orgasm happens, it happens, and if it doesn't, then it doesn't matter. He said so. I'm probably too embarrassed to come now, anyway -

Barely is that thought out of my head when my whole body tenses and seizes up with pleasure zinging through my clit. Whatever he just did with his tongue was incredible. It feels like electricity shooting all through my body, warming me as it sparks. "Oh…" I say faintly.

This never happens. Not to me. I usually wait till the guy is asleep and then get myself off as silently as possible. With Eli, I get the strong sense that all I have to do is relax, and wait, and let the magic happen, and I will be rewarded. Can that really be the case?

His tongue flicks at me, all over my core, and I can tell he's playing off my reactions to see what I like best. So I decide to trust him and work *with* him on this and be honest about it, being still when it only feels nice, and sighing when it feels great to encourage him when he gets it *really* right. He doesn't focus on my clit to the exclusion of all else, either, massaging my entrance with his tongue, kissing my outer lips, sucking on me gently, and he makes his own groaning noises as though this is really doing it for him, too, like this is something to savour…

I'm not sure if this has been going on for seconds or hours, but the difference is I no longer care. If this is selfish, so be it; I just want him to never stop. I'm panting. I'm soaking. I'm on fire.

When he adds a finger to resume stroking my g-spot, I'm basically done for, which is a shock because my g-spot has never really done anything for me until tonight. Until Eli Gastright got hold of it and made it sing. My breath comes in fitful pants, crying out as the feeling builds. And it *is* building. I clutch my breasts; I always need something to hold onto when I come, and for some reason they're always my go-to. Always. And I'm doing that now, so this must be…

…*Real.*

My heart rate is picking up, too, and I stretch out my legs, tensing my thighs, straining for it, *reaching*…

And it happens. It's more intense than when I masturbate, the orgasm sharper, hotter, and I can't control the earthy sounds coming out of my throat, nor can I do anything about the way my face screws up. He doesn't let up the entire time, licking and stroking until I end up pushing gently on his head to get him to stop because it's too much. The smouldering, triumphant look he gives me nearly pulls another moan from me, it's that sexy.

"You did it," I gasp, giggling helplessly with genuine pleasure.

"Yeah, I felt it," he whispers, and rests his forehead on my belly with a shaky sigh, kissing the patches of my skin under his lips. I can feel the tension in him. That gorgeous man is rigid with unfulfilled desire and need, and I cannot tolerate that for a second.

I sit up slightly, reaching down and pulling him towards me. He gives me a quizzical frown.

I can taste myself on his lips, and thank god, it tastes fine. Always good to know.

"Your turn," I murmur, pushing him back on the sofa.

He shakes his head. "You don't have to, that was for you—"

"Then let me carry on, if it's for me," I say, pleading a little. I *cannot* leave him hard and do nothing about that. I want to play. I want to see his 'O' face, and know I put it there. "I *want* to..." is all I manage to say, but it's enough.

He gives me a searching look, and, apparently finding what he was looking for, tears at the fly on his jeans. "Then yes, please..."

Grinning with delight, I pull his jeans down and run my hand over his boxers, along his rock hard cock. He exhales deeply at my touch, his eyes burning at me. It sends a tingle down my spine to see him so affected, and I can feel his eyes on my face as I reach into his briefs and pull out his cock.

He's perfect. Long, but not too long: just exactly right. Wide enough to send a chill of anticipation through me, and ramrod straight, with velvety skin over the pulsing hardness. Taking him in my hand, I slide my fingers up the length of his shaft, rubbing the tip with my thumb, spreading the dewdrops of pre-cum that have gathered there. It makes him shiver and hiss through his teeth.

"I want that mouth," he whispers, desperation coursing through his words, and he shakes his head. "Sorry, I didn't mean to—"

"Shh," I soothe him, running my thumb over his lips the way he did with me. He catches it with his teeth, giving it a soft bite, and I grin. For better or worse, this is something I have confidence in, and I can't wait to taste him, to bring him the same pleasure he was so determined to give to me.

He places his hand over mine and shows me the pressure he likes—harder than I usually do—and the right speed for him. I'm grateful for the insight, and give him a long, deep kiss. He cups my face in his hands, and I feel precious to him.

Breaking away, not giving him a moment to prepare, I shuffle down and give the head of his erection a tongue swirling suck, moaning with relish at his fresh, salty flavour. He lets out a loud grunt, throwing his head back and running his hands through my hair. "*Chere*...fuck..."

Smiling to myself, I take a little more of him into my mouth, and then a little more, enjoying the turgid smoothness, gleeful at sounds I'm wringing from him. I thought the phone sex we had was hot as hell, but this makes it look like nothing in comparison. The sense of power is exhilarating, the idea that he's spellbound and at my mercy, that I can push him over the edge *or* force him to bask in the pre-glow, depending on my whim.

Running a hand down his thigh, I reach below to cup his balls, stroking them gently. They're already firm and tight, and the skin bunches up more under my touch. There's no way I can fit all of him in my mouth, so I pump my hand at the base in tandem, hollowing my cheeks as I suck on him, playing with him, massaging his banjo string with my tongue in a way that makes him shout. "Fuck...FUCK...*please*," he begs, and his hips start to thrust upwards reflexively. I can see him try to control it, watching the fierce expressions on his face as he battles to control and master his body's reactions, but it's plain for me to see I can make him come in seconds if I want to.

And I want to.

I sink down again, taking as much of him as I can fit into my mouth, and then dragging my lips all the way up again, swirling my tongue around his helmet. "Oh fuck... If you..." He's fighting for enough focus and breath to speak. "If you keep doing that, I'm gonna... *Chere,* I'm warning you... I'll explode in your mouth, so if you don't want-" I do it again, harder this time. "Oh, FUCK," he grits out, tensing, fighting to hold on...but then I suck him again, and he's done for, moaning out a deep growl of agonised relief as he spills into my mouth, his dick throbbing hard. There's so much of it, more than I've ever known anyone to come before, and I swallow as fast as I can.

He pulls me to him immediately, kissing me fiercely, over and over. We can taste each other, and that's unbearably hot to me. He arranges me so I'm on top of him, my legs along his, tangling his fingers in the hair at the back of my head. "Oh my god," he says, sounding winded and very American, and I giggle.

"Good for you?" I ask.

He gives me the biggest grin I've ever seen on his face. "*Amazing* for me," he sighs, kissing me again. "Are you OK?"

I nod enthusiastically, making him laugh. "That was perfect," I admit. "I'm so sorry about the first—"

"Don't," he cuts me off gently. "Don't give it another thought. It's fine." He plays lazily with a strand of my hair. "We got you there in the end."

"Boy, *did* you," I say, laying my head on his chest, suddenly tired out, smiling at the slightly elevated thud, thud, thud of his heart under my ear. He still hasn't completely returned to normal, and I'm glad it was that powerful for him.

"Baby?" he asks.

"Yeah?"

He runs a hand back and forth between my shoulder blades as the other rests at the base of my spine. "It seems pretty clear where we're headed," he says steadily, "so…we should probably have the talk."

I shift my head up to look at him, smiling as I lean forward to kiss him. "I appreciate that," I say honestly.

He looks a little relieved to hear me say that. "I'm all clear," he says. "I haven't slept with anyone since the last time I got tested."

I nod. "I went and got tested after Gav, because I just didn't trust him when he said he'd only cyber cheated on me, and I tested negative across the board, thank god."

He pulls me to him and gives me the softest of kisses. "OK, so…how would you like to go about this? We'll do whatever you feel comfortable with. If you want condoms, I'll wear condoms."

I think about it for a few beats. "Would you mind if we didn't? I mean, we're both clean, and we're both infertile, so… Just so you know, I'm not on the pill or anything, cos there's no point. I dunno, call me sappy, but I don't want anything between us when we…" I trail off.

His eyes are soft, warm, and alive. "I don't mind," he says, softly biting my lower lip. "I'd like that, too. Was kinda hopin' you'd say that."

I place my head back on his chest. "In the one in a trillion bajillion chance that you knocked me up…?" I ask, just to be sure.

He chuckles and kisses the top of my head. "Well, I'd sue my doctor for providing incorrect information," he jokes, "and that can pay for the kid's education." He hugs me closer. "In all seriousness, though…if the impossible happens, and you got pregnant, we'd deal. Whatever you wanted, we'd make it happen."

I nod. "I've been told it's practically impossible, though," I add.

"Same here."

I look up at him. "So it really isn't going to happen, Eli," I say simply, giving him a searching look.

He meets my gaze evenly. "I meant it when I said I didn't want that," he says.

I let out a long sigh of relief. "So did I. I just…I wanted to be sure you agreed."

He nods, resting his forehead against mine. "You and me… we'll have a happy life, just the two of us, and leave all our worldly goods to Dean and Leo's kids. Or charity. Or whatever we decide along the way."

I snuggle in closer, touched that he's thinking so far into the future with such certainty. "Sounds perfect."

chapter TWENTY-ONE

Emily

I'M STIFF AND ACHY WHEN I WAKE UP THE NEXT MORNING, and it takes me a couple of seconds to process that I'm not in my bed.

I lift my head, and see Eli, fast asleep, looking endearingly peaceful. We're still on his sofa. I must have just passed out on top of him after last night, all of which comes back to me in a rush. The TV is on standby.

I can't stop the grin spreading across my face. *That was incredible.*

I wriggle slightly to have a little stretch, and two things happen: one, Eli starts to stir, and two, so does his already semi-hard cock.

Neither one of us put our pants back on last night, so I can feel it lengthening further against my thigh as he starts to wake up. God bless morning wood.

He opens his eyes, and I get lost for a moment in his soft, loving expression. He looks pleased to see me. I could very easily become addicted to that. "Morning, *chere*," he mumbles sleepily.

"Morning." I kiss his mouth, making him smile. "Sorry, I guess I crashed out last night."

"No problem. I did the same." He runs a finger down my face. "And it ain't like you ain't welcome to sleep in my arms anytime." Looks like his accent is stronger when he's sleepy, too. It makes me smile to my toes. He rubs his eyes and checks his watch. He blinks. "Shit, it's half past nine!"

"What?!" I clamber up. "God, I'm gonna be so late! Unless…I don't think I have time to go home and change, so I'll have to just wear this and wing it…" I wince a little, and then shrug. No walk of shame here, cos I'm not ashamed.

"You use the shower first," he says, "I'll pour the juice." He stands, and then looks down, realising his morning glory is on display to me. Our eyes meet, and we grin, starting to move towards each other before both saying, "No time."

I start towards his en suite in his bedroom, and then stop.

Well, it would actually save *time…*

I turn back.

"Eli?"

"Yeah?"

"Why don't you join me in the shower?"

He pokes his head around the kitchen door, eyes glowing and a wicked grin spreading across his face. "Because we both know what'll happen, and we don't have the time. Plus, I don't want our first time together to be hurried with one eye on the clock. Screw that."

I lean against the wall, suddenly keenly aware that, although he's put his boxer briefs back on, I'm standing here in just a long vest top that just about covers everything with maybe a millimetre to spare. "Well, yeah, but…it'd be quicker, and I'm sure we can control ourselves." I lift my chin. "I don't want a hasty fumble in the shower to be our first time, either. We're both adults. We have self control." How I managed to say that with a straight face is beyond me.

He quirks an eyebrow and trails his eyes down my half

naked body. I can almost hear his thoughts as one corner of his mouth slowly lifts, and my pussy warms immediately. "It would save time," he agrees, marching forward and grabbing my hand, pulling me to the shower as if he's scared I'll change my mind. "Babygirl, you're on."

What was I thinking…

Heaven help me, this is torture. I've been mentally undressing Eli for weeks now, but the reality is better than anything I could have conjured up with my own imagination.

And there isn't time to touch him.

Not those thighs, muscular enough to make me wonder what he does to stay in shape. Not that arse of his, which is Swayze standard and beyond perfect. And not that gorgeous cock, which looks painfully hard as it strains towards me, balls tightening as I watch.

We're not even washing, we're just staring at each other's bodies as the water beats down on us, trying not to reach out for each other. Focusing all our energy on not touching, not giving in to the out-of-control need roaring its way through us both.

His tattoos are now fully visible to me, and they're beautiful. I saw a hint of a skull on his stomach once before when his t-shirt rode up. I can see the whole thing now, and it's stunning, lifelike enough to make me feel like I could reach out and pick it up, could smooth my hands over the surface of bone and do my best Hamlet impression. And I can see that the sleeve of crosshatches and chevrons, and what looks like shark teeth, travels all the way up his right arm and over his right pectoral, almost like armour.

"That's amazing," I say weakly, pointing at it.

He takes a deep breath. His breathing has been coming

faster since we ducked into this cubicle, and baby, the feeling is mutual.

"It's a Pe'a tattoo. Samoan tradition," he mumbles. "My mother was from Samoa." He pronounces it authentically: *SAH-moa*, the final 'a' barely even a suggestion, and I love it.

His fists are clenching and unclenching, and I realise that mine are doing the same. My clit is throbbing like a heartbeat. I can't take this.

"This was a bad idea," I whisper.

His cock pulses at my words, and he lets out a growl low in his throat as he lunges for me, pressing me against the cool tiles and kissing me ravenously.

"Fuck the parlour," he bites out. "Fuck being on time." He bites my lower lip. "We are not leaving this shower until you've come."

I grab his erection and give it a firm tug, making him gasp. "You're not getting left out, boo," I murmur against his lips, and he grins wolfishly.

"Counting on that," he replies, running a hand down one of my breasts, squeezing the nipple between two fingers, before dipping his head and biting the other gently. Positioning my legs to open them a little more, his fingers find my pussy again, and he grunts and bites my neck when he finds me wet quite aside from the shower. He slips first one finger, then two, inside me, unerringly finding the part I didn't think I even had and massaging my g-spot firmly as his thumb finds and toys with my clit. I was already turned on, so there's a tinge of relief to the aching pleasure, and I gasp. He covers my jaw and my neck in kisses, whispering the sweetest, filthiest words in my ear: that I'm so beautiful, that I feel amazing on his fingers, that he wants me more than anything and he's going to spend hours tonguing my pussy the first chance he gets.

I run one hand over his intricate Samoan tattoo, lightly

scratching my fingers down, catching the flat disc of one of his nipples and making him groan in my ear. With my other hand, I rub the full length of him, loving how his hardness seems to reach breaking point. I squeeze him, momentarily overcome by the bright jolts of pleasure gathering in my pussy as his fingers work, and I cry out. My climax is within reach, but I don't want to get there alone. I want him to come, too. So I pick up speed as I jerk him off, trying to bring him with me.

His hand leaves my waist, where it has been clutching at my skin, and grabs my wrist to hold it still. His eyes are screwed up, his teeth gritted against the pleasure I'm trying to give him, and he's holding his breath. His entire body is rigid. I've never seen someone fight so hard for mastery over themselves. And, amid the zinging arousal, I feel a glow of pride that it's *me* that got him this crazed.

"I want you to come," I breathe, almost begging.

"Not until you do," he growls, resting his forehead against mine and letting go of my wrist. He resumes working my pussy in earnest, shoving me closer and closer to the edge. I fist his cock frantically, determined to hold my own in this race, until the bubble bursts and I pulse against his fingers, a ragged moan leaving my lips as I ride the orgasm out. At the feel of the first clutch and flutter of my pussy, he lets out a raw shout and comes hotly on my skin, his dick surging hard.

I'm dizzy, weak-kneed, leaning against the shower wall for support. I feel his lips on my jaw, my cheek, trailing to my lips, gentle as only a man this huge can be. *I love him,* I think, and mentally jump slightly at the direction my mind has gone. *Isn't that a bit…soon? Take it bloody easy…* But when he lifts his head and we gaze at each other, his bright blue into my grey, blue skies to my rainclouds, I just give in. *Even if it is fast, it's still true.* This gruff, gentle, kind, and patient man has my soul in a warm embrace, and that's just the way it is.

I can't ignore how much better I feel, how *right* I feel, when he's with me. After all that I've been through, that's worth everything. Even the fear.

I'm done being afraid.

I'm in. All the way.

But there's no way I'm telling him right now, I think as we smile sleepily at each other, our heart rates returning to normal. He'll think it's the orgasm afterglow talking, and I want him to know I mean it. I don't want him to doubt me. He deserves better than that. So I resolve to tell him another time, when our heads are clear and neither of us are naked.

It's kind of a shock when he pulls back and his skin leaves mine. The steam from the shower has a cooling effect, and I shiver a little. I want him back again, but if there wasn't time before, now there *really* isn't.

He hands me some shower gel, and it smells just like him: clean, a little woodsy, with a hint of rosemary.

"We really had better get this show on the road," he says with a rueful grin, echoing my thoughts. He guides me closer to the shower and gently wipes his semen from my skin, kissing me one more time before lathering up.

Eli

I've been sexually active since I was 16 years old, and I had no idea it could be like this. No idea at all.

Even though it's only been hurried minutes since we came together, I want to pick her up so that her legs are wrapped around my waist, my hands grasping that hot-as-hell ass of hers as I bundle her into my bedroom. I want to lay her down on my bed, and make sweaty, blurry, can't-quite-catch-our-breath love to her until we're both too tired to move. And then I want to nap with her in my arms, and do it all over again when we wake up, and again, and again.

I'm still reeling from the effect she has on me. It's stronger than anything I've ever known, even when I was a teenager discovering sex and desperate to have as much of it as possible, seeking out any opportunity to get laid. I think it's because it's now totally clear that we're great together, and that the sex between us is going to be *good*. Off the charts good. A small shiver of anticipation tickles my spine as I think about next time, about actually sinking my bare dick into that gorgeous wet pussy I've been playing with, before I turn my mind resolutely back to putting clothes *on*. We're getting later by the second.

Still…as we get ready, rushing around like speeded up film, our eyes keep catching and trading knowing, smiling looks, full of the secrets we showed to each other via touch and lick and kiss and moan. I know what she sounds like in the full throes. I know what she feels like when she comes. I know what she looks like naked. I have no idea how I'm going to be able to concentrate on anything else today.

I nearly lose it and tell her we're both calling in sick when I see her stuff her panties into a zipped up inside pocket in her jacket. She grins at the look on my face when she sees that I know her secret, that my *chere* is going commando in her jeans today.

And I just can't hold it back any longer.

She gives me a quizzical look when I catch her hand just as we reach the front door. My thumb is less than an inch from the red ladybug tattoo I gave her, and I run my thumb over it, feeling pride that it's there. I've marked her with my tattoo needle. I marked her with my come just minutes ago. And now I'm going to put an invisible mark on her, one that I hope she is ready for. One I'm probably slightly insane to give to her after her wobble last night, but I can't not.

"I need to tell you something," I say, my heart pounding like a jackhammer, squeezing her hand gently to steady myself. I wish now that I'd thought this through more and practiced some nice speech or something. I'm not the best with words as a rule. But I don't think I can hold this in anymore, and moreover, I don't want to.

Her face stiffens with alarm. "What's wrong?"

"Nothing," I hurry to assure her. "Nothing at all, everything's...great. *So* great. It's...better than I've ever had it." I feel her relieved smile like glowing embers in my gut, and suddenly it all falls into place, and everything seems so simple. "I'm in love with you," I murmur, touching her hair with slightly shaking fingers.

Her eyes widen. She looks stunned. I think in a good way, but it's hard to say.

I sigh, and go for it. "I know we've only been a couple for a few days," I say quietly, winging it and trying not to stumble over my words, "but...I've spent nearly every day with you for weeks since you got here, and I've been falling for you more and more every single one of those days. So I know this might seem fast, but..." I run a thumb over her cheek. "It's true."

Her eyes are still huge as they look up into mine. I let her go and clear my throat awkwardly. "You don't have to say it back, you know, if...if you ain't there yet. I may have read our book a few chapters ahead of you, and if that's that case, I promise you, I *promise*, it's fine—"

She stops me running my mouth by covering my lips with a kiss. Her tongue gently licks into my mouth, firing me up all over again, and her hands slide across my shoulders until she's on her tiptoes with her arms wrapped around my neck. I gather her to me, holding her as close as I can because it just feels so good to have her body pressed against me and I'm so relieved that this hasn't freaked her out.

She breaks away first, and the look in her eyes has my heart jumping.

"I love you, too," she says, and she looks almost amused. "I was going to say it in the shower, but I didn't want you to think it was only because I was addled with that outrageously good orgasm you gave me." She kisses my mouth again, which is spreading into a grin, and I softly bite her lower lip. "It *is* kind of soon," she adds quietly, "and I'm not going to lie, I'm a little scared...but I'm happier more than I am scared, and this just feels...*right*."

Well, holy fuck.

My fingers are in her hair and I rest my head against hers, sighing with relief. This is beyond doubt the best moment of my life. So far. With her, I have no doubt that, day by day, it's going to keep getting better and better. I've known the shitty side of relationships, and she has, too. I'm never taking this for granted.

My cell interrupts us by ringing. I grumble as I take it out of my pocket, reluctant for the moment to become the past, and she giggles.

"It's Leo," I tell her, and she winces. I swipe up. "We're on our way," I tell him, hoping he just leaves it at that.

"Oh, good, you're both still alive," he teases.

"Yep," I say with an eye roll, "now leaving. Be there in ten."

"My, how the mighty have fallen," he jokes. "It's payback time, Mr Never Late. You know the drill. And I am going to make the most of this." He sounds over-the-top exultant. Man, I'm going to be given the runaround today...

"Thought you might." I end the call.

"What was all that about?" Emily asks.

I guide us both out of the door and lock up. "It's a tradition at Wishbone," I reply, slinging my arm around her shoulder as we start walking. "If you're late for work, you buy lunch for everyone, and they can be as fussy and elaborate with it as they want. Like, a hugely exacting sandwich order, with like a triple venti decaf half fat no foam what-the-fuck from another place across town, that kind of thing. Wasted time for wasted time, Leo calls it."

She bites her lip. "I'm so sorry, this is all my fault-"

"No, it isn't," I insist. "I overslept, too. No taking responsibility for everything, *chere*. You're *my* girlfriend now, and that shit ain't happening." I smile down at her, pick up one of her hands, and kiss the back of it. It makes her smile, and right now I don't think life could be any more perfect.

chapter TWENTY-TWO

Eli

WE'RE THERE IN TEN, LIKE I TOLD LEO WE WOULD BE.

"I'm so sorry, Leo," Emily says as soon as we arrive and she sees him in her chair covering reception.

"Oh, pumpkin, no worries," he assures her, seeing that she feels genuinely bad, and gives her an affectionate cuddle. "Eli led you astray with his shenanigans, that's all. But you're still my angel." He winks at me. "Thinking about how complicated I can make my lunch order."

"Do your worst," I say, grinning defiantly. His eyebrow raises, but I can see he's just happy to see me happy. And that means a lot to me.

"I'm paying my way," Emily pipes up as she gently nudges Leo off her chair.

"Nope, this one is on me," I insist.

Leo shakes his head and points at me. "It's his fault, so he's fixing it. I've been waiting for this day for *years*."

"Hey, it takes two to tango. It's just as much *my* fault as it is *his*. And we'll be able to get it done much quicker if we split the list," she argues.

"But then I miss out on your company. Nah." I shake my head.

Her eyes narrow at me playfully, and I can't help but smile. "We'll see."

"Uh oh, the lovebirds' first fight," Leo laughs, "I'm outta here. Just don't smash up the place." He wanders through to the corridor, and I see him pause by Sadie's open door.

I lean across and crook my finger at my girl so I can reach her for a kiss. I can feel her starting to smile as I brush her lips with mine. *I love you,"* she mouths at me.

There's something my mother always used to say in Samoan to my father: O *se va'ai lava e malie ai le loto*. A rough translation, as I understood it, would be *simply looking at you makes my heart happy*. I get it now, Mom, I think. I'm glad she had that with my father, and I wish she could meet this woman who's made my life right again.

I love you, too, I mouth back, and pull myself away, heading to my studio to set up for my first client of the morning.

The peace doesn't last.

I'm stealing a few moments with Emily on reception after my first appointment—a Spiderman symbol on a regular client's arm—when the shouting begins.

It's Sadie and Leo.

Em and I frown at each other, unable to make out the actual words they're shouting at each other behind the now closed door of her studio. But they both sound seriously pissed.

And then her door bursts open just as Leo yells, "He's an *ASSHOLE!*" Both of them storm into the corridor. It's been a while since they had a fight, but they do happen now and again. Inevitable, really, with their fiery personalities *and* Leo's unrequited feelings pouring gasoline on the bonfire.

But this sounds like the worst one yet.

I tense my jaw. *What is it this time?* Em looks worried.

"Don't you *dare* call him that," Sadie snarls, clenching her fists at her sides.

Leo rakes his hands through his hair in clear frustration. "What…would you…*call* it, then?!" He sounds incredulous, and livid beyond anything I think I've ever heard from him.

"I call it something I should never have mentioned to you," she retorts. She's almost breathless with anger, very unlike the easygoing Sadie I know. She's never been shy about calling it like she sees it, but I've never seen her so raw before. "You think I don't know you don't like him? Yeah, dingus, I see the eye rolls. I hear the pointed comments. You've never given him a fair chance, like some weird inverse snobbery… Like he doesn't have tattoos or listen to your kind of music, so he's not worth bothering with. You just decided you didn't like him and that was that. And now you're laying into him way more than he deserves, and it sucks! It's beneath you."

"More than he…" He sounds stunned, and stares at her for a long moment before pulling his shirt off.

"Oh, for fuck's *sake,*" Sadie growls, rolling her eyes and crossing her arms. But Leo cuts her off.

"Here," he says, pointing to his lower abdomen on the left, where there's a tattoo of a scene from a Moomins cartoon from the nineties. "And here," he points to the Japanese style maroon peony on his left arm, one of Sadie's best in my opinion. "*And* here," he says, turning around to point at the intricate mandala tattoo with the head of a walrus she inked onto his shoulder blade. "Here," he points to the fleur de lis mandala she drew delicately on his neck as a tribute to New Orleans, "*here,*" he points at the skeleton from some British cartoon she did on his hip, "and now *here,* when it's only half finished because you're pissed at me," he ends, pointing to his right wrist, but I can't see what the new tattoo is.

She glares at him, but her anger is dimming and being replaced by something else. Something colder.

"I would *never, ever* have *any* of these removed, for *any reason*, because *you* did them. And *I'm just a friend of yours.*" He huffs with anger. Em tenses up and starts biting one of her nails. "What the *hell* is his excuse?! He says he loves you, and he's…he's…*fucking destroying* your tattoo on him? He's lasering that glorious artwork off? For what? There is *nothing* that can justify that, and you're still with him? You're still thinking of saying yes if he ever gets off his arse and proposes? You still think he cares even *one tiny shit's worth* about you?!"

Sadie is silent for a moment as he finishes ranting. "That's…"

"That's what? Fair? The truth? Something you just don't want to admit to yourself?!" Leo interrupts her angrily.

When she speaks again, her voice is dripping with ice. "That is *rich*. You're a fine one to talk about giving a shit about anybody."

"What the fuck did you just say to me?" Leo spits, his eyes flashing with fury.

"You heard me." She takes a step forward, and their eyes are in a death lock together as they square off. Neither of them blinks. Neither of them would ever be violent, but rage is sizzling in the air around them. This has been a long time coming. "Peter has his faults, but he doesn't sleep with half of Foxton and then never call them again. He wouldn't pull that kind of selfish, lame-arse fuckboy shit with anyone because he understands basic courtesy and thinking about other people's needs and feelings. The other day I covered Emily's lunch break, and your last one night stand called in hoping to see you. Asked me if you'd mentioned her, and what could I say?! I had no idea who she was, and that was obvious. And it was really, really sad to see this poor woman's eyes when she realized she was just one of many, and you'd been perfectly able to call her and just hadn't. It was depressing to watch." She sneers at him with contempt. "You take what you want from these women, and never consider how it makes them feel when you drop them like a hot rock after you got yours. So yeah, actually, jackass, giving a shit about other people is not something you're qualified to comment on. I will not be buying a ticket to your TED talk. *Back the fuck off, you fucking hypocrite.*"

Em inches a little closer to me, and I can feel she's trembling ever so slightly. When I look down at her, she's staring at the ground, but she's gone pale. They're triggering her.

That does it.

"*Knock it off,*" I bark at them. "You," I point at Leo, "back in your room, and you," I jerk my head at Sadie, "back to yours, and deal with this shit later. This is *not* the time *or* the place."

Sadie scowls at Leo one last time before turning and flipping her door closed. They all have soft close mechanisms to accommodate Dean's PTSD, so it's not quite as dramatic as she was probably hoping, but the message is loud and clear.

I've never seen anyone put their shirt on angrily before, but Leo manages it, glaring at me as I look back at him evenly, and then at her slowly closing door. "He's still an ungrateful philistine, and a prat, and you *fucking know it,*" he grinds out before he, too, stalks back to his room.

Dean sticks his head out of his door, rolling his eyes. *WTF?*

Wish I knew, I sign back, keen for them not to hear me talking about them. The last thing I want to do is start them up again. *Had to do something. The yelling was upsetting Em.*

He nods. *You did right. Is she OK? Emily, I mean.*

Just going to check now. He nods again, and I return to the reception area.

Her color looks a little better, and the trembling seems to have stopped. "Are you OK?" I ask her, walking up to her and pulling her gently into my arms, checking for signs of a panic attack. I'm relieved to see there are none.

"Yeah," she replies. "Sorry about that, I just…me and yelling…you know, it's not a good mix." She sighs, resting her forehead against my chest. "I need to get over it."

I just quietly hold her, gently rubbing her back until I feel her relax. "I've got you," I murmur.

She snuggles in. "Thank you." She says it so quietly I almost miss it.

"It's OK."

She leans back and looks up at me wryly. "For real, though," she muses, "I don't think people argue like that without a spark, and it takes two. She might not admit it even to herself. She might not even realize. But that was too much of a humdinger for all those feels to be one sided."

I raise an eyebrow. "You think?"

She nods. "It's definitely not just him."

Emily

In the aftermath of the Sadie and Leo row, everyone mostly keeps to themselves to avoid the tense atmosphere, so the epic lunch forfeit just didn't happen. Postponed, I guess. The air in the parlour is tight and strained for the first time since I've been here, and I really don't like it. It makes me fidgety and uncomfortable.

But I don't freak out. If this had happened a few weeks ago, I'd have been a mess by now. I'm proud of the progress, of the way I've built and expanded my inner resources.

In fairness, having the most gorgeous, sexy, and considerate man on the planet, who just that morning told you he loves you for the first time, and is treating you to your favourite Subway meal deal, makes it hard to feel down for too long. We both have a twelve inch sandwich because we skipped breakfast, grinning at each other in the queue as we remember why.

The wicked light in his eyes when he looks at me throughout our break is the kind that make a person squirm and giggle like a schoolgirl. I touch his hair, and he leans into me unselfconsciously. Several times, he takes my hand and kisses my knuckles. He welcomes any affection I want to lavish on him, and it makes me glow.

And there's a definite promise in his expression, and I just know, even though neither of us say it out loud, that there's no way either of us are spending the night alone.

His place or my place; either way, tonight, it's on.

chapter TWENTY-THREE

Emily

THERE'S STILL A COLD AND STONY SILENCE WHEN WE GET back to work, entirely out of character for the usual cheery bustle of the parlour. I don't think either Sadie or Leo have left their studios once since they stormed back into them earlier, but they both have clients booked later this afternoon, so they'll have to come out. I steel myself for the atmosphere when they do. Conflict is a part of life, and I cannot expect to always avoid it. I need to toughen up and re-harden myself to it.

Eli hangs around with me on reception while we wait for his first client of the afternoon. These days, if he doesn't have a client, or isn't preparing for one, he's next to me. And I love it.

There's a message on Wishbone's Instagram page that turns out to be for me, from Eli's Aunt Wendy:

Hey y'all, this is a message mainly for the lovely Emily! Glad to know you, honey, and I'm really looking forward to Eli bringing you to come visit us :) Eli, you look after her, you hear? You too, Dean. And Leo. Sadie, honey, that tattoo you did of that dandelion clock on that lady's shoulder was DARLING. I want you to do that for me the next time I visit, which will hopefully be around the fall. Love to you all xxxxx

"That's so lovely," I say. What a lovely woman for being so welcoming. It's been a long time since I've had any involvement with a proper large, loving family, and it's making me feel warm to be taken in like this. Eli is beaming fondly at the screen, and again I am struck by how much love he has for them all. I tap out a reply, thanking her and saying I'm looking forward to meeting her, too. Because I really am.

The door opens, and two women walk in. Number one, Eli's client, a smiley and friendly woman with an awesome Studio Ghibli t-shirt, and I instantly want to ask her about it so I can buy one too. And number two, Melissa with the blue hair, who scowls at me when she sees that Eli's holding me from behind and stooping to rest his chin on my shoulder. Speaking of handling conflict...

I sigh inwardly. *Ugh, not her. Thanks a heap, universe.*

"Eli?" Melissa's friend asks. With the pushy, tactless way she acts, I'm stunned Melissa has friends at all, especially one who seems so pleasant. "Hi, I'm Jess, your 2:30?"

"Hey," Eli says, taking her offered hand, and squeezing my waist a little, comforting me. "Nice to meet you."

"You, too. I thought I'd stop by a little early so I can show you a photo of what I'd like..." Jess digs out her phone, and I'm dimly aware of them discussing sizes and options as Melissa glares at the two of us. Eli pays her no mind, concentrating on his client like the professional he is. I can feel my stomach churn slightly as I wonder what the blue haired peril is going to say or do, but I'm not going to allow her to intimidate me. I've dealt with far worse people than her. Compared to Gav and his friends, she's nothing, and she's ultimately unable to do any real damage. I won't even give her the satisfaction of showing her I'm uncomfortable. So I look back at her speculatively, not willing to be the first to look away.

"I'll come with you," she insists to her friend when she and Eli make tracks towards the corridor.

"Oh, no, that's OK," Jess replies, seeming oblivious, "I don't need my hand held this time. Don't wait for me, I'll text you when I'm done and meet you at H&M."

Melissa glowers, thoroughly annoyed. "Well, I need to speak with Eli anyway—"

"Book an appointment, and I'll see you then," he cuts in firmly, unsmiling. He turns to me and gives me an almost imperceptible wink before coming back, cupping my face in his hands, and giving me the most knee trembling kiss. It's one that cannot be mistaken for anything other than mutual ownership, no room for doubt. A clear signal that he is fully taken. I pinch his butt in acknowledgement of what he's doing, unseen by anyone, and he grins against my lips.

He rubs his nose against mine. "You gonna be OK?" he whispers, flicking his eyes towards the bristling woman. I nod. I've got this. "See you later, baby," he murmurs, his voice husky but loud enough for her to hear.

I watch him go—especially his arse, because it's beautiful and I am definitely an arse girl—and beam broadly before turning back to her.

I'm not intimidated anymore, and I know what I have to do.

I clear my throat. "Right, then. When would you like your appointment?" I ask brightly.

If looks could kill, I'd look like pulverised lasagne on the floor.

"After Jess's," she says with an unspoken 'duh', as if that should have been obvious.

"Ooh, sorry," I say without looking at the appointments calendar on my screen, "he has clients back to back all afternoon. He's got a ten week long waiting list currently. Let's see when his next available appointment is..." I turn to my laptop and take my time. My pulse is thudding a bit, but...I'm kind of enjoying this. That's a surprise, but I decide to just revel in it.

She rolls her eyes at me rudely. "I just need a few minutes, for fuck's sake. Just squeeze me in after Jess."

"I can't do that," I say calmly. "I'm sure you can appreciate his next client won't want to be kept waiting. You wouldn't like it if it was your appointment being delayed, would you?" My tone is sweet, but my gaze is even. *I'm not going to be bullied, sweetheart.*

She huffs. "He screwed up my tattoo. He needs to fix it. I'm sure you wouldn't want me to give you guys a bad review for poor customer care, would you?" Her smile is dripping with venom.

"What's wrong with your tattoo?" My voice has gone matter of fact. I don't appreciate threats.

"I'm not dropping my kecks in front of you," she scoffs. "Unless you want me to strip off where everyone can see." She points to the huge windows at the front of the parlour.

"If you don't tell me what's wrong, I can't pass it on to Eli, and he won't be able to judge how to sort it," I reply with a shrug. "And then it will be ten weeks." I put subtle emphasis on the last two words.

Her eyes take on a curious light, as though she's just had a wicked idea. "Oh yeah? Well I'll be showing in ten weeks' time, and won't that be lovely for you?" Her smile is vicious, her face alive with malice.

I raise my eyebrows. "I don't follow."

She leans forward as though she's imparting a secret she knows will sting me. "My tattoo is fine. This was meant to be private between me and Eli, but since you're being such a pissy little jobsworth about it, and given that display you both treated me to just now, I guess I'll have to just come right out with it, won't I?" She leans back, her nasty smile growing. "I'm pregnant. And it's Eli's."

A couple of seconds pass, and then I burst into loud,

uproarious laughter, unwilling and unable to stop myself. *You have GOT to be kidding me…*

She frowns, clearly having anticipated a vastly different reaction. "The fuck is so funny?"

I try to calm myself, but it's difficult. "I'm sorry," I gasp, "say that again."

She narrows her eyes. "I said I'm pregnant with Eli's kid, you smug bitch, so tough shit," she says, every syllable harsh and overdone.

I ignore the name calling. From someone this pathetic, it means nothing. "No, you aren't," I advise her between giggles. "Well, I don't know, you may be pregnant, but it's definitely not *my boyfriend's* baby. Run along." I stare at her with a huge grin on my face.

Her lip curls. "Sure, keep telling yourself that. Just book me the fuck in after Jess so he and I can sort out the…*arrangements*. You know, custody, birth plan, that sort of thing. And I don't want *you* involved in *our child's* upbringing. Sorry to ruin your 'new love' and all, but a baby's a baby, so—"

"What the hell is so funny?" Sadie has appeared and is leaning against the doorway, looking intrigued.

I grin at her. "Not much, just our friend Melissa here is being desperate and pathetic." Melissa gasps a little.

"Yeah, what else is new?" Sadie asks dismissively. "What is it this time?" I could kiss her.

"Apparently, Eli is the father of her unborn baby." I'm not sure if Sadie knows that Eli's infertile, but I'm pretty sure she knows this is absolute bullshit.

And I'm right. "Nah, he's too picky for that. And even if he had gotten desperate enough that even a shit lay would do, he'd never have gone in *her* bareback." I wince comically, and risk a look at Melissa's face. She's gaping and spluttering, and struggling not to stamp her feet like a toddler.

"This—I—you both think you're so awesome, both of you, and you're not… This is between me and Eli, you skanky—"

"No, *you* are the skank." I've snapped. Enough is enough with her. "Only really shitty, heartless, nasty people use fake pregnancy to get a man, and you obviously have no shame." I see her blinking at me, but I just can't stop. "That was *really* low. And what were you going to tell Eli, having told us this stupid lie? You haven't slept with him. What the bloody hell is wrong with you? And let's say he *had* screwed you, what were you going to do when there was no baby? Fake a miscarriage? That *happens* to people, and it's awful and traumatic and *not* a cheap trick to use to cause trouble and get your way, you absolute *plank*. So go home, look in the mirror, check out the awful person you've become, and just *give it up*. Get. The. Hint. Eli is not interested. Never was. *Never will be*. So gather up what's left of your dignity and get the hell out of here."

Wow. I…don't know where that came from, but I like it.

I like the adrenaline rush of putting her in her place. I don't care what her comeback is, or if it squashes anything I've said. I'm in the right here. For once in my life, I feel like I'm on solid ground. It feels good.

"YES," I hear from the doorway, and Leo's there, next to Sadie and clapping his hands, "what Emily said! Christ almighty, that was awesome…" He's laughing with Sadie. *With* her. That's nice. Maybe they'll make up now?

Melissa backs away, bright red in the face in a way that clashes brilliantly with her hair. She looks at us all with total hatred and a hint of well-earned embarrassment. "Whatever," she mutters, and leaves. I make out the words 'stupid' and 'bitch' as she shoves the door open.

Sadie throws her arms around me, laughing. "That was *brilliant*! Look at you, putting that ho-bag in her place like a total *badass*! I'm so proud!"

I laugh, a little cringey after the fact but still riding high. "Is it bad of me that that felt *so* good?"

"No, it's *wicked cool*," Leo assures me, putting his arms around us both. "You don't mess with Em, folks, cos she don't pull her punches." He kisses the top of my head, hesitates, and then kisses the top of Sadie's. "I'm sorry," I hear him whisper to her.

Awwwww.

I step back so that the hug becomes a 'them' thing instead. It's actually pretty touching, watching them hold each other tightly. I wish for the millionth time that things were different for them. "You're still a jackass," she mumbles in his arms, but it's clear now that they're going to be OK, and that they've found their way back to each other.

chapter TWENTY-FOUR

Emily

THE REST OF THE AFTERNOON IS MUCH LESS STRESSFUL. Once the make-up hug finally ended, Leo called Eli out of his studio to tell him what happened, and I grin when I hear Eli's loud, scandalised, delighted laughter. The next thing I know I'm in his arms while he's cupping my chin and kissing the life out of me, letting me know that he's very proud of me indeed. And I imagine he's probably grateful that Melissa will surely be too embarrassed by her shameful and inexcusable behaviour to come by anymore.

Jess doesn't give any indication that she's embarrassed when she leaves, just smiles and pays and wishes me a good day, so I don't think she knows what went down. Yet. How is such a nice person friends with such a stupid, lying cow?

And peace reigns once again. Leo and Sadie go back to normal like this morning never happened. I will always be bewildered by the way some people can do that, just snap back to normal with no residue from their fight. It would take me days, possibly weeks, to recover from a row like that, and I'd probably never see the friendship the same way again. But I guess different people handle things in different ways. I'm just glad they're both OK.

I also decided to re-open my own Facebook and Instagram pages, because it's been great fun looking after the parlour's accounts. I can easily block people if I don't want them to have access to my page, and I do miss having social media. So I block Gav and anyone else I can remember off the top of my head that I don't want to deal with anymore, and make a mental note to come back to that because I know I haven't thought of everyone. And then I friend my Wishbone tribe, gratified by the speed with which my requests are accepted. I smile. I'm back, baby.

Eli immediately sends me an 'in a relationship with' request on Facebook. He beat me to it. I grin as I confirm it, and he immediately hearts the announcement. Ugh, he's so cute.

Oh, and another highlight of the afternoon: turns out I can expect to meet celebrities as part of the job. Nate Woodruff, the exceptionally handsome son of Mac Woodruff the uber-famous multi-Oscar winning actor and director, contacted Leo and booked an appointment with Leo for six months time; it seems he's a semi-regular client. Plus, Chris Richards, the drummer from the American rock band Turn It Up, also called Leo directly, and Leo got me to book out an afternoon for him in a few weeks' time, scoring us all front row tickets for a date of Turn It Up's UK tour as part of the deal. I was open mouthed, but apparently Chris and Leo are best buds. Leo was laughing too hard as he recounted the story for me to one hundred percent get it, but I gleaned that it's something to do with a music festival, a ton of fruit flavoured cider, an amp, and an inflatable sheep. OK, then.

When it's finally six p.m., I breathe a sigh of relief. It's been an exhausting day, one way or the other.

And it's looking like it may be an exhausting night, too.

I freshen up when we're around ten minutes from closing, and can't help beaming at myself in the mirror. *Look how far you've come,* I think to myself. *Look what your life is like now.*

Look at what you've got to look forward to tonight...

Eli

I'm so proud of her. For real. I trusted her to be able to handle Melissa, even though I felt bad for having to walk away and attend to my client. And she did it, even better than I would ever have dreamed.

And I smiled big when she took back her social media accounts. I'm so glad that she's feeling so much safer, and able to have this again. I like to think I've helped, but at the end of the day, it's all her.

Gotta say, I couldn't be prouder to be listed as In a Relationship with her on Facebook. Hell, I'd put it on a billboard in the center of town, or stick a full page ad in the paper.

The second we get home—hers or mine, I don't care—I don't think I can do anything except fall on her like a caveman and do literally everything I can think of to blow her mind and have her screaming with pleasure. I don't care who she shared her bed with before me; I'm going to be her best, or die trying.

I head upstairs to the flat above the shop that Leo sometimes stays in for a quick shower. I'll be damned if I'm going to be sweaty after a day's work for our first time. Leo never minds when we use the facilities up here; in fact, he considers this to be everyone's flat, not just his, free for any one of us to use as needed. Which is why I'm a little surprised that he's left one of his sketches of Sadie's face lying around. It's some of his best work, her eyes jumping off the page with unmistakably Sadie-ish mischief, hair curling down her shoulders the way it does. This is really good work. But she could easily have come up here herself and found this, and wondered why he'd drawn this with such care and feeling.

Ah well. Not my business.

Em's just putting her jacket on when I head back down the

spiral staircase, and she gives me a smile that sends the blood rushing straight downwards.

Thank god it's quitting time.

The thought of the night ahead is giving me butterflies, and I take her hand, squeezing it to steady me a little. It's been a couple of months since I've fucked anyone, but it's been years since I made love. Although... now I think about it, it's debatable whether I ever truly have. I've never felt this strongly about anyone before in my life. She squeezes my hand back, and something settles within me. I know it's all going to be fine.

Better than fine.

The two of us start to head out, and this time I'm going to leave Leo to lock up. If he sets the alarm wrong, he's going to have to deal with it himself, I don't give a shit.

"Don't forget to come up for air once or twice," Sadie stage whispers to Emily, making her giggle and blush. I grin and flip her off, and then, by some unspoken agreement, Em and I walk off in the direction of her place rather than mine. Dean's been fine the past few nights, so hopefully that'll hold true for tonight, but he knows he can message me if it gets too much. Dean in crisis is maybe the only thing that'd tear me out of Em's bed.

I find myself walking quickly. She's having to jog to keep up, and she laughs. "In a hurry?"

"Baby, you have no god damn idea," I reply, and spontaneously sweep her into a fireman's lift, making her yelp, not caring if I'm making a scene. We're about halfway through the short walk to her home, and the sooner we get there, the sooner I can pull all her clothes off and slide into her.

The thought of such a deliciously tight, soaking wet welcome as the one I know is waiting for me makes me growl a little and pick up my pace even faster, ignoring her protestations that she's too heavy for me to carry (she isn't) and that people are staring (let them).

I only put her down when we reach her door, and I'm kind of gratified to see that her hands are shaking as she inserts the key into her lock. Even that action is filled with eroticism, and I honestly don't know how I've made it through today without grabbing her, pulling her close, and doing what I'm about to do.

We get inside and I pull her to me immediately, pressing her against her hallway wall and kicking the front door shut behind me. My mouth is irresistibly drawn to hers, and I cannot, for the life of me, *cannot* stop kissing her. Her mouth slides against mine, and I manage to capture a few of the soft little noises she makes between my lips. I'll keep them forever, somewhere inside me, like memories.

The present moment is a flurry of hands, pulling each other's clothes off, and it's blurry and breathless and exciting. More exciting than with anyone else I can remember. The anticipation was hot and pleasurable then, sure, but there wasn't this fever of need that I feel for my Emily. I need her skin on mine, everywhere. Need it. Now.

I become dimly aware, as we stumble across the hallway, that she's pulling my boxers down, and I need to step out of them, my pants, and my boots. I refuse to let go of her to do so, so I toe out of the boots and step carefully out of everything all at once. I'm naked.

I want her to be, too.

Once I remove her jeans, she will be. She's not wearing panties, after all…

Heart pounding, pounding, pounding, hard enough to make my temples throb, I waste no time and slip my fingertips under the waistband at her hips, easing them gently but swiftly down. I can feel the warmth of her skin almost humming against mine, and it's magic, an electric feeling that says one thing to me:

More.

I lift her so that my hands cup her ass and her legs wrap around me. Her tongue in my mouth tastes sweet and fresh. She's so warm, and her skin and hair are both so soft and smell sugary and delicious. We're up against a closed door. In the flurry of gasps and clutches and gentle bites, almost without us realizing it, our bodies take over and my cock is at her silky wet entrance, and though I don't even intend to do it, I'm nudging inside her already…

"*Fuuuuck,*" I breathe, squeezing my eyes shut helplessly at the gorgeous, tingling feeling, the warmth spreading through me, the soft moan she gives as one inch, then two, penetrates her. I pull back, but my body is demanding to get back inside her. I shake my head resolutely. "No, not against the door…not our first time…" I'm kinda dizzy with need, and she gives the most adorable little soft whine of protest.

"Please," she begs, biting my lower lip persuasively.

"No. Bed." Words are failing me, but touch…touch is good.

She reaches behind her, searching blindly for the door handle, and eventually fumbles it open.

Purple walls. The bed is made, and the sheets are white with pink flowers. A mirror on the far wall. I can only pick up the vaguest details as I carry her to the bed and set her down, turning her to face away from me. She's on her knees, looking over her shoulder at me in curiosity.

It makes the blood slam through my cock, still damp at the tip with her slickness from before, and I pull her back towards me, her back to my chest, and I can finally, *finally* touch this woman the way I've wanted to since the moment I laid eyes on her, and I can't decide what I want to do first.

So I do it all.

Kisses down her neck and along her shoulder. One hand massaging her breasts, fingers plucking lightly at her nipples until I figure out which way makes her breath catch. The other hand smoothing down her stomach, to her hips, down the inside of her thigh…back up…she's holding her breath. I think I am too as my fingers find my own personal paradise between her legs, smoothing her wetness everywhere until it's covered her clit. I gently but firmly massage it until she's trembling in my arms.

"Oh my god," she mumbles in a high voice that sounds like it's being torn from her.

"Good?" I ask breathlessly in her ear. Now is all that exists. My racing pulse is throbbing in my fingertips.

"Uh-huh," she manages, squirming against me, and I can't take it anymore. My dick is painful with need, and again it finds her pussy of its own volition, and once again I'm pressing inside her. It's like a magnet that keeps drawing me back, deeper this time. I just can't not anymore.

We both groan with a mixture of relief and a desperate need for more as I slide slowly, slowly all the way in. "You feel so fuckin' good," I whisper truthfully in her ear, and she shivers lightly. It'd be easy to just give in to the glorious push and pull, the hot, wet, tight feeling clamping and squeezing around me, but I need her to enjoy this as much as I am. I need it more than I thought possible, more than I want my own climax, which my whole body is yelling and raging for. So I keep rubbing her clit, battling for enough focus to try new motions, new speeds, new pressure.

Firm, steady circles seem to win the day, and the noises she's making are the sexiest I've ever heard. Her breath comes faster, and little grunts and cries build until she's squirming against me, and I feel the first flutters of her walls clenching around me, and…and…

I grit my teeth hard and hold on for everything I'm worth as she breaks and gushes and shudders, crying out in a way that gets me right in the feels, pride flowing through my veins. But god, it's almost too much, and I growl a little as I withdraw, holding her up as she collapses against me, fighting off coming myself. *Not yet.*

Not. Yet.

Emily

Well, that's a first.

Two firsts, in fact.

One: I've never had a first screw that didn't start off in missionary. I love love LOVE missionary, don't get me wrong (and anyone who says it's boring simply isn't doing it right, end of, don't even @ me), but this was hotter than anything ever in my life, OH MY GOD...

And two: confession time. I've never once come while anyone has been inside me before. I can't come from penetration alone, I need some clit lovin'. And he just gave me the best of both worlds.

I can't believe how amazing that was.

It makes me want to pounce on him and bite and lick and ride him until he explodes.

And what's stopping me from doing exactly that?

As I float back down to earth, I turn and meet his blazing gaze. He's sweating a little, vibrating as he brings himself back under control. My smile makes his eyes light up, and I reach to undo the messed up man bun just about holding his hair in check.

I tug, and all that gorgeous dark hair spills down. He smiles back at me, leaning forward for a kiss.

I kiss him back. Once. Twice...

And then pull him towards me so I can push him back on the bed.

He lets out the sexiest throaty chuckle, and, without thinking about it any further, I straddle his body and reach under me to take his erection in my hand. He's just such an ideal size, and his girth makes me want to crow with filthy joy. He gasps a little, and his head lolls back onto the bed. Oops. He's kind of half on and half off the pillow, so I put my hand under his neck and lift slightly. Amused, he leans up and allows me to place the pillow under his head, his eyes softening.

"Thank you," he says in that Cajun rumble that got me into this bed with him, and leans up to kiss me again. I will never get bored with these kisses. Or with the gorgeous body art under my fingertips. One day I will trace every line of his Samoan tribal tattoo with my tongue. One day I will kiss every inch of the lifelike skull on his tight abs. But not now. I can't wait any longer to have him back inside me again. So those pleasures will have to wait for another time.

Without further ado, I place his pulsing cock at my entrance, and slide down in one smooth motion, all the way to his root.

And that's when it hits me.

I haven't done this position in years. I always used to enjoy it, but Gav never liked it (which, of course, was my fault), so we never did it with me on top ever.

But now I want to. Because it feels right. And so *good*...

I watch his face carefully as I undulate my hips, sliding up and down, and the best phrase I can think of to describe the look on it is 'blissed out'. He groans. He pants. He groans some more. He clutches at me. He even smiles, his eyes sleepy as he looks up at me, thrusting upwards to match my rhythm.

God, this really does feel good.

And finally, the demons are gone. I'm not magically cured—even Eli's magnificent dick can't wipe away the scars from all those years—but I'm done making comparisons between him and my ex. Because it just doesn't compare. Gav's shitty opinions don't matter to me anymore.

What I felt with Gav isn't in the same league as what I feel for Eli. Not even close.

And I know now that it's time to let the memories of all the emotional abuse go. *That's enough, now.*

I say a little goodbye to the sad, grey, nervous person I was, and ride my love until he's groaning with pent-up, unrestrained desire. He pulls me down so we are nose to nose, raking his hands through my hair, and tugging it in a way that turns me on more than I can express with words.

With my body, however, I can, and I frantically grind into him, but I can't quite get the pressure and motion right enough to trigger the second orgasm I'm craving.

He notices, and then rolls me over onto my back. Both my wrists are manacled above my head in one of his hands—hot—and with the other, he plays with my clit again as he drives into me, too shrewd by half. He's paid attention and learned me already. He knows what I need without having to be told. And I think that's what makes me holler a little when his fingers do everything right and push me over the edge into bliss again, because this is fantastic and he's wonderful and I'm so very, very lucky...

"God...*chere*," he grinds out, his movements becoming jerky, a shudder running through him. I love that he roars hoarsely when he comes. I love that he rests his head in the crook of my neck as he lets go, letting me hold him together as he shatters. I love that I can feel the hot flood of his semen inside me.

I love him. And I'm not afraid to say it.

"I love you," I murmur unabashedly as our heart rates slow their juddering paces. I can feel his beats and mine clashing, out of perfect sync but still together, and it feels like the best kind of chaos.

I feel his smile against my neck as he raises his head, his hair falling down to shield both of us from the world. It's just him and me.

"I love you, too, *chere*," he replies without hesitation, and I believe him. "So much."

Eli

I've never basked in the afterglow like this before.

My fingers trace up and down her spine as I roll her on top of me, her head resting in the crook of my shoulder. She traces patterns on my chest with her fingertip, and her hair tickles my skin as she lifts her head to look at me.

"I wish I could visit Past Emily," she says softly. "Tell her about you." Her eyes are sleepy, but filled with happiness, and I take a mental snapshot so I can sketch them out later for a tattoo. I'll get Leo to do it, maybe over my heart.

I smile. "What would you tell her?" I'm curious.

She thinks for a moment, leaning her chin on my chest. "That it's all worth it," she decides finally. "All of it. Every single one of the days I spent with Gav, the tears, the bullying, the gaslighting...every moment. Because it meant that I left at the exact right point to move here, find this job, and be led straight to you. And knowing what I now know—that the best guy in the world was waiting for me at the end of it—I'd do it all again. It would have just made things easier to know about you in advance," she chuckles. "It would've given me something to hold on to."

Wow.

I can't speak. Emotions I don't think I've ever felt are clogging my throat, so I brush her hair back behind her ear, openly gazing at her. My girl. My happily ever after, I just know it.

I gently pull her face towards me and kiss her, rolling her back underneath me where I can keep her safe, always, cherished the way she deserves to be.

I have the sense of home, the way I haven't felt since I left New Orleans behind. That city has personality and verve and color like a living, breathing entity, and I thought I'd never have that warm feeling of home here, ever, but I was wrong. It *is* here, in her arms.

We're both home now.

chapter TWENTY-FIVE

Leo

THANK THE GREAT GOOD LORD, THEY'VE FINALLY BONED.

It's plain to see. Their smiles have an added intimacy in them. When their eyes meet, there's that special kind of *knowing* in their gaze, the sort that says, "I've seen you bare-arse naked and I'm thinking about it right now and RAWRRR". And, of course, the fact that they can't keep their hands off each other for longer than a few minutes is a massive indication, too. Snogging and excessive cuddling at the front desk, tut tut.

Couldn't be happier for them.

I whip out my phone and head to the EmEli WhatsApp group chat. If nothing else, this gives me a reason to message Sadie under the guise of gossiping so I can check up on her. She called in sick with a menstrual migraine this morning, but hopefully her meds have kicked in enough so I can cheer her up with a message.

I hate when she's ill, for a whole parade of reasons, but mostly because I'm not 100% sure she's being taken care of, and I want to be able to do that myself. You'd better believe I'd do a bloody *great* job.

From the EmEli WhatsApp group (members: Sadie Stewart, Leo Mills, Dean Gastright)

Leo Mills: Liftoff

Leo Mills: [GIF of a phallic looking rocket taking off]

Leo Mills: EmEli have ridden the bone pony together into the sunset

Leo Mills: PDAs all the way and it's frickin' adorable

Dean Gastright: Yep. Surgically attached.

Leo Mills: Twenty bucks says they'll be engaged by New Year's Day

Dean Gastright: LOL that's months away. Not sure he'll be able to hold that back for that long.

Leo Mills: Lol fair

Sadie Stewart: Sounds cute :) I'll take that bet, I don't think he'll last until Christmas

Leo Mills: Hey, princess, how are you feeling?

Sadie Stewart: Meh :(but at least I can see again :) hate when the aura kicks in

Dean Gastright: Hugs. Hope you feel better soon

Leo Mills: Poor sausage. Do you have everything you need?

Sadie Stewart: Well, I just took my last two painkillers, so it's eased a lot. If this bastard migraine comes back when they run out I'm screwed lol

Leo Mills: Fuck that, I'll go out and get them for you. Can pop by with them in a few.

Sadie Stewart: Aww, thanks, but that's OK, I'll ask Peter to pick them up in his lunch break :) he'll drop them round

Leo Mills: If you're sure. The offer's there x

Sadie Stewart: Thanks, boss :)

If that dickhole douchecanoe sonofabitch doesn't at the *very fucking least* bring her that medicine, I am going to whup his ass into next year and smile as he cries for his mama.

Emily

Having my man wrapped around me whenever he's not busy with a client is giving me borderline illegal levels of happiness. Seriously, if Eli's not occupied he's got his arms around me, his lips on my hair, my neck, my face. I've never been given this much affection, and I am revelling in it. I think anyone in my shoes would.

Plus, I keep having the most delicious shag flashbacks. The memory of his skin sliding against mine, a soft grunt of pleasure he made, a gentle bite on my neck, his hair tickling my chest.... These thoughts keep coming back, and I'm amazed I can focus on anything else for longer than a few seconds.

There was a really sweet moment after lunch when I was watching Eli walk back to his studio with his latest client, admiring my boyfriend's butt (again) far less subtly than I thought, and I looked back to see Leo watching me with a goofy, amused grin on his face. I giggled like a total schoolgirl, and he gave me a big, growly bear hug with both arms around my shoulders, swaying me from side to side.

"Happy for you," he mumbled to me, before his phone buzzed. He took it out and read a message which made him frown, clench his jaw, and look like he wanted to murderize something. "That jackoff piece of shit," he muttered darkly, before reaching in his jeans pocket for his keys. "I'll be back in a few. Sadie needs some painkillers." And just like that, he was out the door. Sadie's off work with a migraine today. Guess she messaged him? And he dropped everything and came running because she needed him. I sigh. I wish Leo could be as happy as me and Eli.

It's gearing up to be a very quiet afternoon for me. Eli's halfway through his latest appointment. Dean's probably around twenty minutes away from finishing his. The phone is quiet. We're plenty stocked up on supplies. Not much for me to do but wait.

I check out my social media, because Leo won't mind, especially since I'm going to check the parlour's accounts, too.

Cool. We have a couple of new tags from happy customers on Instagram, and a few messages. I giggle as I read some rather amorous PMs from some women about the three boys, offering all sorts of, ah, treats to them. It's all, *Dean, you are so lush, text me,* and *Leo, get me pregnant,* and *Eli, you can have me any time you want me, just PM me where and when…* Sorry, NakedYoga985, he's taken.

There's one from a woman from my home county asking about parking near the parlour, as she's booked an appointment with us while she's on holiday in Foxton next week. Small world. I send her some information about the nearest parking options, and head back to checking notifications.

Oh, joy. Some bitter comments from MelRoseDarkLight:

Don't believe the hype, shitty service, RUDE staff, overpriced, don't waste your time…

They photoshop their tattoos to make them look better, mine looked nowhere near as good…

Rude as shit, all of them—don't know the meaning of good customer service. Avoid.

Wow, I wonder who that could be.

I roll my eyes and block Melissa from all of the accounts and delete her comments. Bye, honey.

The phone rings. "Wishbone Tattoos, how can I help you?" The line is silent for a couple of seconds, and then the caller hangs up. That's happened a couple of times today. My guess is, someone is trying to pluck up the nerve to book an appointment, but their courage keeps failing them. I smile to myself. They'll get there. If I could do it, they can.

Facebook has a couple of queries and requests for contact, and by the time I've finished up with them, Dean is just seeing his client out.

"Show me," I ask, always enthusiastic to see new ink. The client, a huge guy in a Budweiser t-shirt, shows me his clingfilm covered forearm, and I can make out the words *Si vis pacem, para bellum* in flawless black typewriter script. "Lovely, are you pleased?" I ask him.

"Yeah, very. This is my birthday present from my son. I can't wait for him to see it." He fistbumps Dean. "Mate, you are a legend, as ever."

Dean returns the fist bump, waving his other hand modestly with a 'no big deal' look on his face.

As the client leaves, promising to be in touch, Leo comes back, looking better than when he left. Dean smiles, leaning on the counter next to me. He's giving Leo a knowing look, for some reason.

"All OK?" I ask.

"Yeah, just needed to—"

A car outside slows down outside the parlour, stuck in traffic. Its windows are rolled right down, and *The Power of Love* by Huey Lewis and the News is playing at top volume. It's just getting to the chorus, and by the time the traffic clears enough for it to move on, the chorus is over. I smile, because I like the song, and because it makes me think of Doc Brown and his crazy hair. I used to love *Back to the Future.*

Leo's face is not smiling. It's full of horror and concern. "Dean," he says urgently. He holds his hands up, as though trying to calm someone down. "Dean, look at me. Look at me. It's OK," he says quietly, a desperate edge to his voice.

I turn to face Dean, confused, but then I'm shocked by what I see: Dean, white as a sheet, shuddering from head to toe, a glazed, absent look in his eyes. He's totally rigid with terror, his breathing becoming heavy and fast like he's starting to hyperventilate. He backs away on shaking legs, his fists clenching, before he hurls himself towards the nearest window behind him, scrabbling to open it and then trying to punch the window to break it, like he's desperately trying to escape the room, even if it means hurting himself to get out. The window rattles, and then, to my alarm, cracks.

"Dean!" I shout. He's going to hurt himself. I'm panicked, unsure what's going on. I've never seen Dean look so terrified out of his mind. I've never seen *anyone* this scared before.

Leo launches himself at him, restraining his arms as best he can; no mean feat, as Dean seems to be fighting him with the same ferocity he would for his life as he struggles frantically against him. "GET ELI!" Leo shouts at me as he tries to maintain his tackle hold.

I sprint for Eli's studio, only to see him open his door. He must have heard some of the commotion. "It's Dean," I tell him in a shaking voice, "he…he's panicking, I think, I don't know…"

Eli's eyes clear as he obviously realises what's happening. He turns his head back towards his room, where he has a client waiting. "Stay here, I'll be back in a moment," he says to him in a voice that brooks no argument. He rushes past me, and I follow him, my worry supersizing when I see Leo on the floor grappling Dean, his arms and legs wrapped around him from behind to try to stop him from moving. Dean is sweating, clawing at his throat where the scar is, and gasping and choking for air, looking like he's trying to scream. It's one of the most distressing sights I have ever seen in my life.

"Dean," Eli says in a clear, calm, steady voice, "I know you can hear me. It's Eli. You're having a flashback. What you're seeing right now isn't really happening." He kneels about a foot away from him. "I wasn't there that night, was I? And you can hear me. You're safe, *frère*. Leo's got you. I'm here. Emily's here. You're in the parlour, and you're safe. It's not real, what you're seeing right now. It's a memory being replayed, like Gabriel says. I promise you, it's not real. I'm here. We're all here. You made it out. You survived. He's gone." He turns to me. "There's a bottle of perfume in the top left hand drawer in my room, *chere*. Please could you go get it?"

I nod numbly, glad for something to do. The man with the almost finished tattoo asks me what's going on, and I don't know what to tell him, so I just say, "Nothing to worry about, just another staff member needs help with something. Please, stay here until Eli comes back." I hope he listens to me. I know I probably don't sound that reassuring, likely quite the opposite, but I just don't know what else to say.

Sure enough there's a bottle of that perfume where Eli said it would be, around half full. I grab it and bring it back straight away, shaking a little myself as I hand it over.

"They fixed your throat. It's not bleeding. You can breathe. He's not here, he's gone. You're safe, and we love you." His voice is low and soothing, and though it's clear from Dean's eyes that he's not fully in the here and now, and is seeing terrible things that no-one else can see, he's not fighting against Leo so hard anymore. He's listening as best he can.

Eli squirts a few puffs of the scent into the air, near Dean, but not right in his face. "I just sprayed some of your mom's perfume," he says gently. "You'll be able to smell it in a moment." He watches Dean carefully. Dean's face freezes when the scent reaches him…and finally, mercifully, he relaxes. "Let him go," Eli says to Leo, who gently, slowly complies, watching carefully and ready to go again if need be. Leo looks pretty shaken up himself, but his focus is entirely on his cousin as he catches his breath.

My heart is in my throat, but Dean doesn't struggle anymore. He just…breathes, and stares, and stays lying on the ground, slumped and bewildered, trembling in a way that makes me want to cry.

I've never asked anyone for details of what happened to Dean at the Nolan High shooting. Partially because I haven't wanted to hear it. I knew it must be truly terrible. But seeing him having a flashback episode really brings it home. Just watching it was terrifying. Living through it… and then living it again as a waking nightmare… My friend, my Dean, who's always ready with a smile and treats people so kindly and talked me out of my problems, is suffering. He needs us to rally around him. I understand now; he lives with the equivalent of a hand around his throat, and it sometimes squeezes its grip, without warning, and chokes him.

I've seen him pale with tiredness sometimes, so I understood that he was still affected by what happened. And that was bad enough. This, though…this is in another league. And all I can feel for him is admiration. Carrying on with life, knowing this could happen at any moment? That takes strength the likes of which I've never seen. It makes my own issues seem like small fry.

A tear slips down my face, and I discreetly dash it away. He doesn't need to see this.

"I'm going to help you up, OK?" Eli says to Dean. Eli has remained calm and steady throughout. I'm sad for both of them that this is a regular thing. And I feel my heart swell with even more love for my boyfriend. For his gentleness and how solid he is, and how kind. Dean manages to nod, one small, jerky inclination of his chin, and Eli steadies him as they both slowly, carefully stand. Dean has gone a horrible waxy colour, and he's still sweating. "Need to throw up?" Eli asks him. Dean shrugs. "That's OK. We're going to go back to your room, and we're going to watch an episode of *Friends* on your iPad. How about *The One With All the Resolutions*, sound good? And everything's going to calm down for you. OK?"

Dean nods dully, and seems to be absent-mindedly wiping at the front of his shirt. I'm not sure he realises he's doing it, but Eli notices. "It's OK. You've got a change of clothes in your cup-board. Let's go get 'em, yeah?" He turns to Leo but doesn't take his eyes off Dean. "Leo, cover for me with my client?" Leo nods, not as winded as he was, but still on high alert.

Eli's focus is entirely on Dean, who is still holding himself rigidly and fidgeting with his clothes as they slowly make their way back to the studios.

Leo sighs and runs a hand over his face, looking done in. "That motherfucking song," he mutters as he looks up at me.

"Huh?" I'm trembling and can't really think straight, too worried about my friend to understand what Leo is talking about.

He moves towards the counter, stretching his neck slightly and rubbing the scar on his eyebrow. "That car that drove by. Sheer chance, but..." He braces his hands on the counter. "*The Power of Love* was playing when his teacher opened fire at his Prom. Dean's girlfriend was one of the first ones to get shot. Died in his arms right there on the dance floor, and that god damn song just kept playing. That's why he was pulling at his clothes. He thinks her blood is on him again."

Oh my god... I can't bear to think of it. Leo walks round and puts his arms around me, seeking comfort for himself as much as offering it to me. "I know, honey," he says quietly. "It's scary, especially the first time you see it." He stiffens. "Shit, I just got back in time. If you had been alone on reception when that happened...Christ on a cracker."

"Poor guy," I say sadly.

"He'll be OK," he promises me. "Eli knows the drill. There's a tried and true sequence that helps return him back to the here and now. Dean will be fine." Sounds again like he's reassuring himself as much as me. "I'll tape up the window in a moment. Get it replaced this week. Does he have any clients booked for the afternoon?"

I glance at the calendar. "Yes, one at three o'clock."

"Call them and rebook. If they kick up rough, give me a shout." He sighs. "Now you know why we're so careful with the team Spotify account. Some songs just...do that." Looking tired out, he walks back to Eli's studio to take care of the client, who by now must be wondering what the hell is going on.

Taking a deep, steadying breath, without further ado, I pick up the phone and call Dean's last client of the day. They can be annoyed all they like; I'm part of this family now, and I will speak to aggy people if my family needs me to, however uncomfortable it makes me.

chapter TWENTY-SIX

Eli

I'm relieved when Emily agrees that it goes without saying that we're staying at mine tonight. That was the worst episode Dean's had for a while, and, though he was calm enough for the rest of the afternoon, even sketching out some new designs alone in his studio once his hands stopped shaking, he's not OK.

He wants to be left alone when we get back to our apartments, which isn't unusual, but I know he'll feel better knowing that I'm downstairs if it gets too bad. And I reassured him over and over again that Em wouldn't mind if he needed me. I know she won't, at all. I can see she's dying to mother him, but she's also anxious not to make anything worse. She's just watchful and careful and quietly there if he needs anything. My angel.

I follow him up to his flat to make sure he's all set, and to assure him one more time that he can come down if he needs anything at all, but he shakes his head at me. *I'm good. Go have a nice evening with Emily. Seriously.*

He gently shoves me out the door and, with a final tired smile, shuts the door in my face.

Sometimes he just needs to be by himself so he doesn't have to mask for anyone, even me. Tonight is one of those nights.

I head back down to my own apartment, where my wonderful girlfriend waits on my sofa, her face creased with concern. "How's he doing?"

I sigh. I can talk to her about this. "He gets very tired and withdrawn after an episode. He'll be fine." I sit next to her, wanting to shake off the worries and just have a nice evening with her, like Dean suggested. I also kind of want to put my head in her lap and tell her everything. And there is something I need to make clear upfront. "Dean's probably always going to need me, to one extent or another. He's never going to be all the way recovered. It's not that he doesn't try, because he does, he works *so* hard. But he's had a *lot* of therapy, and the trauma is still so deep. Episodes like that are just going to happen now and again, and I need you to know that I'm always going to be there for him, and I mean *always*."

"Of course," she says, like it's completely obvious and natural.

"So, someday, when we have our own house, it's going to need an apartment above the garage for Dean to grow old in." I'm deadly serious.

"Screw that," my girl says, "he lives inside the house with us, if he wants."

And that, folks, illustrates completely why I'm so in love with her.

I lean forward and kiss her gently, grateful that I have her support. Inwardly, I sigh. It's the evening after our first night together. I would love to continue romancing her like she's never been romanced before…but, as gorgeous as she is and as much as I want her, I'm tired and heartsore for my cousin and his neverending struggle. She smooths my hair back and gives me a sympathetic look full of understanding.

"Baby, I would love to be ravishing you on this couch the way you deserve," I say, "but I just..."

"It's OK," she reassures me, "I'm kind of tired, too." She nestles a little closer. "It must take a lot out of you."

I nod slowly. I hate admitting that. "Honestly, yeah. Don't get me wrong, I'm happy to always be there when he needs me, whatever happens. He'd do the same for me. I just hate seeing him suffer. He's more like a brother to me, and I can't stand watching him in so much pain, and knowing there's nothing I can do to stop it."

"You were amazing, though," she comforts me. "You were so rock solid and calm. I really admire that."

I kiss her shoulder. "I've seen him through so many episodes, I just know what to do. But I wish I didn't need to." I feel a little choked up all of a sudden when I remember that night, the call, the race to the airport to get home. My cousin, my best friend in the whole world, covered in tubes and wires. Holding his hand. Watching him go to pieces when he finally woke up and remembered what had happened.

A small part of me has never fully recovered from seeing him lose it when we told him about Callie...and his voice...

...And Mrs Oberman.

My own mind immediately backs off from that name.

Emily wraps her arms around me, sensing that I need it. I stay like that, just enjoying having someone to comfort me for a change. I don't begrudge Dean a thing, but having someone to talk to about this stuff is a relief beyond words.

"Leo told me a little about it," she says quietly. "About why that song triggers him like that."

"Song?"

"*The Power of Love*," she says very quietly, as though Dean might be able to hear through the floor.

"Oh, was that what kicked it off?"

"Yeah, there was a car that drove by with their sound system on top volume."

"Yeah, that'd do it," I sigh. Having her close to me like this makes talking about it a little easier, and if we're going to be together for the rest of our lives, she needs to know this stuff.

"Shouldn't he…I mean, I'm sure he has a therapist, or…?"

I run my hand over my face. "Yeah, he does, but he won't go unless he's really desperate. He's told me he's sick to death of it, and I try to persuade him, but…" I shrug. "His therapist is good, but to Dean, it's just the same old same old, over and over again, and he hates it, so he'll only go very reluctantly, and not regularly." She squeezes my hand sympathetically. "I've never stopped feeling guilty," I admit finally. I've never said that out loud before.

She pulls back, a frown of confusion on the face I love so much. "Why?"

"I should have been there." She starts to speak, but then stops herself, seeming to understand that I need this, that I have to let it out at last. "He was always my best friend, from my earliest memory. I'm a year older, and when I moved up to high school, I spent my freshman year just waiting for him to move up too. I had friends, sure, but it wasn't until Dean arrived at the beginning of my sophomore year that I felt good about high school. He was always so alive and full of fun, never moody, never an angry word for anyone. Everyone liked him, and for good reason. And he and Callie, his girlfriend, were voted Cutest Couple. They were very happy together. I mean, who knows if they would have lasted beyond high school, but… they were really happy." I pause as I remember Callie, the sweet, beautiful, cheerful doe eyed girl who got snatched from us by one man's insane cruelty.

"And when I graduated and went to college, I missed him." I let out a shaky breath that I may have been holding for the past fifteen years, until now. Until I felt safe enough to let it go, with her. "I know I'd have had no business being at his senior prom, but I nearly went home early for it, just to take the pictures if nothin' else. And then I got caught up in an art project for my course, and so I just didn't. No real reason. But I can't get past the feeling that if I'd been there, I'd have been able to protect him, you know? And it's not like I even had a ticket to his prom. I wouldn't have been actually *there*, at the shooting. I'm just being ridiculous, but the guilt still eats away at me."

There is a world of sympathy in her eyes. "I understand. But you couldn't have. There was no way of knowing. And if you'd been there, you might have been killed yourself."

"I know. But if I could have taken the bullet, even if I'd died, maybe I could have kept him safe, and he wouldn't be in the situation he's in now..." I shrug.

She looks horrified. "I'm so glad you weren't there." She squeezes both my hands. "Never wish that on yourself. And besides, if you'd died saving him...that would have destroyed him, too."

I take a shaky breath. "Or maybe..." Can I even say this? "Maybe I could have led him to a different room, and he wouldn't feel like he had anything to feel guilty for."

"What room?"

I look and look at her, and I know she will never see Dean the same way again when I tell her this, but I need to. I never told Charmaine, never trusted her with this knowledge, which should have said something to me. But I know I can trust Em with it. I find myself opening my mouth and telling her everything. The worst part of it all. The real reason why Dean will never, ever allow himself to get over the shooting, or forgive himself for surviving it. I watch her face change from shock and horror, to deep, aching sorrow, and understanding.

And we quietly cry for him together.

Emily

Neither of us felt much like cooking after that, so we ordered a pizza. We have the same favourite toppings, which is handy. I also insisted we ordered some for Dean too, to make sure he had something for dinner, so I texted him and said it was on its way so he wouldn't get startled by a random knock at the door from the delivery driver. We ordered what Eli said was his usual. Even if he leaves it to get cold outside his door, I wanted to make the gesture. I need to do something to care for him tonight, even though he wants to be alone.

I am absolutely dying to go upstairs and wrap my arms around him, now I know more about what happened. I had no idea of the weight of everything he carries. It wasn't his fault. He was a kid. A frightened kid trying to survive a *mass shooting*. It wasn't his fault at all.

Eli and I have a quiet evening, just the two of us. We have the TV on, but don't really watch it. I think my love needs some quiet comfort tonight, so that's what I give him. I may be sat between his legs, being cuddled, but I'm holding his arms tightly in return, tracing my fingers along the tattoos on his skin, resting my head on his chest, kissing his fingertips now and again. That sort of thing. Simply loving on him, letting him know that I'm here, and he doesn't have to be strong for everyone all on his own anymore.

He cried in front of me.

I love that he let me in and showed me that side of himself. Love that he wasn't ashamed to wear his heart on his sleeve in front of me. He's intimidating to look at—tall, built, and gruff on the outside—but my big guy has an even bigger heart, always giving, always looking out for other people first and foremost, even though he has his own wounds. I'll never let anything hurt him.

I get the impression that not much is going to happen tonight. It's been a rough day, and, while I won't lie and say I'm not a little bit disappointed, a part of me also really loves that sex is not a compulsory part of every day anymore. If either of us don't feel like it, that's totally cool, and not a punishment or a comment on our feelings. It's too easy for sex to become a chore when it's treated like an obligation. I can't wait to jump his bones again, but just snuggling up on the sofa for a quiet evening in is also beautiful in its own way.

Once again, we end up falling asleep where we sit, wrapped up in each other.

He wakes me very gently a couple of hours later. The only light is from the Netflix screensaver on the TV. I feel his hand gently stroking my rib cage and my stomach, easing me slowly into wakefulness. He kisses my hair, and one thumb moves along my face.

I lift my head and our eyes meet, mere inches apart. He gives me a long, intent look, and seems to find whatever he was looking for, whatever consent he needed, because without further ado he gathers me in his arms, lifting me as he stands in one fluid motion. I'm wrapped around him, hanging on tight, and he carries me to his bedroom.

He kisses me the entire way there, not removing his lips from mine for a second, even to open the door. Though I cling to him, it's not in fear of falling. There's no chance of that. He'd never allow me to drop. I'm safe in his arms, so I can just enjoy the ride.

He doesn't rush. I am set down gently onto the edge of his bed, and he removes my clothes one by one. Once I am naked, bathed in the moonlight pouring in through the window, he gives me a thoughtful, almost dreamy smile. I reach for him to return the favour, but he catches one of my hands and gently bites my fingers, his smile taking on a smouldering quality that makes my pulse leap and my pussy warm with anticipation. He undresses himself quickly and efficiently, and then gathers me in his arms, skin on skin, shifting us until my head is on his pillow.

I tug on his hair tie, and once again I relish the feeling of his long, thick dark hair curtaining us, tickling my breasts as he kisses down my neck, along my collar bone, and back up to the spot just under my ear that makes me tremble. I understand why he ties back his thick, dark mane during the day, but I will always pull it loose in our bed. I want it free and untamed. I want to be able to run my fingers through it, clutch it, and smooth it back.

I sigh with contented pleasure as his mouth travels further down to my breast, and almost whimper as the tip of his tongue teases my nipple. My hands run restlessly over his back, and I marvel at how warm, how satiny smooth his skin is. There's a very subtle change to the feeling of his skin where he is marked with ink, almost too easy to miss, but it's there: a certain texture, almost like wood grain. I can feel his hardness against my thigh, and my breath comes faster as I anticipate him nudging into me. I want it now. But I also want him to take his time kissing every inch of me, because he's making my skin feel vibrantly alive.

His hands travel down my ribs, my stomach, my hips, and his touch is almost reverent. I swear I can feel the love in his caresses. Finally, at the age of almost 30, I understand why this act is described as an act of love. His affection dances along my body wherever he kisses and touches, wherever he licks and softly bites, and I tremble with the intimacy of it. My whole body jolts at the feeling of his fingers playing in my wetness, that most delicious feeling that makes my blood burn in my veins. This seems to trigger something within him, because he shifts back up to my face and I am kissed, long and slow and hard. I open my legs to cradle him with my body; the motion notches his cock at my opening. We both gasp at the feeling, and I can feel him pulse and throb at my folds. He wants me badly, I know it.

With one hand he cups my face, looking down at me like I'm precious to him, like I'm everything he's ever wanted or looked for in another human being. The eye contact between us is scorching straight through me, leaving nowhere to hide. He sees *me*, and what he sees, he unabashedly loves.

I don't want to hide from us. Not anymore. I want him to look his fill, because he's melting my heart.

With his other hand, he grips himself and lines up, pushing into me one slow inch at a time. It feels like heaven. Like I'm being savoured. Like he's taking the time to relish every unhurried thrust. I lock my legs around his waist, and cannot resist kissing him, scraping my teeth gently down his jaw, like at the club. This time, though, I'm doing this because he's *mine*. I can feel his pulse skip in his throat as he chuckles. He's loving it.

The hot glide of his full length, in and out of me, over and over, slow and methodical, sends me wild. I claw at his back, torn between begging him to speed up and just ram us both to the edge, and wanting him to spend forever doing exactly what he's doing because it's making me throb. My limbs tingle, up and down, and my core is on fire. I cannot stop my quiet cries of pleasure any more than I could stop breathing in and out. One of his hands comes up to mine, lacing our fingers together and squeezing. In reassurance? In dominance? Affection? Comfort? Probably all of the above. And, because he knows me so well already, his other hand reaches down to give my clit the stimulation it needs as he flexes his hips above me.

All possibility of me being silent is gone. The mix of his deft, sure fingers confidently stroking the *exact right place, holy god*, and his perfect thrusting has me gasping, rigid, then moaning as the most all-consuming orgasm I have ever felt rages through my entire body, leaving me weak and dizzy and entirely euphoric. I can feel my walls rhythmically clutching at him, for real, no pretence necessary or even occurring to me, and he lets out a soft moan of his own as he loses control and empties everything he feels deep inside me, coming so hard I can feel him pump and pound with it.

He kisses my lips, my cheekbones, even my eyelids, like he doesn't want to leave an inch of my face unloved as he carefully withdraws. We both shift to lie on our sides, simply looking at each other. The feelings coursing through us both are beyond any words that exist. His hand smooths my hair in that way he has that I'm coming to adore, in a way that I could enjoy each day for the rest of my life. I kiss his lower lip, enjoying its softness.

"Mo laime toi," he whispers.

"Hmm?"

I feel his breath on my cheek as he exhales a soft chuckle. "Means I love you. Louisiana Creole."

I smile sleepily. "I ashaya du," I murmur back.

He thinks for a moment. "I give in. What language is that?"

"Vulcan," I say, snuggling closer, and the last thing I remember before I fall asleep is his mellow laughter.

chapter
TWENTY SEVEN

From the Gaming Night WhatsApp group (Members: Eli Gastright, Dean Gastright, Sadie Stewart, Leo Mills)

Eli Gastright: Everyone still on for tonight?

Sadie Stewart: You bet

Dean Gastright: Yup

Leo Mills: [GIF of Oprah Winfrey cheering]

Leo Mills: Been practicing my Star Wars observations to impress her with my nerdery

Eli Gastright: Awesome

Sadie Stewart: So she doesn't know?

Eli Gastright: No. I still want it to be a surprise so don't let on during the day

Dean Gastright: I promise I won't say a word.

Dean Gastright: [Wink emoji]

Leo Mills: Dude [Laughing emoji]

Eli Gastright: LOL

Sadie Stewart OMFG [Three laughing emojis]

Eli

Nobody let on all day.

We agreed they'd all come over at 7pm together, as that gives people a chance to shower and change. I'm making Aunt Wendy's famous chili, and managed to explain away the larger amount I'm making with a single word: 'leftovers'.

I don't think she suspects a thing.

She's standing behind me with her arms around my waist, resting her face against my back. So cute. I turn my head. "Wanna try some?"

"Mmm," she assents, and I ladle up a small amount, turning to feed it to her. She blows on it delicately, and how is even *this* turning me on? The chili gets her seal of approval; she moans, "God, that's good," and if I didn't know the crew were just about to arrive, I'd text them to cancel, strip her naked, and just ravish her next to the hob.

"I'll tell Aunt Wendy you approve next time she calls."

She grins. "Promise I can listen in?"

"You just want to hear me do the accent," I tease.

"Duh," she giggles. "It's hot."

I sigh, pretending to be long-suffering and tolerant. "Well, you know what they say..." I lean forward so I'm a breath away from her lips. "We gon' pass a good time bein' *beaucoup crasseux, chere,*" I murmur softly, and she shivers in the most gratifying way. I love making her squirmy like this. Horny Em is one of my favourite Ems.

With perfect timing, just as I'm about to kiss her giggles away, my buzzer goes. "Would you mind getting that for me?" I ask.

She frowns, puzzled. "Sure. You expecting anyone?" I shrug. She wanders away to answer the door, and I bite on a smile. I really hope this works out as well as I think it might.

I hear Leo and Sadie chorus in an enthusiastic exclamation of "HEYYYY!" and I smile wider, joining everyone in the hall.

Em looks stunned. Our three guests have arrived, and have congregated just inside the door. Leo is wearing his long black leather coat, and I know immediately he's planned something like the over the top jackass he is. Him winking at me just confirms it. I love that crazy bastard.

"What's this?" Em asks, looking at us all in turn. I hug her from behind, resting my chin on her shoulder.

"It's gaming night," Leo says, like it happens all the time and she just forgot.

She looks adorably confused.

"I mean," Sadie says with a breezy shrug, "your boy there bought you some awesome games. Be a shame to let them gather dust, right?" She beams as Em's eyes light up with realization.

"Plus," Leo adds, "I hear you've very kindly offered to run us all a Dungeons and Dragons campaign. Curse of Strahd, right? With the vampire dude?" Awesome. He got the name right. Em nods, still astonished, but starting to look real happy. *Perfect.* That's the reaction I wanted. "Great," Leo continues, shrugging off his coat to reveal a medieval style shirt and fucking *leather armor* underneath. He's even got a rubber sword in a scabbard, and twirls a wooden looking stake in his hand that looks like it's made out of the same sort of stuff. "It's cool, I've seen Buffy sooooooo many times. I've got this."

"You DICK," Sadie hoots, undoing her jacket to reveal a blue Dungeons and Dragons t-shirt underneath, "I thought I was such hot shit with this t-shirt! Stole my thunder..." But she's only play-grumbling, her smile still spread across her face. She shrugs at Emily. "I made the effort, babe, but this..." she nods towards Leo. "Just can't compete."

Dean grins at them both looking much brighter than he did a few days ago. It's been a week since his episode, and he seems mostly back to normal. I've sat up with him a few nights, off and on, but it's been worse in the past. I've been trying to get him to contact his therapist again, but he insists he's fine, and I can't force him.

Em is still ecstatic. "Awwww, you guys," she says, smiling ear to ear, and Sadie gives her a big hug.

"Thank Eli," Sadie replies, "this was his idea."

"But you all agreed to come," Em points out, and hugs Leo and Dean as well, before giving me a smooch on the lips I won't soon forget.

"Ah-ah-ah," Leo scolds, "no wenching until we've left. Now, where is the vampire's dungeon and/or dragon? And also, is that Aunt Wendy's chili I smell there, bruh? Because if so, it should already be inside me." Sadie snorts with laughter, and it makes him grin. "Yeah, I heard it as soon as I said it, pervo. And I'm gonna slut it up for that chili. It can have me *any way it wants*."

Emily

"Guys, I've got this," Leo crows, holding one arm up in triumph. He's playing the deck for Ra the Sun God, and I can definitely see that. "I'm gonna play Fire Blast, which does *five* damage, and *then* I'm gonna use the Staff of Ra to boost it by one, *and* I'll top that up with the Solar Flare card which increases the damage done by *two*, and *that* means I've dealt the eight damage needed to reduce Baron Blade to zero, and you can all *suck it*!" He stands and throws his cards down with a flourish, holding both fists in the air like an undisputed champion.

"Leo," Sadie says, pinching the bridge of her nose, "for the final time, this is a *collaborative game*. We *all* win." But there's an amused smile playing at the corners of her mouth, in spite of her best efforts to smother it.

She loses it entirely when Leo starts to sing *You're Welcome* from the *Moana* soundtrack, doing a creditable impression of The Rock.

Kill stealing bastard, Dean says as he carefully gathers up his deck, and I am delighted that I am able to pick a good 80% of his signs up now. I've worked so hard, and I'm still learning every day. Eli's been helping with that, too. *I had him on my next turn, I swear to god.*

"That was fun," Leo says, sitting back down and grinning at me. I know I must look like a sentimental idiot, smiling at them all so fondly, but I can't help it. Eli had mentioned the possibility of a gaming night when he first gave them to me, but I mentally wrote it off as kind intentions, and told myself not to expect it to actually happen. And yet, here they are, taking an interest in the stuff that means a lot to me, taking part, and having fun with it.

We spent the first part of the evening making their new Dungeons and Dragons character sheets for a campaign of The Curse of Strahd, which is apparently also really going ahead. Dean deciding with a wry grin to name his Wizard 'Teller' just about ended us all, and Leo is still considering calling his Bard 'Penn' in tribute. As an added bonus, having to explain the mechanics to them has refreshed my own memory, and I'm coming up with several ideas for everyone to enjoy. I can hardly wait.

Eli lifts my hand and kisses the backs of my fingers spontaneously, giving me a warm smile. I can't take my eyes off him as I smile back goofily. We have a whole conversation without speaking a word; his eyes look hopeful, asking me if I'm enjoying myself, and whatever response he sees in my own make him beam.

"So, Em," Leo pipes up, taking a swig of his drink and banging the glass back down again, "how hard do you think Obi-Wan Kenobi smacked his head between Revenge of the Sith and A New Hope?"

I blink, and we all stare at him. "Er…go on?" I say with a surprised chuckle. That was unexpected.

"Right, so," he begins, stretching like he's readying himself for a fight, making some of his leather armour creak a little. My phone pings with an email alert, but I'm too intrigued to even glance at it. "Obi-Wan helps to deliver both Luke *and* Leia, right? So why does Leia's existence come as news to him? Cos he's all, "oh, Luke is our last hope," and Yoda says, "nah, bro, there's another," and surely he would know that? He was armpits deep in placenta for them both. He must have had his memories thumped out of his head since that time, so whose wife do you suppose he was boffing to get punched that hard?"

"And," Eli points out, "he didn't even recognise C3PO and R2D2 in New Hope. I mean, they're machines, so they could have had their memories wiped, y'know, maybe for security purposes. But Obi-Wan should have known them both immediately. He spent years with them." He nods at Leo. "You're right, he got amnesia somewhere along the line. It's the only explanation."

They both grin at me as I gape at them, and I burst out laughing. "Or, whoever was in charge of continuity screwed the pooch a few times."

"That, too," Eli agrees.

It's not just Obi-Wan, Dean says. He signs some more, and again, I catch most of it, Eli filling me in on any blanks. *Darth Vader has this weird mental block about Leia. Think about it. He knew Luke immediately. He knew when Obi-Wan was just in the area. But Leia? She's face to face sassing him at the beginning, and nada. Zero recognition.*

I laugh. "Wow, I didn't know you were all such Star Wars aficionados!"

Leo grins. "So…are you impressed? Do we get our official nerd cards in the mail, or…?"

"I think you've earned it," I agree, winking.

"Gotta say, the nerd uniform suits you," Sadie says to Leo with a cheeky smile.

He quirks his scarred eyebrow at her. "Oh, reeeeeeeally? The Lamellar look doin' it for ya, Sades?" I make an approving noise at his correct naming of his gear, and he gives me a smug look. "Oh, that's right. I know my shit."

Sadie smirks. "What can I say, I was always a sucker for the Viking-esque look. I mean, Conan the Barbarian? Birth of my libido." She fans herself comically.

Leo's grin widens. "Tell you what. Halloween this year, I'll dress as a Viking, you dress as a Valkyrie. Or I can be Conan and you can be Red Sonja. Deal?"

She giggles. "Maybe."

Hello.

The eye contact between them is going on just a little too long for it to mean nothing. Sadie looks away first, but her megawatt grin remains. I've been very much enjoying watching her reaction to Leo-with-a-sword. She's been wisecracking with him more than normal all night, leaning her head against his shoulder now and again on the flimsiest pretexts, and I also think she'd be shocked if you pointed it out to her. I still say there's something there on both sides, not just his, and I will die on that hill. I'm just keeping my fingers crossed for them both. They are *so* right for each other that it's agonising to watch.

I'm gonna tap out, Dean says, finishing his drink. He's seemed a lot better tonight, and it was good to see him relax and join in. He's been a little subdued over the past few days, especially around me. I get it. I was the only person in his life who had never seen him have an episode, and now I have. But things will work out, I know it. I've made a point of treating him exactly the same. No coddling, much as I would love to. No well-meaning sympathetic gazes. He's just Dean, and the only thing that has changed is my admiration for him. I'm not making that obvious, either. Just being normal for him. I think he appreciates it. Eli sure does.

"Alright, man," Eli says, "thanks for dropping by."

Dean nods. *See you all tomorrow. Thanks, Em.* He smiles and winks at me.

"Thank *you,*" I reply. "It was great. Thank you *all,*" I say, looking at Leo and Sadie as they say goodnight to Dean.

"I enjoyed that," Sadie says, stretching her neck. "Should probably head out myself."

"I'll give you a lift," Leo says, grabbing his leather coat.

"Ooh, please. Thanks."

"Of course, milady," he replies with a smile and a theatrical bow.

She rolls her eyes and giggles fondly. "Here we go. Sir Leo is now a thing we're all gonna have to deal with."

He shrugs. "What can I say? Sir Leo likes to treat a lady the way she deserves to be treated. Courtesy and common decency all the way." There's an undertone to his voice, and judging by her silence, Sadie has picked up on it, too. After the hugs goodbye and the pleasantries, she gives him a thoughtful look as they make their way to his car.

I shut the door and sigh. "She *needs* to dump Peter and jump on Leo," I whisper to ensure they don't hear.

Eli makes a rumbly noise in agreement. "*Chere,* you are preaching to the converted."

I lean back against the door and look him up and down. *Yum.* "Thank you so much for this evening."

He smiles at me, taking me in his arms. "Anytime. I thought that went real well. Everyone had a good time."

I lift on my tiptoes and kiss him. And not just a peck on the lips, either; I pour all my happiness about the evening into it, plus a healthy dollop of what I'm planning to do to him when we get to bed to say thank you for the surprise.

He growls quietly against my lips and presses me closer to

him. "I'm just gonna put a few things in the sink to soak overnight," he purrs like a panther, "and then I'm taking you to bed and pickin' up a little more of that." I grin and bite his lower lip playfully. "OK, a *lot* more," he chuckles, kissing my forehead and heading back to his kitchen.

Every kiss still gives me that delicious fuzzy feeling in my chest.

I let out a happy sigh, and then decide to make myself useful. I head to the table so I can gather up the glasses and chili bowls. My eyes fall on my phone, so I check my messages, remembering the email alert that pinged earlier.

Holy shit.

The email is from Rich, Gav's brother..

I put the crockery down quickly and sit down in Eli's chair, taking a deep breath and bracing myself. Rich is highly charismatic and was always OK to me, but he wasn't someone to mess about with, and I was afraid of him. He was notorious in the area for his loud parties and for being a bit…unhinged. He used to square up to people at the slightest provocation, and was thrown out of court-mandated anger management classes for being *too* angry. His family always laughed about that, like it was a badge of honour, but I always found that to be really worrying. And he tried to push ecstasy on me that one time at one of his house parties. Thankfully he took my refusal in good part, but I didn't drink anything else for the rest of the night because I didn't trust him not to spike my glass. My heart is thudding with genuine fear. I can't imagine there's a heap of sympathy for me in this unsolicited email.

Oh, look. I'm right.

I have to say it's fucking disgusting that you haven't had the decency to reply to Gav. Get over yourself and at least have basic manners. Always thought there was something off about you. Didn't say anything because you seemed to make Gav happy. Wish I had now, might have saved my little brother a lot of time and heart on someone who clearly wasn't worth it. Running away like that, like he was a thug or something, was pathetic. If things were that bad you could have come to any of us for help. You didn't. So all I can think is that you're just another heartless fucking bitch. Rest assured, we all hate you, and all of us think he's better off without you. You better pray I never see you in the street, cock sucking whore. Don't bother replying, I don't want to hear your lies, and don't you fucking dare come back.

"Is everything OK?" Eli's frowning in the doorway, drying something with a tea towel.

"Um..." I sigh, putting my phone down. "Yeah, I'm fine." I don't sound convincing, even to my own ears. I tell myself not to let it bother me, but that much venom out of nowhere, and from someone with such a volatile reputation, is jarring. Especially when the hate is so unfair. Eli wanders closer, still frowning. "I just got an email from Gav's brother." He freezes. "It's...not very nice." I hand him my phone, and he reads it as I try to calm down. I'm thankful beyond words that Rich doesn't know where I am, otherwise I wouldn't put it past him to come to Foxton and do something like put a brick through my windows out of spite. Gav would love to set his creepy brother on me.

Eli reads silently, and a muscle ticks in his jaw. He knows about the email Gav sent me, but I've never really mentioned Rich, so I tell him everything about him, too, so he can understand why my hands are shaking when he hands my phone back.

"What would you like to do?" he asks softly. "I can take care of this if you want—"

"No," I say straight away, shaking my head. "Don't engage with him. I'm just going to delete and block him. It's just...not a nice thing to receive."

He kneels next to me and places comforting hands on my thighs. "I can imagine." Eli's really mad—I can tell by the way his jaw keeps twitching—but his first concern is me, and whether I'm OK, and what *I* want to do about it.

I squeeze both his hands. "I'm so glad he doesn't know where I am," I mumble. "I just have to hope that it stays that way."

He takes his hands off my thighs and smooths my hair back from my face, cupping my jaw on both sides and tilting my head up to make sure I look him in the eye. "If he does find out where you are," he says quietly, "I'll take care of it." I start to protest, and he shakes his head. "I'm serious. He's not going anywhere near you. I don't care how much of a bully he is. If need be, I know Leo and Dean will get involved, too. And Sadie would rip his balls off. Trust me, you will never have to be afraid of him again." He kisses the top of my head. "Rich might be a big guy, and he might be volatile, but I'm not exactly small," he says, one corner of his mouth pulling upwards wryly, "and if *I* wasn't enough, I have good backup. We can handle him, I promise."

I let out a breath. He's right. Eli is *built,* and with everyone else at Wishbone on my side…maybe I *wouldn't* have anything to worry about. I give him a shaky smile, and his face softens. "Now, about that kiss you gave me in the hallway…" His face takes on a wolfish quality.

I smile, happy to be distracted. "Sure, I'll just put the dishes in the—"

He cuts me off by taking my top off, giving my black lace covered breasts a hungry look and leaning forward to softly bite my collar bone. "In the morning…"

chapter
TWENTY EIGHT

Emily

After saying goodbye to Sadie after our girls only lunch, I find Eli's number and press call.

"*Chere*," I hear after a couple of rings, and I honestly don't think I will ever get sick of hearing him call me that.

I smile. "Hey. I'm just stopping by my flat before I come back. Didn't want you to wonder where I was."

"Everything OK?"

"Yeah, I just want to pick up some painkillers."

"Aww, baby, is your head still bad?" I've had a nagging headache all morning. I'm due to start my period in a couple of days, so I think it's probably that.

"It's not too bad, just want to knock it on the head for the afternoon. Plus, I forgot those cookies I bought for everyone."

He chuckles. "Did you just say cookies?"

I laugh. "So I did. You've been rubbing off on me, Nawlins boy."

"Day and night," he rumbles, sounding like he's grinning. "Hopefully tonight, if you're feeling better..."

"Well, rampant sex is supposed to be a good cure for a headache," I purr.

"Baby, I am at your service," he says instantly, and I laugh loudly, making a passer-by give me a strange look. "Oh, yeah—could you pick up my wallet? I left it on your nightstand," he adds.

"Yeah, sure."

"Thanks, Em. Love you."

"No worries. Love you, too. See you in a bit." I ring off, place the phone in my jacket pocket, and quicken my pace. I have to be back in fewer than ten minutes.

It's a rare lunch hour that I don't spend with Eli, but Sadie wanted some girl talk. Peter has started the tattoo removal process, and he hasn't made any noises about getting engaged after she saw engagement rings in his internet search. Personally, I'm quite relieved for her about that, as I'd like to delay her making that mistake for as long as possible, and hopefully avoid it altogether; however, I can understand her frustration. She just needed to vent. From what she said, she isn't planning on talking to him about it. I think that's a bad sign, if she can't talk to him about things that bother her. But I've long since decided to just stay quiet and be there for her as things crop up. As much as I'd love to save her from a bad situation, like no-one did for me, I also know from experience that you have to *want* to get out of it. It doesn't matter what anyone else says; you can only leave when you're ready, when *you personally* have reached *your* limit.

I unlock my front door and head in, closing it behind me. I bought lots of packets of biscuits from the Pound Shop over the weekend and I keep forgetting to bring them in. We stay at Eli's more than at mine, but last night we ended up here. I grab them, a packet of paracetamol, and Eli's wallet, before heading back out.

When I open my front door, it takes my brain a few seconds to catch up to what I'm seeing. Golden brown hair, slightly longer than the last time I saw him. Hazel eyes, sharp and narrowed. I actually find myself smiling instinctively at Gav, out of habit I suppose, before I come to my senses and realise that he's actually there. Gav. At my front door. And his jaw is tight, his face intense. Why is he here?

I let out a cry as the panic sets in and I try to close the door as fast as I can, but his arm lashes out and bangs the door against the wall. Unfortunately for me, my fingers get trapped between them and bear the full brunt of the slam. There's a sickening cracking sound. Pain shoots up my arm, and I cry out, dropping everything. My bag, the packs of biscuits, everything scatters on the floor, and I back away, bent double as I cradle my fingers. I've never broken a bone before, but this horrible, stomach turning thud of odd pain tells me that's exactly what I've probably done.

"Emmy?" he asks, dashing over to me and trying to lift my hand. I back away frantically to stop him from touching them. I don't want anyone near them; and cradle them against my chest.

"My fingers," I manage to squeak out, "they're broken." *You* broke them, I want to shout at him, but I don't. There's no point. He's not going away, but surely, surely he's going to help me…?

"Ohh, baby," he says contritely, kicking the door shut behind him, "I didn't want to do that. That's not what I intended. I just didn't want you to slam the door in my face." He's a bit too close to me. "Let me have a look…"

"No," I whimper, turning away to shield my hand, "let's just…I need to go to hospital." That's the most important thing right now, more important than anything he might have to say, and even Gav will recognise that. We can talk there, if he really insists, though I wish he wouldn't.

"They might *not* be broken," he says, walking me backwards into the kitchen, still trying to take my hand.

"No, let's just…I have to get this looked at." I'm a little dizzy, which I suppose is hardly surprising. The pain radiating through my hand is nauseating, and the horrid crunching noise I heard as my fingers got trapped between the door and the wall keeps playing through my mind over and over. I feel like I could retch.

And Gav's *here*. That alone is disorienting, and I want him gone. I don't want to listen to whatever it is he's so determined to say that he's come all this way. How *did* he track me down?

I'm backed up against the kitchen counter as Gav looms over me. He's not as tall as Eli, but in my current state he seems huge and intimidating. He's a lot thinner in the face than the last time I saw him, and his skin looks pallid and dry. Unhealthy.

"We need to talk," he insists firmly.

"Gav…not *now*," I wail, gingerly holding up my hand, cradling my wrist. "I need a doctor!"

He makes a frustrated huff. "For fuck's sake, Emmy, I've *found* you, driven *all this way*, and all you care about is your hand! It's just a bruise, I bet you anything. Just more of your drama queen fussing about nothing!"

The penny drops. I could smack my own forehead for being so slow on the uptake, but it's hard to think when your worst nightmare is standing in front of you, lighting a cigarette. And my hand is killing me.

He's obviously not going to help me. It doesn't suit him to do so. He'd rather my fingers weren't broken, so he's decided they aren't, and that I'm making a massive drama just to piss him off.

"Don't smoke in my home," I say quietly, coldly, but it's empty defiance. He ignores me, like I never spoke, and takes a long drag.

"I mean, not even a hello?" he asks with a forlorn smile. "Come on, babe." The smoke makes me cough, and I move away a little, but he follows me, so I don't gain any distance from him. It feels menacing.

I wish Eli was here.

I need Eli now. I need him to come and help me deal with this bastard. I can't sort this out on my own.

I slowly put my uninjured hand in my pocket, hoping like hell that he doesn't do anything to jostle my fingers while they're unprotected.

"You just tried to slam the door in my face," he carries on with jittery, self-righteous anger. "You move without a word, you won't respond to me, you block me on everything…and why? *Why*, Emmy? I never laid a hand on you. I didn't cheat on you."

"Yes you did. I saw the messages," I say, trying to tap my phone buttons in my pocket while he paces in front of me. I don't think he's aware of what I'm doing; he's too consumed with his own indignant ranting. I press what I hope are the right combinations of buttons to redial Eli, and pray like hell that he hears part of the conversation and comes looking for me. They'll be wondering where I am soon, anyway, I soothe myself. I'm supposed to be back at work in five minutes. They'll come looking for me.

Gav gives me an incredulous look. "But I never actually *fucking touched them*," he yells, frustrated, like I'm being unfair, and picks up the nearest item he can grab from my draining board. My colander crashes into the cabinet door to the left of my head.

I'm really scared now. Gav was emotionally abusive, but he never got this physical before. He's completely lost the plot. Snapped. My mind races, and I don't know what to do. "Get—GET OUT! *GET OUT! GET OUT OF MY HOUSE RIGHT NOW!*" I yell as loudly as I can. *Oh, please, let Eli have heard that, or even a neighbour,* I think feverishly as I duck away, trying to get out of the kitchen and maybe, if I'm quick enough, out of the front door. But I don't stand a chance. He grabs me around my waist and slings me to the corner of the kitchen work surface, boxing me in. I cradle my hand protectively, grunting in pain at being jolted.

"You," he snarls, his finger in my face, "are going to shut up, and you're going to listen to every fucking word I have to say! Is that clear?" I can smell the harsh scent of alcohol on his breath. It explains a lot. His spittle hits my face. I really believed that I'd left that all behind, but there it is again, the taint of the angry drunk on my skin, making me want to puke. All I can feel is that fleck of spit. "IS. THAT. CLEAR?!" I haven't heard him yell like this for a long while. In fact, this might be the angriest I've ever seen him. Much as it pains me to do it, I decide my best bet is to appease him, play along, and hope that help is coming. I don't want to be submissive to him ever again, but I need to buy time and try to help myself. At least this time this is me being smart, rather than just a brainwashed reflex. I take some comfort in that.

"Yes, I'll listen," I whisper, and he seems satisfied.

"Right. *Finally.*" He takes another pull on his cigarette, and I loathe the smell. "You know, you've been so unfair. I can't believe you'd treat me this way. Just…just *look* what you've reduced me to. Having to track you down like a fuckin' criminal. You act like I'm some kind of girlfriend beater or some shit. What the fuck is wrong with you?!" He's in high dudgeon now. "Sick, twisted little victim fantasist. I was seriously good to you, Emmy. Let you move into my home, didn't I? And before I was ready. But *you* insisted. Remember that?"

I say nothing. It's not true. He wanted me to move in so he could add my earnings to his household finances, and hid that hard fact with romantic words and promises.

"And what have you done with your hair?" he asks, like the change is a personal affront. "I almost didn't recognise you." *I wish he hadn't.* He sighs. "Doesn't suit you." He takes a strand and tugs on it none too gently. I pull back, not wanting him to touch me anywhere, now even my hair. His face hardens as he takes offence, and he tangles his hand in my hair, viciously yanking my head back because he won't be told no or denied something he wants. Seriously, I've never seen him like this. He normally uses cutting words, not physical force. Something is really, really wrong. "What the fuck are you being like this for?" he yells in my face.

"You don't get to leave me like I'm nothing. *Nobody* does that, least of all you. You owe me."

I don't owe you shit, I want to yell at him. Instead, I cringe, hating myself for it. Sadie would never tolerate this. What would Sadie do?

He's crowding me too much for me to be able to kick him in the nuts, so that's not an option.

"I'm trying to tell you that..." He takes a deep breath, as though calming himself down, and leans forward to rest his head against mine. The stale stink of his nicotine breath repulses me, and I wish I had space to back off, even if it does rile him up. I just don't want him near me. When he next speaks, it's in a quieter, softer voice. "I'm trying to tell you that I've thought about it long and hard, and...yeah. I can forgive you. And I can even deal with your broken plumbing. I'll sacrifice having kids for you. For *you*. See? I'm not a monster." *My broken plumbing?* Disgusting piece of trash, saying that to me. He brushes my hair away from my face, but it's nothing like when Eli does it. There's no tenderness. There's just...insistence. Ownership. "It's not going to be easy on me, but I can get past everything you've done," he says, wheedling now. "I know this isn't like you, so there must be something, you know...wrong with you. Other than your messed up..." He gestures towards my womb. "So after we get your fingers looked at, we'll see if we can get you looked at, you know, and get you some therapy as well, OK, Emmy? It's going to be OK." I nearly vomit on him when he kisses me wetly on my forehead. Maybe I should, maybe if I did he'd go away, I think crazily. "I'll forgive you," he continues, his voice cloying. "I'll wipe the slate clean, and we'll start again. It'll be like nothing ever happened..."

I feel cold. My stomach churns at the thought of leaving Foxton, where I've grown, where I've been happy...only to go back to my old life. The life where I was such a nervous wreck that I could hardly breathe. Where I cried myself to sleep every night. Where I shuffled through life, a grey, shapeless thing, staying quiet and trying to fade into the wallpaper to avoid attracting Gav's anger, always unloved and despised. Having to drop my knickers to appease him at any given moment, even if I was tired or sick or just didn't want to. An emotional punching bag at the mercy of his permanently bitter moods…

And then he lifts his hand to my neck, and strokes down, finishing with his fingertips at my nipple.

"No," I growl, shoving him away suddenly, not caring that this hurts my injured hand almost past endurance. If anything, I let the pain spur me on. I glare at him, his shocked face looking so outraged that I would dare push him. "No, not ever, *ever, EVER AGAIN!*" I scream in his face, almost squaring up to him, wild rage in my eyes. He will not drag me back down. I'm not the woman he abused. I've changed. I am stronger. I *won't* cower before him for another second. I am going to do whatever it takes to rid my life of this pathetic bully.

I'm dimly aware of a crashing noise, like a door being kicked in, as Gav grabs my face, his fingers biting hard into my chin. He stubs his cigarette out on my cheekbone just under my left eye. I scream like a wounded animal as the pain bursts across my face in a hot spike. *He burned my face. He burned my FACE. What's he going to do to me…*

The cigarette is pulled back all of a sudden, thankfully missing my eye, and the air hitting the burning injury stings horribly.

When I look back through streaming eyes, I almost start to sob with relief as I see Eli grappling Gav. He came. I dialled the right buttons on my phone, and he came running.

He's bristling with fury as he throws Gav onto my kitchen floor like a rag doll and digs his knee into his back. With one hand he grabs Gav's hair, much like the dirtbag did to me; with the other he pulls one of Gav's arms back and up. Gav yells helplessly and struggles, but he can't really move in this position. I look at my boyfriend, the love of my life, and I vaguely wonder if he's going to snap his neck. If I thought Gav was angry with me just now, that was barely even a flicker when compared to the white hot rage I see in Eli's face in this moment. His eyes are blazing and wild; his teeth are bared like an enraged wolf, and he's muttering, biting out words I don't understand in a voice so low and menacing it can barely be heard. He's beside himself, like a red mist has descended.

I feel arms holding me upright as my legs start to give out on me. They belong to Dean. He's here, too? I grasp onto his arm, and yes, he's real, looking over me with concerned eyes. There's a fine sheen of sweat on his forehead. They must have run all the way. *Are you OK?* He mouths at me. He stares at the burn on my face, gently examining it. Even though he keeps his fingers far away from the wound, it still stings, and I wince. "It was his cigarette," I whisper, feeling lightheaded now, "and…I think my fingers are broken." I definitely feel odd. My knees sink again, and I'm fighting not to faint. Oh god. What if my face scars? Gav will have marked me forever. Every time I look in the mirror, I will remember…

Dean's face changes before my dizzy eyes as he helps me to sit on the floor. All expression drains from his eyes, which is so weird because he's the *most* expressive person I know. It rattles me somewhere deep inside myself, the part of me still watching my surroundings as I fight to regain my composure. This looks wrong. His blank, vacant look is not right.

As I watch, he turns and walks slowly towards Eli and the still yowling and swearing Gav. The arm that Eli isn't holding backwards is scrabbling on the floor, looking for purchase on anything so he can fight back. There's none to be had. Eli has him safely trapped.

"RICH!" Gav screams out. "*RIIIIIIICH!*" I start to tremble. Rich is here, too? Please, no…he'll hurt Eli…he'll hurt Dean…

His screams for his psycho brother are replaced by yells of pain as Dean thoughtfully, coldly stamps on his fingers, grinding them with the heel of his heavy biker boots.

I gasp, but Eli doesn't even flinch. "Thank you," he mutters to his cousin. He looks up at him with a clear, assessing gaze, and then nods once. "Go back to Emily," he says calmly. "The police will be here any second." Dean nods, and walks back over to me, crouching down and checking my fingers as gently as he can as I stare at him.

"Em," Eli calls in an urgent tone, "talk to me, baby. Are you OK?"

"I..." My head is spinning right now, and it's hard to form answers. Eli turns his head to look at me, and I've never seen that expression on his face before. Rage and regret. Desperation flooding his eyes as he searches mine frantically. Dean signs to him, his movements jerky and fast, but I manage to recognise the signs for 'broken hand'. Gav yells as his arm is pulled back harder. Eli is making him *pay*.

"Police!" I hear someone shout at the door, followed by a more familiar voice yelling, "Em?" in a tone of extreme concern. *Leo*. He's being told to stay back, and Eli yells, "In here!" Some uniformed police come into my home and I suddenly feel terrified that they're going to arrest the wrong person. Eli is a huge guy with tattoos holding someone down, and he looks scary when you first meet him and they could easily get the wrong idea, and I can hear Leo yelling, and I'm scared, so I cry out, "The man he's holding down attacked me!" But I don't know how loud I was, and everything seems very far away all of a sudden and all I see are swirling colours surrounding Dean's face as he grabs me—and then there's nothing...

chapter TWENTY NINE

Eli

IN MY HASTE TO GET TO EMILY, I DIDN'T GIVE LEO ANY IDEA what was going on, so he had no clue *why* he was calling the cops. This meant there was plenty of explaining to do when they arrived. One of them called an ambulance because Em passed out, which just about finished me, and I was so relieved when they took Gav from under me so I could go to her. I cooperated with them in every way, to show them I wasn't the problem here, no matter how much Gav was ranting. Em came around very quickly, thank god; when I saw what he'd done to her face and her hand, it took Leo, Dean, *and* Police Constable Tyler to restrain me from ripping his head clean off his body with my bare hands.

He hurt her.

That motherfucker laid his hands on her and burned her face.

I wanted to kill him, and if the three of them hadn't held me back so well, I probably would have. At that point, they took him outside to a waiting police car, and I was told to calm down or I'd be arrested, too. Em's frantic, terrified response to that threat got me back in the right headspace immediately. She needed me. So I complied, and I calmed down. Kinda.

Once Emily explained that she'd called me for help when

her violent ex showed up, the officer in charge, Sergeant Badimi, agreed that, although I would be required to make a statement and it would need to be investigated thoroughly, it was a clear case of me defending my girlfriend from a violent attack. After all, I'd held him down and restrained him; I hadn't beaten him up. He, on the other hand, had actively attacked her, and what he'd done had constituted what Badimi referred to as 'actual bodily harm'.

None of us knew what had happened to Gav's hand. It must have been hurt in the scuffle...

That went without saying. We didn't even need to glance at each other to know that we weren't going to rat on Dean.

Once the ambulance showed up, it was clear that Em needed an X-ray, so PC Tyler went with us to the hospital to continue questioning me so I could be with her. I shook their hands in appreciation for that kindness.

Gav had broken two of her fingers. It made rage boil in my gut and throb at my temples to see her hand all strapped up and the dressing under her eye. They took plenty of photos of both injuries as evidence, because you'd better believe we were pressing charges all the way. He wasn't getting away with this, *at all*. We were later warned by the victim support team to prepare ourselves for the fact that, as this was Gav's 'first offence', he'd probably get a fine and community service, which is a fucking joke. But we got a restraining order against him at least. And I'm sure as hell never allowing him the opportunity to violate it. I've barely let her out of my sight in the two weeks since it happened. And if I'm not with her, either Leo, Sadie, or Dean is. Not negotiable.

It was Dean who remembered seeing the car parked immediately outside Em's home that day when we first got there. At our approach, it sped away, burning rubber. Gav's brother punked out on him when he saw us. Gutless shit.

During questioning, Gav denied everything, of course. He claimed they were just talking, and that I assaulted him unprovoked when I saw them together. He tried to brush her hand injury off as an accident, which, from the way Emily tells it, it may have technically been. But the cigarette burn on her face couldn't be so easily explained, so his story lacked credibility. And when he accidentally let slip about his brother being there, Rich got hauled in for questioning as well. There wasn't enough to charge him with anything as well, but we did manage to secure a second restraining order based on the verbal abuse he emailed to her shortly before the attack.

When Dean stamped on Gav's hand, I thanked him at the time for doing something I was burning to do when I was too busy holding the bastard down for the police. Since then, though… I'm keeping my eye on him. I think he just got mad when he saw his friend's injuries and lost it for a moment, but… I don't know. His mind is a fractured tangle of trauma, and I'm wondering if I should make sure he sees his therapist for a while again. Violence is not really his style, and though this was heavily provoked, it was out of character. I'm a weird mix of grateful and concerned.

Both Emily and I had two days off afterwards. I couldn't stand to leave her side for a moment, let alone a full shift, and I'd have been worried the entire time that something would happen again. Leo immediately updated the security cameras in the parlor and added a couple more panic buttons. He can't do enough for her. He even talked about hiring a temporary security guard during opening hours, but Em put her foot down and told him no. But he's working on her. None of us close our studio doors anymore, and we all check on her regularly, and hang out in the front with her if we don't have clients. Leo, Sadie, and Dean have really stepped up, and I don't have the words to thank them.

They're the best family in the world.

Emily

They're treating me like glass.

Don't get me wrong; I know why they're doing it, and I really appreciate being so loved, but it's been two weeks and they're still babysitting me and handling me with kid gloves. It needs to stop now.

I am by no means ungrateful for their thoughtfulness, but nor am I a victim. Not anymore. I refuse to be. I got out of Gav's house when I moved to Foxton; I won't live my life like I'm still locked inside it.

I'm not going to pretend that the attack didn't shake me up pretty hard. It did. I'm still jumpy, and I don't think I'd want to be on my own in my flat (not that I've had the opportunity). But I've also thought long and hard about this, and the thing is, the worst happened. The thing I dreaded so much, even worse than I ever dreamed it could be. That was Gav's worst shot. And I survived. My fingers were clean breaks and it's anticipated they will heal perfectly well. My facial scar from the cigarette burn can be lessened with plastic surgery sometime, if I want. I probably will. And I have a wonderful group of people in my life who have my back. *Gav* has a brother who ditched him. I'm not naive; a lot of survivors will tell you that restraining orders are often ignored by their subject, and aren't worth the paper they are written on, but the reality is, Rich took one look at Eli and Dean and backed off. So much for the big bad wolf. And Gav had his arse handed to him. On balance, I think they're both self-interested enough to never darken my doorstep ever again. Like all bullies, they are cowards.

I heard from Kayleigh. She sent me a panic-stricken apology message, explaining that she told Gav I was back on social media because she knew he had been 'struggling to cope' without me, and she was trying to be a good friend to him. She didn't mean any harm, and she didn't realise he'd gone berserk. She just thought he and I could talk and then work things out. He made a fake Instagram, found out from Kayleigh where I was listed as working on Facebook, and that's how he tracked me down, waiting around until he could follow me home. The woman who asked about nearby parking, earlier in the month, was actually him with his fake account. As were the dropped telephone calls that I mistook for a nervous client.

Kayleigh apologised to me profusely, saying she didn't know what he was really like, and I believe her. He always used to put on an amazing act around his friends. It's why I never told any of them what was going on; they would never have believed it of their mate Gav. Even now, I'm sure many of them are going to back him up, say it was a misunderstanding that I blew out of proportion, but I think some of them will think again. You can't easily excuse burning someone's face with a cigarette. I don't really care about their opinions anymore, though. I told her I understood, and didn't bear her any grudge. Truth be told, I don't want anything to do with my previous life anymore, so I think that's the last time she and I will ever be in touch.

I just want things to be the way they were before he attacked me. That was my new normal, and I loved it, and I want it back.

I just need to convince them all—especially Eli—that this is the right thing. No more talk of security guards. No more wrapping me up in cotton wool.

Eli is the worst culprit for that, of course. He's so anxious about hurting me that, if it wasn't for the fact that I'm absolutely gagging for him to throw me down and make mad, crazy, so-passionate-I-can't-see-straight love to me without holding anything back, I'd find it adorable. It took days for anything more than the gentlest of kisses. In the days after the attack, it was all painkillers and ice cream and hot water bottles and cuddles on the sofa, which was lovely and I'm not complaining. But since I've recovered enough, we've only had slow, careful sex, with him asking me every five seconds if I'm comfortable and if he's hurting my hand and if I want him to stop. I know it's the sweetest, most thoughtful, considerate thing, and it makes my heart melt, but I *just want him to pound me into next week like the dirty girl I am.*

And I have a plan to make it happen.

It's Saturday, and nothing is booked for tomorrow. I'm wearing some of my best red lacy underwear underneath this cute skirt and top, and Eli is about to find out that there are black hold-up stockings, not tights. I got changed in his bathroom this morning so he wouldn't see. I want the element of surprise to work in my favour.

I've waited and plotted all day, and once Dean, Sadie, and Leo have left, I'll lock up, head back to Eli's studio, and pounce on him.

I think Leo's twigged. I'm not sure what gave me away, but hell, if there's one thing I've learned about my boss, it's that he doesn't miss a thing. Ever. And from the twinkle in his eye as I see them all leave, he knows exactly what I'm up to.

"Show no mercy," he whispers to me as I am hugged goodbye. They all do that all the time, now, even when they're just going to lunch. It's so sweet.

I wink at him, and he grins at me. "Welcome back," he murmurs.

"I never left," I laugh.

He chuckles and nods. "Fair." He turns and calls to Sadie and Dean, who have already wandered away. "Hold up, folks." They stop, and he turns back to me. "Don't forget to turn off the security cameras in his room," he says quietly with a dirty grin, "unless, of course, you *want* to leave it on and make a cool home movie? I mean, that's fine, but you'll owe me a new tape..." I shove him out the door with a laugh, and he holds his hands up, yielding. "Just saying," he says, giving me a look filled with affection. I have a rush of love for my friend, who welcomed me into his world with open arms, no questions asked, and gave me so much. He gives me finger guns, clicking his tongue, and then catches up with the others, slinging an arm around each of them and steering them away from where they were headed and into the direction of the pub.

I pause in the bathroom on my way to Eli's room to check my appearance, after shutting off the cameras. My top has a hint of cleavage, and I pull it down so it's less of a hint and more of a shout. No lipstick on my teeth. Eyeliner still straight... I'll do. The strapped up hand doesn't really fit in with the sexy look I'm trying to create—not to mention having to put my American Sign Language studies on hold for now—but I only need one good hand to show my guy a good time.

I feel the flutter of butterflies in my stomach when I head to his studio, and it makes me smile. I've wondered how to go about this all day, and I think the direct approach will be best.

He looks up and smiles warmly when I enter. "Hey. Still want Italian tonight, or—"

I cut him off with my lips, backing him up against the nearest wall and kissing him, hard, deep, fast, as passionately as I can. I put the full force of my frustration over the last few days into every pull of my lips, and snake my good hand down to the front of his black jeans to give his cock a friendly squeeze.

Startled, he kisses me back, matching me shot for shot, but then pulls away a little. "What are you doing?"

I give him a 'duh' look. "What does it look like," I murmur against his lips, licking the seam of his mouth so he'll let me back in, and to goad him into responding. I grin as I feel a shiver pass over his skin, and he groans quietly.

"*Chere*," he breathes, eyes flashing, sounding a little desperate, "I don't want to hurt you..."

I lean back and look him dead in the eye. "Then why," I purr, "have you been making my hoo-ha all achy this entire time? Cos that's been *agony*." I take his hand and place his fingers up under my skirt, letting them brush the tops of my thighs to clue him in about the hold ups. His eyes widen, and then close when I place them at my core. I think the hot slipperiness he finds there is more eloquent than anything I might say. "Seriously, just *do me*. Throw down. It's what I want." I can't help my pleading tone. I love him, and all, and the slowjam touchy feely gentle sex is nice, but *dear god just have me and be rough about it...* After all, it's only my hand that's hurt.

He looks at me for a long moment, and just as I'm about to start pleading again, he yanks me closer to him and kisses the life out of me like he just can't resist it anymore, pushing my underwear to one side and plunging two fingers inside me, stroking my walls *juuuuust* right, in perfect rhythm with the sweeps of his tongue in my mouth. *Oh, thank GOD...*

"That what you want?" he growls, and it's so hot I can hardly stand upright anymore. I squeeze his cock again, which has gone from interested to flint hard. "Uh-huh." Slowly, I give him my dirtiest smile, and something sparks in his eyes that lets me know I've won. I've told him what I want, and he has never been able to resist giving it to me.

I decide to up my game a little, catch him off-guard and show him just how recovered I truly am.

Turning him, I shove him hard, and he falls into his leather chair. I can see from the flash in his eyes that this has really turned him on, seeing me so strong and assertive, and I don't give him a chance to think before I pull at his fly, tugging his jeans and his boxers down together. He lifts his hips a little to help me, and I hear him mutter, "Jesus..."

The second his hard-on is free, I grab it and wrap my mouth around it, eliciting a groan from him. He tastes so good. I've missed the sweet, salty tang of him; over the past few nights, it's all been for me, and he's distracted me every time I've reached for him. Well, screw that. I moan loudly for his benefit as I lick up the rapidly gathering pre-cum at his tip. I put more of him in my mouth, swirling my tongue. Another inch. Another...

"Oh, *fuck*," he breathes, and my mouth vibrates with a filthy little chuckle. It makes him throw his head back and groan again. That. That's how I want him: panting and out of control and dazed and utterly beside himself. That's when he's at his most beautiful.

I drag my tongue up his shaft, and it pulses in my mouth. *Good boy*. He loves when I play with his banjo string with the tip of my tongue, so I finish my lick with that. He swears through gritted teeth like a demented sailor. I've never heard such language in all my born days.

Good. This is fun.

I grasp his thighs and dip my head again, fitting as much of him into my mouth as I can, fisting my hand around the rest, rubbing in tandem with every dip of my head until I have a good rhythm going, one I know from experience will have him cross eyed with need.

He's gasping now. "Fuck, Em...suck me harder," he begs.

I pause, to make him wonder if I will or if I won't, teasing him. But to be honest, this is hot as hell for me, too, and I'll do whatever it takes to keep him in this zone. So I do exactly as he asks, like a good girl.

Before long, he grasps my shoulders, fingers digging in a little, and pulls me upwards. Before I can protest that, excuse-me-very-much, but I'm not done, he rolls me in the chair until I'm underneath him and kisses me hard until I'm dizzy and writhing beneath him. Pulling my skirt up, he yanks my knickers to one side and positions himself at my entrance.

He lifts his head, and if he asks me if I'm sure this is what I want, I swear to god I will *brain him*.

I tilt my hips, and the first inch of him slips inside me. His jaw clenches. "Don't you dare be gentle," I growl at him, reaching down to grasp his arse and squeeze it, hard. To provoke him further, I lift my head and bite his lower lip until his breath hisses.

I am rewarded for my warning when he slams inside me as hard as he possibly can, harder than he ever has before. It hurts, but it's a nice hurt. The best kind. I cry out, and he smothers the sound by kissing me again, thrusting inside me like a man possessed. We don't bother removing any more clothes. Our bared flesh slaps against each other as the pace picks up, and I find myself squealing with the intense build-up of sharp erotic sensations. We grunt. We growl. We clutch and rake at each other, animalistic and wild, any thought of gentleness long gone.

I'm so close.

So is he.

I can see he's struggling to restrain himself from letting go, and he reaches between us and pinches my clit between his fingers, providing me with the extra friction I need. "Come on," he snarls, pleading, and no sooner are the words spoken than I start to feel it, the tingles, spreading and building and fizzing...

My walls clamp around him hard, and my whole face is screwed up on a silent scream because this is beyond anything I've ever felt before, and I am coming so hard I feel certain I'm going to lose it completely and pass out, but I don't care, it's worth it.

He roars like a crazed animal, burying his head against my neck as he shoots his load inside me. I can feel every throb, every pulse, and I float back down to earth into a bed of gleeful smugness.

I knew I could convince him.

We take a few moments to catch our breath and relax. He rolls us back so I'm resting atop him, and I listen to his heartbeat return to normal, slowly but surely.

"Are you telling me," he whispers, "that you've been wearing stockings all day?"

"Yup."

"God damn," he sighs. I giggle, lifting my head to look up at him.

"Well, I mean," I point out, "you barely got the benefit of them."

He grins. "That's true. Give me a minute, I'll see what I can do about that." My eyes widen, making him laugh. "Oh, no, *chere*. Don't give me that look. You called down the thunder, and I'm gonna make sure you and your 'hoo-ha' get every last hit of it." He runs a thumb over my lower lip. "I'm sorry, by the way."

"Hmm?" Not what I was expecting.

"I've clearly not been giving you what you wanted lately," he says with a rueful smile. "It's just that..." A shadow passes over his eyes. "What happened...it scared me. I heard you scream... and I saw what he did to you..." He's struggling to get the words out. "I just couldn't bear for..." He trails off, at a loss. But I know what he's trying to say.

"It's OK," I whisper. "You made him stop. And I'm fine. I'm healing. And I'm more myself than ever." I kiss his jaw. "I don't want to be the poor little victim anymore. I want to be *me*. I'm stronger than I have ever been in my life, and I want to revel in that. And I can't if everyone is cosseting me, however well-meaning. I appreciate it, please believe me. I've never had such good friends. But it's time for it to stop." I lean up and look down at him, resting my head on my good hand. "I want to be your partner, not your burden. Not your poor little wounded bird."

His eyes soften, and he plays with a lock of my hair with a single finger. "I am so proud of you," he says quietly. Leaning up to kiss me, he slides his hands underneath my top and starts to pull it up. I lift my arms, and once my top is off, he scoops me up into his arms, hands on my butt, and lifts me up, making me yelp with surprise. "Now, about those stockings..."

I keep them on for him as he screws me up against the wall by his shelves, thrusting in and out of me with such force that most of their contents crash all over the floor. Inks, framed photos, equipment, my ripped knickers, everything is everywhere by the time we've both come for the last time. Turns out, he's definitely a stockings man.

EPILOGUE

Eli

Six months later

"ALRIGHTY, ROLL FOR INITIATIVE," EMILY DECLARES, AND we all groan happily and grab our dice. I gotta say, D&D dice are a lot more ornate and decorative than they were when I was a teenager. We've each of us got our own set, because this has become an institution for the Wishbone team. Every other Tuesday, here we are at my place (Em has long since moved in with me), trying to figure out how the hell we are ever going to stop the Vampire Lord and his evil schemes, and having great fun every time. Emily loves running the game for us, and that would be enough for me, but in all honesty, I have a real fondness for my Ranger, and I look forward to each game.

Even with Leo dressing up and being all…*Leo* about his Bard. He still wears his leather armor every time, but usually that's just over a t-shirt these days.

It's almost time. I'm gonna do this.

My palms are sweating a little, and my heart is pounding so fast and so hard that I'm actually a little dizzy. My stomach is jumping with nerves. I take a sip of my beer. My mouth keeps going dry.

I look where I am placed in the initiative order once everyone has rolled their dice, and I'm third. That's...perfect, actually. Gives me a chance to take a few deep breaths. No-one knows my plan, not even Dean.

Speaking of Dean, he and Sadie take their turns first, and they both do a decent amount of damage to the pack of wolves we're fighting. If I was at all invested in this fight, I'd be punching the air, but I just sit quietly and wait my turn.

"OK, babe, you're up," Emily says finally, and looks up at me with a smile.

Here we go.

"I'd like to make a persuasion roll," I begin.

She frowns, a little puzzled. "OK, talk me through it." She's a good dungeon master, always willing to listen to your ideas, and if she can find a way to make them work, that's exactly what we do.

"What are you planning to do? Persuade the wolves not to attack us?" Sadie asks, laughter tingeing her voice.

"No," I say, reaching into my pocket for the ring box. I've been checking and double checking that it's there all evening, all through the gumbo dinner, all through the hour of play we've had so far. "I'm making a persuasion roll to break the fourth wall..." I get off my chair and go down on one knee next to my girl, my heart in my throat as I open the ring box and place my mother's diamond engagement ring on the table in front of her, "and ask the dungeon master to marry me."

"Oh my god," Sadie gasps, and Leo lets out a "HOLY SH-" before Dean claps a hand over his mouth, cutting him off.

Em's eyes are huge and stunned, her mouth open. "Oh my god, are you serious?!" she bursts out in a delighted voice, and she gives me the biggest smile I've ever seen on her beautiful face.

Thank god. I was pretty certain she'd say yes, but it's good to see that reaction all the same. I chuckle. "Yes, I am," I reply, and take her hands in both my own, hoping that'll stop mine from shaking so much. I run a thumb over the tattoo of a tiny elephant I inked on her a couple of months ago. Her tattoo collection is growing, and every one of them is mine. I look into her eyes that I love so much, and take a single deep breath. "I adore the fuck outta you, Em," I say, any semblance of any speech I toyed with in my head just gone in the moment. I'm not one for fancy words, but the ones I say, I mean. Especially the ones I just said. And here's four more: "Will you marry me?"

Her eyes are glistening, but she's giggling. "Yes," she says, kissing me once, and again, "yes, YES! Of course I will..." And then she's wrapped tightly in my arms, or maybe I'm wrapped tightly in hers, but either way, this is the happiest moment of my entire life.

I can hear Sadie squeaking happily, and Leo lets out a loud, booming "YES!" as he stands and takes a twenty out of his wallet and hands it to Sadie before swooping over to us and wrapping us both into a hug. "I've never been so happy to lose a bet," he crows, rubbing my back so hard I swear I'll have friction burns on my skin by the time he's done.

"What bet?" Emily asks, her voice vibrating because he's doing the same to her.

"I said he'd do it at Christmas or New Year's Eve. Sadie didn't think he'd be able to wait that long." He gives my fiancée a loud kiss on the top of her head. "I'd say welcome to the family, but you're already family, so this is just making it legal, but aaaaaaagh, I'm so fuckin' happy for you both!"

"I've never seen a proposal before," Sadie says happily, "and I've always wanted to! I can tick it off my bucket list!" She hugs Em while I endure more of Leo's affection. "Show me the ring, lemme see..."

"Leo, let me go, I need to place it on her finger," I say in a mock strangled voice.

"You got it, buddy," he says warmly, and *then* lets me out of his bear hug.

I start to reach for the ring, but Dean stands up and holds up a hand to make me pause. He walks up to me and hugs me, too, hard but brief. When we pull back, his eyes are ever so slightly damp, and I won't lie, so are mine. We've seen each other through a lot, and we don't need words for me to know that he's happy that I've found my best life.

I can only wish the same for him.

I pick up the black leather box off the table and take the ring out. I inherited it when my mom died. It's a platinum solitaire diamond, set on an ornate band shaped like vines, with a fleur de lis where the rock sits. A traditional New Orleans offering. My dad went all out with it, keen to impress both Mom and her huge, forbidding Samoan family. It worked.

I didn't give it to Charmaine. She chose her own.

And, in all honesty, I couldn't imagine giving it to her. Or giving Emily anything that wasn't as special as Mom's ring is to me.

I place it on Emily's ring finger, and for a moment, as we gaze at each other, it feels like we're the only two people in the room. "Thank you," she whispers to me, "I love it, it's so beautiful."

"It was my mom's," I say, and there's a lump in my throat as I smile at her. "She'd have loved you."

Her fingers on that hand clench into a fist, as though to keep it from slipping off. It won't. It's a perfect fit, thank god. "I'll keep it safe," she promises me.

"I know," I reply, kissing her forehead. "I know."

There's a brief silent moment. And then Dean very rapidly signs something that makes me, my fiancée, and Sadie laugh riotously. Leo growls, as Dean smirks at him in triumph.

The words are, *I call Best Man*.

And then Leo grins bigger. "Fine. That's totally fine. I call *officiant*."

Uh-oh.

THE END

ACKNOWLEDGEMENTS

I am grateful to have so many wonderful people to thank for all their love, help, and support in helping me publish my first book and make a bucket list dream of mine come true. I've put off writing this to the last possible moment, because I know that, by the time I send this off and it's too late to amend, someone else will have done something tremendously kind that deserves a mention here! To anyone this may end up applying to, please consider yourself well and truly thanked and appreciated.

This is in no particular order, but thank you to the following people:

To my wonderful editor, Wendy, for taking the raw text and polishing it until it shone. You gave it to me straight, always put the manuscript first, and your advice was priceless. Thank you so, so much.

To my 'book wife', Natalie Parker, for always getting it, always being there, and always encouraging me to send her more of my work in progress. Alpha reader, I recognise your claim on Leo—you loved him first.

To my other alpha/beta readers, Autumn, Jamie, and Katy, for being so enthusiastic and so gratifyingly eager for more, and for saving me from an embarrassing continuity error involving knickers.

To Matilda at Cover Girl Design for doing such an amazing job on the cover—it looks just the way I pictured it in my head, but better! And the logos you designed for me are BOSS—you're a talented woman!

To the excellent Stacey at Champagne Book Design for doing such a beautiful job with the formatting – I am still headlong in love with the idea of using wishbones as scene break separators! Thank you for your meticulous work and rapid turnaround times. You rock.

To Anastasia, the fairy godmother of aspiring romance writers, and the rest of the wonderful women behind Me, Myself, and Romance Books: Fi, Geornesha, Grace, Jessica, Maria (who added me to the Goodreads Most Anticipated March Releases List!!!), Michelle, and Tara. Your encouragement and support has been truly staggering and heartwarming, and you are all amazing. Big love.

To my awesome street team: Aimee, Anna, Brittany, Carly, Cat V, Cat W, Jenifer, Jessica, Kerri, Kirsty, Leanne, Marla, Melissa, Nina, Vy, and Zainab - thank you for jumping on board with such enthusiasm and dedication. You've all been brilliant.

To my lovely ARC readers for taking a chance on a newb. You've all been so welcoming and so gracious, and I am so grateful to you all.

To Jamie Schlosser, for being a fantastic mentor. You've been warm and patient with me and my many questions, and from the word go you've always had open arms, and I appreciate that a whole lot.

To Carian Cole, who has been amazingly kind, informative, and patient with me, saved me from Facebook ad woes, and gave me the benefit of her experience and honest advice. You're tops.

To my other author friends who have been so gracious to me: Tempest, Cait, Garry, Nola, Paula, Shauna, ML, and all the other fabulous indie authors who have reached out with kind words. This is a truly amazing community, and I will never lose sight of that. It's my privilege to be a part of it.

To the wonderful Give Me Books and Enticing Journeys for their hard work promoting my book baby. Thank you so much for all your help.

To Avery and Cole, who know why.

To all my many lovely friends, who have encouraged me every step of the way, cheered me on, supported me in every way they possibly could, and haven't been mad at me for being MIA so much lately! Thanks for your understanding, folks—normal service will resume someday!

To my unutterably amazing parents, for reading to me every night since the day I was born, for loving me every single day, and for always believing in me no matter what. You two were the first people in the queue to get let into the hall on the day I graduated, beating out all the other parents. I hope you know how very much I love you (it's to the moon and back).

And of course...to my Mark. You were life's best plot twist for me, and I know you'll know exactly what I mean when I say... MUSHROOM.

ABOUT THE AUTHOR

Lizzie Stanley realised the other day how long it had been since she graduated from university, and resolved never to think about it again. She has a demanding but satisfying day job, and still manages to find pockets of time here and there to write. She lives in the UK with her Very Sexy Husband and her Doc Martens collection, and enjoys binge reading, watching true crime documentaries on Netflix, playing Dungeons and Dragons, singing the music of the eighties very badly in the shower, and tormenting her friends with puns.

Lizzie loves to hear from her readers, so if you'd like to make her day by dropping her a line, her email address is lizziestanley-author@gmail.com. You can also hit her up on Instagram: @ lizziestanleyauthor. She is still getting the hang of Twitter, bear with her. Please also feel free to join her Facebook group, Lizzie Stanley's Wishbone Readers, where she will post info on the upcoming titles in the series. And photos of hot guys.